a mother's confession

Also by Kelly Rimmer:

The Secret Daughter
Me Without You
When I Lost You

a mother's confession

kelly rimmer

bookouture

Published by Bookouture, an imprint of StoryFire Ltd.

23 Sussex Road, Ickenham, UB10 8PN,
United Kingdom

www.bookouture.com

ISBN 978-1-78681-065-6
eBook ISBN 978-1-78681-064-9

For S and J

When I look around the life I have now,
I see so many blooms from the seeds of kindness that you planted
back then, and I will be forever grateful.

CHAPTER 1

Olivia

Most of the time, people try to avoid talking about what happened. Even when their conversational acrobatics fail and the subject arises anyway, they stay within the very narrow subject of warning signs... specifically, warning signs that *I* somehow missed.

I get it, I really do. If there were warning signs and I missed them, that makes this my fault. It's a lot easier to blame me than it is to blame a dead man. If there were warning signs, that means that this whole situation was entirely preventable – and *that* means people can stop it happening to them. All they have to do is be a little more vigilant than I was – poor, foolish Olivia... so blind to what was happening right there in her own husband's mind.

I want to talk about it, but I don't want to talk about bloody 'warning signs'. I just want to say his name. I want to scream it in anger, and I want to wail it in grief. Mostly, I just want to hear myself say the words aloud – without feeling like I'm making whoever is in the room with me unbearably uncomfortable.

My husband's name was David Wyatt Gillespie. When he died, he was thirty-seven years old. He was on the town council and one day he was going to run for mayor. He was the captain of our town cricket team for ten years, and when he was at university, he played representative football. He always said he might have gone pro if he hadn't been so focused on his business degree. Here in Milton Falls, David ran a full-service car dealership – the only one in our small town. You might not think that a tiny Australian village would be the right place for a prestige dealership like that, but David found a way. He was so good at what he did that people came from miles around to buy their new cars from his team, and they usually returned for their servicing too.

David was just over six feet tall and in recent years, a little overweight. He had thick black hair that stubbornly held onto its colour, but it had just begun to recede in the year before he died. David was charming and effortlessly persuasive; a salesman through and through. He could take on an irate customer and, with a flash of that smooth grin and some well-placed words of consolation, turn them back into a devotee. He was *that guy* at high school – the one all the girls wanted, the one all the boys wanted to be. Out of my league – for sure – or so I thought, until we met again at university. The night we got together, our eyes locked across a crowded room and it was as if we were seeing each other for the very first time. I felt like I was a character in a romance novel or a princess in a Disney movie, somehow brought to life.

It's funny how even the memory of that first night is no longer pure; it's tinged with guilt and uncertainty. Did I feel that overwhelming tug of attraction because of genuine chemistry with David, or because I wanted to be swept off my feet? I was no passive participant; this was no case of 'falling' in love, it was entirely 'jumping' into love with both feet; well before checking that it was safe to do so. I wanted to live a fairy tale, and I told myself that's what I was doing, even long after it became apparent there would be no happy ending.

Even now, when I think of him, I'm scared. He's dead and I'm safe, but I'm still scared. Perhaps the strangest thing about all of this is that there's no denying that I loved him too, at least at one point. Sometimes I actually miss him, but then in the very next breath I find that I hate him so much that I hope there is a hell, just so that he can be suffering like he left me here to suffer.

David's parents live seven houses away from me. His father, Wyatt, usually walks past my house just after 6 a.m. each morning with their small brood of Pomeranians. David's mother, Ivy, generally walks past again with the dogs just after 6 p.m. If I am on the front lawn, they throw a stiff 'hello' in my direction and walk a little faster. If I'm not, they glance at the house but they don't stop. I know this, because I watch the time and even if I do happen to be outside at either edge of the day, I rush inside when they are due to pass. I usually watch from behind the curtains in the living room to make doubly sure they *don't* stop.

That's exactly what I'm doing now, actually. I'm standing in the living room with my daughter Zoe in my arms, and I'm peering out at the street as Ivy approaches. She dresses well and she looks after herself, and as a result, she looks much younger than she actually is. She used to hint at me sometimes that I could pay more attention to how I looked. I glance down at my yoga paints and the stained T-shirt I'm wearing. When I brought Zoe home from the hospital, I pulled this shirt on and took it right off again because it was uncomfortably tight, but now it is miles too big. I can't remember the last time I washed my hair – it's in my now-standard messy bun. Ivy would be mortified if she happened to see me tonight.

I see her reach the letterbox and in addition to her regular glance at our house, she pauses. That's unusual enough that my heart starts to race and I feel the pounding of my pulse all through my body until I can hear it in my ears. I bounce a little, rocking Zoe gently in my arms, and when I see Ivy look towards the windows where I am hiding, I step back to make sure she doesn't see me.

This means I don't see her walk down through the garden, and when the doorbell rings after a few moments, it is a burst of too-loud sound in my too-silent house and it startles me into an adrenaline rush. I consider ignoring her and pretending I'm not home – but the lights are on, and besides which… I'm pretty sure she still has keys. Would she have the keys to the new lock, the one David installed just before he died? Probably not. I'm probably safe. I could *probably* ignore her.

I won't, though. I'm as ambiguous about Ivy as I am about her late son. I miss her, and I love her but… I'm not entirely sure that I trust her. Ivy wasn't ever able to see David's flaws, even when they were right under her nose. I know I can safely assume she believes that what happened was entirely my fault.

Maybe she's right about that. I certainly feel guilty enough – and he did tell me exactly what would happen if I ever left him.

I gently shh-shh towards Zoe out of habit as I approach the door, and then rest her into a reclining position against my body as I swing the door open with my spare hand.

'Ivy,' I say, as warmly as I can. 'How are you?'

'I'm fine,' she says, stiffly. She raises her hand towards me and offers me an envelope. 'Ross brought this over this morning. It's from the probate people so I thought you might need it.'

I take the envelope and look down at it. It's addressed to *The Estate of David Gillespie* at 15 & 16 Winter Street, Milton Falls. Ivy and Wyatt are at number 21 Winter Street, just around the corner, but in the last few months Ross the mailman has been making executive decisions about our mail on a regular basis. Some mail addressed here has turned up at Mum and Dad's house, and some mail addressed to me there has come directly here.

It is a well-intentioned gesture from Ross, but one that is irritating as hell, and I make yet another mental note to go into the post office and tell him to just *stop* and put the mail in the mailbox it's addressed to. Maybe one day soon I'll go through with it.

But then again, the post office is right in the village centre – a hotbed of other well-intentioned acquaintances and shameless gawkers – which is exactly why I haven't yet managed to go there alone.

I adjust Zoe to cuddle her a little higher in my arms and glance at Ivy, and see her staring at the baby, and her lips are twitching as if she wants to say something. With my other hand, I reach for the door, and I try to wrap things up with a careful, 'Well… thanks for dropping by… '

'Listen, Olivia… ' Ivy says, and she's frowning so deeply that I feel a twist in my gut. I see David in the shape of her icy blue eyes – but I also see pity there, and judgement, and the same gut-wrenching misery that follows me everywhere I go these days. Then Ivy stares at Zoe and I think that she's going to ask to hold her, and I just *can't* let her. My arms tighten automatically around my baby. 'Do you… don't you think it's time—'

'It's only been a few weeks,' I interrupt her. 'It's not *time* for anything yet.'

'You're still carrying on as if it only just happened. You don't even leave the house; I heard that you don't even get your own groceries.' This accusation is flung at me with casual disgust, as if this due to sheer laziness; a character flaw. It's not even true – I *do* get my own groceries… sometimes… when Mum or Dad or Louisa have time to walk to the store with me. But Wyatt owns that store – surely Ivy understands how difficult it is for me to walk in there, even flanked by protective family members. And besides which, I just don't *need* to do the groceries very often because people are still constantly bringing me frozen meals. The chest freezer is full to the top with them, and the little freezer beside the fridge is almost as bad. Ivy's nostrils flare a little, but she presses her lips together and then adds tightly, 'You *can't* carry on like this forever. It's not what David would have wanted.'

The skin on my face is burning up and I close my eyes briefly to block out the sight of her – but when I do, I see David. It's like the moment when I found him has burnt itself into my mind so deeply that if I close my eyes, I can still see the ashen tones of his face and the way he had slumped behind that steering wheel. I don't have anything like a photographic memory and I keep thinking the image is surely going to fade eventually but, so far, time has done nothing at all to dim the detail in my mind.

And the absolute worst thing about this situation is that Ivy is actually dead wrong – because this is *exactly* what David wanted. Does she really not know that – or is she just throwing those words out as a platitude?

I open my eyes and I stare at her. I just want her to go away, and so I say what I think she wants to hear.

'I'll give it some thought.'

'Have you at least considered seeing a therapist?' she asks, and I'm about to tell her that yes, *I-do-have-a-grief-counsellor-not-that-it's-any-of-your-business-thank-you-very much* but then she adds, 'I mean… perhaps… maybe if you had asked David to see a marriage counsellor instead of—'

'No.' I say the word slowly and flatly, but it sounds weak even to my own ear. I tell myself that Ivy means well, but I am actually dizzy with outrage at her patronising tone. And I want to rage at her, but I can't. Ivy lost her son – her only son and he was the apple of her eye too – but I don't need to hear an accusation from her. I know all too well that what happened was entirely my fault. My indignation fades at this thought, and now all I feel are the feelings that run beneath my days like the foundation to my life; weariness and shame.

Ivy is staring at her feet, and she looks miserable too. So I can't rage at her, but I won't comfort her either. She speaks to me as if I am a child, but if I was really a child, wouldn't she offer me sympathy, or grace to grieve as long as I need to, or even a modicum of support?

'I'll think about it, Ivy,' I tell her, and I step back into the lobby of my house.

'Olivia – it's just that Wyatt and I... we really are—'

'I have to go. Zoe needs to go to bed.'

I close the door, and I lock it. First I close the bottom lock – the original one, then the middle one that David installed to keep me here after Zoe was born, and then the sliding lock I had installed myself just after The Tragedy when I felt so unsafe everywhere and I was trying everything to make myself feel better again. I listen for the sound of Ivy's footsteps on the path, and then I rest against the door and I close my eyes and I breathe deeply until I'm close to calm again.

I look down at Zoe – she's the one thing that keeps me going. I might have stopped altogether by now – maybe I still will. The thought of crawling into a hole and disappearing somehow is still the most appealing idea I have for my future.

But I just can't do it, because I have a baby to think about, and she needs me.

'Come on, sweetie,' I say to my daughter, as I force a singsong tone into my voice. 'Let's get you to bed.'

CHAPTER 2

Ivy

My life was never supposed to go the way it did.

I was supposed to finish high school and go straight to uni. I was going to do something with my brain – maybe law, maybe business, I wasn't really sure. But I was the smartest kid in my year, the perpetual teacher's pet, a high achiever in every domain. I was also the quintessential nerd, and I made it all the way to the last year of school without a single boy so much as offering me a second glance.

But then Wyatt Gillespie asked me if I wanted to watch a movie with him one weekend.

He was the school captain, and also the captain of just about every sporting team worth a mention in that year. Wyatt had a shock of thick, wavy black hair and deep blue eyes that seemed to sparkle whenever I dared look into them. Everyone wanted Wyatt, and then suddenly – for some completely unfathomable reason – Wyatt wanted *me*. It was the most startling, amazing thing that had happened in all of my seventeen years.

'Come to the pictures with me,' he said. We were walking out of the school gates, and I assumed he was talking to someone else, so I ignored him. 'Ivy. Come to the pictures.'

I frowned at him.

'Why?'

'Because I want you to,' he said, and he stared at me in a way that made my stomach dance. What I was thinking was *What on earth would you be interested in me for* and *why don't you ask one of the pretty girls instead?* – but what I said instead was a rather dumbfounded, 'Okay.'

Even in the heady haze of lust and excitement that Wyatt brought to my life, I was lucid enough to think we were being cautious – but I underestimated our easy, youthful fertility. I had realised that I was pregnant by the time our final exams rolled around, although I prolonged the frankly awful conversation with Wyatt himself until after my final assessment. I said the words as if they were a guilty, distasteful confession – *I'm so sorry, Wyatt, I seem to be pregnant.* As I expected, he reacted with horror – staring at me in an aghast shock for some time before he managed to whimper something helpless like *My Dad is going to kill me.*

He was wrong about that – they didn't kill him, but his parents were suitably outraged. Wyatt's parents owned the local grocery store, at the time named simply Gillespie's Goods and Groceries. My Mum ran the local branch of the Country Women's Association and Dad was a farmer – humble occupations all round, but in a small town like Milton Falls, each set of parents were as well known as celebrities. The end result was that there were no two ways about it – Wyatt and I were having a baby, so we were going to be married – and the ceremony needed to be arranged for yesterday if possible. The day the uni offers came out, I was at the courthouse suffering through our shotgun wedding.

It wasn't that I didn't want to marry Wyatt, or even that I didn't love him – I did. The problem was that I was smart enough to know that this was infantile love – shallow love – and its roots ran only as deep as the physical attraction between us. I feared it would fade, and indeed – even in all of the stress of the pregnancy and the hasty wedding – we stopped sneaking kisses and quiet moments alone together. Wyatt and I had never really talked. We'd skipped the conversational step in building our relationship and leapt all the way to flirting and making out.

So when we found ourselves pregnant and married, it was rather a shock to realise that we had almost nothing in common. It certainly wasn't that Wyatt was stupid – but he was a simple man with simple interests and tastes. I desperately wanted to travel, and he was happy to consider the possibility – as long as the end destination of our journey involved some kind of cricket match or football game. I wanted to go to the theatre, he wanted to go to the movies. I'd spend hours balancing spices to make a curry from scratch, and he'd walk in from work, sniff the air suspiciously and ask me to make him a ham sandwich. I told him that once the baby came, I wanted to try to figure out some way to study, but from the get-go he told me that would be a waste of time – what did I need a degree for? *He* would support us, and he was perfectly content in the knowledge that his entire working career would be spent at his father's supermarket.

I could barely believe that in the space of only a few months, I'd gone from a life of infinite possibilities to a future where our tiny little town would be my *whole world* forever. Possibly the only thing that saved me from despair during the early months of our marriage was the realisation that out of all of the chaos and shock of it all – a miracle was about to emerge. All was not lost; there was still a way that I could make my life worthwhile.

Our family and the baby would be my purpose.

Right up until the birth, Wyatt desperately wanted to name our baby 'Wyatt Junior', or 'Brenda' after his mother. I loathed both names, and wanted to call the baby David or Selina – names which I hoped would not shackle the child with the Gillespie family history from the very moment of its birth. After sitting quite helplessly in the room staring at me while I suffered through twenty-three hours of labour, Wyatt had the good sense to capitulate and allow me to choose the name, and so our son David Wyatt Gillespie was born. I'm not an unreasonable woman – I did at least compromise on the middle name.

It wasn't what I planned, but from the moment I laid eyes on that baby, the disappointment and frustration I felt at the situation I'd landed myself into all but evaporated. Until David was in my arms, I'd felt trapped – but as soon as I saw him, I was free. He was magnificent – not just *a* reason to make the most of things – but The Reason. All it took was one moment with him snuggled against my breast and everything about my life made sense again. The agony of his birth, the disappointment I'd felt at the accidental pregnancy, the uncertainty about my relationship with Wyatt – all of that became inconsequential in a single, defining moment.

David was my perfection – and raising him was instantly my purpose. I threw myself into motherhood with great abandon, and even in the fog of the early sleepless weeks and months, I found a startling joy in his presence in my life. I delighted in every coo and took satisfaction in his every smile, and from my mild depression during the pregnancy I found myself entering a golden age of my life during David's early years.

And that was the way of our early family life. Wyatt went off to work each day at Gillespie's Goods and Groceries as his father's assistant manager and he continued to immerse himself in sports each weekend, and I stayed home to keep our house and build my life around our son.

And it wasn't at all the life I'd wanted, but that really didn't matter – I was blissfully happy anyway.

CHAPTER 3

Olivia

The doorbell rings again the next morning just after 8 a.m. I know who it is the moment I hear it. I also know I won't answer it.

I walk to the door anyway and when I look through the peephole my gaze momentarily focuses on his. Sebastian McNiven is standing as he's always standing when he visits – hard up against the door, his expression guarded, hints of both hope and resignation battling in his hazel eyes. Today, his thick red hair is still damp, and the beard that had grown a little out of control has been freshly trimmed since his visit yesterday. He's my boss and my friend, my *best* friend – maybe even my only friend. Seb is on his way to work – wearing the uniform I helped him revamp when he first took over the clinic. The logo of the Milton Falls Veterinary Clinic is over his heart, which is fitting, because he truly loves that place.

'Livvy? Sweetheart, are you there?' he asks very gently, and I rest my forehead against the door and close my eyes. 'Liv?'

I still can't convince my voice box to work when Seb is at the door. Instead, I tap the door with my fingertip. It barely makes a sound, but I know it will be enough that he knows I'm there. I'm sure of this because we've done this almost every day for the last few weeks. Sebastian comes past on his way to work. I go to the door, but I can't bring myself to open it. He calls out until I knock to give him a sign that I'm here. But I don't speak. I can't speak. I haven't said a word to him since I finished up at work, all of those months ago.

'Hi, Livvy,' he says softly. 'How are you today? Just called past for a chat. If you want me to leave, you just let me know, okay?'

He always says that, and I know he means it. If I asked him to leave, he'd turn on his heel and disappear. That's just the kind of man Sebastian McNiven is.

But I don't ask him to leave, and so he sits on the step just as he always does, and I lean against the door as he talks for a while. His deep, quiet voice floats through to me, and I don't just listen – I soak in the words and they infuse into me. Today, he talks about work – to a level of detail that might be mind-numbing if I wasn't desperate for something safe to occupy my brain space. But I am desperate and in some ways I'm actually bored too, so I love hearing about how he walked through the mud to Rafe Thomas's cattle yards to do the insemination because he couldn't get the ute down there, only to remember he left the sperm at the clinic. I manage half a smile when he tells me that he sat up until midnight last night trying to catch up on billing because he's been slack with it lately, as if *that's* anything new. He asks me for my advice on a case – a Labrador dam had to have a C-section and she's not bonding with the pups, what should he do?

I don't answer, but he's not really expecting me to. Still, he waits a while before he says softly, 'All right, Livvy. I'd better get going. I'll catch you tomorrow?'

And I tap again, just so he knows I've been listening, and then I pull myself up off the floor and I watch through the peep-hole as he walks away.

I love the days when he talks about work. They are the days when I really feel like I should just pull the door open and let him inside. If I had milk, I'd make him a cup of tea with two sugars, just the way he likes it. We'd sit at the table and I'd stare into those hazel eyes and feel comfort in his presence.

If there was a way I could let him in but keep strict control over the subject matter we addressed, I wouldn't be sitting behind a door hiding from him. But some days he doesn't talk about work, and on those days, even sitting on the other side of the door to him is a struggle. There is so much Sebastian and I need to discuss, and somehow, I don't have the language yet to face the conversation.

So I sit on the other side of the door when he visits each day, and I miss him even though he's there, and I don't let myself think about why.

❖ ❖ ❖

I fall into the routine I've accidentally developed. After Seb's visit, I make breakfast, and sit on the floor with Zoe. Inane chatter echoes through the room from the television that I have on merely for background noise, and I leave the bowl of cereal on the coffee table beside me but I don't touch it. I'm already onto my second cup of coffee though, and it's as I'm lifting this to my lips that I am hit quite unexpectedly by an epiphany.

I can't live this way any more.

The concept rises to my consciousness like a bubble of air, but as it bursts, it hits with the force of a steam train. I'm flattened completely by the idea, so much so that I sit dumbfounded for a long while before I even ask myself what it might mean. All that I really know is that at present I live in a house that I hate, separated from everything good in my life by physical barriers like doors and emotional barriers like grief, and I'm stuck around the corner from a pair of ex-in-laws that I can't bear to face either. And I feel trapped, but am I? Do I actually *have* to be here at all?

Milton Falls is home. It's safe – well, safer than anywhere else might be. This is where my family are, and after seven years of semi-estrangement from them, I'm only just rebuilding my relationship with my parents and my younger sister – I *need* them in my life. And then there are friends... colleagues and acquaintances at least... and Sebastian. Plus, just about everyone in town knows me and they all know my story – I am nurtured and somewhat protected here, my freezer full of meals and even the meddling postman is a testament to that. I have to stay, but there's no way I can disappear here.

How do I move on, without moving away?

I *can* move – maybe not to another town, but certainly I could shuffle myself from David's house and all of the memories that linger here, into a new place that I could call my own. Find a new place to build a real home for Zoe, who now rests safely on my lap, and who really *does* deserve a mother who at least has her shit together enough to shower on a regular basis.

I spend the rest of the day wondering about it all. The house is mine now – despite the fact that I had left David before his death, there wasn't any time to change his will so I automatically inherit what's left. I've instructed the solicitor to sign David's business over to Wyatt and Ivy because I just can't even begin to think how I might deal with *that*, but the house and even the savings accounts I was never allowed to touch have all defaulted back to me. This has felt like a curse until now, like I've been trapped in a gilded cage. I thought about donating all of his money – all of *our* money – to charity, just so I could rid myself of his presence in my life. But now, as I consider a fresh start, I realise that I'm actually blessed in at least one small aspect. I have a million things to worry about, but at least money isn't one of them.

So I don't *need* to rush back to work to support myself. But just as soon as I consider this, it occurs to me that maybe going back to work isn't actually a bad idea. I wanted a way to control the conversation with Seb, didn't I? What better way than donning my uniform, and returning to work alongside him in a professional setting? I could engage with him just like I used to. We could discuss cases and customers, and if he tried to talk about anything else, I could steer him right back to the business at hand. After all, the office isn't really the time nor the place…

And God, would I ever benefit from a reason to bathe on a regular basis?

I walk into David's study; one of the rooms that I have mostly stayed out of over these last months. I lie Zoe gently onto the carpet and I walk to the whiteboard. David's scrawl is still on it – lines of 'to do's and thoughts – all related to the business and his work with the council. It takes a good amount of window cleaner to clean off the whiteboard, but once it's a blank slate, I pick up a marker.

What to call my list? I ponder this for a moment, then I start to write – *Olivia Gillespie's Plan for A New Life*. I stop at the G at the start of Gillespie. I've been Olivia Gillespie for years – but was that ever really *me*? Why *did* I take David's name? At the time, I remember feeling almost sentimental about the tradition. I liked the idea of us sharing a surname, and there was a great lot of talk from Wyatt about David 'carrying on the family name'.

But now, knowing where we wound up, the Gillespie surname feels like a mark of ownership upon my life and I know I need to leave it behind – as soon as possible. I wipe out the 'G' with the back of my hand, and instead, I write:

Becoming Olivia Brennan
1. *List David's house*
2. *Buy new house and move*
3. *Find Zoe childcare*
4. *Go back to work*
5. *Adopt a dog*

I stare at the list. The thought of that top task, selling this dungeon of a house, makes me feel nothing but joy. I'll do that first because I know that I will go through with it. The second line, buying a new house, is nerve-wracking but I know that it will feel like progress if I can actually get it done. The thought of finding childcare is enough to send anxiety flooding through my body, but I know this has to happen too – I haven't been apart from Zoe since the days after the funeral, but the time has to come eventually.

There are two childcare centres in town – a new one, and an older one. I went to school with the director of the new one – her name is Taylor Wager, and I know that she's a very kind, nurturing woman. Still, when I picture myself handing Zoe over to her, I actually feel like I'm going to throw up. I stare down at my daughter and I wonder how on earth I'm ever going to go through with it.

But it has to happen. There's no way forward without loosening the vice-like grip I've held onto my daughter with since The Tragedy.

I look back to the whiteboard. I'll get through the business of listing this house and then buying a new one before I put myself through the trauma of looking into childcare. I haven't made a single life decision on my own in over a decade. I need some runs on the board… some confidence in myself again. Achieving the easier tasks will be proof to myself that this isn't a false burst of enthusiasm. It will be evidence to the people who love me that I really am ready to start to move on.

And then, of course, comes the most significant step of all – going back to work. I smile just at the thought of the return of something normal to my days… something to occupy my thoughts and drag me out of my own mind. And there is only one veterinary clinic in town, so it's not like I have an alternative.

It's going to be hard – but all of this is going to be hard. That's why I need to keep a carrot dangling before my nose, to force myself to move forward. My eyes drop to the last line on the list, and something close to a smile rises on my lips.

A dog of my own – it's something I've dreamed of for years.

I bend to scoop Zoe up into my arms, and I carry her towards the whiteboard.

'Look, Zoe,' I whisper, as I stare at the list. 'I'm sorry I haven't been much good to you lately, but Mummy's going to make a new life for us… a better life. I promise.'

CHAPTER 4

Ivy

When David was three, Wyatt decided he wanted another baby. I was actually open to the idea at first – I loved motherhood. Only one thing was holding me back, and that was David. I remembered how intense those early months were, and how little time I had for anything else, even with just one child. I simply could not imagine how he would adjust to sharing me with a needy newborn, nor how I could live with myself if my David suffered for having to share my attention.

So I told Wyatt that I didn't want any more children. He was disappointed, but as soon as I'd made my decision, I knew it was the right one. Over the years that followed, Wyatt would ask me every now and again if I'd reconsider – but the older David got, the more certain I was that I should focus my energy on him. And that's what I did.

David was the kind of child who reached all of his milestones early. He walked at ten months, he was speaking in full sentences by the time he was two, and he showed remarkable mathematics skills from a very early age. As soon as he learned to talk, my days were filled with an endless series of 'why's that made my head ache sometimes. I'd occasionally get exasperated with the demands of his limitless curiosity, but I was quietly very proud of the way he seemed to be interrogating the world as he learned it.

'Mummy, who decided what order the numbers go in?'

'Mummy, how did the moon get in the sky?'

'Mummy, why is Grandpa Gillespie old?'

'Mummy, when I eat food, how does my belly turn it into poop?'

'Mummy, where do butterflies go at night?'

I kept him at home with me until he was four. Other mothers in our social set had enrolled their children at preschool, but I couldn't bring myself to do it. On the odd occasion when he'd gone to my mother's so I could run an errand, I fretted dreadfully for him – there was no way I wanted to commit to a weekly period where he was out of my sight. I loved the way that as soon as the slightest thing would go wrong – if he couldn't find a toy or he stumbled or there was a loud sound – he'd scan the room, frantically searching for me. Then he'd make a beeline for me, and his chubby little arms would loop around my neck, and he'd press his face against mine. So instead of preschool, I tried to meet the demands of David's inquisitive mind with trips to the library and on the odd occasion when we ventured beyond Milton Falls, I'd ignore Wyatt's eye rolls and take our son to museums.

David was a clever child, but he was also quick to develop strong gross motor skills, and, unfortunately, Wyatt wasn't about to miss a thing like that. Soon they were spending hours in the backyard, kicking the ball back and forth to each other. I loved that they were becoming close – what mother wouldn't want to see her son and his father build a relationship? But I used to stand at the kitchen window and watch them play together, and tell myself that the twisting in my gut was something other than jealousy.

Soon David was old enough to start kindergarten. He was so excited to be a 'big boy', but all I felt was anxiety. He was going to be away from me for thirty hours a week, and I knew that he didn't realise the major shift that was about to take place in the way that our lives ran. On that first morning, he was positively vibrating with energy and anticipation. He settled quickly into the class, but I waited outside for almost an hour, peeking through the window to ensure he was okay. Eventually, one of the other clingy kindergarten mothers gave me an equally teary hug and suggested we go get a coffee.

As I left the school gate that morning, I really felt like I'd left a part of my soul behind. I knew it was all a part of the journey of parenthood, but it felt like it had come too soon – like my role in his life was starting to fade already. And that idea was terrifying.

CHAPTER 5
Olivia

Natasha Green is my grief counsellor. Our family doctor, Dr Eric, wanted me to see a psychiatrist instead but there isn't one in town – the closest is at Bathurst, a regional city an hour's drive away. They booked me in to see him, but then when Mum and Dad tried to bundle me in the car to drive me over there I completely lost my mind.

I still can't bear the thought of sitting in a car. Every time I do, I see David behind the wheel instead of whoever is actually driving, and I spin into a panic. I keep telling myself it's going to pass... maybe it already has passed, and I just don't know it yet because I can't bring myself to get in a car to see.

I'm waiting out the front of the house with Zoe when Mum arrives to walk with me to my appointment with Natasha. She'll sit in the waiting room for the hour I'm in the session, then she'll walk me home, pick up her car and go to a shift at the little hospital where she's a part-time registered nurse on the geriatric ward.

Mum and Dad were supposed to retire next month. Dad owns a small accountancy practice. He was going to install a manager at the business, buy a caravan, and travel all the way around Australia with Mum. He told me a few weeks ago that they've decided to wait a year, and I know that's entirely my fault.

'So you're staying in town, but will you still retire?' I asked him.

'Ah, no point sitting around doing nothing. We'll just work another year, it's fine.'

But it isn't fine, and I feel guilty whenever I think about how hard they've worked to get to this point and how much they deserve to make the most of their retirement years. It hardly seems fair that I barely spoke to them for seven years, and then I burst back into their lives and dropped a bomb on them. Even Mum chaperoning me to this appointment each week is a huge inconvenience. She only works part-time, but Natasha only works part-time too, and we couldn't line up my appointments for a day when they were both off.

So Mum goes to work an hour late every single Thursday and it's all because of me. She says her boss is fine with it. It must still be a huge inconvenience.

'How are you feeling, Olivia?' Natasha always asks me at the start of our session. She is younger than me, which I find challenging. I'm thirty-five this year, and judging by her flawless skin I'm pretty sure Natasha is only in her late twenties – maybe early thirties at a real push. I can't help but wonder why there isn't some rule that psychologists have to live some other life before they take up this occupation and start trying to *fix* people's minds. If she was sixty, I might feel more confident about her ability to give me advice. But instead, she's younger than me, and what would *she* know about life? I know she has a family, two young children of her own. She hasn't told me anything at all about herself, but I can see her likeness in the children in the photo on the wall beside the window.

Natasha is quite beautiful, and her children are absolutely adorable. I'll bet her husband is wonderful too. I'll bet he's never so much as raised his voice at her. I'll bet if he did, she'd pack up those beautiful babies and march right out the door. She'd never stand for it, not a woman like Natasha – no, she'd be better than that. Smarter. Stronger.

'Olivia?' she prompts me now, and I shake myself and shrug.

'I'm okay,' I say, but I never know if I'm lying when I say those words these days. People ask all the time, and they don't really want to know the answer, so why shouldn't I reply with something I don't necessarily mean? It's habit.

'Is there anything in particular you want to start with today?' she asks me gently.

Of course there is. I flick my gaze over Natasha's angelic children and then focus on my own. Zoe is on my lap, and I tighten my arms around her and raise my chin. I brace myself, in case Natasha thinks this is all a terrible idea. It will take so little to discourage me. If she isn't enthused…

Everyone treats me as if I'm fragile these days, maybe there's a reason for that, maybe I *am* fragile; if I'm so uncertain about these things that I could be shaken by the potential of a single discouraging sentence from a woman I barely know.

Pathetic. Pathetic enough to stay, even when I knew I had to go. And look where that got me? Something has to change. *Something has to change.*

At the very last second, a burst of motivation resurges and I blurt,

'I'm going to move house and try to go back to work.'

'Really?' Natasha says, and her eyebrows lift, temporarily wrinkling that baby-smooth forehead. I scan her expression desperately, still terrified she will shake her head or frown, but instead, she offers me a soft smile and I release my breath in a rush. 'Well, okay then. So – moving house? Talk to me about that?'

'Ivy came to see me to drop off some mail and I just… I need to move away from her. I need to get out of David's house.'

'You could move back into your parents' house for a while?' Natasha suggests, and I shake my head automatically.

'I can't. I need my own space – and I need to *make* my own space.' I look down at my lap, then back to her and ask hesitantly, 'Do you think it's a terrible idea?'

Natasha stares at me, tilting her head just a little, but then she shrugs and offers me a smile as she says, 'Actually, I think it's a fantastic idea.'

I return her smile and my enthusiasm grows.

'I want a dog. I've always wanted a dog of my own.'

'So why haven't you had one?'

'David,' I say simply, as if his name explains everything. Natasha gets that gleam in her eye – the one she always gets when we're about to talk about him, as if she's thinking *Now we're getting to the juicy part*. I'm sure she's dying to understand, just as everyone else is – the difference is she can ask me about him without things getting awkward.

'Tell me about it?'

I remember David, sitting up in bed late one night early in our marriage, a year or two after we finished building the house. I had mentioned so casually that I'd done a health check and vaccination on a litter of Dalmatian pups at work that morning. The mess of squirming puppies had been such a delight – all six of them pressed into a box, tumbling over one another, a blur of white fur and black spots.

'They're selling them soon, and at quite a good price. Don't you think our yard is big enough for a Dalmatian? We have all of this space.'

'I don't want a dog shitting all over the turf,' David said. He was peering down at the business magazine that rested on his lap, and he seemed relaxed. I decided I would press just a little harder.

'You said when we finished building the house we could look into it. I think now would be a really good time – we're coming into the spring, and the landscaping is really established now so—'

'Liv. No. It's not happening.'

'But, babe—'

'I said no.'

'Perhaps we could consider—'

'Olivia – would you drop it? Christ, you're harping on about it like I'm being a monster – you're around animals all bloody day. Why would you want a dog at home too? *No.*'

'How did that make you feel, Olivia?' Natasha asks me, as she drags me back to the present with that question. Maybe part of the problem is that I don't really *feel* anything these days, not at the surface anyway – only numb, although occasionally I'm aware that there's a swirling turmoil deep down somewhere that I just can't connect with yet. That's probably at least in part because of the anti-depressants Dr Eric is insisting I take, and also... maybe I'm still in shock. But Natasha isn't asking me how I feel now, she's asking me how David's refusal to let me get a pet made me feel back then, and there's no avoiding *that* emotion. My arms are still around Zoe, but my hands clench into fists. I watch this happen, and I focus hard to release them, but as soon as I do, there are heavy, hot tears in my eyes.

'It was such a small thing, wasn't it?' My voice breaks, and then the crack becomes a sob.

'A reasonable request,' Natasha agrees quietly.

'He used to tell me we'd get a pet as soon as we built our own place, but he never really meant it. He didn't want to share my attention.'

'And that made you feel... '

'*Angry.*'

I didn't bring it up again with David for months, but the next time I did, he silenced me with a fierce wave of his hand and a raised voice. By then, I knew what came after that raised hand. I knew that it meant tears from me, and then guilt from him later. I didn't know which was worse, physical pain when he struck me, or his pitifully pleading remorse afterward. By then, I *knew* that it was my fault he hit me. He'd told me so many times... I was so beautiful and so brilliant that I drove him to distraction – his love for me so intense, he actually lost control because of it. *My fault.*

At first, I knew that all of this was nonsense and I simply expected that I'd change him. I was lucky to have him. I was living every little girl's dream, a handsome husband, plenty of money, a comfortable life. And I genuinely adored him and believed the best of him – I believed the best in me. I thought if I stuck around and was patient enough, I'd learn to help him control his anger.

Hadn't David told me that, a million times? I was his soulmate. He *needed* me to overcome this problem. I just had to stop provoking him, and then I could help him.

It's humiliating to look back now because it's all so obvious. But if you hear something often enough, and if the lie is repeated to you with enough sincerity by someone that you love with all of your heart, rationality eventually does give way to trust. Self-belief is a fragile thing – it can be bent so easily under the right circumstances; a closed-circle like a marriage is the perfect environment for that. There was never a single day when I was finally convinced by David's warped logic – never a single moment when I realised that *Aha! So this is my fault after all.* It was a subtler process, the gradual intermingling of his perspective with mine, so slowly that I was completely unaware of it happening. Little by little, over weeks and months and years, my confusion and shame turned to a confused acceptance and even gratitude – somehow, I came to believe that when he hurt me, he was doing it *for* me. I bought into the lie that I needed his correction. I bought into the lie that it was simply tough love from a husband who wanted the absolute best for his wife. I fell victim to a twisted psyche of my own. I began to mirror David's perspective on the ugly aspects to our marriage – he was a good man, and I just kept on goading him, so who was really to blame in the end?

'A person is always responsible for their actions. Even if they are provoked, and given what you've just said, I'm not even convinced David *was* provoked,' Natasha murmurs.

'If it wasn't really my fault,' I ask her, 'why did I keep asking him about a pet, even when I knew it made him angry? Because I did keep asking. Even when I knew it enraged him, I'd still bring it up from time to time. Why would I do that, if I didn't know on some level that I needed the punishment, or if I didn't like it somehow?'

'How did you feel *after* David hit you?'

'He loved me harder after he had hit me,' I say, around the lump in my throat.

'He was remorseful?'

'I knew I could look forward to several days or even weeks where he would almost drown me in care. The pain became secondary to the nurturing.'

'Do you feel guilty that you liked the attention after he was violent, Olivia?'

'Of course I do!' I gasp, and the shame is so intense I shift away from her a little to face towards the window. I would come home from work to find David home early, having run me a hot a bath with exotic bubbles, a glass of wine sitting at the edge and candles all around as soft music played in the background. Or he'd surprise me on my lunch-break with jewellery, or a romantic weekend away where I would have his fullest attention. David was a charming man, but he was *never* more seductive than when he was guilty. And that's absolutely the right word for it – he'd seduce me all over again, with excuses and with gifts and with promises of a better future.

Sometimes, I actually believed that the post-violence David was the real David.

'The two things don't cancel themselves out. It's not a transaction – he hurt you, but it was all made okay because he did something you liked afterwards. That's not how life works.'

'But I kept asking about the dog,' I tell her. 'I knew that he'd hurt me and I asked him anyway. So can I really blame David, if I was the one who initiated the argument even though I knew it would make him angry?'

'Sometimes in an abusive relationship, the victim convinces themselves that they are responsible for the trauma as a way of feeling in control again. Do you think that might be what you did, Olivia?' Natasha asks me now, and I look at her blankly. She offers me a gentle smile. 'You're a *vet*, Olivia – obviously you love animals, and you wanted a pet of your own, and David had already told you that he was supportive of you getting one earlier in your relationship. You were simply reminding him of a very reasonable request that he'd actually already agreed to. The dog became a battle ground for you not because it was a big deal, but simply because David used it to control you.'

I don't wear glasses, but I imagine if I needed them, the first moment I pulled them on might be like this one. It's like I see ideas that I think I understand, but they are blurry until Natasha fixes a different lens to my eyes, and suddenly the ideas come into focus. I think about all of those conversations with David about dogs and all of the times it enraged him and all of the guilt I had that I was driving David to hurt me, and I realise that this is yet another thing I have misinterpreted in the way that I understood my life. And I'm angry, but it's not the same futile, helpless anger at myself for being so stupid – finally, I'm angry that *he* treated *me* in this way.

I hate these sessions, but this is why I come. Once you see something for how it really is, you don't unsee it. It's in refocusing my life like this that I'm starting to find healing. I sit up a little straighter, and my tears – for the moment – slow.

'He can't control me now.'

'No, he can't.'

There is absolutely nothing to stop me from taking ownership of this small thing now. There is no reason at all why I cannot have what I have *always* wanted, why I cannot satisfy this simple need which has been denied.

'I'm going to get a dog,' I say, but then I remember the whiteboard. 'But not yet.'

'Why do you need to wait?'

'Because I have to do all of the hard things first, and then once I've finished them, I'll get the dog as a reward.'

With five minutes left in our session, Natasha turns the conversation to the same topic she's always hoping we'll get to. Today, she seems impressed with my plan to move forward, and there's a hopeful lilt to her voice as she asks,

'So, are you ready to talk about Sebastian yet, Olivia?'

Even the sound of his name is both a relief to my ears and a source of torture. Maybe I want to talk about David, but on some level, I do wish I could *hear* about Sebastian. I can't even help the way my heart beats faster at the sound of his name. If David brought me pain and control, Sebastian only ever offered me love.

I wish he could say the same about me.

But I can't think about that yet, let alone talk about it. I hold Zoe closer to my chest and I shake my head.

'Soon.'

✦ ✦ ✦

I get out of bed on Friday morning and I shower and wash my hair for the first time in months. I even blow-dry it.

Perhaps that achievement doesn't seem worthy of celebration, but it's actually a significant milestone. I dress myself in an entirely fresh outfit, in clothes that have actually been washed, then I put proper shoes on. Not flip-flops, not slippers – *closed-in shoes*.

I stare at myself in the mirror and I can't help but be disappointed by how tired and aged I look these days. There's make-up in the cabinet in the en suite off the master bedroom… The foundation would go a long way towards hiding at least the ghostly paleness of my skin. But that was the room I shared with David, and I haven't been able to bring myself to go in there yet. Besides, the bottle represents too many memories. I used that very bottle of foundation to cover my bruises for work in the past. Not that it ever fooled Sebastian. Maybe the vet nurses might have noticed marks too from time to time, but they were all too polite to ever mention them. Not Sebastian.

I dismiss the thought of make-up. So I look tired, well… I am tired. Besides, I'm not ready to try to emphasise my features or try to make myself shine. To start with, it's enough of a stretch just to let myself be visible again.

Next, I clip Zoe into the baby carrier. I love carrying her within it – she rests right against my breasts, close to my heart. It means that I can hold her but my arms are still free to do things, and over these past awful weeks I've wanted her close to me all of the time. Now, once she is safety strapped against my body, I slide my handbag onto my shoulder and I walk to the front door.

I unlock each latch, and then with my hand on the doorknob, I pause.

This is going to be a difficult day. There is no doubt at all that I will be uncomfortable. I am going out of my house with Zoe, and this will be the first time I've done that on my own since The Tragedy. I've done it with my sister Louisa in tow, and with Mum and Dad a few times… but even with my family to stand guard, trips into the village centre have still been awkward. I see the way that people look at me. I feel their pity acutely, like barbs into my skin. I feel their guilt too, and I hear the questions that they don't dare ask.

But today, I won't let my fear of any of that stop me. I turn the doorhandle, and I step out into David's front yard.

Our house is close to the centre of town, just three short blocks to the shops. David always wanted to live in the established part of town close to his parents – we lived in a rental for an extra two years so that we could buy two small house blocks side-by-side here, rather than one of the relatively cheap blocks of land in the new estate at the edges of town. We then knocked down the old-style houses on both blocks and he personally oversaw the building of the house we came to call home.

That house is two stories of rendered white cement. It is shaped like a giant box, with four flat sides and a flat roof. Other than windows, the only external feature is the huge charcoal door right at the centre for the entrance, and the door at the laundry at the back. There is a high fence along the front yard and the plan was that eventually we would grow hedges all along it – for privacy, David always said – but the hedging plants he chose are taking forever to grow. Our house is probably one of the flashiest homes in Milton Falls. It is the ultra-modern equivalent to the older style, apricot-bricked two-storey house that Ivy and Wyatt own around the corner – both houses bigger than just about everyone else's, as if both Wyatt and David needed their homes to make a statement.

David wanted to fill our house with a huge family one day, but I've never understood why Wyatt and Ivy needed such a large place, given it was always just the three of them. Their home is immaculate – Ivy keeps it like a museum. It is always pristine, decorated and redecorated on a yearly basis. She would never admit that she's bored – but you can see the landmarks through her life that give it away – and the compulsive redecorating is certainly one of them.

David used to say that he was actually born into the wrong region. Because he grew up here, he hated the city – but maybe he *should* have been born in Melbourne, or maybe London or Paris or Manhattan – maybe he should have been a Kardashian, he would have loved all of the meaningless attention. It was a trick of fate that he was instead born to Ivy and Wyatt. They are big fish, but instead of shining in the spotlight of the world stage, they live in a teeny tiny little pond.

I stare at the pavement as I walk past their house. It is 9 a.m. on a Tuesday morning, so I know that Ivy will be home. Most likely she will be doing the laundry – she likes to get it done first thing in the day. She should be out the back of the house hanging the clothes on the line. Just in case I'm wrong about that, I stare hard at the pavement, and I count my footsteps as I pass – saying the number under my breath and focusing on the sound of that counting. Perhaps I look like a mad woman, walking past my in-laws' house muttering to myself, but it stops me from obsessing about whether Ivy is going to try to talk to me and by the time I say the number 'forty-eight', I am into safe territory – out the front of the Walton's house next door.

This feels like a triumph, and I suddenly wish that someone was keeping score of my progress today.

I need milk and that means I'll need to go to the supermarket, and of course, Wyatt still works there – he does own the place, after all. He'll be in the office, and I have been in that room a million times myself, so I know there is an entire wall of security cameras right in front of his desk. He'll see me walking the halls of that store with his granddaughter fixed against my chest. He won't come down to say hello – unlike Ivy, he has been avoiding me with stark determination since The Tragedy. That's why I'm so confident he won't even leave the office while I'm in his store, and that's the only reason I'm going there at all.

I round the corner before the grocery store, but as I pass the little café there, the scent of ground beans wafts past me and I pause. How long has it been since I had a barista-made espresso, let alone sat in one of those familiar padded wing-chairs to read a magazine? The thought is just too tempting. I push the door open and step inside. The place is quite busy – lots of workers are standing in line waiting patiently for their morning caffeine fix on their way to the office.

I tell myself that I am imagining the chatter in the room fading off as I step inside, but when I find the courage to shoot a quick glance around, there's no denying the tension. A couple of men in suits whisper to one another while flicking hesitant glances in my direction. The barista is frothing milk, but she's staring at me as she works the jug and her jaw is hanging open. Two students waiting in the line are facing away from me, but they take turns sneaking a glance back at me.

The barista's gaze is still on me as she calls, 'Can I help you?'

'These people are in front of me,' I point out, and heat sweeps up my face. The students step aside hastily, but the two women in front of them don't move, and I add, 'I'm not in a rush. Honestly.'

So I wait in the line while the barista serves the other customers between stints at the coffee machine. When it's finally my turn, she greets me with, 'What can I get you, Olivia?'

I look at her nametag. *Brontë*. She's new here, and I've never seen her before in my life.

'A flat white, please. In a mug.'

'Okay,' she says, then another bright smile. 'Take a seat, I'll bring it over to you.'

'How much is that?'

'Oh – err – it's on the house.'

'You don't have to give me free coffee,' I say, bewildered, but she offers me a weak smile as she insists, 'Please, I'd like to. Take a seat?'

'Since when do you have table service here?' I mutter, but there's already more customers behind me and the more I protest, the more attention I seem to be bringing to myself, so I walk to an empty set of chairs and I sit down. I push aside a news and current affairs magazine at the top of the stack on the table – *too risky* – in the early days, I know the national media covered what happened. I dive into a glossy rag full of likely fictional celebrity gossip. When Brontë brings my coffee over a few minutes later, she pauses at my table, and offers me another smile. She's young – maybe only nineteen or twenty, which somehow makes her pity harder to bear.

'I think you're *really* brave,' she whispers as she sits the coffee down in front of me. I look at the coffee, then at the well-intentioned, if somewhat patronising barista, and I clear my throat and mutter, 'Thanks?'

I don't intend the question that slips out with the word. Brontë gives me a gentle smile and pats my shoulder as if I'm a tragic invalid of some sort, and returns to the line of customers waiting for her attention.

Fortunately, the coffee is so good that it's almost worth the ordeal. It is creamy and perfectly bitter and a little too hot... The taste is full in my mouth and I savour the feel of it on my tongue. This is one of those luxuries I haven't even thought to miss; a simple enjoyment I once absolutely took for granted.

Perhaps the little pit stop has been anything but ordinary, but this first venture alone into town was always going to be difficult, and I promise myself that every time I come it will be less so. I catch up on celebrity gossip and I enjoy the coffee, and then I rise and I continue on my way.

CHAPTER 6

Ivy

Early in that kindergarten year, I realised that David had a crush on one of the girls in his class. She was a pretty, popular little girl named Rachael. Her mother always styled her white-blonde hair into two bouncy pigtails on either side of her head, right behind her ears.

David's teacher sat him next to Rachael in class at the start of his second month of schooling. She was quiet and shy, and David was more confident and boisterous – their teacher told me she was hoping they'd balance each other out. Soon, David would greet me each afternoon with an anecdote starring Rachael: she'd made a funny joke, or read a really difficult sentence all by herself, or she had an egg sandwich for lunch or had been away sick.

I knew David's crush was obvious when even Wyatt noticed it, after yet another family dinner where the entire conversation centred around David's desk mate.

'What a stud! He's noticing the ladies early, must take after me,' he said, and he winked at me. I rolled my eyes at him, but I had to agree it was pretty adorable.

When David turned six in March, we invited Rachael to his birthday party. There would be ten boys and Rachael at the party at our house on a Sunday afternoon. I ran into Rachael's mother Julia at the school gate on Friday, and I asked if she would be joining us.

'She was surprised that he invited her,' Julia admitted. 'She's been telling us that he doesn't like her – she thinks he's picking on her when they play at lunchtime.'

I looked down at my son, who was standing hard up against my hip. I gave him a questioning glance, but he stared back at me blankly. I looked back to Julia and tried to convey an extra layer of meaning as I said carefully, 'Actually, he talks about her *a lot*.'

She laughed and winked at me. 'I told her that was probably the case.'

Rachael tugged at her mother's hand impatiently. 'I don't want to go. He is so mean to me all of the time. He pushed me over today when we were playing tip! I don't like him.'

'Rachael!' her mother gasped. 'You are being so rude! I told you – this is just how little boys show you that they like you. Mrs Gillespie and David have been very kind to you inviting us to their house.'

Julia looked at me, a flush to her cheeks, and she said pointedly, 'We will be at that party, Ivy. See you on Sunday.'

David was delighted. As we walked home to our house, he talked with such excitement that his sentences ran into each other. 'And Jack is coming… and Alan… and now Rachael is coming so we can play 'catch-and-kiss'! It's going to be the best party ever.'

'I'm glad she's coming, Davey – but you know, you do need to be a bit careful not to upset her, okay? She's just a little girl, and I know you boys like to play rough.'

'Naw, Mum!' David groaned. 'We're just having fun. She likes it, I know she does.'

'Girls are much more fragile than you are – they like different things, and they don't always understand that you're just playing. So you need to be more careful, okay? Have your fun, but don't take it so far that you get yourself into any trouble.'

At the party, Rachael sat sullen beside her mother while the boys thundered through my house. We had the cake I'd fashioned, and then we all went outside for one final game before the children would head home. Julia was immensely frustrated with Rachael by this point, and she pushed her daughter towards the boys impatiently.

'Go and play, for goodness sakes!'

Rachael moved reluctantly towards the rest of the guests, but as the game started up again, she did warm up. I was relieved to see that she was finally smiling, and finally laughing – and I was satisfied by this, and somehow proud that David had been so inclusive as to invite a *girl* to his sixth birthday party, at a time when all of the rest of his friends had a mortal fear of 'girl's germs'.

Just when it was time to leave, I was standing at the door farewelling Julia when David ran up out of nowhere to pull hard on Rachel's ponytail.

'Don't!' she shrieked, and the shrill word still echoed in my hallway as her mother said sharply,

'Rachael! Don't you dare raise your voice inside!'

David laughed and Rachael scowled. I scolded my son gently, 'That wasn't very nice, David.'

He stuck his tongue out at Rachael as he ran back to his toys and I sighed apologetically to her mother, 'Boys will be boys.'

'True,' Julia sighed, 'and *girls* need to learn their manners.'

CHAPTER 7
Olivia

I walk the final block to the supermarket. Everyone who passes me looks at me and then they stare at Zoe. I keep my head down and I try to avoid their gazes, but bizarre moments of pure bravado overtake me, and sometimes I look right at the passers-by – at one stage, I even stare a woman down, until *she* looks away. Her name is Linda and she works at the town council, and once upon a time she would have said hello to me, but today she just looks at the ground and takes off at a near sprint down the street.

This almost gives me a giggle – I feel like I've outwitted Linda somehow, but there's a sting in the tail of the moment and that's the shame I feel as the sympathy in her eyes belatedly registers. The problem with meeting people's gazes is that it's a fast-track way to remind me of just how much things have changed. In all that has happened in the last three months, nothing has been harder than facing people's pity. It feels like an insult – not 'I feel for you', but rather 'I am just so *glad* that I am not you'.

I know this is only going to get worse today – the supermarket is going to be harder than facing near-strangers on the street. But I also know that if I hide from this forever, my whole future will look like a blank canvas that I never found the strength to paint on and I *cannot let that happen*. If I really don't have the strength to do this for myself, then I simply have to find a way to do it for Zoe.

Besides, I only need milk. This will take all of two minutes.

I take several deep breaths at the entrance to the supermarket, and then I step inside.

The shoppers at the checkouts at the front of the store do not stop what they are doing to stare at me. I've been anticipating a much more dramatic reaction and the ordinariness of the scene that greets me is a revelation. Instead of running to the milk aisle and then to the checkout, I walk towards the trolleys and take one, and I decide that, since I'm here, there are a few other things I could do with and I might just wander the aisles for a while.

I walk down the first aisle, pushing my trolley with my baby on my chest and I feel for just a moment like I am someone other than me. I am an average person – a blissfully ordinary person. Maybe it was all a nightmare – perhaps a terrible hallucination – or maybe I've simply gone back in time and I am once again the Olivia from before it happened. For a few beautiful moments, I am not a living reminder of the latest town scandals – I'm just an ordinary shopper, perusing an ordinary supermarket. I pick fruit and vegetables I don't really need, and then I get milk and bread. I am enjoying myself, completely taken by the simple ordinariness of this moment. It could actually be addictive – and I start to wonder why I haven't tried to do this before now. It seemed so insurmountable – the fear of what people would say, the fear that just going out in public alone with Zoe would somehow humiliate us both further. But now, here I am, mere days after I decided to build a new life for myself, shopping in the supermarket like nothing ever went wrong. I wanted runs on the board, and here I am – hitting a six. But then I see Mrs Jones.

She's a seventy-something-year-old widow, and I know her well from work because she likes to collect cats. I stopped trying to keep tabs on her menagerie years ago, because it doesn't really matter – she has plenty of money, and nurtures her pets as if they are children. She's a sweet, innocent old lady with the best of intentions and the startling ability to keep tabs of what every single resident in Milton Falls had for breakfast – exactly the kind of person I do not want to see today.

I try to turn the trolley around when I see her, but she has already spotted me and she rushes at me. She stares wordlessly at Zoe, and then at me, and then her eyes fill with tears and I take an automatic step backward.

'Olivia,' she breathes, and then she gives a little cough that I think might be the start of a sob. 'Dear girl, I am just so sorry.'

In that moment, I make the second momentous decision of the day, because it would be easiest to step away from Mrs Jones, to leave my half-full trolley, and to run home to the solitude and refuge of my house. But if I do that, I won't come back – not tomorrow, not next week, maybe not next year. To fail today is to accept that I will live my life of solitude; it would be to accept that life will not go on.

'Thank you, Mrs Jones,' I say very carefully. Then I put my hands right back on the handrail of the trolley, and I start to push past her.

Mrs Jones hooks her frail hand through the crook of my elbow, and my footsteps stop.

I am staring straight ahead. I don't want to look at her again, in case that encourages her to say something else. I don't want to address what happened, I don't want to hear her say David's name, not here in the supermarket – not in these aisles where he once worked, not with his father watching on the CCTV.

I hear Mrs Jones draw in a deep breath, and I know that she's about to say something difficult or awkward, or worse still – that she's about to say the thing that I hate hearing the most. What if she's about to say something like, 'But dear, didn't you know? Surely there were *warning signs*?' or worse still, 'David was a good man, he just snapped, didn't he?'

Even in my hesitant ventures out and about with my family, even with their intervention and the way that they guard me like a security detail, I have heard these questions too many times already, and I can't bear to hear them again.

Not today.

So I turn to Mrs Jones again, and I stare at her, my gaze hard. I want her to see my pain, and to be frightened away by it. Maybe if I show her just how damaged I am by what I have walked through, she'll run away.

I'm startled when she suddenly, fiercely pulls me against her. Zoe is caught between us, and I gasp and try to pull back, but Mrs Jones is not releasing me. She kisses the side of my head, and then she whispers in my ear, 'Olivia darling, I am praying for you every single day.'

At that, I do pull away from her, violently – I am breathing hard and adrenaline is racing all through my body – my hands shake, my stomach is churning the coffee. I run my hands down over Zoe and it's only when I see that she's fine that I can breathe again. I glare at Mrs Jones, and then I walk briskly past her, straight to the end of the aisle.

I complete the remaining aisles at breakneck speed, staring into my trolley. At least two other people say hello to me, I don't even look to see who they are – I just keep my head down and I walk fast and the whole time there is a relentless litany of questions running through my mind. Am I *sure* this is going to get easier? What if I'm wrong – what if I'm always going to be defined as Olivia Gillespie – the woman who drove her husband to suicide, the woman who found her husband's body? I used to be more than that. Before I was a battered wife, I knew that I was *more* than just a wife. I was an educated, dedicated career woman. I was a friend and a sister and a daughter. I was a lover. I was a mother.

I was a person.

I make it to their checkout. I'm exhausted, my limbs heavy and my muscles sore as if I have run a marathon. I still have to go the post office. Do I do it tomorrow?

No.

That defeatist attitude is what got me into the situation in the first place – still hiding out and hiding behind my family. I have to stop procrastinating about moving on. Zoe needs me to, *I* need me to – even the damned townsfolk need me to. So, I rudely ignore the small talk that the checkout clerk attempts to inflict upon me, and I ignore the way her eyes well with tears when she looks at Zoe.

I carry my four little bags of groceries out the door, and I walk straight across the road and into the post office. I go straight to the counter, and this time, I do skip the small line and I don't wait at the end like I should. I am so tired, drained by all of this exposure – besides which, on some level, I know that nobody will protest. Perhaps they are clumsy about it sometimes, but the people of Milton Falls really have been trying to care for me. It's probably the only reason I've managed to survive this far and I don't take it for granted.

'Hello, Olivia,' the clerk says carefully. Her name is Leah. I can't remember how I know her – but I know we've met before.

'I need you to tell Ross that he needs to stop redirecting my mail,' I say flatly.

Leah stares at me, her eyes wide and her lip trembling a little. She doesn't answer at first, and the store is now completely silent and everyone is looking – I feel their eyes on my back.

'I don't need him to protect me, I just need my mail delivered to wherever it's addressed, regardless of whose name is on the envelope and whether or not he thinks it's going to upset me.' Leah is still staring at me blankly, so I give her a pointed look and I say, 'Can you actually hear me?'

When she nods, I turn and walk right back past the line, and out the door, and I make my way all the way back to David's house. Once I'm inside and I have unbuckled Zoe and put her down into the bouncer, I feel like I have done something amazing. I go to the phone and I call my mother.

'Hello, darling. How are you today?'

'Mum,' I say, and then I burst into tears. They are proud tears though. I'm overwhelmed, but I'm triumphant. I have done it. I have left my house alone, I have gone into the town centre, I have *faced* people. I am moving on. I don't sound like I am moving on, though, because I'm crying great heaving sobs which I imagine must be making my mother quite nervous. I try to explain myself. 'I walked into town and I got a coffee and I bought some groceries and I went to the post office.'

'But... Livvy, sweetheart,' Mum sounds bewildered. 'I would have taken you after work sweetheart – or Dad – or even Louisa would have gone with you if you'd asked. Why didn't you wait?'

'Mum – I *can't* rely on you forever.'

'But that's what we're here for, darling.'

That's *not* what they are here for, and I know it. It seems so brutally unfair that they were the first people to try to intervene, and I hated them for it and all but cut them off from my life – and yet now that David's gone, their entire lives are on hold for me.

'So... did you drive your car?' Mum asks me hesitantly.

'No,' I say, then curtly, 'I'm still not ready for that. I walked.'

'Okay, okay.' Mum pauses, then she gasps, 'But Livvy – what did you do with Zoe?'

'I took her with me,' I laugh quietly. 'What did you think I'd do with her? It's warming up outside at last so I just put her in the baby carrier. It was fine.'

I'm still crying, but I'm fairly sure I'm coherent enough that my mother can understand me. But then she is silent for a long time, and my sobs start to fade off as I wait for her response. I battle a negative voice in my mind that wants to assume that Mum is somehow offended that I've done this, or thinks it's too soon, or that she's still angry with me for not listening to her all of those years ago. I'm relieved when my mother finally whispers, 'Well done. What a huge step for you to take on your own. I am so proud of you, Livvy.'

CHAPTER 8
Ivy

David was always just a little jealous of my dogs. He never said it in so many words, but I could tell. I religiously spent an hour a day with them between their walks and training time, and the inevitable grooming and show preparation. On weekends and in the school holidays, David was sometimes at home to watch all of this happen, and I'd feel his eyes on me from the bedroom window as I worked with them in the backyard. I sometimes asked if he wanted to help, but he'd give me a miserable look.

'You spend more time with those dogs than you spend with me, Mum.'

'I don't, darling,' I'd say, pleading with him. 'The dogs are my only hobby, I need something to do while you're at school, right?'

It was maddening, particularly given that out of twenty-four hours a day, I felt like David already got twenty-three of them. Right from the time he was born, I even seemed to sleep with one ear open, in case he needed me somehow overnight. I'd hear the slightest cough or change in the tenor of his breathing, even if I was deeply asleep. It was almost as though his care and safety became more important even than my own basic biological needs.

When David was eight, we had a litter of brand new puppies arrive right before school holidays. Queenie was a beautiful dog, and she'd had a litter sired by a dog from the city – one of the best champion Pomeranians in the state. They had six pups who were soon scampering around the house making messes and causing chaos. Due to the strong pedigree, I sometimes spent hours a day fielding enquiries from potential homes for them.

David was unimpressed by all of this excitement around the dogs.

'I'm so bored. You didn't organise anything for me to do these holidays, you're too busy with the dogs again.'

'Why don't you help me?' I asked him. 'You could play with them in the backyard.'

'I don't want to,' David muttered. He wanted to sulk in front of the TV when he didn't have a pre-arranged, scheduled activity to go to. It grated on my nerves, particularly when he would interrupt me while I was on the phone to ask me nonsense questions about food or whether I'd buy him a new toy of one sort or another. I finally snapped one day. I was on a call and he physically dragged the phone away from my ear only to ask me, 'What's for lunch?'

'Excuse me one moment,' I said to the caller, and then I muted the phone and I pointed to the back door.

'Take those bloody puppies outside and play with them for a few minutes, for goodness sakes – you *and* the dogs could both do some fresh air – then I'll make your lunch.'

It was only a few minutes later that I heard David give a piercing scream. I hung up the call and ran to the backyard to find David on his hands on knees, right beside a pup lying on its side on the ground.

'What happened?' I gasped, and I ran to the puppy's side and crouched beside it. The dog was twitching, there was a trail of blood from its ear, and David was white as a ghost. Queenie and the other pups were all yapping wildly, scampering around with visible distress.

'Mum, I'm so sorry. I tripped; it got under my foot and I just fell.'

The puppy was trembling, and I wanted to take hope from the fact that it was still moving, but it was clearly in a bad way. We bundled it up in a towel, and raced it to the vet clinic. Years later, David's own wife would work at that clinic, but at that stage it was owned by Dr Ryder Wilson. He was old and infamously grouchy, but he had always treated our pets.

Ryder checked the puppy over while David and I watched, holding our breaths. David was sick with guilt. He could barely sit still, and he had gagged a few times – a nurse passed him a bucket in case he actually threw up. When Ryder eventually lifted the puppy onto its feet we all watched as it fell to its side.

'I don't think it's going to make it,' he said very quietly. Then he looked at David and asked, 'David, what really happened?'

'He just tripped. He accidentally fell on the puppy.' I rushed to answer the question for David, who gave me a stricken look as he nodded.

'I'm so sorry, Dr Wilson. I was playing with them, and I just tripped.'

'I think the puppy's skull is crushed,' the vet murmured. He glanced at David, and his brows knit for a moment before he said very carefully, 'Maybe you stumbled and your foot landed on it?'

'I don't know – I mean, I just panicked – I didn't mean to, Mum. I promise, I didn't mean to.'

I walked quickly to my son, and I pulled him close to me. I could feel his body shaking against mine, and then later, when the puppy died, David cried as if he was a baby again. I cried too, particularly after we came home and Queenie was still running around yapping and trying to find the missing puppy.

Wyatt thought we were both being ridiculous. When he came home from work that night and heard what had happened, he was only angry that we'd wasted money at the vet trying to save the dog.

'Jesus, it was just a stupid puppy. You've still got five of them.'

'It was very distressing,' I said quietly.

'Sometimes, when I was growing up, if the cat had kittens and we didn't want them, it was my job to take them out, put them in a sack, and drown them. You need to toughen up a bit, son. It's a fact of life that puppies die sometimes.'

'Sorry, Dad,' David said, and he wiped at his eyes. 'I just feel bad. I didn't mean for it to get hurt.'

'Well, you made a mistake. That's life, isn't it?' Wyatt said, and he picked up the remote and turned the television on.

'I should have been more careful,' David said, but I could see from the look in my son's eyes that he wanted to talk about this some more. I could see that look as clearly as I could see the guilt, and I couldn't quite tell if the guilt was there because this was just a terrible accident, or because it wasn't. I could only imagine how much force it must have taken to fracture the puppy's skull – could that really have been an accident? Eventually, I'd come to loathe myself for even wondering about that, and I'd shift blame for the incident back onto my own shoulders – I really shouldn't have forced him to go outside with them, or left such a young boy with the responsibility of caring for so many small dogs.

I thought perhaps after what happened with that pup that David would want to get a little more involved with the family dogs, particularly after how upset he'd been when it died. But if anything, David wanted the dogs around even less. He no longer would even take them out to go to the toilet, or refill their water trough when I asked. In fact, after that litter of puppies had all gone off to their homes, and I mentioned that I would breed the dogs again the following summer, David tried to convince me not to.

'They're such a waste of space, Mum. You hardly make any money off them, and they're just *so* annoying. Plus, you never know… ' David shrugged, and said sadly, 'You just never know when they're going to get hurt. Accidents *do* happen, don't they?'

I remember that day so vividly. I could have heard that as a threat, but I was sure that wasn't how David meant it. He was so young – too young to work with nuance. Surely the implied threat was just a mistake - my mistake. I told myself that he was scared that he might accidentally hurt the tiny puppies again. I promised myself that was the case.

I didn't breed the dogs that summer. I waited years, until David was a teenager, and far too busy with his sport and his schooling to be bothered by what was going on with the dogs. I didn't even invite David to the dog shows after that, in fact, I never asked him to help at all.

As a mother, you're biologically programmed to look for the best in your children. It's how we bring out their strengths – how we protect them from people who would criticise and cut them down from a very young age. Who hasn't become defensive when another parent has accused their child of something terrible? Or boasted about a child's achievements, or pushed them just a little harder to reach potential they didn't seem to want to access? It's all muddled up together for a parent – defensiveness and that odd drive we have to help them to be their best. And I was doing what a good mother does – I was believing only in the *good* in my son.

I pushed the incident with the pup right out of my mind, and I wouldn't think of it again for decades.

CHAPTER 9
Olivia

'… Gilly made caramel slice for morning tea but she used that gluten-free flour her husband has to have and it tasted like cardboard. I organised some in-service training for the nurses, they're all going off to Sydney together in a few weeks for this professional development seminar on biosecurity. Let me see… what else has been happening… Oh! How could I forget? Do you remember Alistair's girlfriend Vanessa? They got engaged last night, so I guess I'm going to get a sister-in-law.'

I'm sitting with my back against the door, listening as Seb chats to me from the other side. Zoe rests on my lap.

'I'm thinking of selling this house,' I say, somehow forgetting for a moment that my voice doesn't work around Sebastian these days, and I'm delighted to find that it actually *does*.

'Liv?' I can tell by his tone that he's as startled as I am. 'You are?'

'It's time to move on.'

'Good,' he breathes, and I hear him shift on the doorstep. 'Can I help?'

'Maybe,' I say softly. 'Maybe you already have.'

'So I should keep doing this, Liv? Calling past? Even when you can't speak to me? I don't want to be in your way… '

I can hear how anxious he is to be addressing this directly, and I know if I could see him, I'd see his hands moving compulsively and his expression would be pained. His concern is palpable, and he wears his heart on his sleeve even at the best of times.

'Actually,' I say, my voice a little louder now, 'no, you can stop now. I'm going to come and see you at work soon instead, okay?'

'Are you sure?'

'Yes.'

'You have my number. You'll call me if you need anything?'

'I'll try.'

'Okay, Livvy. Okay,' he says, and I hear the smile I can't see. 'It's good to hear your voice.'

'It's been good to hear yours too.'

'I'll see you soon, then?'

I think of the whiteboard, and I clutch Zoe a little tighter.

'Hopefully, yes.'

I'm buoyed by Seb's visit and by the delight in his tone when I spoke to him. After he leaves, I make myself up a cup of tea and walk to the laptop. I search for 'Milton Falls real estate agent', expecting to find only one result and really only looking for the phone number. I'm surprised when the search returns two entries.

There is the Milton Falls Real Estate Agency, the estate agent that we've used in the past, the big one – the one that I know. It's owned by Todd McKay who went to school with David and me. His wife is Sarah. I wouldn't call her a friend these days, although she certainly was one back when we were at high school. Now she's an acquaintance, someone who'd approach me to say hi at a party, but who would avoid the awkwardness of seeking me out after a major life crisis.

But beneath Todd's entry is a new real-estate agent. I didn't know a new one had opened, but it was probably overdue – Todd's family has had a monopoly on the town's real estate forever. The new business is named Ingrid Little Real Estate, and I click on the website to find a 'Coming Soon' page. But there is a phone number, and my fingers hesitate on the keyboard.

I should really use Todd's agency. I know all of the staff, and they know my situation.

But something about the idea of using the new agency appeals to me. I call my sister. Louisa is a paralegal at the town solicitor's office – if Ingrid Little has sold any houses, Louisa will have seen the conveyancing paperwork.

'What are you up to?' she greets me when I call her mobile phone.

'I'm thinking about putting David's house on the market.'

Louisa gasps. 'But where will you live?'

'I'm just considering it, I haven't made up my mind,' I lie, because Louisa seems horrified and I don't feel like defending myself. 'But… if I go through with it, I'll buy myself a new house. A small house, just a little cottage for me and Zoe – and maybe a dog down the line.'

'But… isn't it a bit soon, Livvy? You're really still coming to terms with what's happened. Can't you let the dust settle a bit more?'

'Anyway… it's just an idea at this stage. I was looking for the phone number for Todd's agency, and I saw that there's a new place in town – Ingrid Little. Have you heard of her?'

Louisa sighs, and she mutters, 'Yeah, I've heard of her. She opened up just about the same time as… as… as when… '

Even Louisa can't bring herself to say it. I hurry her along.

'I know *when* you mean, Lulu. Is she any good?'

'Just use Todd. He knows you.'

'That's exactly why I *don't* want to use Todd,' I mutter, and then I ask again. 'Is there any reason why I shouldn't use Ingrid Little?'

'Only because she's new in town. She has no idea how complex your situation is. If you use Todd, he'll know to be sensitive. Plus he and Da… Dav… ' she breaks off, then groans impatiently. 'You know what I'm trying to say, Liv. They were friends. I'm sure Todd will look after you.'

'Louisa, just tell me – is there any good reason why I should not use Ingrid Little to sell my house?' I ask, more firmly now. 'I really like the idea of using this lady if she's new to town and if she has no idea about what happened.'

'Olivia, *everyone* knows what happened. I just think that Todd might be more sensitive. He won't ask you any awkward questions.'

I sigh.

'I'll think about it.'

Almost as soon as I hang up the phone from my sister, I dial Ingrid Little's phone number.

'Ingrid Little Real Estate,' a chirpy voice says, 'you're speaking with Meg.'

'Oh, hello Meg,' I say, and suddenly I'm nervous. 'My name is Olivia Gillespie – Olivia Brennan, I mean. I need to sell my house, and I need to buy a new one.'

'Certainly!' the voice says. 'I'll just put you on hold. Ingrid will be right with you.'

I listen to the hold music for a minute or two, and then a voice says, 'Hello, this is Ingrid. How can I help you?' There is no denying that this is the exact same voice that answered the phone the first time. I smile a little to myself, and I say, 'Hi there, Ingrid. My name is Olivia Brennan. I need to sell my house and I'd like to buy a new one. Can you help me with that?'

'Of course I can!' Ingrid says, and she's positively bursting with enthusiasm. I like her already, and even better, I like that she didn't gasp or say something awkward as soon as I identified myself. 'When can I come and take a look at your house, Olivia?'

'Um, when are you free?' I ask.

'How about now?'

I look around my living room and survey the filth. Mum and Dad have been coming to help me clean occasionally, but I really haven't put much effort into maintaining their efforts between visits. The house is mortifyingly dirty, which would have driven David completely insane, and maybe that's part of the reason why it hasn't bothered me one bit until now.

'Erm, I'm pretty free this week, but I do need a bit of notice. I'll need to tidy the house up.'

Ingrid laughs. 'I won't take the photos today. Let me just come and have a look. We can talk about what you're looking for in your new house, and I can give you an indication of price for the old one. What's the address?'

CHAPTER 10

Ivy

Those tender primary school years passed us by quickly. David was a great student – and Wyatt made sure he was a strong sportsman, too. We were the family who were always running off somewhere – soccer training on Mondays, piano lesson on Tuesday, scouts on Wednesday, athletics on Thursday and then Friday night was generally football or cricket training.

Sometimes people commented that we pushed David too hard, which I found completely bewildering. He was just so *good* at so many different things, and I wanted to give him every opportunity to succeed.

'He needs time to be a kid,' my mother said to me one Saturday morning. We'd invited her and Dad to watch David compete in an athletics carnival, but almost from the moment of David's first race, she sat by the sidelines in stony silence. While I was cheering him on and giving him pep-talks between events, Mum was scowling.

'He has plenty of time to be a kid,' I sighed, and Mum raised her chin.

'Rushing around to activities every day isn't good for him.'

'Wyatt and I are in a position to let David explore a lot of interests. It's good for him.'

'Perhaps,' Mum said, but then after a pause, she muttered, 'but I'm not at all sure it's good for him when his mother tells him that he should have come first every time he loses a race.'

'Mum,' I groaned, and shook my head at her. 'You don't get this at all, do you? I'm not pressuring him. He *wants* to be the best. It's just my job to help him do it.'

'He can't be the best at everything, Ivy. He's a kid – this is meant to be fun. Isn't all of this sport about learning how to win and lose? How to play nice with the other kids? How to try and fail and accept when things don't go his way?'

'Of course! But he's a special little boy and—'

'Every kid is special,' Mum said flatly. 'If he doesn't understand that, he'll think he's entitled to special treatment his whole life.'

'You don't get it,' I snapped at her, and I shook my head in disgust. 'What kind of grandmother wants her child to feel *less* special?'

Mum stared at me for a moment, then her lips compressed and she turned back to the field.

'You're right, Ivy. I *don't* get it. So maybe I should keep my thoughts to myself.'

'Maybe you should,' I muttered. It was my turn to scowl. I should have known Mum would be like this. She and Dad never really took much interest in my hobbies or education, beyond the routine pat on the head when my report cards were good.

Later in the day, David moved from the races to compete in the long jump. On his first jump, he positively nailed his technique and flew through the air to land a good way in the sand. I leapt into the air and cheered, but just as I landed, the referee shook his head.

'Foul,' he called. David turned and looked straight at me, so I saw the way his triumphant smile faded all the way to nothing.

'What?!' I gasped, and left the spectator's area to approach the judge. 'Why was that a foul?'

'His foot was over the line.'

'David knows the rules, he's always careful about that. You must be mistaken.'

'Mrs Gillespie,' the referee sighed. 'I know what I saw. I'm sorry, but the jump was definitely a foul. Look, he's still got two jumps left—'

'No!' I exclaimed, and I planted my hands on my hips. 'David definitely jumped correctly. I'm sorry, I have to insist you reconsider.'

'You can insist all you want,' the referee said pointedly. 'My decision is final.'

'I'll take it up with the organisers, then.'

Then he exhaled forcibly, and leant towards me and said, his voice low and urgent, 'Look, Ivy – it's a social comp. This isn't even being recorded. It's just for fun, okay? David misplaced his foot, it wouldn't fair to the other kids to let him get away with it. Just leave this one. Pick your parenting battles, hey?'

'Don't you dare patronise me,' I snapped, and just when I was ramping up to give him a piece of my mind, I heard a hesitant voice beside me.

'Mum,' David said quietly. 'Maybe I did foul.'

'Don't be ridiculous, David,' I frowned at him. 'I was watching; you were well behind the line. Let Mummy talk to Mr Jacobs quietly, okay?'

'But what if I slipped a bit?'

'David, you *didn't*. That was a terrific jump and it should count.'

Right then, I happened to scan past the little spectator's area looking for the head of the organising committee. My gaze stalled on my mother's face. She was wearing a look of such stern disapproval that I stiffened. She had *no idea*! Her generation didn't advocate for their kids, and maybe... just maybe that's why *I* didn't know to advocate for myself when I'd found myself seventeen and knocked up. Well, I wasn't about to make that mistake with David. I looked right back to the referee and was about to launch into another appeal for a reconsideration, but then David tugged at my hand.

'Mum, *please*. Everyone is looking.'

I sighed and shot the referee one last glance to let him know I still wasn't happy, and I let David lead me back to the spectator area. He trailed behind me, his head down and his feet dragging along the ground.

'Listen, Davey,' I said quietly, and I crouched so that we were at eye level. 'You're a special little boy, and that was a really great jump. It should have counted. Mr Jacobs is just jealous because his son isn't as clever at sport. And I'm always, *always* going to try to make sure people do the right thing by you, okay? I *know* you wouldn't have fouled that jump.'

David stared at me, his brow furrowed, his expression unsure. I caught his upper arms in my hands and shook him gently, forcing his gaze to mine. 'You didn't foul it, did you?'

Something in his blue eyes sharpened. He raised his chin and shook his head. I was proud of the sudden confidence in his gait.

'No, Mum. I didn't foul it.'

'Then next time, you make sure Mr Jacobs knows it. Got it?'

'Okay.'

'Go back and get ready for your next jump.'

He ran down the hill, and I sat beside Mum again.

'Ivy,' she said carefully. 'Just be careful, love.'

'He was robbed, Mum,' I muttered.

'Kids *need* to learn how to fail, Ivy.'

'I'm not going to sit on my hands while he's being victimised,' I said abruptly. 'Look, you said it yourself earlier. Maybe you should keep your thoughts to yourself.'

Mum sighed and shook her head, then went back to watching the competition.

She did have some funny old-fashioned ideas, my mother.

❖ ❖ ❖

They *were* busy years, but they were such happy years too. I was watching my little boy become a little man. I took pride in his every achievement, and pride even in the way that *I* could see his potential well before others did.

When David was at school, I had a regular routine of chores around the house – laundry first thing, often then I'd bake, train the dogs around lunchtime, and enjoy some downtime in the afternoon. In winter, I liked to read by the fire. In summer, I liked to read on the back deck near the pool. I had to be militant with my downtime during the day because the afternoons and evenings were always full. I was the president of the Parents and Friends Committee at the school for most of David's primary school years, I was often the secretary for his sports team, and he needed my hands-on tutoring. I really had to push him to keep progressing with his schoolwork. He tended to get bored quickly, and sometimes, his grades came in low – which was ridiculous, because he was by far the smartest child in his class most years.

'This happens with gifted children,' I told Wyatt. 'They just need extra challenges… extra stimulation. His teachers just aren't meeting his needs.'

Wyatt tended to just go along with whatever I suggested when it came to David's schooling, but his teachers were a whole other matter. It was a constant battle to convince them that David *needed* constant challenges. His third-grade teacher streamed the class by spelling ability and at one stage, actually sent David home with the easiest set of words.

'That's ridiculous!' I exclaimed. David grinned.

'Easier is *better*, Mum, don't worry.'

'I'm not having it,' I said flatly. 'You use that brain of yours, Davey, or you'll lose it. Trust me.'

So the next morning I walked him to the classroom and I asked his teacher for a word in private. Mrs White sighed as we sat opposite one another at her desk. We wasted no time on pleasantries, instead, she opened her palms wide and prompted, 'What can I help you with this morning, Ivy?'

'David is not working to his potential in your class. I wanted to let you know in person before I speak with the principal. I'm going to request he be switched to the other class.'

The teacher's eyes widened and she sat back in her chair, surveying me with something akin to disbelief in her eyes.

'Ivy, David is settled and happy here in my class. He's working right on the levels we expect of a child in grade three, I have plenty of parents who'd kill to see a report card like David's. Is there a particular problem we need to address?'

'David should be with a teacher who can see his potential, not one who is willing to let him coast along as if he's an ordinary child.'

She protested very little in the end, and the principal switched David to the other class without much fuss; I assume because he could see that I was right.

And once I requested it, the new teacher moved David into the advanced spelling group. It took a lot of work for us to catch up on the work he'd missed in those months with the sub-standard teacher, but I didn't mind at all; I worked intensively with David at home on his spelling until his assessment results were back on track.

Wyatt's influence on David seemed to trump mine sometimes, and I could never understand why, given I provided for all of David's essential needs. Maybe Wyatt earned the money, but I was the one who used it to keep the house. I was also the person who organised David's schedule and tended his hurts and offered hugs when he was sad.

But Wyatt was still a *god* to our son, and as the primary school years ticked past us, I began to see his influence shaping David's interests and opinions. Sport was everything to Wyatt in those days, and David became borderline sport obsessed too. In the summer they watched the cricket, in the winter they watched the football, and in the window between seasons, they taped European soccer matches to watch later.

But nothing was more exciting than going to watch the town representative teams.

'The Milton Falls Blazers are playing the Orange Tigresses in the rugby this weekend,' I heard David telling Wyatt excitedly one evening. 'Can we go?'

'Orange Tigresses?' I repeated from the kitchen. 'Is that a women's team?'

The sound of riotous laughter greeted me.

'Women's team? In the *rugby*? It's the Orange *Tigers*, Ivy. You need your hearing checked,' Wyatt was laughing hysterically, and David's laughter mingled with it, like a little shadow of his father's mirth.

'What's so funny about that?' I said, and I walked to the door to the living area so I could frown at my husband.

'Girls can't play rugby,' Wyatt chuckled with a smile. 'It's a sport that requires a particular kind of strength and power, and speed is important too. But all of that aside, it really does boil down to the mental game – I just don't think women are built to be able to think the right way to play rugby.'

'Wyatt Gillespie,' I said, shaking my head at him. 'You are *such* a Neanderthal! I'm sure women play your precious "rugby" in the city all the time.'

'Ah, love,' he sighed, and he rose and crossed the room to pull me close for a hug. I resisted initially, but he held me until I softened against him and then he brushed a kiss against my forehead. 'Don't take it personally – I'm not saying women aren't as good as men. I'm just saying they're better suited to other things, that's all. I mean, look at you with Davey – you juggle so many things, and you make it look easy – I wouldn't stand a chance of doing half of what you do with our boy. You were *born* to be a mother, it's clear as day. But put you on a rugby field… well, you're going to struggle, that's all I'm saying.'

'Girls play netball, Mum, not rugby,' David piped up. 'If you really want to play some sport, you should try that.'

'Yeah, Mum,' Wyatt winked at me, then turned to David. 'Does Rachael play netball, Davey? Maybe she could teach Mum.'

'I can ask her if you want?'

'No, thank you, David,' I sighed, and I shook my head at Wyatt, who laughed again.

'Hurry up with dinner, love – I'm starving,' he said as he went back to his recliner. I glanced at my watch and swore as I realised how late it was. I hurried to the kitchen – Wyatt always liked me to have the food on the table by six, although that was often difficult when David and I were at after-school activities until late. I planned out our meals weekly and picked up the groceries on a Sunday from the store, and then I pre-cooked what I could, for nights like that one when Wyatt would be hurrying me up and I'd be trying to help David with his homework while the veggies cooked.

'Come on, Ivy!' Wyatt would call, groaning in exasperation, if the clock ticked even a minute or two past six without the food being on the table. 'Jesus, woman, what do you do all day, can't you be more organised?'

'Nearly ready,' I'd call back. David would inevitably be mucking around with his toys at the table again and the dogs would be yapping around our feet waiting for their dinner too and the whole evening routine could be so stressful, with so many competing demands and me at the centre of it all, trying to hold the family schedule together.

If I was running really late, instead of sitting down with the boys to eat, I'd stay on my feet – picking at a plate of food on the bench as I cleaned just to make up a bit of lost time. Wyatt rarely noticed when this was the case, although one time, David did.

'Why aren't you eating dinner, Mum?'

'Mum's hips are getting so wide, she can't fit in her chair tonight,' Wyatt grinned. I looked at him and bit back a retort – Wyatt too had started to pile on weight, in his case, when his focus shifted from *playing* sport to watching it. 'Maybe if she skips dinner for a few nights she'll be able to join us again.'

'Mum's hips aren't wide, Dad,' David frowned, confused. 'And she does fit in the chair, she was just sitting in it earlier to chop up the veggies.'

'I'm joking, son.' Wyatt laughed. 'It's fun to have a joke now and again, isn't it?'

'Ah,' David said, but then he laughed too. 'Yeah. I get it.'

They both sniggered, and I rolled my eyes and kept right on tidying up.

But I did skip dinner that night, and the one after that.

CHAPTER 11
Olivia

I like Ingrid Little from the moment I open the front door. She is tall and slim, with a flawless blonde bob – she looks like a Barbie doll. But she smiles at me, freely and easily, and after a cursory glance to Zoe – resting in the baby carrier on my chest – she says, 'Hi there! I'm Ingrid. You must be Olivia.'

'Nice to meet you, Ingrid. Come on in and… please excuse the mess.'

I step out of the doorway, and Ingrid joins me in the expansive lobby. She looks around, and I see her eyes taking it all in – the white porcelain tiles on the floor, the high ceiling, the furniture and décor. I follow her gaze around the room and suddenly I'm remembering how we put all of this together. I can see David carrying the hall table in after we bought it in Sydney one weekend, and I can hear the echoes of our quiet discussion as to exactly where it fit best. I see myself opening the unpainted front door one evening while the house was being finished and gasping at the sight of the tiles – I hadn't spared a single moment's thought to keeping them clean until I saw them already fixed to the floor.

I can see David carrying me over that doorstep and I can remember the muscular strength of him – his sheer bulk in moments like that representing a simple safety and security. This was going to be our home – our castle. David was the prince, which of course meant that I got to be the princess.

But then, I can see David standing right there in that doorway and quietly locking the new lock and telling me that he was never, ever going to let me out again on my own. I can hear the click of the latch, and the wheezing of my breath even to my own ears – my chest had felt so tight and the air had somehow seemed so thin. It was as if he hadn't just physically trapped me in the house with those new locks, but also, he'd thinned out the oxygen somehow – making the house completely inhospitable.

'I have to say,' Ingrid drags me back to the present as she murmurs, 'this has got to be one of the nicest houses in Milton Falls.'

'Thanks. I'll show you through,' I say. I sound weak to my own ears, and I clear my throat and force strength into my voice as I say, 'You really are going to have to excuse the mess… I've been… quite busy.'

I walk past the lobby and step down into the expansive open plan living area. I see the house with fresh eyes and I am suddenly mortified by the mess I've grown accustomed to, and for a moment, I really wish I *had* insisted that we needed to do this another day. Ingrid doesn't seem concerned. She stands right next to the white-leather couch, then she turns a full circle as surveys the living space.

'This is beautiful,' she breathes, and she laughs and says, 'Maybe if you were selling this in a year or two's time, I'd have bought it myself.'

'I heard that you're new to town. What made you come to Milton Falls?'

'I don't know if you know Todd?' When I nod, she says, 'We met at a conference last year and he offered me a job, but then after I'd resigned from my old job in the city, and I'd started packing up my things – there was some downturn, or something… supposedly. But I already had my heart set on coming to Milton Falls, and he's the only real-estate agent in town – so

I thought – well, why the hell not start up in competition? So here I am.'

'And how's it going so far?'

'Terribly,' she laughs again, and I can't help but smile at her in sympathy. 'I didn't realise how tight a community like this is.'

'You're not wrong about that,' I tell her wryly. 'But don't worry; Milton Falls looks after its own, and after a while, you'll be a part of that too. But you might need to hang in there for a little while, till people get used to seeing you around. I've never understood why Todd was the only agent here. There are plenty of properties around – if not houses in town, there's farms in every direction around it.'

'I'm hoping to specialise in residential real estate. I know a lot of Todd's business is the farming side of things, so maybe, if I leave him alone in that area – he won't destroy me altogether.'

She laughs again and the sound is musical and free. At first impression, I like Ingrid Little. She seems brave, and I don't freak her out. Maybe she doesn't even know who I am. That thought is completely thrilling.

I lead the way through to the kitchen and formal dining area. Ingrid's eyes skim over the dirty dishes on the bench, but she comments only on the expensive European appliances and on the huge ceramic under-mount sink.

'I think we market this as a luxury property,' she murmurs, and she looks out through the bay window to the backyard. 'I just don't know if we're going to find anyone in town who can afford a place like this. Maybe we need to market this to the city? Try to find someone like me, someone looking for a tree change – although, we *definitely* need someone wealthier than me.'

She laughs again, and this time, I laugh too.

'Actually, I'm more interested in selling this quickly than I am in getting the full value for it. My new house needs to be quite a bit smaller – a much simpler place. I'm picturing a little cottage, somewhere with an enclosed yard – but just two or three bedrooms. And I don't need two living areas, and I don't need a spa bath, and I definitely don't need a pool. A simple, quaint little cottage. So as long as the sale of this place covers the purchase of that, I'm not too concerned about how much money I get for it.'

'Are you really saying you'd sell this for less than market value?'

'I'm saying… whatever you tell me to do to get rid of this place quickly, I will do. If you think I should paint it bright pink or knock down the games room or add a third storey – and if you think that will mean that it will be out of my hands within weeks instead of months – I'll consider it. So I guess, price it as if it's an ordinary house. Someone will snatch it up, and I can wash my hands of it.'

Ingrid stares at me, and then she crosses her arms over her chest, and she peers at me curiously.

'You see a lot of things working in real estate. I've had families in the city who are selling up because they're going bankrupt – I've had men selling their homes after a marriage breakdown – and I've dealt with some heartbreaking widows over the years. People get a bit of a scent about them when they're just ready to move on. Sometimes, life drags us out of places – other times, we leap out of places, and we make our own futures. That's exactly what I'm doing here in Milton Falls. I feel like that might be what you're doing too.'

'That *is* what I'm doing,' I say, and I'm actually delighted at her assessment of my situation. 'It's is well and truly time for me to leave this place behind.'

'Well, let's make it happen then, Olivia Gillespie. What else do I need to see?'

'Olivia Brennan,' I correct her, and it's an automatic reaction that pleases me, although Ingrid winces as she nods and that makes me wince too. 'Sorry.'

'No, *I'm* sorry. Olivia *Brennan*. Should we look upstairs?'

'Let's do it.'

We walk back towards the stairs, and I lead the way to the second floor. Zoe's room is first, overlooking the front garden. The door is open and I lead the way inside.

Zoe's name is on the wall, in big wooden letters I hand painted myself – the Z is striped diagonally, the O has spots, the E has checks. Behind the letters, the walls are painted in a light salmon. David hated the colour I picked for this room, but once I knew I was having a girl, I had such a clear image in my mind for the nursery I wanted to bring my daughter home to. There's a huge built-in wardrobe, and cream woollen carpet, and a change table and toy box – and then finally a white sleigh-style cot which, like the rest of this room, is unused these days.

I can't let her sleep in here. It's too far away from the spare room where I sleep now. Instead, Zoe sleeps in the bed next to me. I prop pillows all around her, so she can't roll off the bed, and then I wake several times every night to check that she's still there.

'Seen enough?' I ask Ingrid, and she nods curtly, and follows me to the next room. This next door is closed, and I pause before I push it open. I have not opened this door in weeks. This was the room I shared with David. This room contains just as many happy memories as disturbing ones.

Now that David has gone, entering our bedroom feels like disturbing a grave. I know that it needs to be done, and so I take a big, deep breath, and I push the door open. The master bedroom is a triple sized room – a stupidly large room. There's our king bed right there in the middle, unmade – and I've not been in here, not since The Tragedy – so that means the unmade bed is from him. The sheets are twisted. Was he in torment? Was he scheming? Was he missing me so terribly that his mind wouldn't rest – is that why he did this to himself, and to me?

The unmade bed is somehow a message to me that I don't know how to interpret, and I don't even want to try, so I drag my eyes past it to the floor. *This* is why I need to get out of this house so badly. His ghost lives here, echoes of his past stretch forward into my future – the simplest things contain layers of meaning that I shouldn't ever have to force myself to unpack.

I want to get out of the master bedroom quickly, but I have to show Ingrid the en suite. So I walk stiffly from the door to the bathroom and I push open that door too and I let Ingrid poke her head inside.

'That's a seriously big spa bath for a bedroom,' she says, and I nod.

'My – my ex-husband loved the idea of having a nice hot spa after a football game.'

I called him my *ex*-husband. I haven't referred to David in polite conversation since he died. And although he wasn't technically my ex, not yet, I feel empowered just by saying the words – and by having someone hear them who didn't know me well enough to question the accuracy of the term. Suddenly, I'm actually smiling. I sweep my gaze over the bathroom bench, and see my side – almost clear except for a deodorant can. My clutter used to drive him insane, so I worked hard to hide it out of sight. David's side of the bench is decorated with a perfectly ordered set of bottles: cologne, soap, aftershave – and as soon as I see those things, I can smell him, and I feel a clench in my chest.

I *did* love David Gillespie, once upon a time. I think back to a moment – one of the ordinary days that didn't seem memorable at the time. I think back to us standing side by side at this basin, me putting on my make-up, him getting dressed for work too. I glance over to the toilet – and I remember the morning I took the pregnancy test. I didn't even realise my period was late – David had been tracking it himself, and he was the one who insisted I test, so my heart was sinking. When the second line came up, David was so excited that he had swept me up into his arms and twirled me around and around. He wept that morning, and he was embarrassed about it after – telling me I needed to forget about it, that he was going to be a father now and repeating that line he always trotted out when things were hard or emotions grew too big: *real men don't cry*.

But there are other memories in this room too, and they start to swamp me and I'm suddenly scared I'll drown in the torrent of the scenes that flash before my eyes. There was the time I ran in here, and I locked the door and cowered behind the toilet, terrified that he was going to kill me because he had checked my Facebook account and some random man in a uniform had sent me a friend request. There's the time when I was in here getting dressed, and he walked in for no apparent reason, and he wrapped his arm around my waist and pulled me against him, and I felt his hot breath against my ear as he whispered, 'I'd kill you if you ever tried to leave me. You know that, don't you?'

And *so* many arguments about having a baby – the time he slammed my face into the mirror and chipped my tooth because I asked for a few more months, and the time he spat in my face and then the worst time... the one and only time he gave me a monstrously visible black eye. We'd been at our routine Sunday night dinner with his family and Ivy had made a comment about wanting a grandchild, and when we got home David told me for the umpteenth time that I needed to come off the pill. I refused because I didn't want to leave work and I knew as soon as we had a baby, he'd insist upon it. But that night, he was absolutely determined that he'd been patient enough and he wasn't taking no for answer – and when I begged him for just a little more time he accused me of cheating on him with Sebastian.

That's why you won't give me a baby, isn't it! You need that fucking job so you can see your boyfriend!

He raised his hand to slap me, but then he clenched his fist instead. I thought at first that he'd broken my eye-socket. I sank to the floor and I cowered there – dizzy and terrified, he popped every single pill from my packet of contraceptives into the toilet and then he flushed it and left the room, without even checking that I was okay.

When we woke the next day and he saw how bad my eye was, I expected him to beg for forgiveness as he usually did. But that time, he simply shrugged and said, 'I gave you plenty of time to do this the easy way. You didn't really leave me any choice, did you?'

And I wasn't sure – because once things got worse, they usually stayed that way, and did his lack of remorse that morning mean that he would now hit me and not even express regret afterwards? And if that was the case—

'There are other bedrooms, right?'

I turn to Ingrid and I blink, trying to reorient myself. She's smiling at me patiently, expectantly, and autopilot kicks in and I walk out of the master bedroom, my steps fast enough that I'm almost jogging. The other end of this floor is safer – there are only the three spare bedrooms left to show her. The first was David's office, the room that I have since re-appropriated as *my* office. I push the door open and Ingrid peers inside and remarks that all of the rooms are such a good size and wouldn't this house make a great B&B for the right buyer? And then we walk through the already open door into the guest room – where my bed is. This bed is made with simple white linen and I've even managed to place the scatter pillows at its head. Ingrid surveys it, and then I show her the *other* spare room – which is all set up, but has never actually been used. David had no intention of letting people sleep in our house with us. This was his domain, and we rarely even had people over for dinner – generally only Ivy and Wyatt, and even then it was rare.

Finally, I take Ingrid through to the main bathroom – and after she surveys this, she plants her hands on her hips and she nods at me.

'How serious were you about selling this below market value?'

'Deadly serious. How quickly can you sell it?'

'Let me go back to the office, and I'll take a look at some historical pricing data. I'll have a look at what else is on the market, and then I'll come back to you – probably tomorrow?'

'And what about my new house?' I say to her. 'Do you have anything I might be interested in on your books already?'

Ingrid laughs quietly. 'I'll be frank with you, Olivia. I have two other houses on my books so far, and neither of them are what you're looking for, but what I can offer you – if you're interested – is to act as a buyer's agent. I'll list this house for you, and we'll figure out your budget, and then I will go through all of Todd's listings, and find some houses close to your criteria. That'll save you having to visit lots of places, and then I can just take you to the ones that seem a good fit. What do you think?'

'Perfect. But there's just two things I *really* need in the new house.'

'Go ahead.'

'It needs to be as far away from this street as possible, and the yard needs to be dog friendly.'

CHAPTER 12

Ivy

I figured that I knew pretty much everything that was going on in Davey's life because I was so involved at the school. When he met me at the gate one afternoon, in tears and sporting a black eye, I was completely bewildered.

'What on earth happened?' I gasped, and I took his shoulders into my hands and crouched before him to stare into his eyes. He avoided my gaze, so I caught his chin and turned him back towards me. His big blue eyes swam with tears and his chin had such a miserable wobble to it that I thought my heart was going to break.

'One of the big kids hit me,' he whispered, and a tear ran down his cheek. I wiped it away and pulled him hard up against me. 'I was playing soccer but he took my ball, and when I asked for it back he hit me.'

'What was his name, Davey?' I whispered.

'I can't tell you, Mum. If I tell you, he'll get in trouble, and then it'll get worse.'

David was breaking down by then, and I felt a surge of anger run through my body. I clutched his shoulders again and said fiercely,

'You will tell me, David. And you'll tell me now.'

When he only shook his head, I rose and took his hand, and then I dragged him towards the school administration office. As we entered, the receptionist shot to her feet.

'Hello, Mrs Gillespie,' she said brightly, and then she glanced at Davey and gasped.

'I need to speak to the principal, Clara, please. Now.'

The principal at that stage was Mr Jenkins. He was well into his sixties – probably past retirement – the kind of career teacher who lingers out of habit in the system rather than any genuine desire to be there. He had an old-fashioned approach to running the school – the children were encouraged to be seen and not heard. The school was not a fun place during that period, but I assumed that Principal Jenkins would clamp down hard on the bully who was picking on my son.

'Someone has hit Davey, during the lunch hour,' I said to Principal Jenkins, and he looked at Davey curiously

'And what did you do to this boy?' he asked David, and I snaked my arm around my son's shoulders and pulled him close.

'Davey didn't do anything. He's been bullied. I need you to intervene,' I said tersely.

'Davey, you need to tell me what happened. What did you do?'

I gasped. 'Principal Jenkins – don't you dare blame Davey for this.'

'Your son is no angel, Mrs Gillespie. I regularly have to speak to him about his behaviour in the playground. This time I suspect he just happened to pick on someone his own size.'

'How dare you!' I gasped, and my arm contracted around him. 'Are you going to do something about this situation, or not?'

'It wasn't my fault, honest,' Davey said, and his eyes filled with tears again. He sniffed miserably, and looked up at me, pleading.

'Davey,' I whispered, 'please tell Principal Jenkins who did this, and what he did to you. I know it wasn't your fault.'

'It was Tim Bryson,' Davey muttered, and he looked at the principal. 'But I really didn't do anything this time, I promise. I was just playing soccer with my friends, and Tim wanted the soccer ball, and so he hit me and he took it.'

'Well, if that really was the case, tell me; did you fight back?' Principal Jenkins demanded, and I frowned at him as he continued to stare at Davey expectantly.

David shrugged uncomfortably and shuffled from foot to foot as he muttered,

'I tried to… but he's so much bigger than me. It's just not fair… '

Davey dissolved in a flood of tears, and I'd had enough.

'You'll do something about this, won't you?' I snapped at the principal, who sighed heavily and assured me he'd look into it. I took David home after that – and as we walked the short blocks to our house, I wished he was just a little smaller so I could scoop him up onto my hip as I'd done when he was little. Instead, he walked beside me, holding my hand and wiping his nose on his sleeve when the tears came in waves. I tucked him up on the couch with a blanket, and I sat next to him while he watched his cartoons. I gave him biscuits and milk, and I coddled him – because I could *see* that was what he needed.

But then Wyatt came home.

'What's going on here?' he frowned. 'Davey, did you let someone hit you?'

'It was a big kid and I tried to stand up for myself —'

'Well, David, you're a big boy too now. You need to defend yourself. Haven't I taught you better than this?'

'But, Dad—' Davey was starting to cry again, and to my horror, Wyatt gave an incredulous snort.

'Jesus, son – what are you: a girl? We are Gillespie men – we don't let bullies pick on us, and we sure as hell don't cry about it if they try to.'

I held David even closer to myself. 'Wyatt, he's upset, and fair enough. Show a little support!'

'Ivy, let me handle this, all right? This is the kind of thing a boy needs to get through to toughen him up.'

'Then you can "toughen him up" tomorrow,' I said pointedly, 'But today – he needs some comfort.'

'Do you think they're going to make you captain of the footy team if you cry every five minutes?' Wyatt said, ignoring me altogether and directing his comment to David. 'Tomorrow, you'll go to school, and you'll punch that kid right back. Got it?'

'Sorry, Dad,' David muttered, and I felt him stiffen as he sat away from me. He still had tears on his little cheeks, but he wiped them away with the back of his hand, and he straightened his spine. 'I'll do better, Dad.'

Once David had gone to bed, Wyatt took his usual place in the recliner in front of the television, but I flicked the set off with the remote. Wyatt frowned.

'What's wrong, love?'

'David is only nine,' I said pointedly. 'You were too hard on him today. That kid is three grades above him. What did you expect him to do?'

'He needs to learn to be a man, Ivy. I know you don't understand, but trust me – I had a similar thing happen when I was that age, and my dad was tough on me too – it's how I learned to stand up for myself.'

'He was so upset. He needed us to support him today.'

'And we did. You babied him, and I told him to man up. Perfect balance. He's not going to be nine forever, love. He needs to grow some balls before he gets to high school or he'll be in for a world of pain.'

I sat there and worried while Wyatt watched the news that night. I wanted to protect David, but Wyatt had a point – high school *could* be tough for boys who didn't know how to stand up for themselves. This was the first time he'd come home from his school in tears, but we couldn't really afford for it to be a regular event.

The next day at breakfast, I said quietly to David, 'How about you stay away from that big kid today, huh?'

David looked at me. His eyes were clear, but hard. There was a little fear in him, but he hid it well – no one else might have been able to see it, but I was his mother – there was no hiding it from me.

'Don't worry about me, Mum. Dad and I had a talk this morning, and I'm going to handle this like a man.'

I got called to the school that afternoon. Clara the reception-ist told me I needed to come right in, so I literally sprinted from the house to the school. When I got there, I was out of breath and shaking with fear – expecting to find David with another black eye, or worse.

Instead, he was sitting in the visitor's chair opposite Principal Jenkins's desk. The black eye was still visible from the previous day, but he was otherwise unharmed.

'What happened?' I gasped.

'I was just sticking up for myself,' David said, raising his chin. 'From yesterday.'

'What did you do?'

'David kicked Tim,' Principal Jenkins muttered. 'Given this is obviously a retaliation for yesterday, David will go home today but he can return tomorrow. As long as this is the end of things, David, I won't put you on detention. Do you understand?'

David nodded, but then he flicked a glance at me, and the corner of his lip twisted upwards into a smirk. I was relieved that David was unharmed – annoyed that Wyatt's advice had potentially sent our son right back into a situation where he *could* have been in danger – but I was also confused by David's smugness.

'Your father should never have told you to do that,' I said stiffly as we walked out of the office.

'Well, Tim Bryson won't bother me any more, will he?' David said, and his arrogant, unaffected tone to his voice was suddenly a comfort, because finally, I could see Wyatt's logic. That older child really wasn't going to hassle my son in the future, not now that David had humiliated him.

'I guess he won't,' I conceded.

As soon as he walked through the door that night, David greeted Wyatt with a proud announcement.

'On the lunch break, I walked right up to Tim Bryson and I kicked him in the nuts. He went down like a sack of potatoes and he cried like a *girl*.'

'Well done, son,' Wyatt beamed, and he patted David on the back. 'You handled yourself like a man. I'm proud of you.'

◆ ◆ ◆

There was an unexpected battle to be faced as I watched my son morph from boy to man. Life was a constant balancing act. I took so much joy in the ordinary comings and goings of our life together, but at the same time I was frequently conscious of moments of sheer terror that his tender years were passing, and with every new day, he slipped away from me a tiny bit more. The sweet little boy with the big blue eyes and thick black hair gradually shifted into a true-blue pre-teen. By the time he was finishing primary school, David had a mild case of acne, and I'd stopped hinting at him to use more deodorant and started sending him right back to his room for a second application before he left for school. He was still doing reasonably well academically, but it was an outright struggle for me to keep him at the top of the class. Left to his own devices, all David would have cared about was making sure he was the captain of the football team.

It's Milton Falls tradition to hold a 'formal' for the students at the end of sixth grade, the year before the kids move from primary school into high school. I was chair of the organising committee, and David was the primary boy's school captain, which meant that over several weeks he and I spent every Wednesday night at the school with the rest of the committee planning the dinner. It was as we drove home from one of these meetings that David told me with great solemnity that he'd been doing a lot of thinking and he'd decided to ask the girls' school captain, Jennie Sobotta, if she would go to the formal with him.

When he came home from school the next day, he burst into the living room, leapt into the air for a fist pump and shouted, 'Mum! She said yes!'

'That's great, darling!'

David threw his schoolbag onto the staircase and then nearly toppled me over as he embraced me in a hug.

The end-of-school formal was an event which dictated much more formality than the children had generally experienced before, and David decided that he wanted to buy Jennie a corsage for the night of the dance. He asked her what colour dress she was going to wear, and then he used his pocket money to buy her a pink and purple arrangement. There seemed to be general consensus among the other mothers that David was possibly the sweetest twelve-year-old in town, but later, he admitted to me that he'd just seen corsages exchanged on an American TV show, and he just didn't realise it wasn't a tradition Australian school children tended to follow.

Still, my David wasn't the kind of kid to back away from an idea just because no one else was doing it, and so right after school that Friday night we went to the florists together to pick the flowers up. After David was dressed, I drove him to Jennie's house. She was waiting out the front, and I left them a quiet moment alone together while he gave her the corsage. She wore a dress her grandmother had sewed – the off-the-shoulder neck-line was already slipping around and driving her crazy before we'd even left the house. The dress was every twelve-year-old girl's dream at the time – swirling purple and pink roses in the fabric, stiff boning at the waist and a skirt held artificially out-wards by just a little too much tulle. Like most of the year six girls, Jennie had her hair curled and a dusting of make-up on her cheeks for the first time, and like most of the boys, David wore a white shirt and black trousers with his freshly polished school shoes. That was the first time he ever wore a tie, and when I was making the knot, I had to keep turning away so he didn't see the tears in my eyes. He looked so much like Wyatt when I first fell in love with him – the same athletic build and thick dark hair.

I took a few of photos of David with his date as they stood together in front of her mother's rose garden. At first, they stood stiffly side-by-side but for the last photo, David suddenly slipped his arm around Jennie's waist. When I had the film developed, Wyatt and I were in stitches at the expression on his face. David seemed somehow startled to find himself touching a girl.

The world was a golden place the night of that formal dance, and not just for the kids, who were too young to know how fleeting those moments of innocent excitement would be. I chaperoned and supervised the ever-popular soft-drink stand, so I was there that night for every single minute. I saw the way that the kids danced and the way that they laughed together hysteri-cally over the simplest things, and I delighted in watching them create their memories. I knew that they'd all look back at the formal once the inevitable adolescent angst of high school hit and wonder if life would ever be so simple or so beautiful again. There was something magical about the school hall that night, with the crepe paper pompoms hanging from the roof and the lighting that Evan Drysdale had borrowed from his cousin in the city, to give the room some 'atmosphere'. I felt lucky that I got to be there, to see my son dance out the end of his last primary school year, and to witness his joy and exuberance as he celebrated with his friends… and those awkward first dances with Jennie.

When we arrived back to her house, David offered to walk Jennie to the front door. I was impressed with my son's sense of chivalry. I waited in the car, and I tried not to look – it seemed appropriate that I give them some privacy. For a while, I stared down at my lap, but the minutes stretched until curiosity got the better of me. I looked up just in time to see David place a very tentative, chaste kiss on his date's mouth as Jennie pulled away, protesting furiously. As he straightened, she muttered something at him from beneath a frown. I frowned too – what game was she playing, exactly? David had been such a considerate, attentive date – and she'd led him on all night – how dare she get annoyed with him when he offered her a kiss! I was going to tell him so, too – to point out how unfair she'd been to react that way, but then Jennie went inside and David turned back towards the car. He was positively strutting, apparently totally unfazed by Jennie's reaction, and I relaxed. All he said on the way home was that it had been a great night, and he didn't take the grin off his face for days.

A few weeks later, David told me that he and Jennie were now 'officially' boyfriend and girlfriend. I liked Jennie for the most part; she was a nice girl: positive, bubbly, and, of course – most important of all, apparently – quite athletic. Soon she was at our place after school every spare afternoon the kids had, and my weekends were spent ferrying David to his sporting activities, and then racing across town so we could watch Jennie play netball or hockey. They were a sweet couple, and at first, I thought the whole thing was adorable.

When the high school years came, they were so different for me – David now walked to and from school by himself, and he *really* didn't want me to work in the canteen, or be involved in the Parents & Friends Committee. In fact, by the end of his first year of high school, he didn't want me at the school at all – and if he did see me there, instead of my usual hug when he greeted me, he would put his head down and mumble something as he walked past. I knew this was all ordinary teenage behaviour, but of course, it stung. And then when the time came to refill his winter wardrobe, he asked if he could take Jennie shopping instead of me.

'But, Jennie isn't going to pay for your clothes, is she?' I said pointedly. David rolled his eyes at me and said, 'Jennie knows what's cool, Mum. You don't. So, I'm going to go with her on Saturday morning.'

Later David came home with an empty wallet and a completely impractical wardrobe – one expensive jacket, two pairs of shorts, and a singlet. The following weekend, I quietly took him back to the shops, and bought him clothes that would actually see him through the winter.

'Sorry, Mum,' David said to me, as we drove home. I looked at him in surprise.

'That's okay, love. But I guess you might need to remember for a little bit longer yet, Mum really does know best. Okay?'

David's relationship with Jennie was another little reminder to me that parenting is investing everything you have into another human being, and then gradually releasing your grip on them. You need to let them make their own mistakes right there in front of you while you're still around to pick up the pieces afterwards, and trust them to find their way eventually. But as David's mother and until then, the only real female presence in his life – it was much harder than I'd anticipated to make way for another woman in his world, even when the 'other woman' was actually a thirteen-year-old girl. Over their first year of high school, David and Jennie were inseparable and I gradually became concerned about how attached he was getting.

'Davey,' I cautioned him. 'Take things slowly with Jennie, won't you? Girls tend to have big feelings for handsome boys like yourself, but you want to make sure you don't limit yourself.'

'Limit myself?' he repeated blankly.

'Well,' I shrugged and I distracted myself with my cross stitch. 'I mean, she's not the *prettiest* girl in year seven, is she? Part of the fun of being your age is getting to know lots of girls… and there really are some beautiful girls at your school… girls worthy of your attention. Just something to think about.'

I knew what it felt like to settle. I knew the frustration and resentment that came from tying myself down to someone who was beneath me – although in my case, my mismatch with Wyatt was intellectual. But in any case, there was no way I'd ever stand by and let my son get himself wrapped up in a girl who wasn't a worthy partner for him, not even in junior high school.

But it didn't seem to matter what I said, David still only had eyes for Jennie, and towards the end of year seven, there was a distinct shift in their relationship. A subtle intensity arose and lingered. I could never really put my finger on it; but there was a gentle fading to Jennie's easy grin. She was still at our house often, but every now and again, there'd be an afternoon where it was clear that she didn't actually want to be there. I'd think back to that awkward first kiss on her porch, and wonder if my initial concerns about Jennie leading him on were right.

'David, I just want to go with my friends. It's just a milkshake.'

'I'll come with you.'

'No! Sometimes, I just want to hang out with the girls. You're *always* at training or games with your friends – this is just the same.'

'It's *not* the same. I go to training because the team needs me, you're just going for a milkshake. Why are you trying to avoid me? Don't you love me any more?'

I was standing in the new kitchen while the kids sat in the lounge room. I paused in the kitchen, waiting to hear where the conversation went, but their discussion dissolved into hisses and whispers and then Jennie left in a huff.

'Is everything okay with you and Jennie?' I asked David, later that day.

'Of course it is.'

'Things can get a bit intense, sometimes… with teenage romances, I mean. You're both young. Remember you've got a lot of life ahead of you – you're just having fun for now, right?'

'Yeah… '

'If Jennie was a good girlfriend, she'd be more supportive of you. I've heard you two arguing, David. You shouldn't have to beg her to spend time with you.'

'I know!' he exclaimed. 'That's what I said.'

'Just you remember that she's lucky to have you. And if she doesn't realise that then… ' I trailed off, then shrugged, leaving the unspoken suggestion to ferment in the silence that lingered. David glanced at me, uncertainty.

'But I really like her, Mum. A *lot*. I think I love her.'

'You'll love plenty of girls. That doesn't mean you have to let them treat you badly. You're better than that,' I said, and when he hesitated, I flashed him a gentle smile. 'You are, David. Don't let her make an idiot of you, okay?'

'Okay, Mum,' he said, and I thought maybe that was the end of it – maybe I'd said just enough that he'd end this silly dalliance once and for all. I was relieved when, over the next few weeks, things between David and Jennie became very rocky indeed. There were plenty more arguments to be overheard from the kitchen, and it became something of a habit for David to call her at night only to wind up slamming the phone down after an argument. I kept wondering when the day would come when he would walk through the front door and tell me that they had broken up. I had a moment of hope at a football game one weekend when I overheard David talking to his friends about Jennie.

'I think I'm going to dump her,' he said, and then he shrugged nonchalantly. 'Have you seen the size of the arse on her these days?'

I wasn't concerned about the coarseness of his comment – I was sure he'd said worse when he thought no adult was listening – he *was* a teenage boy, after all. No, when I heard David make that statement I felt only relief that David's oddly discordant relationship with Jennie might be coming to a close. I was disappointed though when still more weeks passed, and the relationship lingered and the arguments continued. I wanted her gone – out of our lives, the sooner the better. I decided that since Wyatt and David were always telling me that there were some 'men things' I couldn't understand; this might be something his father needed to address.

'I think we need to talk to David about Jennie.'

'Is there something wrong?'

'They just don't seem very happy at the moment… She's becoming quite high maintenance. Maybe she's even cheating on him, I mean… I've overheard some of their arguments and she certainly seems to be hiding *something*. But you know how loyal Davey is, I think we need to tell him it's okay to let her go if he's not happy.'

'Okay,' Wyatt exhaled. 'Aren't you glad we had a son? Imagine having a teenage girl in the house. It's constant drama, isn't it?'

I shrugged.

'Maybe he just picked a bad egg.'

CHAPTER 13

Olivia

Not long after Ingrid leaves, there's a knock at the door, and I open it to find Dr Eric standing on my doorstep. He peers at me over through his thick glasses and offers me a smile.

'Hello, Olivia. It's been a few days, I thought I'd pop by to see how you're doing.'

I sigh and step aside to let him in.

'Dr Eric, you know that I'm always glad to see you, but at what point are these unscheduled house calls going to ease off?'

'I think we'll both know when the time comes. How are you feeling today?'

'I'm fine.'

'Good, good.'

He walks automatically through to the couch and sets his medical case on it, then withdraws a manila folder with my name on the side of it. He rests the folder on the armrest, and I sit beside it because I know the drill.

'Have you seen Natasha?'

'Yes, I went on Thursday.'

'Have you been taking the antidepressants?'

'Every morning.'

'Have you needed the sleeping medication the last few days?'

'Yes, but not every night.'

'Have you had any incidents of panic or anxiety attacks since we last spoke?'

'No.'

'What have you eaten today?'

As I'm pondering this, my eyes wander past the coffee table behind Dr Eric, and I see two bowls of untouched cereal. I'm pretty sure one of them is from today.

'I had a very large bowl of cereal for breakfast, and I was just about to get lunch when I heard you knock,' I lie, and Dr Eric frowns at me.

'You've never been a very good liar, Olivia. Not since you told me that *Louisa* put that pea up your nose when you were five.'

'Fine,' I sigh. 'Yes, I'll eat when you go. I forgot, okay? I'm excited – I've just met with an agent and I'm selling the house. Time for a fresh start, isn't that progress?'

'Yes, I've heard you've been out and about this week.'

'From who?'

'There's a lovely young barista at the coffee shop named Brontë who mentioned she saw you.'

I laugh weakly.

'And how do you know Brontë, Dr Eric?'

'She's Kerry's niece, visiting from Sydney for six months to help with Yvette after her hip operation.'

'Who's Kerry? And who's *Yvette*?' I'm still laughing, but I'm also well accustomed to this kind of thing – Milton Falls is close-knit, and Dr Eric is one of the cogs right at the centre of the wheel – he knows everyone. 'And how *do* you keep track of everyone at your age?'

'Kerry is that very efficient nurse at my clinic who does the vaccinations, and Yvette is her mother. Besides which, I'm only seventy-one, and I bet you'll still remember every animal you've ever treated when you're my age. It's the same with my patients. You're all like my children, or in your case, like my grandchildren.'

'So, do I pass today's health check?'

'I'll do your blood pressure and check your pulse and be on my way.'

'Maybe soon we can revert to our usual schedule, and I'll book an appointment with you and actually come into the office.'

'I think I'd be less determined to make so many of these house calls if you'd just agree to stay with your parents again.'

'You know I can't do that. I need some time alone with Zoe for now.'

'In that case, I'll keep right on popping by. It's not forever, Olivia,' Dr Eric smiles kindly at me as he slides his stethoscope into his ears. 'We'll both know when you don't need me to call in any more. Until then, I drive past your house all the time on my way from the nursing home to the clinic, it's really no trouble at all for me to just stop in sometimes.'

'Fine,' I sigh, and he smiles at me.

'Good girl.'

❖ ❖ ❖

Ingrid returns the next day. She is carrying an iPad and a small folder and she positively beams at me when I open the door at her.

'Hello, Olivia! So great to see you again. Can I come in?'

'Hi, Ingrid, and please do,' I say, matching her bright tone. I am starting to suspect that positivity is like a muscle that wastes without regular use. It takes a lot of energy to keep my voice lilting, but I don't want to bring Ingrid's mood down – and I need the practice. One day, I want to genuinely be as cheery as she is.

She comes into the house, and I lead her to the dining room table. I already have Zoe waiting in there, reclining in the high chair.

'Well, I've already found a few houses that I think you'll really like,' Ingrid says brightly.

I take the seat opposite Ingrid and accept the folder she turns towards me. I look down at the paper it contains and my heart starts to race. Am I really doing this? I was so hoping that Ingrid Little would work at a million miles an hour, charging ahead at full steam – because if I am going to do this, I will need to do it quickly before I lose momentum and change my mind. But now, Ingrid has prepared a contract – something that's going to need my signature – something that's going to commit me to this course of action.

Am I actually ready?

'Let's look at the contract in a minute. First, the exciting stuff – the new house. What do you think of these?'

Ingrid reaches across the table and flips the contract over to expose a single page with some colour photos at the top.

'Hey… I actually know this place,' I say, and I pick the page up and bring it closer to my face. When Louisa and I were kids, Mum worked at the hospital, and Dad was setting up the accounting practice he still owns today, so there were plenty of times when their work schedules meant we had to go to a babysitter. Her name was Mrs Schmitt, and she was in her fifties by then – an ex-teacher who had to stop work because of issues with her eyesight that I never really understood. All I knew was that Mum constantly used to remind Louisa and me that we needed to behave for Mrs Schmitt, and we adored her so much that we would never have dreamed of doing otherwise. We'd walk to her house after school and she'd greet us with hot milk and scones, and when Mum and Dad came to pick us up, we'd complain that we wanted to stay.

Despite extensive renovations, I immediately recognise Mrs Schmitt's house in these photos and I am swamped by marvellous memories – a smile immediately covers my face. It's a beautiful home: small, cosy, comfortable – perfectly *ordinary*. My memories of that place are all accompanied by the heavy smell of baking in the air and the rhythmic click of Mrs Schmitt's knitting needles.

'When can we visit?' I ask Ingrid, and she raises her eyebrows at me in surprise.

'You want to see that one?' she says to me, 'It's beautiful, but quite small, perhaps this one—'

She pushes another piece of paper towards me, but I shake my head. I have already decided, and somehow, this feels easy – and it feels right. Mrs Schmitt's house is the kind of house that I wanted all along – the kind of house that David loathed. It's an older style, a narrow California bungalow, double brick – tin roof, small rooms, no open-plan living.

In short, it is everything this house is not, which makes it *perfect*.

✦ ✦ ✦

'So, are you ready to go?' Ingrid asks me the next morning. We're standing at the front of my house and the morning sun beams down on me, making me squint.

'I am,' I say, and I am positively vibrating with excitement… there is just one tiny hurdle I need to overcome first. I don't move from the front step.

'So… are we going to take my car?' Ingrid says, trying to prompt me to move I think, but I shake my head, and then I point towards the garage.

'I was hoping that we could take mine,' I say. 'Zoe needs to go in the car seat, and it's such a pain to move it between cars. But… ' I take a deep breath, and I admit in a rush, 'I haven't actually driven in a while, so I was hoping that you wouldn't mind driving for me.'

'Of course,' Ingrid says easily, as if this is an everyday request which I'm pretty sure it is not. But I open the garage and then I stare at my car.

It's a red BMW sedan – David's choice, from David's dealership – and my palms are so sweaty when I go to open the door to put Zoe inside that it takes me several attempts to grip the handle, but then I open the door and I take Zoe from Ingrid. As I buckle her into the car seat, my vision fades in and out and I have to stop a few times to force myself to breathe.

There's something about the sight of Zoe in the car seat that makes me feel sick, and I pause, trying to grasp it. Is it because I found David in the car? Is it because I haven't been in the car for so long? It's right there – like a word right at the tip of my tongue – but then it's gone, and I straighten out of the car and stand straight.

'Are you okay?' Ingrid asks me after a while. She's sitting in the front seat already, adjusting the mirrors with great care just as if it's a complicated task, and I blink slowly and clear my throat.

'I will be.'

Another deep breath, and my heart rate starts to slow. I lean back into the car and check Zoe's buckles once-twice-*three* times, then I close the door, and check to make sure it's properly latched. I need to be sure she's going to be okay.

But I also need to get myself to Mrs Schmitt's house, and to do that, I need to stop obsessing over the car and put myself in the passenger's seat. I walk around to it, and then I slide in, and I pull my seatbelt on.

'Hey, Olivia, if you're not ready to do this... ' Ingrid says quietly, and I shake my head resolutely and I say, 'I am absolutely ready to do this.'

My hands rest on my lap now, in painfully tight fists.

'Are you sure?' Ingrid asks me gently, and I look at her. She is so well made-up; how does she do that? Maybe she was a beautician before she was a real-estate agent. One day, maybe I'll ask her.

'Do you know who I am?' I ask her instead, and she winces as she nods.

'I moved into town on the sixth of June, Olivia. I swear to God it was two whole weeks before I heard a single sentence that *didn't* have your name in it.'

I laugh weakly.

'I haven't been in a car, not since… well, a few days after it all happened. And suffice to say the pharmaceutical industry assisted with the first few trips so I didn't really notice them.'

'And you're sure you want to do this? We can walk, if that's easier.'

I glance down at her feet. She's wearing patent-leather stilettos with an enormous heel. I'm not even sure how she's going to drive in them, let alone walk all the way across town.

'In *those* shoes?'

'These old things? *Please*. I could run a marathon in these without so much as a blister. I don't exactly have a lot on today, so I have time. I don't mind.'

I take a deep breath, and it comes out as a nervous, slightly elated giggle. Ingrid looks at me in alarm.

'I think I'm fine,' I say.

'Are you sure?'

'You know how sometimes the thought of something is worse than the reality of it?'

'Okay, well, let me know if you need to stop,' Ingrid says. I can tell she's still unsure, but then she starts the car and then we are driving down the street past Ivy and Wyatt's place. The further we get away from David's house, the more relaxed I feel.

By the time we park at Mrs Schmitt's house on the other side of Milton Falls, I'm no longer anxious at all. I slide out of the car and unclip Zoe, and I carry her with me as I walk through the wrought-iron gate towards the front door. As I approach the house, I stop to brush my palm over the foliage of hydrangea bushes in the garden bed along the front walls. The plants are huge and I wonder – are these the exact same bushes that Louisa and I picked blooms from when I came to this house as a child? These bushes will need a trim in the spring, and I can imagine myself working at them with shears with Zoe lying on the grass beside me. I can even imagine some years down the track, Zoe picking the blooms for me as a gift just like Louisa used to do for Mum.

I can make a home here. I know that I can. I stop before I step onto the veranda and I stare at the heavy front door.

There is only one lock.

Even *that* small detail endears me to the place.

'Hello, ladies.'

I recognise Todd's voice before I see him, and I turn around and frown. 'Why are you here?'

Ingrid reaches forward and snatches a set of keys from Todd's hand, then skips ahead of him towards me.

'Well, this is Todd's listing. But he's very kindly agreed to let me show you through the house,' Ingrid says pointedly. Todd half nods, but he's staring at Zoe.

'How are you doing, Olivia?' My skin crawls at the tone he uses – it's beyond patronising, almost *slimy* because it's drenched in so much pity and awkwardness. He presses his lips together into something like a pout. 'I was very surprised to hear that you'd engaged little Miss Ingrid here.'

He speaks to us as if we are five-year-old girls – he could almost could be patting us on the head.

'I thought I'd give the hot-shot city agent some business,' I say, with forced politeness. 'So, can you give us a few minutes? Or better still – can Ingrid drop the keys back to you when we're finished?'

'Look… I know it's all… *difficult*, but David was a good friend to me and he really was a top bloke, so I know he'd want me to look out for you. So I'm going to come with you and make sure this really is the right place, yeah?'

It is habit and instinct to simply agree. In fact, I open my mouth to do so – but then – I feel the rising tide of fury and indignation *surge* within me. Does Todd really think I need his approval now that my husband is dead? Like a woman can't buy a house because she likes it, she has to have some *man* tell her it's a good decision?

And the worst insult of all – David was a top bloke? *Really?* Do David's footy buddies really think that, even now?

Once upon a time I'd have deferred to Todd simply because of his tone. I'd have ducked my gaze and forced myself to be demure, deferent to his confidence.

But I am not the same woman who smashed my way out of David's house all of those weeks ago. If Todd thinks I'm going to stand here and let him patronise me and Ingrid Little without saying anything – he has another thing coming.

'That won't be necessary. We'll drop the keys back to you afterward.' I glance at Ingrid. 'Let's go.'

'I just think it would be better if I just show you a few—'

'*No,* Todd.' I stare into Todd's wide eyes and I raise my free hand towards him, pointing a finger towards the road, just as if *I'm* the school marm. If anyone is going to be doing any patronising in my new house, it will be *me.* 'I don't need you to do anything else. Thank you very much for bringing the keys over, and for allowing my agent to show me through personally. I don't need any more of your "help", so have yourself a great day.'

Behind me, I hear the sound of Ingrid opening the door, but I continue to stare at Todd until he holds his palms up towards me and backs quickly away to his car. Then I turn on my heel and I march inside, and Ingrid makes a point of gently slamming the door behind us.

I face away from her, into the house, and I blink hard against automatic tears.

'Well,' Ingrid says with a laugh, 'Aren't you a bundle of surprises, Olivia Brennan? What a fucking *jerk*.'

'He doesn't mean to be like that,' I sigh, and I have cleared the last of the tears so I turn back to her. 'He just grew up here – and sometimes the men around Milton Falls have these archaic country attitudes.'

I hear myself excusing Todd and it disgusts me. Why did I do that? He had no right to treat me that way – no right to treat *Ingrid* that way. Yes, Todd grew up here in the country – just like David did – just like *I* did. But it isn't 1950 any more. If Todd has a small town, backward attitude, that is his fault, and it's not something that I need to just 'let go'.

I look at Ingrid.

'You know, you're right. Todd *is* a fucking jerk, so don't let him push you around. We have a lot of big fish in this little pond, and it's time that you take some of that pond for yourself.'

Ingrid laughs, and then she extends her hand towards the hallway.

'Shall we go look at your new home, Olivia?'

The house is perfect. It's been painted and the floors redone, and the kitchen has new granite benches, but otherwise it's just as I remember it: even the cast-iron stove Mrs Schmitt used to cook on is still right there – left in place as a feature piece because there's also a gas stovetop now. The cast-iron stove is the kind of thing that would have driven David crazy, *dust collector,* he would have said, and I can almost hear the scornful tone he would have used.

When I look at that stove, I see both the past and the present – and I am sure that *both* can be beautiful. I'm going to put a silly, dust-collecting vase full of chaotic, dust-collecting silk flowers on that beautiful, dust-collecting stove and I'm going to leave it all undusted until I can *see* the dust all over it and then

I'm going to write David's name in it and then I'll rub it out and erase him altogether.

'Can you make an offer on my behalf?' I ask Ingrid as she's pulling the front door shut.

Ingrid smiles at me. 'It would be an honour.'

CHAPTER 14

Ivy

A few days after Wyatt's chat with him, David came home from school and made a quiet announcement.

'I broke up with Jennie today,' he told me.

'I'm so sorry,' I said, and he shrugged nonchalantly.

'It's time to let her go. We had a fight today and it just kind of happened,' David muttered. The hoarse edge in his voice was subtle, but there was no mistaking it. Now that I really looked at him, I could see a slight redness to his eyes.

'Are you okay?' I asked softly.

'Of course I'm okay,' he said abruptly. He passed me and walked to the lounge, flicking the television on as he passed it. Next, he threw himself into a sofa, putting his feet up on the cushions and dumping the school bag on the floor beside him. I dragged my gaze from the dirty school shoes on my sofa to the out-of-place bag on the tiles then back to the expressionless set of David's face. I clamped down on the urge to remind him of the house rules, and instead I asked gently, 'And was Jennie okay?'

'This is much worse for her than it is for me. I'll find another girlfriend; loads of girls want to be with me. *No one* else wants Jennie.'

'Exactly,' I said softly. 'You'll find someone much better. Someone suited to you.' But then I looked again at the red-rimmed eyes and the hard set of his jaw and I added softly, 'But it's okay to be upset, Davey.'

'I'm *not* upset,' he scoffed, without shifting his eyes from the television. 'Can you get me something to eat? I'm starving.'

I handled him with kid gloves for the next few days. I let him sulk in his room when he wasn't at training, I made his favourite meals and let him slack off a bit with his homework and even bit my tongue when he left his towels on the floor of the bathroom. Whenever Wyatt and I talked to him about Jennie, he insisted that he was fine, but I could see that he wasn't – the spring in his step was gone and he wasn't sleeping nearly enough. He'd go to bed right after dinner, but at all hours of the night I'd wake up to see the light on in his room.

The more I thought about it, the more I wondered if Jennie was having a hard time letting go, and I thought seriously about calling her mother, Andrea. In the end, I decided to talk directly to David.

'Listen, Davey… ' I said at breakfast one morning. 'Is Jennie giving you a hard time at school? About the breakup?'

His gaze was wary.

'Why?'

'You still seem upset.'

'I'm not.'

'Well, I just wanted to say… if she is… you don't have to take it. You make sure you don't let her get away with any nonsense, okay? You're a good boy – a sensible boy. You're too good for a girl like Jennie – and you make sure she knows it if you need to.'

David nodded curtly, but I could see in his eyes that I'd given him something to think about, and I was pleased. He *did* still need me, and despite the fact that I sometimes felt he was slipping away from me as he grew up, I was comforted by this evidence that I could still influence the direction of the decisions he made when I needed to.

'Yeah, thanks Mum.'

He perked right up after that day. I was surprised a few days later when the phone rang and Andrea was on the line.

'Hello, Ivy,' Andrea said, and I could hear the hesitation in her voice from the moment I answered the phone. I sank into the chair beside the telephone table and braced myself for awkwardness.

'Hello there, Andrea,' I said carefully. 'How are you going? How's Jennie?'

'Jennie's not doing so well. I guess David told you that she broke up with him?'

I frowned, and I said carefully, 'Actually – I think David broke up with *her*.'

'No, I'm afraid that's not what happened.' There was an awkward pause, then Andrea's tone sharpened, 'Is that what he told you?'

Of *course* David had ended the relationship – hadn't I heard him planning it? Hadn't Wyatt and I encouraged it? I didn't want to rub that obvious truth into Andrea, so instead, I said hastily, 'Well – it doesn't matter anyway. Who broke up with who is irrelevant.'

'Actually… I think it *is* relevant. I'm calling because I think David has sent Jennie a few really upsetting notes and the last few days has been making life quite difficult for her at school. I could talk to Edward, but I don't want to make trouble. Do you think you could talk to David?'

I hadn't really thought too much about it until that point, but Andrea *was* a teacher at the Milton Falls High School – a foreign languages teacher. She had easy access to Edward Parker, the principal – and if she wanted to cause trouble for David, she wouldn't have to try very hard.

'What do you mean David is making life difficult for her?' I asked defensively.

'He's been harassing her in the playground. She's been coming to the staffroom in tears every day.'

'I'm sorry, Andrea, but I do find it very hard to believe that David would ever do that,' I said sharply. 'And what about these notes? Is it possible that Jennie's writing those herself? You know what teenage girls can be like, they do love their drama. Perhaps she's having trouble letting go – because David broke up with her.'

'Listen, Ivy,' Andrea sighed. 'I know how hard it can be to hear these things about your kids, but David's behaviour lately has been terrible. He was so possessive of Jennie, he started to really frustrate her – that's why she broke up with him… and these letters? And now the playground harassment? I really don't want to have to go to Ed Parker – I don't want David to have to get a formal discipline at school, I *really* don't… but this can't keep on. Please just talk to him.'

'Well, you show me one of these letters, then. I'll recognise the handwriting if he really wrote it,' I said. I tried to convince myself that I needed to at least consider the possibility that David really had been sending these letters – but I just couldn't bring myself to do it. How could this woman suggest that *my* son – the same son who had bought Jennie that beautiful corsage and given her that sweet little kiss just a year earlier – would ever harass her like this?

'I know David's handwriting, and I know my daughter's handwriting,' Andrea said sharply. '*David* wrote these letters, Ivy, there is no doubt about it. Would you like me to read you one?'

'Yes, fine,' I sighed impatiently, and just a minute or two later I heard the rustling of paper in the other end of the phone. Andrea cleared her throat, and then she paused. 'Well?'

'Are you sure you want to hear this, Ivy?' Her tone had softened just a little, but I was impatient by then and I said tightly,

'Please just read it to me, Andrea.'

I listened for the next thirty seconds as Andrea read a letter – a stream of clumsy, adolescent nonsense.

'Who do you think you are? I was too good for you anyway. Don't you realise no other boy is going to put up with your shit? I did you a favour going out with you in the first place.'

'Oh, just stop!' I exclaimed impatiently and Andrea trailed off. 'David did *not* write that. What utter rubbish. Jennie is trying to cause trouble for him.'

Maybe David wasn't an angel, but I couldn't even begin to imagine him ever sending such a letter to anyone. It was nonsense, the very idea of it.

'I'm really sorry, Ivy,' Andrea said, 'You know what teenagers are like, especially teenage boys. Their blood runs hot. It's very hard for them to distinguish a good idea from a bad one, particularly when they're hurt. But David simply has to stop this. Jennie can't exactly leave school, but at the moment it's hard for me to get her out of the house in the morning. I really hoped that I wouldn't have to call you—'

'Andrea, I don't know what's going on, but I do know that my David would never have written those things. So yes – I'm glad you called so we could clear the air, and I will talk to David – but you need to keep an open mind too. Jennie is almost certainly behind this herself somehow.'

I hung up before she could answer me, and when I turned around, David was standing behind me. He was staring at me, and there was a question in his eyes.

'Did you hear that?' I asked him, and my heart was racing. I fanned myself a little – and my breaths came in short bursts because my chest felt oddly tight. I was embarrassed, and completely bewildered.

'Was that Mrs Sobotta?' David asked.

'Yes. Somebody's causing some problems for Jennie at school, and Andrea seemed to think it was you. But it isn't, is it?'

Just for a millisecond, I allowed myself to entertain the idea that the tension in my chest was because maybe… just maybe

David *had* written that note. After all, didn't the note *echo* my own words to David at breakfast a few mornings earlier?

You're too good for a girl like Jennie – and you make sure she knows it if you need to.

David gave me a confused smile. I assessed his posture – he was completely relaxed, seemingly unfazed by this entire situation.

'Of course not,' David said easily. 'I told you. I broke up with her. She's trying to get me in trouble, probably just upset because I told her a few days ago to stop bugging me at school, just like you told me to.'

Relief flooded in at me. I smiled back at him and patted my hair down as I pondered the situation.

'Okay, Davey. Can you do something for me?'

'Yeah?'

'Can you please just stay *well* away from her? I don't want Andrea causing any trouble for you at school – she was talking about going to speak to Mr Parker. You and I know this is all nonsense, but if one of his own teachers tells him it's true – I just don't know if he'll believe us.'

'Okay, Mum.'

David turned and walked away, down the hallway towards his bedroom. If there was *any* doubt in my mind that he was innocent in all of this, it disappeared as I watched him walk away. In those days right after the breakup, he had been skulking around, dragging his feet – but now, he was back to his usual, light-hearted self.

Not a heartbroken boy at all, certainly not upset enough to send such an awful note or bother an ex-girlfriend at school. I was satisfied by these realisations, and completely confident in my assessment of the situation. No one knew my son better than me. If he was up to no good, I'd know about it.

When I told Wyatt about Andrea's phone call, he was livid – but not at David, at Andrea herself. He threatened to call

Edward to have her disciplined for getting involved in nonsense that her daughter was making up. I convinced him to leave it, but I heard him talking to David about it the next morning before school

'Listen, son. Girls can be *lots* of fun, right?' My husband and son shared a knowing laugh. I was at David's door, about to knock, but I paused to listen. 'But you need to realise, they also like to stir shit up. Girls tend to create drama; you know? It's not as simple with women as it is with your mates. They like to play games... God only knows why... but you'll find it all through your life – even when you're older and you meet someone and you get married. They never say what they mean. It's always 'Maybe' and 'No' – but the *no* sometimes means yes, and the maybe sometimes means yes – and sometimes a yes can even mean no! Then you have situations like this one, and who really knows *what's* going on? At the end of the day, a young boy like you doesn't need to be tied down to a girl like Jennie and it's over now and everyone has to move on. You've got to stay in that school for another four years, so do exactly what Mum said – stay away from Jennie. If she tries to talk to you, ignore her. Do what I did at your age – hang out with the boys, but don't tie yourself down to any one girl – there are plenty around, just have your fun with them and enjoy life. You don't need a girlfriend to do that, got it? You'll be old and married soon enough, so make the most of it now, okay?'

I dropped my hand away from the door and backed away, frowning. I was glad Wyatt was talking to David about those things, but I wasn't impressed with his tone, or the undertone of innuendo. David was simply too young for those concepts... wasn't he? Later, I asked Wyatt about the chat.

'He's only fourteen. I'm not sure you should say those things to him,' I said carefully.

'You're a wonderful mother – the *best*. But you have to recognise that now David is getting older, there are some things that he's going to need to deal with as a man, and you're going to have to trust me to speak to him about those things.'

'I just don't want David to think all girls are going to play games with him, Wyatt.'

'The truth is, love – girls do play games with boys. That's just the way of the world, right?'

'That's not true—'

Wyatt interrupted me by raising his eyebrows and offering me a pointed look.

'Every year you tell me you don't want a birthday present. The one year I didn't get you one, you had the shits with me for *days*. Tell me that's not a bloody game.'

I sighed impatiently. 'Wyatt, that's a completely different scenario.'

'*How* is it? Blokes don't do that kind of stuff, love. We just don't, and David just doesn't understand yet how different girls are. Whatever went on with Jennie, I'll bet he's just trying to bumble his way through the maze of messages and grey areas that you women set up for your men. I'm just trying to explain to him that girls are complicated and messy and it's not going to get any easier for him, not even when he's picked one and been married to her for fifteen years. Right?'

We saw Jennie often over the years that followed, and she'd always say hello to me, but I noticed the way that David could never acknowledge her. It was like they had never been together – like his first ever romance had blossomed, and then somehow disappeared.

He had other girlfriends over the years at high school – but they never lasted as long as the one with Jennie had and the relationships always seemed to implode. It was never David's fault – after Jennie, he always seemed to pick the same kind of girl – pretty, vain, and *complicated*. He had a terrible run of relationships in high school where the girls cheated on him and after a while, he quite naturally became jealous. That anxiety often came across as protectiveness, and in that regard, I was actually proud of David. He was the guy at the party who would always make sure his girlfriend never walked home alone – once he could drive, I'd watch at the window when he'd bring a girl home, and he'd leap out of the car as soon as he parked to rush around to the passenger's side to open the car door. David was just like that with his girlfriends, inevitably thoughtful and affectionate. I'd see him sitting with his arm loosely around his current girlfriend's shoulders whenever they were together, or holding her hand in public and lingering at her side when they were in a crowd.

And while there were romances that ran very hot for a short time and then very cold overnight, there was never another drama as big as the one with Jennie.

It was easy for me to dismiss the whole affair as an aberration; a bad combination of a young, enthusiastic boy, and a girl who twisted the story she told her mother to get revenge on my son for breaking up with her.

CHAPTER 15

Olivia

'Well, you've had a big week then,' Natasha says, when I update her on my news about the houses. She seems more shocked than impressed, and I get a little defensive.

'No point wasting any more time.'

'Do you feel like you might be rushing things?'

'Do *you* think I am?'

'It doesn't matter what I think.'

'I'll take that as a "yes".'

'Have you started packing up the house?'

'Yes. I'm not taking much.'

'So you're sorting through your belongings deciding what to take?'

'Exactly. I want the new house to *feel* new, so I'm hardly going to take anything that has a memory attached to it. Except things for Zoe, of course.'

I started packing as soon as I walked in the front door from Mrs Schmitt's place. I didn't have any packing boxes, so I walked through the house with a laundry basket in my arms and I picked up the things that called to me – a few photos, one of Louisa and me at her twenty-first, one of me alone with my parents on my wedding day. There were plenty of other photos, but David was in all of them, so I turned them all face down as I walked around, even though it did nothing to cleanse his presence from the room.

I can't wait to get out of that house.

'What do your parents think about all of this?' Natasha asks me quietly.

'I haven't exactly told them… not yet,' I admit.

'Hmm. That's interesting.'

'Well, Natasha,' I say pointedly. 'You'll probably recall that they didn't even want me to go home to David's house. I did call Louisa to ask her for advice about which agent to use and she didn't seem thrilled, so I'll bet she's mentioned it to Mum and Dad… but I haven't really discussed the detail with them yet.'

'Are you afraid of disappointing them?' she asks me.

'Why would they be disappointed?' I frown.

'You tell me.'

'They want to protect me – that's what they've *always* wanted.'

'And… how do you feel about that?'

'I've never let them,' I admit. 'It feels a bit too late now, the damage has been done.'

'I know you were estranged from them for a long time. You've never really explained to me how that happened.'

'It was Christmas morning, maybe seven years ago,' I murmur.

The day was so hot – and we were supposed to have lunch with Mum and Dad, who didn't have air conditioning, so I'd worn a singlet and skirt. Louisa had just started seeing a new guy she'd met at the pub. Johann was a German backpacker, in Milton Falls only for the summer to work on the cherry harvest – not likely to be a long-term relationship, but still, my sister was excited to have a date for Christmas for the first time in a while.

I was so happy that day, which made everything somehow worse – the contrast between joyous morning and miserable afternoon seemed cruel, the timing unfair – wasn't Christmas supposed to be the happiest day of the year?

We'd exchanged gifts and Dad was barbecuing seafood for lunch, so we were all sitting outside under the awning complaining about the heat and wishing for a breeze or rain or *something*. We'd already had a few glasses of wine, and Louisa and I were giggly and generally having fun.

Then Johann decided he'd start a water-fight. He approached Louisa and I with a bucket of water and threw it right over us – catching us by surprise. We squealed and dissolved into fits of laughter and promises of imminent revenge, and just as I stood to go for the hose, David announced, 'I'm so sorry, I have a headache coming on.'

Everyone stopped. They all looked at him, and so did I, only to find his gaze had settled right on my cleavage. I was genuinely confused because there were storm clouds in his eyes and he was hiding it well from the others, but *I* could see that he was enraged. He offered me a tight smile. 'Why don't you stay and catch a cab home?'

His words didn't match his expression, not one little bit. I was bewildered, but while I didn't want to leave, I *knew* the safest option was to go with him. So I looked at my family and I gave them an apologetic shrug, then turned back to David.

'No, I'll come with you now and make sure you're okay.'

'I'm absolutely fine,' he said, 'It's just a headache. Maybe the cheap wine.'

It *hadn't* been cheap wine at all, and it was unlike David to throw barbs at Mum and Dad – generally he was cordial to them, his usual charming self. That's when I realised that whatever I'd done, David was absolutely furious. He took my hand then, and squeezed it – *hard*. Too hard for a warning. It was a precursor.

'I really don't mind if you stay,' he said quietly, but his eyes still said something different altogether, so I apologised too and we walked out, hand-in-hand. As soon as the front door closed behind us and we were alone on the street he released my hand and started to walk faster, his footsteps heavy and fast. I fell behind him, my own steps hesitant. My heart was thundering against my chest, and I was frantically replaying the morning in my mind, trying to figure out what I'd done wrong.

Then he turned, and he grabbed my shoulder – his grip was too hard, the movement too rough – and he pulled me hard against his torso. He stared down at me, a long and intense stare, and it only broke when he pulled his head back, his nostrils flared, and then he spat on my face.

Public displays of anger were very rare from David. He was always so controlled – even later in our life together once things escalated, he'd hold off until there was no one around to witness his rage. For him to dare to treat me like that on the street in front of my parents' house meant that he was completely out of control.

'You wore that top just to turn him on, didn't you? *Slut.*' David hissed at me, and then I finally looked down. The bucket of water had left my singlet virtually translucent. 'You knew he was going to be here. You loved his attention all morning.'

'Get your damned hands off my daughter!' Dad shouted and I stumbled away from David, shocked and humiliated. I turned towards the house and I saw Dad running at us – his face beetroot, from the heat or the exertion but also, undoubtedly, the hard set of fury I could see in his jaw and his posture. I knew then that Dad had seen the whole thing play out. *Dad saw him spit on me. Dad heard him speak to me like that. Dad is going to lose his mind. David is going to kill him.* Dad stopped between David and I, drew himself up to his full height and said flatly to me, 'Get inside. Now.'

'Fuck off, Tom,' David snapped, and reached around to grab at my wrist again. Dad pushed him back, and although he barely even budged at Dad's attempted to protect me, it seemed to give David a shock. He drew in a long, slow breath, then raised his eyebrows at my father, the mask of rage he'd been wearing calming until he once again looked cool-headed and aloof. I knew that was an act, but I doubted Dad would see through it. David then tilted his head towards me and said quietly, 'This is none of your business. I suggest you take yourself back inside and leave me with my fiancé.'

'She's *my* daughter, David,' Dad was livid now, so angry he could barely form words. 'You'll never lay a hand on her again, do you hear me? I won't have it!'

'Olivia,' David said, and he looked right into my eyes. 'Get in the car.'

'Don't you dare, Livvy,' Dad gasped, and he pointed towards the house. 'Why are you still out here? Go inside to your mum and Lulu.' When I didn't move, Dad raised his voice, but it was rough with his desperation to get through to me. 'Go on! Get inside so we can keep you safe!'

I was standing between them now, and I looked from Dad to David and then back again.

'Did you think of going inside, Olivia?' Natasha asks me quietly.

'We'd just gotten engaged,' I say, gnawing my lip. 'The announcement had just been in the papers a few months earlier. Everyone knew we were going to get married.'

'So you felt loyal to David?'

'Yes. I knew that if I did go inside with my family, David would lose his *mind*. If he was already angry enough to spit at me on the street, there was no way he was going to stand idly by as I walked away from him. And I really didn't want them to know, I was just so embarrassed at what I was putting up with, even then. I knew my parents and Lulu would be devastated if they knew how bad my relationship with David was, so I thought if I could leave with him and calm him down, I could just explain it all away later... somehow. I'd tell them he was under a lot of pressure with the business and he was tired and hot and he had a migraine and he didn't mean it and it was a one off. Plus, I guess... ' I swallow, and start to pick at the cuticle on my thumb so I can avoid Natasha's patient gaze. 'I had this awful feeling if I went back inside, Dad was going to cop it instead of me. And David had a good foot on Dad, not to mention twenty-five years of youthful athleticism. I knew Dad would come off second best and be humiliated in the process.'

So I got into David's car. My whole family was screaming at me by that stage, and as David drove furiously out of the street, I stared out the window and I cried silently. I didn't realise what I'd done – it was days before it sunk in that I'd made a choice that was bigger than the moment.

'They bombarded me with texts,' I murmur. 'Calls, texts, visits to the house and Mum even came to work. They tried so hard to get me to leave. I couldn't risk anyone at work finding out what had happened, and honestly, I couldn't bear to hear their desperation. I tried to keep in contact with them by making my relationship with David off limits when I spoke with them, but they couldn't help themselves. They did come to the wedding, but only after I begged them to, and Dad refused to walk me down the aisle... Louisa refused to be a bridesmaid.'

'How did you feel about that?'

'Abandoned,' I whisper. 'I understood that they thought they were doing the best thing for me, but it just made me feel like they'd given up on me. They hadn't, of course, they were just sick of me telling them to stop trying to *help*... but it just made me feel all the more isolated. After that, David always told me that even if I left, they wouldn't help me – and of course, I believed him because I knew how disappointed they were in the decision I'd made. It felt like he was all I had left.'

'How do you feel about it all now, Olivia?'

I inhale and then exhale on a groan as I run my hand through my hair.

'When I look back on it, I feel like I'm looking in on the life of a woman with no spine – a woman who mustn't have known any better, but the thing is, I *did* know better. I was raised in a great family by two strong, amazing parents. I was university educated, David wasn't even my first boyfriend. If you'd asked me before I met David if I'd ever let a man control me, I would have laughed at you. I suppose I didn't realise that's what was happening at the time.'

'These things can evolve gradually. Is that what happened?'

'Yes. Like maybe there were just tiny seeds of it in the early days of our relationship, but over time, it grew into a vine that wrapped itself around my whole life.'

'When you finally left David after Zoe's birth, you went to your parents, didn't you?'

I clear my throat and nod. 'Yes.'

'Why did you go to them? You just told me a minute ago that David had convinced you they wouldn't help.'

'I was prepared to beg them if I had to. Besides, I had to get out to keep Zoe safe, and I really only had two options. Them, or… '

I trail off, and Natasha finishes for me.

'Sebastian.'

'Yes,' I nod.

'So, why Tom and Rita?'

I shift awkwardly on the chair and try to shrug nonchalantly, but instead, I hiccup and I realise I've been sobbing as we talked and I'd barely even been conscious of it. I reach for the tissue box, clean myself up a little, then admit in a whisper, 'I couldn't let him see me like that… I was a mess, my throat was black and blue with bruising and I was quite hysterical. Plus, I felt like Mum and Dad were the first people to try to get me out, so as scared as I was that they wouldn't help me, I still wanted them to know that I'd finally found the courage to leave.'

'And they've obviously been supportive in the months since.'

'They have, they're amazing. And I know they don't mean to, but sometimes... they do crowd me. Even this morning I told Mum I didn't need her to walk me here today, but she insisted and she's in the waiting room right now.'

'Why *did* you go back to David's house?'

'Well, there was media in town swarming around like flies, and Dr Eric kept giving me tablets to take that made me feel so spaced out I couldn't even summon the energy to *want* to move anywhere. But I hadn't so much as visited Mum and Dad's place for almost seven years and it didn't feel like home any more. Eventually I realised that what I actually needed was to be alone. So I went back to David's house, and then everyone *really* started freaking out.'

'They were scared for you, weren't they?'

'They thought I was going to top myself,' I say wryly. 'I almost had to throw them out of the house just to get some time alone.'

I had to promise Dr Eric I'd call him – 'anytime, day or night' – if I had suicidal thoughts, and I had to agree to stay on the antidepressants and the other catalogue of drugs he gave me for various things, but eventually the fuss all died down and everyone stopped freaking out about it.

'Tell me why you needed to be alone.'

'I wasn't used to having people around me like that. I'd just grown so used to solitude during my life with David. There was work, and there was each other, and the rest of the time I was alone. And as hard as it was on my family, I knew that it was only natural that I needed to withdraw back into that shell to grieve.'

'David isolated you, didn't he?'

'I didn't see it that way at the time, but… yes. The only real friend I've had over the last few years has been Seb… ' I break off, and glance at the clock. Three minutes to go. I look back to Natasha, and she gives me a gentle smile because we both know what she's going to say.

'Are you ready to talk about him yet?'

I shake my head.

'Today has been tough enough.'

'Despite everything you've been through, I don't think I've seen you cry like you have today. Why is *this* topic so upsetting?'

'Because… ' I tear at the tissue in my lap for a while as I plan the words to explain, then I admit, 'My family is the best, you know? And when I think about what I've put them through… '

'What *who* has put them through?'

I shake my head sadly.

'No, I own this one. It was my decision to choose David that day.'

'I'm not sure I agree with you there, Olivia. Maybe next week we can talk some more about power and control.'

'Well, that sounds super fun,' I say wryly, as I take one last tissue to dry my face, then rise.

❖ ❖ ❖

Later that night, I tuck Zoe into my bed and I wander across the hall into the study. I look at the action list on the board, and my stomach spasms – did I eat today? I can't remember, Dr Eric is not going to be impressed. I promise myself I'll do better tomorrow, and I pick up the green marker, and I put a big green tick beside 'sell David's house', and another one next to 'buy new house'. I smile to myself, but then I hover the marker over 'find care for Zoe' and if I had a single thing in my stomach, I'd probably throw it right up.

I set the marker down, and I tell myself that I'll try again tomorrow.

As I'm lying in bed with Zoe in my arms, I'm not actually sure if I can take the next step. I know that I need to find someone to look after Zoe so I can go back to work, and I *need* to get back to work. It's the next step – the only way to move out of this phase of grief and isolation and back into the community in a very real way.

I think about what it's going to be like to work alongside Seb again. I don't even know if it's at all fair of me to go back to work there with him. He loves me, and if there's a single shred of me left that *can* love in that way, it's set aside only for him.

But love isn't always safe. Sometimes, love can hurt, and sometimes, it can cause immense pain and even chaos. I know because the love I had for David has done this to me, and I'll bet Sebastian knows it too now, because the love he has for me has done this to him. I shiver closer to Zoe at the thought of this. I feel a lot of regret, but the crushing weight of my heaviest shame comes from the way that I have hurt Sebastian McNiven.

And still, he's visited me – or at least my doorstep – almost every day since I locked myself away in this house.

And if I want to work, it has to be with him – unless I want to commute an hour each way to work in the clinic over in the regional city nearby, Bathurst. Two extra hours a day away from Zoe, just to avoid meeting Sebastian's gaze? Leaving her at childcare is going to be hard enough – I struggle to even imagine what it's going to be like to let her out of my sight. I haven't done it at all – not even with Mum. When pain comes that close to your family, you have to adopt a whole new level of protectiveness just to survive.

And I do *need* to face Sebastian. I need to force myself to figure out how to apologise to him for everything that has happened between us, and maybe take one of the baby steps towards letting him back into my life again, even in this small way.

Olivia Brennan, you can do this.

It's a long time before my eyes drift closed, but I don't reach for the sleeping pills Dr Eric has prescribed me – I wait it out, until I can go to sleep all on my own.

CHAPTER 16

Ivy

In David's final year of school, he began to focus on his studies in a way that we had never seen before. He had decided that he was going to study business management and marketing at university, and had the goal to return to Milton Falls one day to set up a business of his own.

'As long as it's not a rival grocery store, that sounds like a great idea,' Wyatt laughed.

I assumed that David meant to go to university at Bathurst. That campus was within driving distance so he could live at home with us. When the time came for him to put in his university applications, he filled in the paperwork by himself and then asked me check it over.

'But, David,' I gasped, 'all of these universities are in Sydney or Melbourne.'

David looked at me blankly.

'Of course they are. Where else would I study?'

'I assumed… I mean, your father and I just figured that you'd study at Bathurst. Are you really ready to leave home just yet?'

'Mum, I'm eighteen now,' he laughed easily. 'I'm not staying at home.'

'But, David… we've given you plenty of freedom. You have a car, you come and go as you please. What more do you want?'

'Mum, I just need to spread my wings. I'll be back during the holidays, and most likely I'll be in Sydney – it's only four hours away.' He gave me a consoling hug and said softly, 'Look, this is happening, okay? So can you just check the paperwork, please?'

I tried to talk him out of it. There were dozens of reasons why Sydney was not a good option for David. All of our family lived around Milton Falls for a start, so he would have no support network there, and although David couldn't see that he needed one, even Wyatt could see why I was concerned. In typical fashion though, once David had an idea in his head, he was going to head towards it regardless of what I or anyone else thought.

He aced his end-of-year exams, and that meant he got accepted to the uni of his choice in Sydney. Before I knew it, we were packing up a ute, and with David in his car behind us, we made the trip to Sydney. I sobbed the entire trip, and while Wyatt and David were amused at first, when the time came to leave him there, Wyatt almost had to drag me back to the car.

David spent his first undergraduate year in a dorm on campus. This was an expensive accommodation option, but I was happy to foot the bill, particularly given it meant that there would be food, electricity, and at least a roof over his head for the entire school year. At least he kept in touch with us. David called every single week without fail, even if the calls were sometimes short.

'How are you?' I'd ask.

'I'm really good, Mum. How are you?'

'Well, I've been updating the kitchen, you'll love it. New benches, more modern. And Dad's had the stocktake on so... you know, we've been busy.'

'That's great.'

'And tell me about your week. What have you been doing?'

'Ah, the usual. Study, footy, a party last Friday but don't worry... ' I heard his chuckle, and it made me smile. 'I was well behaved.'

'Of course you were.'

'Can you tell Dad I called? I'll call at night when he's home next time, I just had training tonight and I was missing you guys.'

'Oh, we miss you too,' I said, and there was a pinch in my chest at the sadness in his voice.

'Anyway, I'll be home at midterm break, only a few weeks. See you then?'

'See you then, Davey.'

I couldn't believe the *hole* David's absence left in my life. I lived for those phone calls, and between them, the house had never felt so empty or so vast, and it wasn't long before I began to wonder why I was there at all.

Wyatt and I had never been much for talking, and when we did talk, it was generally about David, but with the absence of David in our lives, there was this insurmountable chasm between us. Some days, I'd crawl into bed and realise that Wyatt and I hadn't spoken a single sentence between us over the full day. He wasn't one to come in through the door and greet me, just as I wasn't one to greet him. More often than not, I was angry with Wyatt about one thing or another: leaving the toilet seat up, putting his whites into the dark bin in the laundry or leaving his plate half full of food because he wasn't impressed with what I'd cooked – but he also wasn't man enough to tell me what he *actually* wanted.

I stewed over all of this in the spare time that David's leaving had left me with. It started as a small idea – a possibility for the future – maybe I'd move to the city too at some point, to be closer to David. I thought about raising it with Wyatt, but I couldn't predict his reaction and that made me nervous, and so I put it off again and again over several weeks and months, until it was no longer a small idea – it was a huge one, and behind it was two decades of resentment and frustration.

By the time I spoke up, I had actually convinced myself that Wyatt was going to be very pleased to see me go, since he clearly didn't love or even like me any more.

'Doesn't seem much point to me staying here, now,' I said to him over dinner one night. 'So I'm thinking that I might pack up and get my own place.'

Wyatt stared at me as if I had suddenly grown a second head. 'What?'

'I'm going to leave.'

'Don't be bloody stupid,' he said, and he blinked at me, clearly dazed. 'Ivy – love – why? And where would you go? Your place is in this house.'

'My place was with David, and he has his own life now so there's no reason for me to stay here. You and I haven't really been married for a decade.'

'What do you mean – "haven't been married for a decade"? Have you lost your mind?' Wyatt said, and he rubbed his forehead, then he blinked again. 'I have no idea what you're talking about, love. Can you slow down, maybe rewind a bit and start at the beginning? What's this about?'

'I've done my hard yards, Wyatt. I raised our son. I've looked after your house. I don't want to be here any more – I want to go and live my own life. I've earned it. Why would you even stop me? We don't talk, we don't have much of a life together – it's just time for me go.'

'Ivy, don't do anything rash. Let's just think about this for a while,' Wyatt muttered, and he looked down at plate and played with his vegetables for a minute, before pushing his plate away. 'I think this is what they call empty nest syndrome. Sometimes women go a bit crazy when the children leave... don't know what to do with themselves. Maybe you should get a new hobby.'

'*Wyatt!*' I slammed my hands onto the table, and pushed myself into a standing position. I was shaking – not with fear, not with regret – but with rage. 'I have been waiting for years to do this. I don't want to be with you any more. It's not too late for me; I'm only thirty-seven. I could go to uni, or I can move away, and train and get my own career. There's nothing to keep me here with you any more.'

Something of what I was saying was finally penetrating Wyatt's thick skull. He looked at me in shock, and then, he carefully extended his hand towards me, and he said, 'Let's just a take a minute. Take a deep breath. You're clearly hysterical… is this a hormone thing?'

When I growled at him, Wyatt raised both of his palms towards me, surrendering quickly.

'Look, Ivy… just… don't do anything rash.' I could almost *see* the way his mind raced as the implications of my announcement sunk in, and it surprised me. Wyatt was panicking. I really thought he would let me go without a fight. 'Maybe… ' he said thoughtfully after a moment. 'Maybe we could go on a holiday? You always wanted to travel. Let's go overseas.'

'*Now* you want to go overseas? I've been asking you for two bloody decades!'

'We were raising David, love. We were busy with the family – and I know that it's scary with David gone, but let's think of it as an opportunity – this is *our* time now. We can focus on each other, have some new experiences—'

'It's too late for that, Wyatt,' I said, but I was no longer angry, I was simply pitying my husband. He wasn't exactly pleading with me, but he was visibly upset. He had always resisted the idea of travelling overseas. So this one small peace offering, as silly as it was, meant something to me.

If only he'd made it ten years earlier.

'I can't believe you'd give up on us this easily,' Wyatt said then, and at last he sounded both hurt and more than a little pissed off. 'I can't believe that you'd let me look after you for all of these years, and then the minute our son leaves home, you abandon me.'

I went to move out of the room, but Wyatt gently put his arm in front of me – blocking my path. I looked up at him in surprise, and found his eyes were full of shock and confusion and hurt. He reached to touch my cheek, very gently, and I wondered when the last time we had showed each other affection was. Years before, possibly even decades. If Wyatt thought that a tender touch of his hand could change that now, he was kidding himself.

'I'm going to move into the spare room,' I said quietly, and I stepped past him and out of the room.

I thought Wyatt was adjusting to my decision. Days passed, and although we didn't speak about it, he was smiling at me, greeting me warmly. He ate all of his dinner, he was careful to put his socks in the right place in the laundry, he didn't complain when I ironed his shirt too crisply.

And then David called.

'Mum, tell me this isn't true,' he pleaded, without identifying himself. His voice was hoarse, as if he'd been crying but... surely not. Not David. 'Dad said you're leaving him? That's not right, is it?'

'David – Dad shouldn't have – I mean; I was just—' I was embarrassed, and confused. I wasn't prepared for this, not at all. I was going to sit David down in person and break the news to him gently at midterm break. Just as anger started to rise in me at Wyatt's lack of sensitivity, I heard David's sigh, and he sounded completely heartbroken. 'I'm so sorry, Davey. I was going to tell you in person.'

'Mum, I can't even begin to tell you how upset I am about this. It's been playing on my mind since Dad told me... it's *all* I can think about.'

'I'm sorry, Davey. I really am. But... you don't live here any more, and well – the truth is – your father and I haven't been in love for a very long time. I think it's time for me to go and live my own life. I had you so very young—'

'I know you did, Mum. I really do get it. It's just *so* upsetting to think of you two apart. Our home and our family have been everything to me, you know? And having somewhere to go *back* to… Uni is great of course but life is so different out here… it's just been such a comfort to know that home was always there waiting for me.'

'You'll always have a place, Davey,' I said urgently. 'Both with me *and* with Dad.'

'Yeah,' he said, reluctantly. 'I suppose so but… it'll never be the same again, will it? Sometimes, I think all that's got me through this year has been the thought of coming home and seeing you guys on the breaks. When I'm studying or going to training, I get distracted by parties or girls and it's just the thought of making you two proud that brings my focus back, you know?'

'Oh, Davey… '

'I mean, Mum, you have to do what you have to do,' he said miserably. 'I understand. I just can't stop thinking about what Christmas will be like now.'

'I guess… we'll have two Christmases,' I said unsteadily. David had fallen silent. I paced the kitchen with the cordless phone at my ear, and I was bewildered. I didn't realise how much David would care. I didn't realise how upset would be. As the silence stretched on and on, a rising sense of guilt enveloped me – I felt quite queasy with it. 'Say something, David,' I prompted urgently, when the pause became just too much.

'I… I think I better go,' he said, his voice a bare whisper. 'I… Dad told me yesterday and I didn't study last night and I didn't get much sleep… I don't want my grades falling because of this.'

'Of course,' I whispered, and now there were tears in my eyes. 'I'm so sorry, Davey.'

'It's… well, I won't say it's okay. But… I understand. I support you, Mum. Even if the timing of this isn't great, I understand.'

'The timing?'

'My exams… I'm studying for my half-yearly exams. At least I, I *was* and now I'm… well, you know. I'll catch up, I guess. I better go. Bye, Mum.'

I hung up the handset, completely numb to everything but the guilt that radiated all the way through me. I walked around the house in a daze, back to the spare room, and I sat on the bed. I thought about what David had said. I hated myself for distracting him, but I hated Wyatt for telling him – why tell him now? Why not wait and let me do it? This was *my* decision – my responsibility – surely Wyatt could have left the conversation up to me.

I would have waited. I would have told David at a better time, when he had more brain space to process it. For a few minutes I think that might have made all the difference, but then I remember the aching sadness in his tone as we discussed it, and my chest tightens. I just didn't realise the impact my decision would have on my son.

When Wyatt came home that night, he walked through the door and he stared at me, and I knew then I wasn't actually going to go through with it. I moved back into our bedroom that night, and when he came to bed, Wyatt pulled me closer to him and he kissed my hair.

Broken as we were, Wyatt and I were David's family. And David, even at eighteen and living four hours away – *needed* his family. Besides which, although he hadn't spoken directly to me about how much he wanted me to stay, Wyatt had sent me a message when he rang David to tell him I was leaving.

He knew David would be upset. And he knew that *nothing* would motivate me like the sound of my son in pain.

I called David the next day.

'Hi, Mum,' he said heavily. He sounded exhausted.

'Davey, I just wanted to let you know, I'm going to stay with Dad.'

'Really?' There was an *immediate* change in the tenor of his voice. Now he sounded excited, like a child again. 'My God, Mum, that's—' he broke off, then he asked me cautiously, 'Mum, this isn't because of me, is it? I was quite upset yesterday; I would hate to think I influenced your decision… '

'No, no… I just came to my senses, that's all,' I laughed weakly. 'It's been an intense week and I did some thinking yesterday and realised how foolish I was being. I'm really sorry to distract you from your exams.'

Later I'd reflect on those phone calls and I'd feel guilt, but also… an odd discomfort. It was hard to put words to it, but it was almost like the outcome I'd chosen wasn't *actually* what I wanted, but I couldn't actually make sense of that. I was sure David would never want to manipulate me. I was also sure Wyatt wasn't smart enough to do it.

But it felt a lot like *someone* had, and I was just never sure who or how.

Wyatt surprised me with an overseas holiday later that year. We spent six weeks going through Europe together, and although it didn't fix things, it did rekindle some warmth between us again. Every year since then, we've travelled for at least a week or two – and we always stay in the kind of accommodation I would never be able to afford on my own – and we eat out at the restaurants that I pick, and we usually do the tours that I pick. Sometimes we manage to stretch the budget far enough for business class flights.

I live in the big house we've owned since David was a boy. I renovate when the whim takes me, and it takes me often, and the renovations are expensive. I get my hair done every fortnight, and I buy premium brands and I never, ever have to wor-ry about how to pay the bills.

Maybe I gave up some things to stay with Wyatt, and maybe even once he was an adult, I did it for David.

I just don't kid myself any more that there isn't something in this life for me too.

CHAPTER 17
Olivia

I am sweating profusely the next day by the time I arrive at the Brighter Futures Childcare Centre. The sweat is not just from the 2km walk pushing Zoe in the stroller, it's from the sheer terror I'm feeling at what I'm about to do.

I'm so anxious that I've almost slipped into a state of shock. My head feels fuzzy, and I'm disoriented – as if I've taken one of Dr Eric's tranquilisers, but I am sober and this needs to be done. It's the next step – the next item on my action list. There is no way to proceed unless I clear this hurdle.

So I take a very long, very slow breath and then I walk along the footpath to the centre. There are cars in all of the parking spots and I tell myself that's a terrible sign – the centre is probably full – wasn't everyone always telling me how hard it is to get childcare in this town? This thought seems so convincing that I actually stop walking at one stage and pause there, right in the middle of the walkway.

No point even asking, really. Everyone says so. *Put your baby on the waiting list the day you find out you're pregnant*, they all said, and David always laughed and said, *Olivia will be at home with our baby, just like my mother was with me. We'll never need childcare.*

That's when I stumble forward again and I keep moving until I'm at the automatic doors. Even the sound of them sliding open startles me, and I scan the area around me anxiously, as if Zoe and I could be about to stare down a physical threat to our safety.

But the area is clear – we are safe – of course we are safe. The only person who ever might have hurt us is long gone.

I push the stroller into the office and walk right up to the counter. Taylor is there – wearing an electric-pink polo shirt with the centre's logo embroidered into it, and she's tapping away at a keyboard. She glances up at me briefly, looks down to the keyboard, and then slowly raises her eyes back to me as the shock dawns on her face.

'Olivia,' she says, and she stands and approaches the counter. 'Are you okay? What are you doing here?'

Taylor looks quite terrified. I rock the stroller back and forth as I take a deep breath and I say, 'I'm thinking about going back to work, so I was wondering if you had space for Zoe one or two days a week.'

'Zoe?' Taylor repeats, and she leans down over the counter to stare into the pram, then sinks back onto her heels and she takes a deep breath. She stares at me for a moment, and the pity in her gaze is too thick for me to tolerate. I look away. 'Oh, Olivia… God… '

She seems lost for words, and I'm embarrassed – mortified. Obviously, even Taylor believes I am making a mistake, and I suddenly wish I'd checked the centre's website. Is Zoe even old enough to go to day care? I'm such an idiot, I should have checked.

'Sorry, Taylor… I'm new to all of this, and I don't want any special treatment, and I know it's complicated. I just… I just need things to get back to normal a little bit, you know? Maybe we could go on a waiting list for when she's a bit older, then?'

'Liv, I do understand,' Taylor says, very gently. She leans on the counter and she is almost whispering as she explains, 'And I'd love to help you – I really would. But I have to think of my families first, and I just don't think they would be comfort-able… '

I realise then that Zoe is not actually too young at all – she's simply too awkward, or at least, her family situation is.

'Wouldn't be comfortable? Because of… because of David?' I repeat. I'm still rocking the stroller out of habit, but now the movement is jerky – fierce with barely restrained anger and embarrassment. I catch myself and force a smoother rhythm.

'Livvy—'

'Don't you understand? If I can't get childcare for her – I can't go back to work. I *need* to go back to work!'

'What about your mum, Olivia? Maybe Rita could help. You said you only need a few days' care – isn't she only working part time these days?'

'I've inconvenienced my family enough – I need to stand on my own two feet,' I say, but the words are constricted and the tears are coming. I pull the stroller away from the counter fiercely and force myself to say, 'I was hoping I could leave her with you because I've known you my whole life, but if you don't want to help us, I'll have to try the other place.'

'Liv… honey… it's not that I don't *want* to help, it's that I just can't. And I'm so sorry – about everything. *Really*. Please – believe me – if we were equipped to help a family with your special circumstances—'

'*Special circumstances?* Because my husband killed himself? No one knows how to deal with me any more because you all think this is my fault,' I'm in a blind panic, and I sound bitter. I scrape together whatever dignity I have left, and I push Zoe out the door. I hold myself together as best I can – I cry a little, but I manage at least to hold back the sobs until I've trekked back to David's house. As soon as I hear the click of the door behind me, I slide down against it and start to come undone. I unclip Zoe from the pram and pull her close, I feel humiliated and desperate and rejected and I want to protect my daughter from how hideous all of that feels.

I'm not at all surprised when Dr Eric shows up an hour later.

'How are you going today, Olivia?' he asks me gently, and I sigh and let him in. He looks around the floor of the entrance way, which is littered with used tissues, but he doesn't comment as he walks to the lounge.

'Let me save you some time, Dr Eric.' I say, as I flop onto my usual place on the lounge. 'I'm taking the antidepressants. My mood is bad. I'm anxious, I'm not sleeping and no, I'm not eating.'

He unclips the medical case and withdraws my file, then he glances at me. 'I see.'

'Are you going to dose me up again? Knock me out for a while?'

'Perhaps I could call your family… for company. And I could give you a sedative, if you want me to.'

'I don't. I just want to feel better,' I admit, and I start to cry again.

'There will be good days and bad ones, Olivia. Only you can decide when it gets too much, and there's no shame when you need to sleep and let your body take a break from the stress.'

'Who from the town rumour-mill called you?' I ask him, and he chuckles and shakes his head.

'No, no one today – I just happened to be calling past and I thought I'd stop in. Why, did you do something outrageous?'

'Kind of,' I sigh, and he slips the stethoscope up into his ears.

'Don't tell me then. Let me find out from the gossips later, and I can report back to you what they say. It's just like Chinese whispers.' I laugh weakly, and Dr Eric pauses and his expression shifts. When he speaks again, his voice is so gentle that I start to cry again. 'You're going to get through this, you know.'

'I'm trying. I'm trying so hard.'

'I *know*. That's how I know you're going to be okay.'

Later, when the storm of emotion finally clears, what's left is a clear crossroads. Taylor's refusal to help with childcare is one very small hurdle that feels like an insurmountable mountain because I am so worn out already – but I could stop here and it would be completely understandable. This is all so very hard, and the only person I'd be letting down is myself – no one would judge me – not any more than they already have, anyway. I could move into the new house in a few weeks' or months' time, and I could stay at home with Zoe, just like David always wanted me to. I could try to find other ways to make myself get out and about again – maybe start smaller – a regular weekly shopping trip or rejoining my mother's group or the little gym at the Police Citizen's Youth Club.

But the alterative is that I can dry my eyes, pull myself together again and give it one last shot with the other day-care centre. I don't know the staff there at all, but it is a little closer to the clinic, and assuming Sebastian lets me come back, that might even be a bonus. Yes, this is a setback, but it doesn't change anything. It doesn't change what I want – which is to wake up one day, in the not-too-distant future, and have something to think about other than the loss and the horror of it all.

So I decide that I will take the day and I'll sulk until the sun goes down. I am embarrassed, and the rejection hurts; fresh pain onto already bruised skin, and I deserve to take the time to lick my wounds. But tomorrow the sun will rise again, and I'll have a new day and a new chance to take a step towards a better future. *That* future is worth digging deep enough within myself to find the strength to press a little harder when I face an obstacle like this. To accept defeat right now would be to submit to the idea that my life is always going to be this way – an endless series of days focused only on my pain. To give up now would mean that my survival this far means nothing, and I refuse to believe that. I simply can't, and I simply won't. My strength is nothing more than a flicker of light… but it's stubborn, and it persists even when it shouldn't.

That's a miracle worth honouring.

So I'm going to get up early, and I'm going to walk across town to the Milton Falls Long Day-Care Centre and I'm not going to take 'it's all too hard' for an answer.

✦ ✦ ✦

I walk with such purpose and focus the next morning that I'm standing in the office of the other day-care centre before I know it, and I'm immediately greeted by a polite, older woman with a smear of purple paint on her cheek. She's at a desk at the back of the entrance area, cutting coloured paper, and I am separated from her by a long, heavy counter.

I don't know her, and the label on her nametag is too small for me to read. Her reaction to my presence is much less dramatic than Taylor's, and that's a great sign. I clear my throat and I say, 'My name is Olivia Brennan. I am looking for someone to care for my daughter Zoe for a day or two each week.'

'Hi, Olivia. I'm Ellen, I'm the director here,' Ellen crosses the room and leans on the desk, then peers down at Zoe and then back at me.

'And this is Zoe,' I say.

'Hello, Zoe,' she says to my daughter, then her eyes raise back to me and she smiles kindly as she says, 'I do so love that name.' Ellen takes a few steps to the right to open a door in the counter. 'Why don't you come through to my office so we can have a chat? I'm sure we can figure something out.'

Now my heart is racing for another reason – because Ellen is clearly more receptive than Taylor was, and if this all works, and everything falls into place, I'm going to have to leave Zoe here and walk away from her. I've not left her for even a second in months. I carry her with me everywhere I go, sometimes even to the toilet. She sleeps in my bed, she watches while I eat and when I take a shower… if I take a shower.

Can I even do this?

I sit in Ellen's office, in the visitor's chair in front of a large desk covered with children's artworks. This centre is less modern than Taylor's – much more cluttered, but somehow more homey. Ellen pulls her own chair from behind the desk to place it near to me and she points towards Zoe.

'Can I hold her?' I don't know what the answer to that question is. *Can* she hold her? I look at Zoe, then I look at Ellen. I clench my jaw and force myself to unclip Zoe from the pram, but I don't lift her out – instead I freeze in place with my hands around her tummy and I'm not sure how to make myself move. Ellen smiles kindly, patiently. 'Let me be blunt, Olivia. I know who you are and I'm aware of your situation – Milton Falls is a pretty small place. I'm so sorry for your loss, and I can only imagine how difficult it is for you to entrust Zoe's care to anyone else. So I'm going to tell you a little bit about me, okay?'

I slowly nod, and then I sit up, bringing Zoe to sit up on my lap. I wrap my arms around her as I nod silently.

'I'm sixty-three years' old. I'm a widower, and I have five children and sixteen grandchildren. I've been working in childcare since I was twenty-four, and I love the children who visit this centre just as much as I love my own little brood. My husband died suddenly from a heart attack five years ago, and although that's very different to your loss – I do know what it's like to lose someone – and I understand the way that all of the parameters that make up your world stop making sense when you have to process immense shock and grief all at once. So you're thinking of returning to work?'

'I just need to,' I croak. 'I don't know if it's the right thing to do, but I have to stop living as if it just happened – to start to put one foot in front of the other, you know?'

'Oh, sweetheart,' Ellen says, and she blinks rapidly, then gives a self-conscious laugh and wipes at her eyes. 'I'm so sorry – and yes, I do know – and that's how I know that you are so very brave. If you're ready – *when* you're ready – I'll be honoured to care for Zoe so you can go back to work.'

My hands tremble as I lift Zoe towards Ellen, but then I feel almost overwhelmed by relief as Ellen lifts my daughter very carefully to cradle her in her arms. She peers down at Zoe, then flashes me a soft smile, and says, 'I promise you, Olivia... I'll care for her as if she is my own.'

'So, Ingrid Little has put the house on the market and the sign is going up tomorrow and I've made an offer on Mrs Schmitt's house – do you remember she used to look after us when we were in primary school? It's been renovated, it's so great – wait till you see it. Also, I went to see the long day-care place and booked Zoe in for two days a week, and I'm going to go see Sebastian tomorrow and ask him if he'll give me my job back part-time. I won't start back just yet – hopefully after I finish moving house. And yes, I've talked to Natasha about all of this and she thinks it's okay.'

I'm sitting at my parents' dining room table when I make the quiet announcement. Perhaps I could have eased it in more gently, but I'm nervous, so I dump all of that information out right after Dad's 'please pass the salt, Rita'.

Mum, Dad and Louisa all stare at me. I try to read their expressions. There's definite shock; Dad had just accepted the salt from Mum and he's still holding it in mid-air. Mum blinks a few times but doesn't move, and Louisa stares until I meet her gaze and then she looks at her plate.

'Day care?' Mum repeats warily. 'But... '

'I know she's young, Mum. But she's too young for separation anxiety yet, so in some ways, it'll be easier if she starts now.
She'll settle in and she'll love the staff before she's old enough to
know any better.'

'Did you… you already went to see the day-care centre,
then?' Dad frowns. 'Which one?'

'The one near the clinic, Milton Falls Long Day-Care Centre. The owner is Ellen and she's agreed to personally watch Zoe
herself. Have you met her, Mum?' When Mum shakes her head,
I say, 'You'd love her. She's so gentle, and so nurturing. Zoe and
I both took to her right away.'

'And… '

Dad tries to speak, but like Mum and Louisa, seems lost for
words. I feel a bristling defensiveness rising, and I straighten in
my chair.

'You all think it's too soon, don't you?'

'Olivia,' Louisa says suddenly. 'If you think you're ready, of
course we'll support you. But… you need to tell us about this
day-care centre.'

'It's the one near the clinic. I told you, I took Zoe in to meet
the owner and it went really well – of course I'm nervous about
leaving her, but it's *time*.'

'Are you sure you wouldn't rather leave her with me, Olivia?'
Mum asks me gently. 'I'm sure Sebastian will be flexible about
the days… '

'Listen – you guys – you've been amazing. I know that you've
all put your lives on hold to drag me through the last few months
and I really appreciate it.'

'We haven't "put our lives on hold", Olivia,' Dad says, but I
see the tautness in the skin around his mouth.

'That's exactly what you've done, Dad,' I say gently. 'You're
only working this extra year so you can be here for me. That's
not right, I'm not going to risk it happening twice.'

'We're happy to do it—'

'Yes, and I appreciate it. But if you want to head off on your trip *next* year, I need to start moving forward, okay? I can't rely on you three to shield me any more. I need to think of Zoe now.'

There are so many concerned glances passing between my parents and my sister that I'm starting to wonder if someone is going to try to put their foot down and tell me it's just too soon and I just *have* to give it more time. I hold myself a little stiffer, against the disappointment at their unsupportive reactions, but then I run out of energy for all of this and I slump in my chair.

'Mum, Dad… Lulu… I *need* to do this. Please, trust me.'

Dad reaches across the table and he rests his hand over mine. I look up at him, and his eyes are filled with tears. I'd never seen Dad cry until I left David. I don't know if I can handle seeing it again.

'Olivia. I trust you. If you say you have this all in hand, I'll do whatever I can to support you. Okay?' he says gruffly, and I sit up taller again and I beam at him.

'Thank you, Dad.'

'Dad's right,' Mum says quietly. 'If this is what you need to do next, Livvy, then you just tell us what day you need us to come help you pack up the house.'

Louisa clears her throat.

'Liv – do you mind if I check this day-care centre out too? I wouldn't mind meeting this Ellen lady myself. It's the one down the road from my office, yeah?'

'You're a good aunty, Lulu,' I smile at her, but she avoids my gaze. 'But trust me, she's wonderful. There's no need for you to do that. And yes, it's right near your office too and if I'm ever running late I fully intend to ask you to pick Zoe up. Okay?'

Louisa laughs weakly and nods. 'You got it, Liv.'

I look down at my untouched plate, and suddenly, I'm ravenous.

CHAPTER 18

Ivy

David visited us at least once or twice a term. He would drive up on Friday afternoon, go out on the town or to parties Friday night, sleep most of Saturday, share dinner with us Saturday night, and then return to the city on Sunday. He often timed these visits to coincide with some convenient town event – the bachelor and spinster's ball, the end of the football season finals, big cricket tournaments. David was frequently invited to be a ring-in on the teams, and even when he wasn't, he would stand with the players and give them coaching advice. Back in Sydney, he was playing for the university football team in the winter, and for the cricket team in the summer. He told us, more than once, that he had been approached by professional scouts in both sports.

'I turned them down. I'm focusing on my studies,' he told us, and he was doing *very* well at university – just as I always knew he would. And David might have been busy with sport and study, but he still seemed to find time for an endless array of friends and girlfriends. He seemed so happy, and I felt like he'd found the perfect balance between studying and making the absolute most of the rich life university offered him. Then, at the end of his second year of study, David surprised us when he announced that he was bringing a girl home for Christmas.

'Well that's a first,' Wyatt remarked when I hung up the phone.

'He wouldn't tell me her name,' I said, and I was inexplicably nervous. This was the first girl David had brought home since that disaster with Jennie all of those years earlier. All I knew about this girl was that she wasn't staying with us, but that she'd be joining us for Christmas lunch. It didn't make any sense.

'Where else would she stay?' I asked Wyatt, and he said, 'Do you think she's a local?'

We stared at each other, and then we started to laugh. It seemed exceedingly unlikely that David would move four hours away, only to hook up in some kind of serious relationship with another girl from Milton Falls. But then the day arrived, and I opened a door and David was standing there with Olivia Brennan.

I'd been aware of Olivia. She had been in David's year at school, a clever girl – a focused girl. He'd never shown the slightest interest in her in high school. As far as I knew, she had no interest at all in sport – and I couldn't ever remember seeing her at any of his games. I knew her parents: Rita was a registered nurse at the hospital, Tom was an accountant. They were a nice family, they lived in a nice, average-looking house on the other side of town, and as far as I knew, they kept to themselves. I'd certainly never been aware of any scandals involving the Brennan family. They were good people. Simple people.

But even so, Olivia was not the kind of girlfriend I had pictured or wanted for David. Not only did I fail to see what they might have in common, Olivia was actually quite a plain girl. After Jennie, David had always gravitated to the prettiest, to the most outgoing, to the most vivacious. Olivia was quiet and gentle, and she had mousy-brown hair, and some freckles scattered over her cheeks. She didn't wear a lot of make-up; she didn't really dress up. She was the kind of kid to blend in, rather than the kind to stand out – certainly not the type to command attention. This was not the kind of woman I pictured David settling down with. I had imagined that one day, he'd finish uni and go on to a highly successful career, and he'd be with the kind of woman who turned heads when she entered a room. Everyone would be jealous of them – they'd be the perfect power couple.

Olivia Brennan was the polar opposite of the woman I'd pictured for my son. But there she was, standing hand-in-hand with him, passing anxious glances in my direction between intense gazes at her shoes.

'Well, hello,' I said.

'Mum, I think you know Olivia?'

I had assumed that if he was bringing a girl home, things between them had to be fairly serious – but then it struck me that if it was *only* Olivia, maybe they weren't actually home 'together' but rather just home 'at the same time'.

I glanced at their hands – tightly entwined, and my heart sank. No, they were definitely *together*, and I had no idea what to make of it at first. So I stared at them, and a sense of unease slowly dawned in me.

Olivia wasn't the kind of girl a boy like David should be dating. She wasn't good enough for him – she was too plain. Too *ordinary*. But she also wasn't the kind of girl a boy like David would just have some fun with. She was no notch in his belt, no fling. And even if she had been, he wouldn't have brought her home to meet us formally like this.

I swallowed heavily. David was serious about her. I couldn't even begin to fathom what he was thinking. He was looking at me expectantly, and I realised I was yet to welcome her.

'Of course, hello Olivia,' I said, and I forced a bright smile as they walked into my house. I watched the way that David brushed a kiss against her hair as he led her gently into the hallway. He was tenderly, gently encouraging her. I remembered how protective he was of Jennie Sobotta all of those years ago. There were hints of that same determined chivalry in those first moments with Olivia.

'How was the drive?' I asked them, and David wrapped his arm around Olivia's waist and steered her into the living room. She sat on the couch, and then he sat right beside her but kept his arm around her. Olivia lent into him, and she flashed him a doe-eyed smile.

'It was great, thanks Mum. How have you guys been? How's the dogs?'

I think my jaw probably hung open for a good ten seconds or so before I could collect myself enough to say, 'The dogs are good. We're having pups again soon. Dad's well, he's busy at the store. I'm good too.'

'Olivia's doing vet science,' David told me, and I looked to Olivia in surprise.

'Is that right?'

'Can I see your dogs?' she asked me, brightening. 'What breed are they?'

'Of course you can!' I said, and I was warmed a little to the situation myself.

That Christmas, David left no doubt in our minds that he was very serious indeed about Olivia Brennan. Rather than going out on the town or even going to sporting events, he wanted to spend every spare moment with her. He doted on her. When she was in our house, he was always fetching her a drink or asking if she wanted anything else at dinner, or cuddling her, or just holding her hand. They weren't the kind of kids to spend a lot of time alone in their room making out. Instead, David seemed respectful, devoted, and completely and utterly in love.

I must admit, I felt threatened. I'd never imagined that David would be like this when he found a serious girlfriend – Wyatt certainly hadn't been. Perhaps I was just a little jealous too – David and Olivia seemed to share the kind of relationship that I had always imagined I might have for myself. They were well matched intellectually, and although their interests were diverse, they found easy middle ground. Olivia went to a few cricket games with David over that summer, and when she volunteered to walk the dogs for me, David willingly went. I even caught him patting one of the dogs, just because Olivia was sitting on the couch beside him patting the other one.

And then there was the fact that David had come home to see *me*, but in that entire visit, he didn't spend a single moment with me alone. We spent plenty of time together, but Olivia was always there... and she was always his focus.

I thought seriously about suggesting to David that perhaps they were moving a little too fast. I went as far as to plan what I'd say, and how I'd bring the subject up. I'd ask him as non-chalantly as I could if he didn't think things were Olivia were getting just a little bit intense. I could point out that they didn't *really* have all that much in common. I could even try an off-hand comment about how her sister Louisa was actually the more *classically* beautiful of the two, and had he met her? All I needed was a little doubt in his mind... a little wedge between them. Then I could expand it later.

During that entire summer, almost every day I thought about trying to find a way to break David's focus on Olivia, but I never once went through with it – and the only thing that stopped me was that I knew I'd fail. I knew instinctively that an attempt to introduce some distance between them would only damage my own relationship with David. The intensity in his gaze when he looked at her was a force I'd not reckoned with before, and I came to the conclusion that all I could do was wait and hope that this honeymoon period between them faded by itself in time. I kept telling myself that this thing with Olivia would pass, and David would move on to someone more suitable. Someone who didn't monopolise his time or energy. Someone who wasn't so needy for it. Someone worthy of him.

On Christmas morning, Olivia came round as soon as she'd finished opening gifts with her family. David presented her with a parcel, a small box, not small enough to contain an engagement ring – and I was so relieved about that I felt a little giddy with it.

When Olivia opened her gift, there was simply a little piece of paper folded up inside.

'What is it?' I asked, peering over to see.

Olivia had tears of happiness in her eyes. She threw her arms around David's neck and hugged him, and then she finally showed me the piece of paper.

'We're going to go do some behind–the-scenes animal feeds at the zoo,' she said, and her brown eyes were sparkling with joy and delight.

She seemed overtly excited about this gift, in the way that a person can only be excited when a gesture truly speaks to something that they desperately wanted to do. I looked at David, and he was so pleased with himself – I could see that her happiness made him happy. There was no doubt at all in my mind then that David loved Olivia. And when I saw the way that Olivia looked at David, I really started to wonder. If this relationship didn't fade, would she do everything within her power to make my son happy? She was at university too, and clearly very focused on her vet studies: would that career come before David in the future? Or if they did stay together long enough to build a shared life, would she do as a good wife should, and lay her own needs down in order to support my son?

I wondered if Olivia knew the unspoken promise she made David when she looked at him with love shining in her eyes like that. I wondered if this clever, quiet girl realised the sacrifices that becoming a good wife and mother would require of her. I wondered if she understood that to commit fully to a man meant a life that sometimes felt hollow, because her purpose one day would be to build and sustain her family. I knew girls of Olivia and David's generation liked to kid themselves about careers and independence and feminism – but equally, I'd seen enough women try 'to have it all' to be quite certain that motherhood inevitably commanded a determined selflessness. That was just the way of the world.

And it was all ahead of her; ahead of *them*, if they decided to walk the path of life together.

I was still hopeful it was just one of those romances young adults tumble in and out of when they're trying to figure the world out. But over time, Olivia became an awkward addition to the fabric of our family.

CHAPTER 19

Olivia

Just arriving at the clinic on Friday morning is confusing. I stand at the front door for a long time, trying to convince myself to go inside. I can't even begin to imagine what Sebastian is going to say when I ask him. I know he'll be happy to see me. I know that beautiful smile will spread over his face, transforming him. But then I'll have to ask him for my job back, and I try to imagine his response to what will no doubt be an unexpected request. I ponder this for a while, and it seems that I can't convince myself to cover the last bit of distance to step inside. I stand in front of the building, just as I have done a thousand times before, just as if nothing had ever happened. Except this time, I'm quite frozen with indecision.

'Olivia, hi.' Gilly, the practice manager and senior nurse, eventually comes out through the doors to greet me. 'Are you coming in?'

I draw in a sharp breath, and I nod. She walks down the ramp and loops her arm through mine.

'So great to see you, Livvy.'

All of the nurses are waiting in the reception area. They stare at me, but no one speaks for a moment or too. Gilly again breaks the silence.

'Just in time for morning tea,' she says brightly, and I shake myself out of my daze.

'Thanks, Gilly,' I say stiffly, and then I look back towards the offices, 'But I'm only here for a few minutes. I just wanted to see Sebastian, if he's free?'

There's an awkward silence, and I suddenly wonder if they all *know.* Would Seb have told them about us?

Surely not.

Definitely not.

Oh God, what if he did?

'He's playing reptile midwife,' Gilly explains, and I shoot her a confused glance.

'We do that now?'

'It's a special case, a pet diamond python. The owner is nine and she read about a case online where a snake got egg-bound and died. Seb tried to explain to her that even if it did happen, it was easily treated and there was no real rush, but she was so upset. So he's been in there for an hour with this kid, waiting for a bloody snake to finish laying her eggs in an aquarium.'

That is so like Sebastian McNiven that I even manage a chuckle.

'How many eggs?' I ask.

'Fourteen and counting, last time I checked, so he should be almost done; you can wait in his office if you like.'

I walk through to Sebastian's office with Zoe strapped safely to my chest, one arm tight around her. I don't go in, though – instead, I walk further down the corridor.

My name is still on the door to my own office.

Olivia Gillespie: veterinary surgeon

I slide the nameplate out of the bracket and as soon as I open the door I dump it into the bin. Olivia *Gillespie* is gone. If Seb lets me come back, I'll order a new nameplate.

The room is just as I left it; right down to the text book open on the desk and a stained coffee cup by the mouse. There was no time to pack up – I left work one day expecting I'd be back the next morning and instead wound up in emergency with a fractured wrist.

Sometimes my wrist still aches when it rains, but so do my ribs, and while I never had an x-ray to confirm it, I know that David broke several of those over the years. I understand the science of the lingering pain – it's a simple consequence of air pressure and bone density and the site of the repair – but I also draw more meaning from it. Bones can heal, but they can also remember, because what's done to the structure of a person can never really be undone.

He broke my wrist.

He fractured two of my ribs.

Sprained my ankle when he pushed me on the stairs.

Gave me a huge, hideous black eye that no make-up could hide.

Chipped my tooth, slamming my head into the bathroom counter the second time I refused to come off the pill. The dentist fixed it the next day, but now, whenever I brush my teeth, I run my tongue over the groove of the repair, almost compulsively.

And then there were the bruises, more than I could possibly count, even if had tried to keep tabs, which of course I never would have. I liked to pretend it wasn't happening at all, or that whatever incident I was recovering from was a one-off, like I had selective memory loss. I never did manage to look back and catalogue my injuries, not while David was alive. It's only now that I can scan back over the years and see how sustained and consistent the pattern was.

But he's gone. And I'm here at work. I give a little giggle of relief as I step inside my office, and I walk behind my desk and sit down, wriggling to make myself comfortable in the chair. I know that the fact that this office is undisturbed means that Sebastian has made the locum use the spare room. It's little more than a cupboard, terribly uncomfortable, and the only reason he would have done that was to save a place for me.

I am suddenly full of confidence. If Sebastian has not even repurposed my office even six months after I took early maternity leave, that means he will certainly not have replaced me permanently. There's no way he would have made a permanent vet use the spare room.

Sebastian McNiven is *loyal* to a fault.

He steps quietly through the door to my office a few minutes later. He is not as tall as David was, and he's actually quite slight compared to my ex-husband. Sebastian is a different kind of man – a man who takes up much less space, both physically, and emotionally. He looks at me, assessing me, and then he closes the door quietly behind him.

'Olivia,' he says quietly, formally, but then a broad smile crosses his face, as if he wants to be solemn but he just can't hide his pleasure at the fact that I'm there. 'It's so good to *see* you.'

The slight emphasis he puts on the word 'see' makes me think of the dozens of mornings he's spent sitting on my doorstep talking to me. It's suddenly embarrassing that I let him come by like that, but didn't even have the courtesy or the courage to open the door or speak back to him.

'I'm sorry,' I wince, and shake my head in self derision. 'It was… I had to do this in stages, you know? I'm really sorry I've been rude.'

'Hey,' he says, shrugging easily. 'You have nothing to be sorry about, I kind of liked those chats. Felt good to talk, even if you couldn't talk back yet. I just had to find a way to let you know I was here if you needed me. I mean, obviously we really need to—'

I know exactly what he's going to say, and so I cut him off, and without preamble I re-steer the conversation to the place I need it to go.

'I know it's going to be difficult for everyone at first – but I'm actually only here today because I need to come back to work.'

Seb's smile disappears in an instant. He stares at me, disbelief echoing across his face.

'But – oh – Liv—'

Well, that confirms it – Sebastian wasn't expecting this request at all. He looks like I've just dropped a bomb on his lap – his eyes are wide and his jaw is slack. I pause and carefully analyse my reaction to his shock.

I'm not deterred at all, and a warm flush of pride washes over me.

Determined. That's what I am. Determined, strong, resilient.

It helps that this is a hell of a lot easier than visiting the supermarket or the coffee shop, or even begging Taylor or Ellen for childcare. I have no issue at all with Seb's uncertainty, and no qualms about advocating for what I know I need. Perhaps the difference is that I'm completely safe here. Whether I deserve it or not, Sebastian cares about me, and again whether or not I deserve it, he absolutely wants what's best for me.

I lean back in my chair, and I pat Zoe's back gently as I say, 'I'm not ready for full-time work. I know that, but I do need to come back part time. I miss the work, and I miss the animals – I even miss the team. I miss morning teas with you guys and beers on a Friday afternoon while we do paperwork, and I miss the nurses laughing at you because you agreed to some stupid request from an overprotective pet owner – like, spending your entire morning monitoring a snake on the off chance she develops dystocia.'

Sebastian grimaces, and I laugh softly.

'If you let me come back, I'll volunteer for the crazy-cases, I'll do as much snake-sitting as you need. I just need something normal in my life again. Surely you can understand that?'

'I'll do whatever I can to support you – but I don't want to allow you to come back to work too soon. You couldn't even speak to me through a door last week, Livvy… and I understand, but

– if you're only just ready to go out in public now, how are you going to handle dealing with clients?'

'I don't know,' I admit, and I slump a little at the thought of this. A vet who doesn't want to deal with owners is not going to be much good to Sebastian, but there has to be a way. 'I know it's going to be hard. But *everything* has been hard. I mean,' I clear my throat, and I stare at the desk as I say, 'If I have to stay at home for another month, I might lose my mind completely. I have to find ways to make my life go on.'

Sebastian crosses his arms over his chest, and he stares at me. It is an intense stare, searching, and I see his affection for me even in that stare. I ignore it – in fact, I push away any thought of it, because to acknowledge it even to myself at this point is going to be too much. Instead, I raise my chin, and then – somehow wanting to make myself feel larger in the room – I stand, and I plant my feet wide at the hips, and I cross my own arms over my chest, around Zoe. I want Sebastian to see my stubbornness. I want him to know how determined I am that I can make this work.

I can be as brave and as bold as a person can be with Sebastian. I'm a completely different woman with him, because I know in my heart of hearts that he would never, ever do *anything* to hurt me.

'Find something for me to do where I don't have to talk to owners, at least at first. You don't have to pay me my own salary. Just pay me as if I'm a nurse, or… don't pay me at all, if that makes it easier. I just need a routine. I just need to come through those doors regularly, and contribute something here. I need something to think about *other* than what has happened.'

Sebastian sighs, and then he steps away from the door and runs his hand through his hair, and I can't tell if he's exasperated or stressed. The mystery is solved only a moment or two later, when he glances down at Zoe, and he says hesitantly, 'Liv, I'm sure we can figure *something* out… but… I know it's hard for you to leave her, but you *can't* bring her to work with you.'

I glance down at Zoe, and then back to Sebastian. He looks so miserable that suddenly, *I* feel sorry for *him*. When I laugh, his eyebrows shoot upwards. 'Is that all you're worried about? Of *course* I can't bring her to work. I've already lined up care for her. It's all under control.'

Sebastian is still not convinced. 'You're sure this is what you want, Livvy? Now? It really hasn't been very long.'

'I'll be healing for the rest of my life. And I *need* this, Seb.' There's a flicker in his eyes, and his uncertainty gives way to something else – it takes me a moment to recognise it, because it's something that's been missing in my life for some time. *Hope.* 'I need the *job*,' I clarify hastily, and Sebastian pauses, then he nods.

'Okay,' he says, on an exhale. 'One day per week?'

'Initially.'

'We'll see how you go. I'm sure I'll find plenty for you to do, maybe you can just assist with theatre work until you're ready for more. I *do* want you to come back, Livvy.'

He looks at me, and he looks right into my eyes. I feel a confused twist in my gut – it's not altogether unpleasant, but there's guilt there, and there's shame there, and regret – all tied up with the pleasant butterflies that looking at Sebastian once gave me. I look away hastily, to the floor. It's a self-protective mechanism.

'There'll always be a place for you here, Olivia, but I was never going to pressure you to come back. I get it. I'm just *so* sorry.'

'It's in the past,' I say hastily, and then I walk around my desk. I'm ready to make a beeline for the door.

'Livvy,' Sebastian says, and he takes a step towards me, but I back myself right up against the bookshelves and shake my head while I fix my gaze to the floor.

I'm going to have address this directly, but I still can't look at him while I do it.

'When I say I'm ready to come back to work, I mean I'm ready to come back to work – that's it. I can't deal with *anything* else yet, I can't even talk about it. I don't know… ' I trail off, and then I flick the briefest of gazes towards him and return my gaze to the vinyl tiles before I finish. 'I don't know if I'll ever be ready to deal with what happened, Sebastian. I really need be sure that you're okay with that.'

Sebastian stills. He speaks very quietly, his voice an urgent and slightly hoarse whisper, 'I'm here for you as a boss and as a friend. I don't expect anything more, not ever. Yes – I'd like to talk when you're ready to, but I'll never rush you. I'd never do anything to hurt you, Olivia. You've had more than your share of that in this lifetime.'

I could cry then. The gentleness of Sebastian's patience is breathtaking, but I turn towards the door. I pull it open, just to make sure that the privacy we've had disappears and the conversation has to stop. Once the door is safely open, I turn back to him and I say as lightly as I can, 'So, I'm moving house… I was thinking I could start straight after that. Once I know when I'm moving I'll give you a call.'

'Why don't you give me a call *before* you move, and I can help you with your furniture?' he suggests.

'I'm not taking any furniture.'

'Oh?'

'This is going to be *my* house,' I say. 'There's not a trace of David Gillespie coming with me.'

Seb's smile returns, dawning slowly over his face. He's proud of me.

I like that a lot more than I should.

'Good for you, Livvy. And you know where I am if you need anything.' He pauses, then he adds softly, 'Anything at all, Liv. And that offer will *never* expire.'

I step out into the hallway, and the last of the butterflies disappears from my tummy. I walk back into the reception area, and then I have a perfectly average chat to the girls there and even share in the morning tea, as if I was just coming back from holiday leave, or maternity leave... as I should have been, one day.

After the chat subsides, I walk back out through the door. As I'm walking home, I pass the long day-care centre, and the nervous tension returns to my gut – but it's tolerable.

I'm *doing* this. All on my own, I am starting over. I look down at my daughter, resting peacefully in the baby-carrier, and I stroke my hand down her back and I whisper, 'I'm really doing it, baby. I'm taking my life back.'

CHAPTER 20
Ivy

After that first visit with Olivia, David mentioned her every single time he called. I got the distinct impression that they lived in each other's worlds, spending every spare moment together. David was certainly happier than I'd ever seen him before. His phone calls back home now were punctuated by tales of Olivia; stories about how he was sweeping her off her feet, about how she ceaselessly amazed him. In time, I came to accept that this was no passing phase.

'You two seem to be getting so serious,' I said cautiously during one of his calls.

'Yeah, I guess we are,' he said, and there was a grin in his voice. I had asked the question for fear of very that answer, but David took such delight in saying those words. I'd spend twenty minutes on the phone to him and all I'd hear about was *Olivia* and I'd get off the phone and I'd stomp around the house doing the cleaning or I'd take the dogs for an extra-long walk to burn the scowl off my face. The lack of control made me feel *crazy*, but I still couldn't bring myself to challenge his commitment to her. I no longer had the power to correct the trajectory of the course of my son's life. Olivia had taken *my* role as the most important person in his world.

David's course drew to a close when Olivia's still had two years to go, maybe three if she opted to do postgrad study, which she was considering. He initially picked up a graduate marketing position in the city, but after eighteen months, he had *really* had enough of city life.

'Why stay if you don't like it there any more?' I asked him, and he sighed heavily.

'I would come home,' he admitted. 'But I can't leave Olivia... '

'Perhaps Olivia needs to revisit her priorities if you aren't happy,' I said, my tone sharper than I'd intended. I paused, but when David remained silent, I seized the opportunity to press the issue a little harder. 'Surely there's some way you can both adjust your lives so that you can both be happy. I mean, goodness, surely Bathurst would have a vet science program, and if you both came back she could transfer easily enough with those grades.'

'She's pretty determined to finish her degree here,' he murmured.

'If she loved you, she'd be willing to compromise.' I heard his sharp intake of breath, and I knew I'd gone too far, so I added hastily, 'But darling, you know what you're doing and I won't interfere. I'm sure you'll make the right decision.'

'Yeah. Okay. I better go. Good chatting to you, Mum,' he said quietly.

'You too, darling.'

It was only a few weeks later that Wyatt's assistant manager called me to let me know that something had happened at work, and Wyatt was being taken to the big hospital in Bathurst. They wouldn't tell me much over the phone, but as I raced into the emergency ward, I found my husband sitting up on a gurney with an oxygen cannula under his nose and leads and machines attached to his chest.

'They think it's my ticker,' he explained. Wyatt's face was flushed, but he didn't look sick – only embarrassed.

'What happened?' I asked him, bewildered, and he shrugged.

'I had some chest pain and I passed out,' he admitted reluctantly, and for the first time, I realised how serious the incident was. Later, we'd learn from the cardiologist that Wyatt had suffered a heart attack and needed urgent bypass surgery. I was sobbing when I called David.

'Dad's going in now,' I choked. 'They couldn't wait.'

'Mum, is he going to die?' David asked me unevenly.

'The cardiologist said it was risky surgery, but Dad's age is on his side – he's young for this kind of blockage,' I wept, and David's uneven tone suddenly solidified.

'I'm coming, Mum,' he said urgently. 'I'll be home in four hours, okay? Hang in there, I'm coming.'

I sat in the waiting room alone for several hours. I thought about Wyatt during that entire time, and how complicated my relationship with him was. I was nothing like in love with him, but I definitely *loved* him, and the thought that he might die actually left me terrified. When David flew in the door, I rose and let him embrace me. I closed my eyes and cried quietly into my son's shoulder, but then when I opened them, I was startled to see that Olivia was also in the room. She hovered just behind David, her gaze concerned.

I slid out of David's arms and drew in a deep breath.

'This is a *family* issue, David,' I said stiffly.

He frowned, and looked from me to Olivia, then back to me.

'Yes,' he said flatly. 'It's a family issue. And the whole family is here now, right?'

'I just want to help,' Olivia offered. I could see the hurt in her gaze, but she forced a smile. 'But I can go if you'd prefer, Ivy.'

David's expression had darkened immeasurably. He stepped away from me, towards Olivia, and I panicked and shook my head hastily.

'Livvy, darling, I'm so sorry – I didn't mean anything by it, I'm just so…'

I let the sobs come unhindered. They'd quietened over the hours that passed, but now, I forced all of my fear and pain out, and both David and Olivia embraced me and led me to the chairs. I was angry with myself – this *wasn't the time* – but I'd been caught off-guard by the sight of her and the words had just slipped from my mouth.

Still, some unhindered sobbing was all it took before everyone seemed to forget about my comment, and given I was genuinely anxious for Wyatt, that was easily enough arranged. We were all sitting together an hour later when the cardiologist came to tell us Wyatt had come through the surgery well.

'There's a long road to recovery,' he warned us, but then he smiled. 'But I'm confident he's going to be just fine.'

❖ ❖ ❖

Wyatt would be off work for at least two months' even if his recovery went well.

'I'm coming home,' David said firmly, the day after the surgery. 'I'm going to move home to help.'

'You don't have to do that,' Wyatt insisted, but David was determined.

'I'm ready to leave the city anyway,' he said, and then he glanced to Olivia. 'Maybe you can transfer to Bathurst uni instead?'

'We can talk about that later,' Olivia said quietly. Even I could see the displeasure in her gaze at the mere suggestion of this.

'It would make a lot of sense,' David insisted, but she shook her head and her frown deepened.

'I haven't worked this hard for the last three years in a top-tier university just to move to a regional university at the end of my degree, David.'

David gave an impatient sigh and muttered that they could discuss it afterwards. I watched all of this unfold with some glee. Maybe *this* was the answer to my prayers – maybe David would come back to help Wyatt with the store, and Olivia would stay in the city, and then the natural challenges distance posed would be enough for them to see how unsuited they were. I could only hope.

✦ ✦ ✦

I'd kept David's bedroom for him just the way it had always been, but it was so strange to have him back under our roof again. Four years of independence had changed him – matured him. He still let me do his laundry and cooking, but he had ideas now about how those things should be done – he liked his T-shirts ironed now, and his taste in food had been broadened by exposure to a wider set of cuisines in the city. He bought me a few cook books, and when he told me he really missed the food at this little Moroccan place Olivia liked to go, I ordered a tagine and after a few false-starts, managed to make a reasonable attempt at using it.

Wyatt took a lot longer than we'd expected to regain his strength and adjust his lifestyle. He'd always eaten the same way that he had as an athletic teen – his diet had been completely unrestricted, and as his activity levels had dropped, he'd quickly gained weight. But the brush with his mortality had been just close enough that Wyatt immediately recommitted to his health. He began walking the dogs every morning and instead of white bread loaded with butter and deli meat for his beloved sandwiches, he enthusiastically devoured grain breads and salad.

'What will you do when Dad goes back to work?' I asked David.

'I'll stay and help him settle back in. Then I have some ideas for revamping the store.'

'And Olivia?' I asked hesitantly, and David sighed.

'She's determined to finish her degree in the city. So I guess we just have to make do until she's done.'

'Hmm,' I said thoughtfully, and I gave a reluctant half-shake of my head. David sighed and nodded.

'Look, I know Mum. It's not ideal.'

'It just seems selfish to me,' I remarked. 'Does she always do that?'

'Do what?' he asked, frowning.

'Put her needs before your own. Your relationship is still young; it doesn't bode well if she's already refusing to compromise.'

'She just wants to finish her degree. Then she'll come back.'

'Well, it's your life, darling. I won't interfere. I'm just disappointed for you,' I said lightly, and I offered him a sad smile. 'You're such a wonderful partner to her. You really do deserve her full devotion… you shouldn't have to share her.'

His gaze narrowed and he repeated slowly,

'Share her?'

'Just in the sense that she's *so* determined to stay in Sydney, hours and hours away from you. Something about her life there must have *really* captured her attention.' His stare was steady, but his eyebrows pulled together, and I added lightly, 'But if you're okay with that, then who am I to comment?'

I couldn't believe how foolish Olivia was being with David. Didn't she realise how lucky she was to have him? But if she was going to be a fool, then I wasn't going to miss the opportunity to give David cause to rethink his relationship with her. It was obvious to me that if he ended things with Olivia, he'd grieve for a time, but it would be a chance for him to find someone more suited to him, worthy of him… someone who'd prioritise his needs above her own. Every time I saw him sulking around the house at night, waiting to call her or staring absently at the clock as he waited for Friday to roll around so he could drive all the way to Sydney to visit her, I'd feel my frustration rise. He was devoted and besotted – a good boyfriend. He deserved better. I wished he could see that for himself.

But the weeks turned into months, and the pattern of him pining for her between those daily phone calls and weekend visits did not abate, and I couldn't deny the strength of the feelings he had for her.

'Things are still good with her then?' I asked one night, my voice thin and high. David nodded and smiled softly.

'She's my soulmate, Mum. We were made for each other.'

I figured I'd always be a little jealous – maybe that was natural for a mother when her son found the love of his life. But even I had to accept that Olivia was in our lives to stay.

✦ ✦ ✦

David had some wild ideas for the grocery store. He convinced Wyatt to engage a very expensive branding consultant, and soon the store took on a whole new name and new look – Gillespie's Groceries and Goods became simply Gillespie's. There was a huge controversy in Milton Falls when they shut down the store for ten whole days for the renovation that came next. Given that in its entire existence the store had only ever closed on Good Friday and Christmas Day, this was a risky move – but during the shutdown, the entire layout was revamped and a small café was added at the entrance. David had sourced new trolleys that had cup holders on the handle, and he'd replaced the old florescent lighting with much brighter industrial-style bulbs. Even the music that piped over the speakers all through the store was updated – rather than the standard local radio station, he ordered a service from the United States which streamed specially selected music.

'Studies have shown that slow music makes customers move through the store slower and overall spend increases as a result.

And we intersperse the slow songs with classical music periodically, which triggers impulses for customers to purchase premium products. We have those at the end of every aisle now,' David told me, as he walked me through the store the day it reopened while we sipped our espressos. And I looked at him then, and suddenly it was all worthwhile – the loneliness of my marriage, the sacrifices I'd made of my own dreams, the way I'd had to *push push push* to see him reach his potential – it had all paid off. David was a strong, confident and capable man. A man I could be proud of.

We were halfway through the detergent aisle, but I sat my coffee on a shelf and I threw my arms around him.

'Mum? What the hell?' he said as he stiffened in surprise.

'I'm just so proud of you,' I said tearfully, and David laughed and hugged me back.

'God, Mum, you scared me for a minute there.' We stayed like that for a while, and when David tried to gently pull me away, I held on fiercely. He laughed again and said gently, 'Come on Mum, that's enough soppiness for one day, there's more to see yet!'

Despite the outrage over the shutdown, the day the store reopened saw the highest takings in its history.

'I must admit, I wasn't sure about some of these newfangled ideas when David first came back,' Wyatt admitted to me as that year drew to a close. 'But our turnover is consistently up by 20 per cent – the renovations will have paid for themselves by the end of next year.'

He was busy with his projects at the store, but outside of work, David spent a lot of time on the phone to Olivia. He'd come home tired or stressed, eat dinner with Wyatt and me at the table and then disappear with the handset into his room, and he'd stay in there for hours. Later he'd emerge with a smile on his face – as if the contact with her had resettled him. Every now and again I'd try to stir the pot a little, just to see if I couldn't remind him of how *unfair* the arrangement was to him.

'It just doesn't seem right to me that it was *her* decision to stay there, but you're always the one travelling back and forth,' I said to David, as he packed his car for yet another Friday evening drive.

'Yeah, I know,' he sighed, accepting the travel mug of coffee I'd made him. He stifled a yawn, and my gaze softened.

'Maybe you could ease up a bit with the travel,' I said. 'Couldn't she could come here? Or maybe you could just go every second weekend?'

'No, I need to be there. She's got to study, and she's got prac. too – she can't come to me, so I have to go to her.' He glanced at me, and he smiled softly at my frustrated expression. 'I *know*, Mum. But like she keeps telling me, it's not forever.'

'Doesn't it just make you wonder?' I said, absent-mindedly plucking a dead flower bud from a plant beside his car. 'What it really is that keeps her anchored there?'

'It's her study.'

'That's never rung true to me,' I admitted, then at his frown, I shrugged and patted his shoulder. 'But I suppose you know her best. I'd better let you get going.'

As he drove away, I growled my frustration and wished not for the first time that he wasn't so besotted with Olivia. If his emotions and hormones were running a little cooler, I could be less subtle in my attempts to make him see sense. But it was such a delicate balancing act – trying to lead him to his own conclusions about her unsuitability, without letting him throw his whole life away on her.

David seemed to know his own mind, and there was certainly nothing about his behaviour that concerned me – he seemed like any young man in love, flush with hormones and enthusiasm. His job at the grocery store was only Monday to Friday, so his weekends were his to do with as he pleased. But I couldn't help but wonder about the way that all of David's hobbies had gradually disappeared from his life after things with Olivia got serious. She was virtually his only interest outside of work – and once he was travelling every weekend, there was no longer even time for sport.

One weekend, he left on Friday night in a surly mood, and returned on Sunday evening with a broad grin – as if the visit had completely refreshed him. As I watched him walking around the house whistling, it occurred to me that Olivia Brennan had become David's whole world. I almost began to hope that they'd never break up, because if they did, I wasn't entirely sure he could handle it. I kept thinking back to the incident with Jennie when David was a teenager, and Andrea's words during that phone call would float back into my mind – a time-travelling accusation I had been so sure I'd already put to bed. But when I watched the intensity of David's devotion to Olivia, I'd have to forcibly remind myself that everything Andrea had said was a lie – and that *David* had ended things with Jennie and he had assured me that all of the other nonsense with the confrontations in the playground and the upsetting notes was all her doing. And then I'd convince myself, only to have the worries cycle back through my mind too quickly for me to be sure that they were unfounded.

I had to believe the best in my son. That's a mother's job, isn't it? So I focused on the good aspects of David's commitment to Olivia – the way he cared for her, the way he nurtured her, the way his face brightened after he spoke with her.

And when my fears just refused to be silenced, I told myself that just as long as Olivia did right by David, everything would be fine anyway.

CHAPTER 21
Olivia

'I want to try something different today, if you don't mind,' Natasha says on Thursday morning as I take my seat. I regard her warily as I make myself comfortable and settle Zoe on my lap.

'Tell me a bit about the early days with David,' she asks, and my frown deepens.

'The early days? What good will that do?'

'I'd really like to understand how you two came to be together. When did you start going out? Where did you and David meet?'

'Well, we actually were at school together, so I had known *of* him all of my life. I even remember rumours about this girl he went out with... Jennie. They had some kind of bad breakup and she was always crying at school for a while afterwards. Then in the last few years of high school, he had a lot of girlfriends and other than leaving a trail of broken hearts behind him, he just seemed like a... ' I break off, frustrated as I search for the right word, then I shrug and admit, 'He was just a bit of a player, you know? A "use them and lose them" kind of guy. Not *dangerous*, just... flirtatious. Superficial.'

'Well, besides his reputation, what did *you* think of him when you were in high school?' Natasha asks, and I shrug again.

'I didn't spare him much thought, to be honest. David and I moved in such different circles, I probably didn't have a single conversation with him alone until the night we got together. At high school, I knew I wanted to get into vet science at a prestigious university and the requirements were so tough – it's very hard for a kid from a small high school like Milton Falls to make the grade, so that was my focus.'

'If he'd expressed an interest in you at high school, what would you have said?'

'I'd probably have been flattered, but I would have assumed it was a joke.'

'Why is that?'

'Boys like David didn't pay attention to girls like me.'

'Why not?'

'He was seriously out of my league. He was handsome and popular, I was bookish and I had good friends but… you know. I wasn't like *him*.'

'Huh… so, tell me about when you did get together?'

'It was at a party. We were both back home for the midterm break and a bunch of guys had been out at some football game, they all came into the party together.'

I was in the kitchen when they arrived, getting myself a drink, and when I came back into living area it was suddenly full of slightly drunk, beefy footballers. I remember wondering where they'd all come from, and as I scanning the room for my friends, my eyes locked with David's.

He was so handsome. His hair was jet black, and his eyes ice-blue. David was tall and muscular, so he stood out even in that testosterone-filled room. And he was staring right at me. When I didn't avoid his gaze, he pushed through the crowd and approached me, wearing that utterly charming smile.

'It's funny how we're at the same university,' he greeted me with, 'And yet, I only ever seem to see you when we're both home.'

'You go to UNSW?' I said, surprised, and he laughed and clutched his chest.

'Ow, my feelings. I hoped you'd been keeping an eye out for me,' he said, his eyes still crinkling with mischief, 'just like I've been keeping an eye out for you, looking for a chance to ask you out for a drink.'

'Sure,' I laughed wryly, but my heart was racing. The room was full of scents – not all of them pleasant, given the boys had been drinking for a while and they'd been at the football before that. But maybe David had showered, because his aftershave tickled at my nose, and I wanted to lean into him to breathe it in. Everything about him was strong and masculine, and that contrast made me feel petite and feminine.

'How did that make you feel?' Natasha murmurs. 'When he said he'd been looking out for you?'

'Oh, it wasn't creepy,' I assure Natasha. 'No, it was flattering. As we got chatting, it was pretty apparent that all he knew about me was that I was at the same university and I was studying to be a vet. But we chatted for *hours*. The party wound down and everyone else either left or went to bed, but David and I sat there and we talked and talked and… '

When I finally said I had to go, he walked me home and he was a perfect gentleman – he didn't even try to hold my hand. And then at the front gate to my parents' house, I turned to him, and we stared at each other before he leant in and offered me a very chaste kiss. Still, the whole thing – every aspect of it was like a dream to me, and my head swam with the full force of his attention. I was a rabbit caught in the headlights of his gaze all night. I'd never experienced anything so flattering in my life.

When I woke up the following afternoon, there was a bunch of flowers on the dining room table.

'Nice, Dad. Charming Mum, are we?' I'd laughed, winking at him, and Dad shook his head.

'No, love. I didn't get them for Mum. They're for *you*.'

There was a card attached, which Louisa promised me she hadn't read, although I could tell by her longing sigh that she was lying.

Liv, loved chatting to you last night. Dinner next week in the city? Please say yes. David

'He was *so* romantic,' I murmur now to Natasha. 'There were no red flags in the beginning. Even once we were started officially dating, he was just like a prince charming, you know? He brought me gifts, he lavished me with attention, and he was always so protective – he was the guy who opened doors for me and pulled out my chair at fancy restaurants and always wanted to walk me in. Everyone was jealous. He absolutely swept me off my feet. I felt *so lucky* to have him.'

'How do you feel about all of that now?'

I swallow hard.

'What should I feel?'

'There's no right answer. Do you still think it was genuine?'

'He loved me,' I say uneasily. 'He did. If things between us had stayed like they were in the city… we would have been happy together.'

'And where did things turn?'

'It was a really, really slow decline. I mean – there was no single day when he started abusing me. If he had, I'd have left then, you know?'

'Yes. The lines grew blurry, right?'

'Yeah… the protectiveness… it really slowly – I mean, like *glacially* slow – it gradually became possessiveness. I didn't even realise it at the time because all of the things he did that were protective could also have a different motivation. There's a huge difference between walking someone to their door because you want to keep them safe, and walking someone to their door because you feel you have a right to know where they are *every* second of the day.'

'That's very true. Well, tell me when you first noticed that his motivation had changed.'

'That's the thing,' I admit heavily. 'I don't even think I ever did notice. He just loved me so passionately, but I loved him too so… things that maybe should have made me nervous just didn't. I trusted him completely. He was always just a *little* jealous, you know? But even that was sweet. I mean, I thought it was just because he wanted me all to himself, and that's how I felt about him too, so why would it worry me?'

'Okay. So when did things *sour* for you?'

'He moved home before me, but right from the day he moved back, he was pressuring me to transfer to Bathurst to be with him.'

'Did you come home?'

'We compromised. I stayed in the city until I finished my undergrad, and I didn't transfer to Bathurst like he wanted me to. But I also didn't stay for the postgrad surgery year I wanted to do.'

'And was that your decision?'

'It absolutely was,' I say firmly.

'So why did you change your mind about the postgrad year?' I look at her blankly, and Natasha prompts, 'Was it that you didn't want to do it any more?'

I hesitate. 'Well, I still wanted to do it. But I realised it was a bad idea.'

'Why was it a bad idea?'

I sit back in my chair and I am getting defensive and I have no idea why.

'There were lots of reasons. The cost, for one thing – and the fact that I was qualified to register as a vet by then and that's all I really wanted, so anything else was just icing on the cake – almost like I was being greedy… *selfish*, you know? Besides, the professors who kept encouraging me to do postgrad just wanted the fees, they didn't really see special potential in me, that's just what they have to say. Academia *is* a business, after all…'

I break off, and then my eyes widen.

'Oh my God,' I say, and I'm numb with shock. 'I sound just like David.'

CHAPTER 22

Ivy

David soon grew bored of working at the store. I'd expected as much, but Wyatt was devastated when he announced that he was applying for other jobs.

'There's a car dealership over at Bathurst looking for an assistant manager. I think I'd be good at that.'

'But then you'd have to drive all the way over there each day,' Wyatt said. 'Don't you think you should just stay a bit longer? I'll retire someday soon and the store will be yours.'

'Dad, the only way I'd want to stay working for the store is if you were really seriously thinking about franchising the brand. I need bigger fish to fry. I'm sorry, but I don't want to manage it. If you want to retire early, I can help you recruit someone.'

I watched the interactions between my husband and son with curiosity. Wyatt hadn't mentioned anything at all to me about retiring, and given he was only in his forties at that stage, he was far too young to consider it anyway. But he had told me that he enjoyed having David at the store, and their relationship had certainly blossomed over the twelve months that they'd been working together. Equally though, I could understand David's need to spread his wings. He hadn't spent three years at university just to run his father's grocery store one day. David was always the kind of kid destined for something better.

'And if I get the job at the dealership,' David told us, 'I'll actually move to Bathurst. Olivia is going to come back at the end of this year anyway, she's had enough of studying – she's not going to do that postgrad course she was looking into.'

'She seemed pretty sure about it when she was back on mid-semester break,' I frowned. He shrugged, but I heard him on the phone to her a few times over the weeks that followed, and his voice would wind tighter and grow louder as the discussions dragged on. One night, he came out from his room and instead of the usual contented smile he wore when he said goodnight to her, he gave a frustrated groan and pressed his palms against his temples.

'Everything okay, Davey?' I asked, and he shook his head.

'I'm going to go to Sydney.'

'Now?'

'Yeah. I need to see Liv.'

'Are you sure that's a good idea? It's so late… why don't you go in the morning?'

'The morning might be too late,' he snapped. 'If I can't talk sense into her, we're going to have to break up, Mum.' His voice broke, and there was something like panic in his eyes as he said unsteadily, 'I just can't let that happen.'

I'd spent years anticipating that moment, but when it finally came, I wasn't even excited. All I could see was the storm clouds in David's eyes, and I was scared for him. As much as I'd hoped that things with Olivia would end one day, now that it finally seemed to be happening, I was worried how he would cope. I told myself that rushing off to Sydney in the middle of the night to talk to Olivia was rational behaviour if he loved her. I told myself that it was gallant – romantic – that one day this would be the story they told their grandkids, and the little girls would all sigh longingly that one day a man might love them too like that.

I told myself the thud of fear that sounded against my chest was just because the drive at that time of night was dangerous, and I told myself that he wouldn't do anything crazy when he got there. David was a passionate, loving boyfriend. I told myself that even if he did do something intense, it would be Olivia's fault anyway – she'd driven him to it. I told myself that even if he did lose control a bit, it would only be to show her how much he loved her.

I told myself he wouldn't hurt her. He was passionate, he wasn't obsessive.

It was well after 10 p.m. by the time David packed his car and tore out of the driveway. I was worried about him driving so late at night and while he was clearly upset, so I made him promise that he'd text me once he got there. It was a four-hour drive, so by 4 a.m. I was frantic. I looked up Olivia's number and I called.

'Hello?' she mumbled into the phone.

'Olivia, it's Ivy – I'm so sorry to wake you up. David – did he make it to your house safely?'

'My house?' she said blankly. 'No, what are you talking about? What time is it?'

I was completely gripped by fear then. I looked at the clock, and did the calculations – he should have arrived at least two hours earlier.

'It's 4 a.m., he left here at 10, so I'm—'

'Hang on a sec,' she said, and I heard the squeak of her mattress shifting, and then after a moment she sighed. 'He's here, Ivy. Everything is fine.'

'He said you two had to talk – is everything okay?'

'He's parked in the driveway, sound asleep in the car, but he's fine.'

'He's not *fine*, Olivia. He's worried sick about your relationship, for God's sakes,' I snapped. 'Don't you understand how upset he must be to drive down there like this?'

There was an awkward pause. 'David can be very protective, that's all,' Olivia said carefully. 'I have to put the application in for my postgrad next week but he still doesn't want me to do it. We had an argument and he convinced himself I had someone here with me tonight. I'll bet he drove all the way here, realised that I was alone after all and felt like an idiot. I'll go bring him in so he doesn't freeze himself to death. Sorry to scare you.'

I wasn't sure how I felt about all of this. This was the first I'd heard of David suspecting Olivia might be unfaithful, and the very thought of that made me angry too. It was no wonder that David had taken off in the middle of the night if he had reason to doubt her fidelity. I was only glad those fears had come to nothing… although still unsure, because the two of them obviously had other issues to sort out if Olivia was still considering staying for the postgrad year. Just how patient did she expect him to be? *He* was wearing the cost of her insistence that the relationship remain long-distance – she didn't even have to juggle the travel.

She still didn't get it. Olivia's tone was calm, almost resigned, as if this whole incident was some silly quirk of David's that she didn't quite get but wasn't too bothered by.

She'd upset him enough to drive to Sydney in the middle of the night to check on her and she didn't even appreciate him.

It was suddenly too much.

'You're lucky to have my son,' I snapped. 'He's a good boy – a good *man*.'

'I know, Ivy, it's just—'

'If you can't give him what he needs, then maybe you should let him go.'

'I love him, Ivy. And he loves me. We'll figure it out, I promise.'

I growled in frustration and hung up the phone before I said something I'd regret. I didn't sleep much that night – I kept thinking about the steel in her voice when she talked about her postgrad course, and how *unaffected* she seemed to be by David's visit.

And then when David came back the next day, he was still wound tight. He greeted me with a near grunt and went straight to his room, just like he was a teenager again. There were more late night phone calls over the days that followed, and then finally, on Sunday night, I heard him shouting on the phone and then there was a thump, and the sound of something smashing. I ran to his room and threw open the door.

The phone was on the ground, shattered on the other side of the room, and there was a hole in the plasterboard above David's bed. He was facing the wall, one hand over his eyes, the other limp against his body. I could see blood on his knuckles.

'David...'

'It's over, Mum,' he said, but he didn't turn to face me. 'She's determined to stay in Sydney next year.'

'Oh, love...'

'She's the one. I just... I *need* to win her back.'

'Maybe if you two have some time apart...'

'I can't, Mum!' David said, and he finally turned to face me. I was shocked by the state of him – the red stain on his face and the tears on his cheeks. He clenched his fists and raised them near his head and started to pace. 'You don't understand how much I love her. I have to get her back. I have to find a way to convince her to come home.'

'Maybe you two could do the long distance thing again then?'

'That's not fucking working! I *need* her with me!'

His voice broke, and all I wanted to do was console him. 'Perhaps you could move to Sydney again then...'

'No, I fucking hate the city. I can't do that again. Plus, I just took that job at Bathurst, it's exactly where I want to be.' He groaned and started to pace, rubbing his forehead with palpable frustration. 'She can just be such a bitch sometimes! She *has* to be cheating on me. She just has to. Why else would she be so determined to stay away from me?'

I cringed at the fury in his voice, but I told myself that his anger in that moment was simply a manifestation of his deep feelings for her, a different expression of the same love that saw him hold her hand even as they walked around my house sometimes.

I approached him to offer a hug, but David looked at me miserably, then he whispered, 'Mum, can you leave me alone for a while? I need to figure this out.'

'I know. And you do need to figure this out,' I said softly. 'I mean… one way or another, you deserve to know, right? There has to be *some* reason she's behaving this way and… well, whatever it is, once you know, you'll feel so much better.'

I heard the pacing on the floor of his room – his steps moving up and down slowly over the next few hours, and then they stopped altogether. When he finally emerged, he seemed calmer, but he had a bag on his shoulder. He was going back to Sydney to see her.

'You were right,' he said heavily. 'We can't go on this way.'

This time, he remembered to text me when he arrived. I waited up for the chime of my phone, then went to bed and lay awake thinking about how their discussion was going. I *was* worried. There were so many possible outcomes, and not all of them were favourable. For David, of course.

Say Olivia refused to move back to the country. David would be devastated, but at least then that would be the end of things and I could console him and things would move on. I thought about all of the hours each week he spent chasing after her, and the way things could be if she was out of the picture.

Maybe he'd walk the dogs with me. Maybe we'd sit at the table and he could tell me about his day. Maybe on the weekends, we could go out for coffee, or he'd start playing regular sport again so I could go and watch him compete.

Still, I couldn't help but feel a pulse of anger at the thought that she'd let him go. How did she still not get it? Plain, dull

Olivia would never hook another extraordinary man like David. She should be willing to drop everything to be with him. She should be willing to give up everything to keep him, just like I did with Wyatt. I felt a sizzling sense of injustice when I considered her situation. I'd been every bit as clever as Olivia when I was at school. I told myself I wasn't jealous that she had the option to continue her studies, but I had not. It wasn't envy that simmered in my gut, but distaste and disappointment. Her behaviour was unbecoming of a woman, unsupportive and selfish. I'd never have done such a thing; I was raised better than that.

I imagined the alternative – that David's visit this time would finally convince her and she would agree to move back. David would at least by pleased by this, and he'd no longer be miserably sulking after her. That was still better than what I'd seen over the past week.

But what if he did visit and Olivia *was* there with someone else? And then, David would be… what?

Sad? Disappointed?

Angry.

I thought about the hole in the wall and the way he'd spat those words earlier that night… *she can be such a bitch sometimes.* There was disdain in his voice in that moment, and while I could understand his frustration, I was also concerned where that might lead him. He'd never hurt her, of course. David wouldn't even be capable of such a thing, he *adored* Olivia.

But she'd encouraged the relationship for the past few years, and if she broke up with him suddenly, well... perhaps he would lose his head… maybe say some things that were unkind, things he didn't mean. He was passionate, after all, and passionate men could say things… *do* things… things they didn't necessarily mean.

I wasn't scared for her. I wasn't. I trusted my son. I really did.

But still, I didn't sleep a wink that night. I thought about so many incidents over David's childhood – Jennie Sobotta, his jealousy with his other girlfriends, even the incident with the puppy – I felt sick with guilt as I did, but for some brief moments over that long dark night I considered that perhaps… perhaps 'possessive' was a better word for my son than 'devoted', and if that really was the case and Olivia didn't come around, how would he react? He wouldn't hurt her – not my David. Not the same little boy who used to throw his chubby arms around my neck and ask me where butterflies slept at night.

By the time the sun came up, I regretted encouraging him to go to her. But then, when David rang just after 9 a.m., I could tell from the moment I picked up the phone that she was going to move home. I was disappointed on one level, but mostly… I was just relieved. It wasn't what I was hoping for, but in the freezing hours before the dawn, I'd feared far worse outcomes.

'Just wanted to let you know the good news,' he said, and there was delight in his voice. 'Livvy's realised she doesn't want to stay in the city after all. Postgrad is so expensive and she's qualified now, it would be a wasted year. So she's going to find a job back at Bathurst or Milton Falls, and we'll finally move in together.' He gave a contented sight. 'We're so happy, Mum. We've cleared the air now, and everything is going to be fine. You were right, you know. Better to bring things to a head and get it all out in the open so… thanks.'

Olivia certainly did seem happy enough when she came back with David that weekend. She was staying with her parents, but on Saturday afternoon David was asked to sub in for the town cricket team, and I sat with her by the sidelines while he played.

'So you're moving in with David, I hear?' I asked her, and she beamed at me. She looked so young – with her dirty blonde hair in a ponytail and her face completely free of make-up, the freckles over the bridge of her nose vivid in the afternoon sun.

'It's so exciting. We're going to find a cheap place so we can save while he works at the dealership. We'll buy our own little cottage one day soon – here in the village most probably, and we're going to get our own dog… I'm thinking a Labrador? Not really sure yet, probably won't be until next year anyway.'

'But… your postgrad?' I prompted cautiously.

'Oh, I was being such an idiot, poor David. It's just so easy to get caught up in that academic life – but really, what's the point of *more* study? I'm qualified now, I don't really need a speciality, and like David said, the professors have a vested interest in convincing students like me to stay on as long as possible. I should know by now not to take their flattery at face value, I mean… a university *is* a business at the end of the day and the students really are their customers. Anyway, things are going to be great, I'm sure I'll pick up some work at one of the clinics here and we can properly start our life together. Plus, I mean, eventually – once we're established here and we find our feet financially – we'll probably rent out our cottage and move back to the city for a year. I can specialise then. Like David said, it would make so much more sense once I have some experience under my belt anyway.'

As she chatted, I couldn't help but identify with her – our situations were so different, but the parallel was undeniable. Twenty-three-year-old Olivia agreeing to move back and skip her postgrad year felt a whole lot like eighteen-year-old Ivy agreeing to marry Wyatt and skip university altogether – and I knew how that panned out. I simply had to challenge the naivety of her viewpoint.

For her own sake, I told myself. Not to cause further trouble between them. Not one last effort to push her away from him.

'It that sounds like a very difficult decision, and… well, I'm really glad for you two that you managed to sort it out but – are you sure? I just mean, once you settle down, it can be very difficult to find opportunities like this one.' Olivia looked at me blankly, and I cleared my throat again and said stiffly, 'I want you both to be happy, and I know that you are, but… I'm just saying, once you plant roots in a place, it's not always so easy as just "taking a year off" to go study. Maybe you're at the only stage of life where you *can* do this course – once you have a house and maybe some kids… it's just not going to be as simple as it is now. Just something to think about, hey?'

Olivia gave me a somewhat patronising smile. 'If you're talking about a family, Ivy, we aren't going to have kids for a long time. David wants to wait until we're ready to raise them – financially ready – so that I can stay home full-time, just like you have. And you know, we *will* go back to the city first, and then David will probably start his own business after that… so it's going to be a really long time before I'm going to be tied down by kids. Our situation is so different to yours and Wyatt's. *We* won't accidentally fall pregnant.'

Perhaps on some level, I had actually grown to like Olivia, despite how difficult it was for me to share the focus of David's attention. She was smart, and she loved David, and I grudgingly admitted to myself that I saw how happy they made each other. But that day, by the football field, she seemed to me to be a foolish little girl. She reminded me of me, in that last year of high school, so flushed with hormones and lust that nothing else seemed to matter. The world seems black and white to someone who is young and hasn't yet experienced shades of grey. And I reminded myself as I sat there that Olivia knew nothing of my life, and that to her, it probably *did* seem like I had built it all around one foolish mistake.

I was hurt and I felt dismissed – patronised by this girl I'd tried so hard to be kind to. I didn't lash out at Olivia that day. I held my tongue, but I sat somewhat smug in the knowledge that one day, Olivia would be caring for my grandchildren, and she'd come to my house in tears because she hadn't slept for weeks, or she'd be frustrated with David about some thing or another, and I'd be the natural person for her to vent to – because I was the only other person on earth who knew David as well as she did. Maybe, as his mother, I even knew him better. I'd enjoy her misery on some level, not because I'm a bad person of course, but because I could see the outcome looming for her from a mile off, and I actually tried to *warn* her, and she'd dismissed me like a silly, insipid old woman.

I knew with absolute certainty that the moment Olivia left the city, her days of studying would be over. Even if he'd promised her otherwise, David would never move back to Sydney with her, and even if she couldn't see it coming, the roots they put down in Milton Falls would also be chains that would bind them to a life together here. Just like the link between Wyatt and me, what started as a flush of adolescent love would one day be a prison she wouldn't escape.

Because if Wyatt – passive, *simple* Wyatt – was willing to go as far as to use our own son to manipulate me into staying with him, I couldn't even begin to imagine the measures a complicated, intense man like my David would take to hold onto his own family. I felt like Olivia had committed to a lifetime with David in agreeing to move back to the country with him, because surely she knew by then that if she came home, and she ever tried to leave him, he would stop at nothing to get her back.

Olivia had seen all of the same intensity I had – and she'd obviously enjoyed it, and she obviously *wanted* it if she was actually willing to take the relationship to the next level.

CHAPTER 23
Olivia

I'm still sitting in the chair in Natasha's room, but reeling from the realisation that 'my' decision to forgo my postgrad course was actually *David's* doing.

'If you asked me to pinpoint the moment when things between us began to darken, that wouldn't have been it,' I say to her, shaking my head. 'No, that decision *felt* like mine.'

'He manipulated you, Olivia,' Natasha surmises, and I pause. I'm racing through memories of that time, other decisions I made… that perhaps David made for me.

'He kept showing up in the middle of the night and he'd be so affectionate and logical and if I tried to express any alternate point of view, we'd end up arguing and I'd feel so guilty about upsetting him.'

'So you came back to Milton Falls.'

'Yes. I mean, I got a job at the clinic here, but we lived at Bathurst at first because David didn't want to commute.'

'So you wore the entire time-burden of the commute because he wouldn't?'

'Well, I mean – he was so busy and—' I break off, and now I'm scowling. *Goddamnit.* 'Yes. I commuted because he wouldn't.'

'Did that feel unfair?'

'Of course it didn't. Isn't that what good girlfriends do, Natasha?' I ask, a little bitterly. 'Aren't good women supposed to be selfless? To stand behind their man?'

I thought of Ivy – the ultimate martyr, the dux of her school who abandoned all plans for a career and even further study the day she found out she was pregnant. Even my own mother – she maintained her career, but before she had Lulu and I, she'd been a nursing unit manager. Then she had kids, and she went back to working on the ward because she needed part-time work and that meant giving up the management role she'd so loved.

For me, femininity and sacrifice are so entwined I don't even know how to separate them, even now. All I know is that I made a decision to follow David back here to the country because I believed that was what *we* needed – what *he* needed – and I didn't spare a single thought to what I actually wanted for myself.

Natasha is silent, but I feel this ball of tension building inside of me as I think about those days. I thought I was happy, but I shouldn't have even *been here*. I should have been doing that masters degree. I was going to do a bovine research project; I'd even planned my study area with a supervisor. Now I feel cheated, and ashamed.

How did I let him manipulate me? How did I even miss the fact that he was doing it? He bent me to his will as if I was nothing – a spineless shadow of a woman – and he made me feel like I was making a noble sacrifice in the process. *How?*

'Trust, Olivia,' Natasha murmurs, answering my unspoken question. 'You trusted him. You didn't see his need for control yet, so you thought he wanted the best for you and you trusted him to help you figure out what that was.'

'But once we were in Bathurst, I was so isolated,' I say numbly. 'We had no friends over there, and I was working so much and then commuting back and forth, so I didn't see my family much. This was long before I became estranged from them, but even then, it really was just David and me.'

'And is *that* where things escalated?'

I hesitate a little.

'The blatant physical violence didn't start there, but the aggression did. If he'd *hit* me then, I'd have just left him.'

'Would you?' She doesn't seem convinced, but I know that I'm right about this one.

'Yeah. I mean, I didn't see them much, but I was still in contact with my family and I think if David had done something violent out of the blue, I'd have gone home. No, he was far too cunning for that. I think, in hindsight, it all started when he changed the way we argued.'

When we disagreed and I was in the city, we'd talk… maybe we'd yell… but one or both of us would always find a way to put a pause on the fight before it got out of hand. But once we were in Bathurst, our fights would rapidly escalate. He'd do something that upset me – like, the day I caught him checking the odometer on my car and I realised it was because he was making sure I'd come straight home from work. And I'd stand up for myself, and we'd start yelling at each other, and David would shift himself physically to block the doorway of the room – making sure I couldn't leave. Sometimes it was subtle… but often it was more overt. Even if we were sitting when the argument started, he'd fall silent and rise, and walk to stand in the doorway with his arms crossed over his chest. He'd puff himself up until he seemed even bigger than he was, and he'd stare down at me.

And in those moments, I didn't feel fear… not yet.

I felt uncertain. I felt intimidated.

So I'd fade out of the argument, because I no longer had any power over when it ended, and I no longer felt sure of myself enough to keep it going. Often, I'd go so far as to apologise.

'And then,' I add, when I finish explaining all of that to Natasha, 'the way he touched me changed. He was always an affectionate boyfriend, constantly holding my hand and embracing me even if we were in public. But one day at Bathurst, he got it into his head that I was flirting with the waiter at a restaurant, and he grabbed my hand quite forcibly and it didn't *hurt*, but it was uncomfortable. It stuck in my head because it came out of nowhere. I hadn't even noticed the waiter. And I thought seriously about leaving him then. *That* felt like a warning sign.'

'Why didn't you leave?'

'Because he pulled the master stroke, Natasha,' I whisper, and I've talked for almost an hour now without a single tear, but I know I won't get through this part without sobbing. I pick up the tissues from the table beside my chair and I hold them beside Zoe on my lap. 'He admitted he had some issues with jealousy. He told me he was so sorry and he wanted me to help him deal with it. He *needed* me.'

It felt so good to be needed. It actually felt very grown-up, we were an adult couple, working through adult things, *together*. But after that vulnerable, tear-filled discussion with David, I was a partner with him in this problem he had.

So he'd get jealous and a little rough with how he handled me, and *I'd* feel guilty because I didn't know how to help him. Soon I was apologising for 'making him jealous' even though I never even realised that's what was happening until David lost his temper.

'He found a way to make *you* responsible for his problem,' Natasha surmises, and I nod and wipe at my face with the tissues.

'So if you want to know when it escalated, that was definitely the start of it,' I say. 'I knew something was wrong between us, but I just kept thinking it would pass... that we'd live happily ever after, because we loved one another so much.'

But it didn't pass, and every time the discord between us escalated even a little, it was a permanent change. I recognised that pattern even at the time. It was like the boundary of what was acceptable in our relationship just kept moving, and my own space to be safe was shrinking around me.

'Do you remember the first time he physically injured you?' Natasha asks me quietly.

I tense all the way from my head to my toes. My gaze drops from hers, and the edges of the room blurs around us. Am I really in her office any more, or am I back there, in our apartment in Bathurst at 3 a.m.? Time passes, and I'm not sure how long – seconds? Minutes?

'Can you talk about it, Olivia?' Natasha prompts me, and I raise my eyes to her – slowly, numbness setting over me. She's kind and patient. I try to ground myself in the gentle concern in her gaze.

'It was when he was getting ready to set up the business. He was under a lot of pressure ... he was at the computer in the middle of the night and I came in to ask him to come to bed.'

Come to bed, Dave. You're exhausted.

I can't! Are you completely stupid? Seriously, do you not see how much pressure I'm under here?

Everything will feel better after some sleep.

And then he stood, and he turned to me, and for the very first time, I was scared – I could see the intent in his eyes as he stepped towards me. He grabbed the collar of my nightgown and he twisted it hard and he pulled me right up into his face.

Who the fuck do you think you are? I am the man of this house and I'll come to fucking bed when I'm ready.

And then he released me forcibly, and I stumbled back and hit the wall with the back of my head. It was an ideal injury for secrecy – bruises beneath my collar bone and a huge egg on the back of my skull. Damage in places that wouldn't be noticed. At the time, I was actually relieved by that – I was confused and upset, but *no one* had to know.

The next day, David sobbed as he begged for my forgiveness. It was an accident, he said. He really didn't mean it. I just had to stop pushing him – I had to trust him – I had to help him control himself. It would never, ever happen again.

But it did, less than a month later, and then on and off for years. We'd have months of peace, and then something would trigger him and I'd cop the brunt of his anger. It was always a little restrained, at least until we moved into the new house. And that's when things became savage.

'Have you seen our house?' I ask Natasha now, and she nods. 'Yes.'

'Did you see how big the yard is?'

'I did.'

'Do you know why? The house is big, but it could easily have fit on one block.'

'I know.'

'He wanted enough of a buffer around us that no one would hear me scream. He planted hedges all around the fence lines. He said it was for privacy.'

'And how does that make you feel?'

'I don't know why he bothered. I never screamed anyway. The more it escalated, the less I resisted. I was too scared to fight back.'

'Feeling words, Olivia,' she prompts.

'Betrayed.'

'More?'

'Stupid. Embarrassed. Ashamed. I was too smart to fall into that trap.'

'Intelligence has nothing to do with domestic violence.'

'But it shouldn't have happened to someone like *me*. I should have known to leave as soon as he really started lashing out.'

'Olivia, you have just laid out for me a devastatingly typical pattern of escalation in an abusive relationship. It doesn't just happen to uneducated women, or to stupid women – hell, it doesn't even just happen to *women*, there are male victims of this type of violence too. It happens in every pocket of society – rich or poor, tertiary educated or not, and everything in between.'

'I never thought of myself as a battered wife. I never thought of myself as a victim.'

'How *did* you think of yourself?'

'I thought I was brave and noble. I thought I was strong – but unlucky enough that the man I loved had some problems. I thought I was the only woman on earth who could save him.'

Natasha nods sadly. 'And now?'

'I feel like every time we talk about this, I see the past in a different way.'

'Good. That's what we want. It's a part of taking the power back – identifying all of the ways he took it from you. Now one thing I'd really like to talk about in the last ten minutes is *why* you don't want to talk about Sebastian yet.' I open my mouth to protest, but Natasha offers me a very patient smile. 'I *know* this is hard, Olivia. Let me give you one little tip before you tell me it's too soon.'

I sigh and frown as I nod.

'Do you think you were in denial during your marriage to David?'

'*Definitely*. At times.'

'Did it feel like you were denying the truth?'

'Well… no. It felt like the way I understood my situation *was* the truth.'

'Exactly. Denial isn't a conscious thing. It's an *unconscious* coping mechanism. So to say it another way, you don't know you're doing it.'

'What does that have to do with Seb?'

'There's a very good reason you're avoiding that discussion with me.'

'Yes,' I whisper, and I stare at the floor.

'How do you feel when I press you to talk about him?'

'Ashamed,' I can barely speak. My chest feels too tight.

'I'm not going to push this any further today, Olivia. But you have one little piece of homework to do for me.'

I look up at her hesitantly. 'Go on?'

'I want you to think about that shame, and ask yourself what's behind it.'

'I don't like to think about that.'

'I know. But I think if you can face it internally, you might be able to start the conversation with me – and as hard as it is, that discussion is going to be a big part of your progress as you move forward.'

CHAPTER 24

Ivy

At the end of that year, Olivia moved back to the country and almost immediately took up a position with the Milton Falls Vet Clinic working for Ryder Wilson. It wasn't long before she and David officially found a small studio apartment in Bathurst, and Olivia commuted the hour's drive each way every day.

And just as I had expected they would, they settled quickly into a grown-up kind of life together. They seemed so happy; two young professionals, ready to take on the world. But they didn't buy the cottage Olivia had imagined. Instead, they stayed squished into that tiny studio apartment for several years because David had decided that his next career move would be to open his own car dealership.

At first, Wyatt and I didn't realise how extensive his plans were, but over time the dream unfolded. He had a crystal-clear vision for their future – one day, he would own a franchise of car dealerships across the state. His first stop would be Milton Falls.

'I'll be a full-service dealership. Utes, prestige cars, eventually farm equipment once I'm up and running and I have the operating capital. It'll be the kind of place where you come to look at a car, and you walk out with a croissant in your belly and a contract in your hand. My target demographic is going to be the agriculture industry – I want every farmer within a two-hour drive to be coming to my dealership for servicing of their existing vehicles, and once that's the case, it'll be a small next step for them to buy their cars from me too.'

It all seemed like a pipe dream to me. Even Wyatt was cynical at first, but David spent several years preparing his business plan. The day he showed it to us, it was hundreds of pages long – comprising a detailed marketing strategy including a branding approach, supplier agreements that were almost ready to sign, a draft lease for the premises he hoped to rent and even position descriptions for his initial staff.

All that he needed was money.

A lot of money.

'I have savings,' he told us. 'But only $100,000. I need another two million.' Wyatt nearly choked on his tea, and David drew in a breath. 'Mum... Dad... I'm not asking you to give it to me. I'm simply asking that you act as guarantor at the bank.'

'Oh, David... ' I gasped. Wyatt looked at me, eyebrows high, almost amused.

'Well, you've got balls of cast iron, David, I'll give you that,' Wyatt laughed.

'If you put the supermarket up as collateral, I'll get the loan easily,' David said steadily. Wyatt's smile faded.

'Maybe so, son,' he said carefully. 'But if we do that, we risk losing absolutely everything if this thing of yours goes belly-up. Are you *sure* that you've done your research?'

'Dad, even the bank said this is a great idea – the manager said it's "gold",' David shrugged. 'They just can't lend me this much money without the concept being proven. If I could start it, and do what I needed to do, but start small or cheap... I absolutely would – but that's just not possible in this situation. *Everything* needs to be top-notch – from the building, to the brands, to my staff. So... yes, Mum – Dad, I know I'm asking a lot. But – don't you trust me? Don't you believe in me? I didn't spend three years at uni, and now these years at the dealership in Bathurst wasting my time. Didn't I prove my skills to you when I revamped the supermarket? That's paid out handsomely for you, hasn't it? It was *all* leading to this. So are you on board, or do I need to find another way?'

I expected Wyatt to say no. The grocery store had been in his family for three generations. It had grown from not much more than a corner store when the town was small, and now it was the only grocery store for an hour in any direction. The turnover wasn't immense, but it was more than enough to provide a stable, very comfortable income for us – as well as the thirty part-time staff we employed.

It wasn't just our future that David was asking us to risk – and as one of the biggest employees in town, I knew that Wyatt would take this very seriously.

'Okay,' Wyatt exhaled, and he looked at me. 'Unless you have any objections, Ivy?'

I was dumbfounded, and I tried to speak to Wyatt with my eyes, so that I didn't undermine David's confidence with my words. But Wyatt didn't react, and eventually I had to say, 'Perhaps we should at least talk about this, before we go ahead?'

'I'm not rushing you – but this is time-critical,' David told us. 'I need to get this paperwork back to the bank. I'm hoping to be up and running within four months. And I want to resign from my job next week, so that I can give them lots of notice. I don't want any bad blood between the dealership in Bathurst and me.'

So it was decided in a single conversation; we would gamble everything we had on a roll of the dice for David. I realised that this is what I had been doing since I learned that we'd conceived him, but this particular time felt risky and dangerous – I didn't sleep a full night for months after we signed the loan forms. I thought back on that conversation and wondered if he'd rushed us into it – although it certainly didn't feel that way at the time. David had seemed so relaxed and confident during that discussion – like this was such a sure thing that we'd be crazy not help him make it happen despite the mammoth amount of money involved.

He worked like a maniac to set the dealership up – twenty hours a day at the computer or at the office, liaising constantly with tradesmen and his new staff and finalising agreements with suppliers; he even managed to screw down a utility company on the price of the electricity. And David was stressed out of his brain, but whenever we saw him, it struck me how patient he was with Olivia. I thought she should have at least taken some time off from her job to help him out or support him, and I was a little annoyed when she didn't. Still, they started coming to our house each Sunday night for dinner and he was still patient with her, still loving with her, and I used to think, *does that girl even realise how lucky she is?*

On the dealership's grand opening day, it would be no exaggeration to say that most of Milton Falls called in at some point. David had activities organised for the kids, a small market area set up with local vendors, he had the press in attendance from all over the region. Olivia walked around like the First Lady, wearing a beautiful pink suit, shaking hands and smiling, as if *she* had some hand in all of this.

I wasn't sure if it was the novelty factor of what David was attempting to do, or even if his age was a part of the reason why people went out of their way to support him. He was only just twenty-eight, far too young for the immense responsibility of owning his own business, and yet there he was, thriving. Perhaps it was just his skill at building networks over the years, but the entire town really got behind him.

As for Olivia – she had really found a place at the vet clinic. Ryder Wilson was so old and cranky, and Olivia by contrast was a breath of fresh air, enthusiastic and pleasant, renowned for her cheerful manner, even when she was called in the middle of the night due to a vet emergency.

A small town like Milton Falls is a close-knit place – so I knew all kinds of things about David and Olivia's life that they never shared with me. The things I knew made me proud – like the fact that despite his own demanding job, David never let Olivia take overnight house calls on her own – he always went with her to keep her safe. I heard about the Sunday when David sat in the clinic with her, keeping her company while she tended to a dog who had eaten rabbit bait and needed intensive care. My David was a doting partner, and absolutely everybody knew it. The two were rarely seen apart, and equally, the two were rarely seen without smiles on their faces.

I was still so proud of David but occasionally I'd be conscious of my own jealousy of Olivia's relationship with him. Their partnership seemed so perfect to me. I'd look at Wyatt on his recliner, munching on his salad sandwiches and grunting in response to my attempts at conversation, and then I'd see David and Olivia and the *connection* they seemed to delight in. When I acknowledged this to myself, I felt guilty sometimes. David deserved happiness, and he had it. Olivia made him happy.

But then I'd think about the way that she had now claimed a permanent place in his life that completely overshadowed mine, and the jealousy would surge all over again. For the most part, I kept a lid on this. There was nothing I could do about it anyway, I had to accept that they were in this relationship for the long haul – I knew it was only a matter of time before David proposed now that their careers were both on track. And I was right, because a few days before Olivia's birthday that year, David called into our house unannounced and told Wyatt and me that he was going to propose.

'I have it all planned, I'll do it on her birthday – if she says yes, which, I'm pretty sure she will – we'll get married in spring up at the Bush Chapel lookout on the mountain near the falls.

She always told me she wanted to get married up there,' he told us.

It was just too beautiful and just too much. I burst into tears – mostly tears of happiness, but also disappointment. Olivia was a part of our lives to stay.

The boys rolled their eyes at me, but as I batted away the moisture from my face, I tried to say what I thought they expected me to say, 'I'm just so happy for you two. You're going to have such a wonderful life together.'

Wyatt and I sat at home and waited for news. When David's car pulled into the drive I didn't even wait for them to come inside – I ran at them.

'Well?' I prompted, and Olivia beamed at me and held up her left hand. I could see the sparkle of the diamond even from several metres away.

Once they came inside Wyatt poured whiskey for himself and David, and Olivia and I opened a bottle of sparkling wine so they could fill us in on the details.

'So we went for dinner in Bathurst, to some fancy restaurant,' Olivia told us, 'And I had my suspicions that maybe this was coming… '

'What! You did not,' David protested, but Olivia nodded sagely.

'I really did. You've been skulking around for days – I figured you were getting ready to propose or throw me out of the house.'

'Never,' David promised, and she smiled at him tenderly.

'So after dinner, David took the wrong road to come back to Milton Falls then I realised he was headed for the mountain.'

'The Bush Chapel,' I murmured, and Olivia nodded at me and beamed.

'So he said something lame like… *it's such a beautiful night, let's just check out the view*. And I was like… huh? It's freezing.

He's lost his mind. But then we came to the clearing and there were candles all over the place, already lit.'

I could picture the scene in my mind as vividly as if I'd been there. The Bush Chapel Lookout is high on the mountain above Milton Falls, deriving its name from a natural circle of rocks that surround a flat clearing. It's a popular place for teenagers to abscond to for make-out sessions, but also for weddings and other intensely romantic occasions – like, apparently, my son's proposal. He'd outdone himself. I'd have expected nothing less.

'How did you manage the candles, son?' Wyatt asked.

'I got the office girls from the dealership in on it,' David grinned, and Wyatt laughed.

'Nothing like dedicated staff.'

'So then we got out of the car and he took my hand and led me to the middle of the candles, and he dropped on one knee and pulled the ring out of his pocket. Behind him, the lights of the town were shimmering and there were stars in the sky and... God, it couldn't have been any more perfect.' Olivia sighed. 'I ask you, did I have *any* choice but to say yes after all of that effort?'

'No,' I said, and I smiled tightly at her. 'No, I don't suppose you did.'

CHAPTER 25

Olivia

The next few days pass in a flurry of activity and this is such a stark contrast to my recent weeks of endless grief that I tumble into bed each night, completely exhausted. It's a satisfied kind of tired, and I sleep so deeply that days pass without me needing to reach for the sleeping pills.

Natasha asks me to think about my feelings of guilt towards Sebastian.

'Did you do your homework?' she asks.

'I did,' I say. And I do think a lot about the way just a single glance at Sebastian can at times leave me feeling dizzy with shame – like he is somehow *my* victim, and that makes no sense. But right behind that thought is a wall that I just can't bring myself to push against, and if I think about it too long, I feel overwhelmed. Trying to untangle why I feel so much guilt about Sebastian is exactly like trying to remember the events of that god-awful day when David died. I know if I press hard enough, I'll be able to remember *all* of the details, but I just can't force myself to. Not yet.

'Are you ready to talk about him yet?' Natasha asks me.

'Soon,' I say. 'But not yet.'

Ingrid brings a mallet and installs a huge FOR SALE sign for the front yard. I watch as the legs of the sign sink through the thick turf that David once nurtured so carefully, and I brace against a shadow of the fear I would have felt if he were alive to see this. David was so house proud. He spent every night for an entire summer hand watering this lawn until the roots took hold, and then he maintained its health with militant precision – plucking the weeds by hand when they tried to invade, and handcrafting a scarecrow when the magpies started picking holes in the grass for some unfathomable reason.

He would have been beside himself to see this. He would have been monstrously angry that I'd allowed that turf to be damaged by this sign.

The fear is irrational, because I know all too well that he is gone. Still, I have to consciously force the feeling away by reminding myself that he can no longer hurt me. This fear is a habit, and it's one that I need to break – David was not immortal and his power over me died when he did. When the sign is in place, I stare at it until I feel a surge of satisfaction. The simple sign represents a rebellion in every way possible and I am just so damn proud of myself for coming even this far.

'Well, it's official,' Ingrid says, and she rests the mallet on the ground beneath her feet and joins me to survey the sign. 'Looks pretty good, huh?'

'It really does. Your marketing leaves Todd's for dead.'

'That's the idea,' Ingrid grins. 'The listing went up online yesterday too. I'm sure we'll have interest in no time.'

'Good,' I say, then I shake off the last shadow of the fear and I smile at her. 'Let's get rid of this place.'

'How's the packing going?'

'I'm getting there.'

'What's going on?' I hear Ivy's out-of-breath accusation from behind us, and Ingrid and I turn to find her running through the gates. 'What do you think you're doing? You can't *do* this, Olivia!'

Thirty seconds ago I was puffed up with pride and hope. Now I'm shrivelling under her gaze, and anxiety and panic flood through my entire body.

'I-Ivy,' I try to say carefully, but the word comes out with an audible stammer. 'I have to do this. I have to move on.'

'This was David's house. This was his pride and joy – you two were so happy here,' Ivy's eyes are wild – she looks from the sign to the house and then to me. 'No, I won't let you. I simply won't let you do this.'

'Mrs Gillespie,' Ingrid says carefully, 'Please—'

'And *you*! Don't you dare speak to me, you're trying to profit from Olivia's fragility!'

'Ivy,' I say, firmer now. 'You have to respect my wishes. I'm trying to do the best I can with everything that's happened—'

'You're not in your right *mind*, Olivia!' Ivy gasps. 'This is not the time to make major life decisions like this! You should stay here, recover some more—'

'Do you really think that staying in the house where he tormented me for years is going to help me *recover*?' I snap, but it's a brutally cruel question, and I may as well have hit my mother-in-law – her eyes widen in outrage and her jaw drops. I feel awful – I turn to walk away, but Ivy calls out after me, 'Don't you dare do that to his memory, Olivia Gillespie,' she hisses. 'David was a good man, and a marriage is a two way-street – if he made some mistakes, you *know* as well as I do it was because you provoked him.'

I stiffen and my footsteps stop dead. Everything within me slows. If I was sure of all of the things Natasha keeps telling me – that what happened to me isn't my fault, that what David did to himself wasn't my fault, that all of my misery isn't ultimately self inflicted – then I would turn around and I would shout that statement down. I'd defend myself. Because I see exactly what she's doing – she's shifting enough of the blame to me so that her son's memory can be blameless. Natural, perhaps, for a mother to want to remember her lost child well but...

Is she right?

That's the question, isn't it? Where does the responsibility for my pain really lie?

'Olivia,' Ingrid says quietly, and when I look at her, I see her through a pea-soup fog of shock. She extends her hand towards me, and on autopilot, I take it. 'Come inside.'

'Don't you dare try to move away yet. I won't let you give his house over to strangers.'

I walk steadily to the house with Ingrid, and as soon as we're inside I slam the door and I work from bottom to top, slamming each of the locks into place. I'm standing in the lobby with my real-estate agent and my breathing is ragged, but she simply waits beside me in silence.

'I'm really sorry about that,' I whisper. I'd be crying now, but Ingrid is here, so I hold myself together. I'll cry after she goes.

'Don't be sorry, you didn't do anything wrong. What a *cow*! How did she even know?' Ingrid asks me. 'I put that sign up three minutes ago!'

'News travels fast in this town. Plus, it helps that she only lives around the corner. Why do you think I want to move so badly?'

'Look,' Ingrid exhales, 'this is just an idea but… the new house *is* empty and it's pretty much ready. We could ask the vendors if they'd let you rent it until the contracts exchange.'

'Do you think they'd let me do that?'

'We can only ask.'

I turn and raise my eye to the peephole. Ivy is walking away, her shoulders slumped. I watch until she disappears from view, then I turn back to Ingrid.

'Please, see what you can do.'

❖ ❖ ❖

When I go to see Natasha the next day, I tell her about Ivy.

'Do you feel guilty?' she asks me. I look up at her warily.

'About selling the house?'

Her eyebrows rise, then quickly fall.

'Well, yes,' she says carefully. 'Let's come back to that question. Start with the house.'

'I don't want to hurt her,' I admit. 'She was a godsend during my pregnancy and when Zoe first came.'

'How was David's relationship with his mother?'

'Bewildering.' I say.

David used to tell me, 'I love my mother, but sometimes she can seriously be a controlling *bitch*. You should have seen her when I was a kid – she was involved in absolutely every bloody thing in my life. Her own life was always empty so she had to meddle just to give herself something to do.'

'She loves you,' I'd protest, and he'd shrug.

'I know. Well, most of the time I know. Sometimes I felt like the mutts were her kids and I was just the hobby.'

I drag myself out of the memory and glance at Natasha. 'They were incredibly close. But when she wasn't around, the way he talked about her just never matched up to the things I saw. He seemed to have some impossible expectation of what kind of mother she *should* have been. Given he had such a peaceful childhood – wanting for nothing, as far as I could tell, his resentment seemed to make no sense at all. I'd ask him to explain why he disliked her so, but instead of reasons, he just had these endlessly vague complaints that she was suffocating and manipulative.'

'What does Ivy do for a living, Olivia?'

'She's at home. She's never worked.'

'Not ever?'

'Nope.'

'That's unusual even for her generation.'

'I think Ivy's generation is the transitional generation around here, from that old model of families where only the father worked to the way we are now where most families have two incomes. Some of her friends worked, many didn't. And she fell pregnant with David in high school and married Wyatt right away. Plus… I'm not sure she *could* have worked even if she wanted to. Wyatt is so old-school – I mean, I've literally never seen him pick up a dishcloth.'

'So David thought her life was empty and that's why she suffocated him?'

'Yeah.'

'But you told me once before that he was resistant to your career.'

'He absolutely was.'

'Isn't that fascinating? The very thing that he disliked about his own upbringing was the same thing he demanded of you for your child.'

I raise my eyebrows at her. Yet another angle to David's behaviour that I'd never considered.

'Why do you think that is?' I ask her.

'I doubt it's any one thing. Most likely it was related to his need to monopolise your attention, but also… well, some abusive men just have a deep seated hatred of women. They want the perfect wife and mother – but their expectations are impossible to achieve. When you don't manage to fulfil the needs they feel entitled to have met, then they get to punish you for failing them. In your case, I'd say David wanted you to stay at home and make your family with him your entire world, but also somehow at the same time, be *completely* unlike his mother when she did the very same thing.'

'Nice to know I was doomed regardless of what I did,' I sigh, and Natasha gives me a pitying smile.

'What can you tell me about the dynamic in their home?'

'It's quite like my family, you know… kind of traditional,' I say quietly. 'I mean, Mum does most of the cooking and cleaning in my house too – but Dad has always done a share. It's like that in David's family, but it's so much more rigid.'

Whenever we went to visit with Ivy and Wyatt for dinner, the boys would inevitably drop straight into the recliners to watch whatever sport was on, and I'd join Ivy in the kitchen. She'd be flying between a dozen things at once – cooking ever-elaborate meals in an unsubtle attempt to try to impress David – and I'd always offer to help.

'Oh, no – you work so hard, Olivia, I've got this,' she'd insist as she shooed me out of the kitchen, but then I was never really sure where I was supposed to go because I certainly didn't belong watching the footy with David and Wyatt. So I'd insist that I remain in the kitchen with her, and Ivy gradually came to accept my offers of help. Her reluctant concessions that I could pitch in a little gradually came easier – until in recent years, it was just assumed by everyone that Ivy and I would cook the meal, and then clean up together.

'How was David's relationship with his father?'

'Oh, they were very close. David absolutely adored Wyatt – although I don't really understand that, either. If David was really stressed about something – and it had to be pretty serious for him to ask for advice – he'd always go to Wyatt. His dad isn't really a talker, so he'd listen to David speak and then grunt some nonsense usually about how David needed to 'stay strong' or 'be a man', and David always seemed to perceive some incredible wisdom from the discussion and leave energised and inspired. But you know, generally, Wyatt's "advice" would be useless and David would *actually* end up listening to whatever Ivy said, but he'd look back on the discussion with me later and attribute the advice to his father.'

'Do you think David was sexist, Olivia?'

'David?' I look at her in surprise. 'No. He's always employed women at the dealership, and he let me work until I fell pregnant.'

'He *let* you work?' Natasha repeats gently and I wince.

'Well, he had some old school ideas... ' I say. 'He wasn't quite as bad as Wyatt at home, but he certainly expected that I'd do the lion's share of the housework. He wanted me to stay home once I had Zoe, but that was just because he thought it was best for her, not because he didn't want me to work.'

'Let me rephrase my question. Did David respect women? Did he ever call you hysterical? Blame your hormones when you were upset about something *he* did wrong? Did he respect your wishes for a career? Did he consider you an equal?'

I sigh, and shake my head. 'Okay. Maybe David was sexist, but never overtly so – not in the sense that he'd ever, *ever* say anything off about men being superior or a woman's place being in the home. He was very socially aware – he was never offensive. But I can see in hindsight that maybe he did have some issues with women in general, he was just too charming to be open about it.'

'Do you think his parents are equal partners in their marriage?'

'God, no,' I snort.

'And do you think David saw *you* as an equal partner in your marriage?'

'He always asked me what I thought before he made decisions.'

'Did he respect your opinion?'

I drop my gaze to the stroller beside me and stare at my daughter. 'No.'

'Do you think that Ivy and Wyatt were aware that David was abusive towards you?'

I swallow heavily, and nod. 'Ivy was. She made sure that I knew she knew.'

She'd caught us out. It was the black eye. Too severe to excuse, too dark to hide, but also simply too fraught for David

and me to discuss, so we'd never synchronised our stories. Ivy
had asked me about it one night when she and I were alone, and
I was somehow caught off-guard – surely she'd noticed other
injuries, but she'd never drawn attention to them so I wasn't
expecting her question. I'd fumbled for a believable excuse and
she dropped the subject, so I thought she'd bought it. But then,
a few days later, she asked David and when our stories were
hopelessly mismatched, Ivy drew attention to it.

I thought you said it was a cupboard door, Olivia?

I felt a bizarre hope rise in me in that moment. Was *Ivy* going
to help me? David said he hated her, but I *knew* he revered her
and I knew if she made a point of telling him to get help – he'd
do it. Hope was like a fragile sprout seeding in my heart, and in
that fraught moment as I tried to think of a response, I saw the
panic on David's face, and I knew that even just for a second,
Ivy held *all* of the power.

But then her expression morphed until she was positively
sneering at me. Before she even spoke, I knew that she wasn't
going to help me.

You silly girl. I suppose you must have been confused.

Oh, God. The humiliation of it makes my stomach churn
even now. I remember looking between her and David, my face
flushed and my heart racing. The guilty secret the three of us
shared after that moment somehow bound us together in a way
that I still can't understand – all of us complicit – me because I
provoked him, David for hurting me, Ivy for her silence.

'Did she ever try to intervene?' Natasha asks quietly.

'No.'

'Surely she must have discouraged his behaviour then.'

'No.'

'*Never?*' Natasha's unflappable façade slips for just a second,
and she actually seems aghast. I shrug and shake my head again.
'Did you resent that?'

'I knew her loyalty was to David. He was her golden child. We've never actually talked about it, but even in that conversation on the lawn the other day, it was pretty clear that Ivy knew—' I catch myself, and correct my careless phrase, 'I mean, she *thought* that if he'd hurt me, I must have done something to deserve it.'

'I wonder what it would feel like to look Ivy in the eye and challenge that?'

I laugh incredulously. 'I could never do that! It would be terrifying.'

'Why?'

'She's… she can be *so* manipulative. And *no one* messes with David. She'd destroy me.'

'I think you underestimate yourself, Olivia. Perhaps, one day when you're feeling stronger, it would be good for you to have a discussion with her about it. To confront her by telling her how much damage her silence has caused you.'

I shake my head violently. 'No. I just couldn't. I would never be strong enough to do something like that.'

'And I certainly won't ever push you to. But maybe it's just something else to think about.'

I wait at my front window that night and I watch as Ivy passes with the dogs on her evening walk, right on schedule. She looks in at the house and at the FOR SALE sign, and I see the way her face falls. The grief and pain in her eyes is so breathtakingly vivid that I want to weep for *her*.

I realise in that moment that there is a real possibility that The Tragedy is actually even worse for Ivy than it is for me. We both lost David, but at least I knew him as a three-dimensional man – I saw him as a person of both great strength and great weakness – a man of love and cruelty, to such a degree that I could love and hate him sometimes in the very same moment.

Ivy saw only good in David, and she simply manufactured it for him at those times when there was no good to be found. She is mourning a perfect son, and that surely makes her loss so much greater.

❖ ❖ ❖

Ingrid calls me the following morning to tell me that she's had a call with Mrs Schmitt's grandchildren and that they are very happy for me to rent the house as soon as I'm ready. She asks me when I'll be wanting to move in, and I pluck a date out of the air – next Saturday. I hang up the phone, look around the house, and then I could almost panic.

I've packed a bit of the house up, but there's so much stuff here I just don't know what to do with; all of David's things – will Ivy and Wyatt want anything? I should ask them, but I don't want to talk to them. I'll get Mum to call… she's good at these awkward discussions. But what about the rest of it – the expensive furniture David took such pride in is worth a fortune. Who would want it? I certainly don't want to take it with me, and I can't very well leave it here to inflict on the next owners of this house.

I'll need to have a moving sale. The thought turns my stomach – I picture dozens of gawkers stomping through, half of them just wanting to visit because of the controversy. I couldn't possibly be here for it – I just couldn't, I'll have to hide out at Mum and Dad's house, or at Louisa's flat. This move will be yet another thing I rely on my family for, and I hate that – but I tell myself that this is one of the last things I'll need from them before I'm on my feet again.

Mum snaps into action when I ask her to help me clear out the house. She's on the doorstep the next morning with two takeaway cups of coffee in her hands and a notebook under her arm. We walk around the house and tag furniture with post-it notes and finish at the master bedroom's door.

'Bin it,' I say, and I write on a post-it note *rubbish pickup service* and I stick it on the door of the bedroom and dust my hands. 'Done.'

I start to walk away, but Mum hesitates at the door. 'Love, do you really not want to go in there at *all?*'

I shake my head, and she shrugs and follows me down the hall and down the stairs. We stand in the living area and she looks down at her list.

'It's up to you, but you've pretty much tagged everything to sell or throw. It doesn't leave much for the new house,' Mum frowns and as she thinks about this, she pauses. 'It doesn't really leave anything, Liv. What are you taking with you?'

'Me. Zoe. My clothes. Her things,' I admit. 'That's it. I'll replace everything else, I need to go to a furniture store tomorrow and order what I need. This is a fresh start.'

'Are you sure, love? You and… you worked so hard to build this place. Isn't there anything here you want to keep?'

'Mum… ' I say gently. 'I *didn't* work hard to build this place. David did. There's nothing here that doesn't have some awful memory attached for me.'

'But – it's just furniture, Livvy. And some of it is worth *so* much money. Are you really sure you want to get rid of it all?'

I swallow, hard. How can Mum not understand my reluctance to hold onto anything from this life? Surely she *knows* how bad it was for me here. Surely she understands why I need a fresh start.

Then it hits me. Of course she doesn't know. How could she? I've never told her. I've never told anyone what my life was like. It's been a shameful secret I've born all on my own.

'See that lamp, Mum?' I say quietly, and she looks across to the corner of the room, where a floor lamp rests. There's a thick, heavy base and a tall black steel pipe that leads to an inverted bowl, and from the top of the bowl, an old-style light bulb is visible. I shiver when I look at it, and then I lift the bottom of my T-shirt to reveal a circular burn on my belly. I run my fingertips over the jagged edges, and my memories flicker to life – I remember the pain, and the rawness of it and how I had to treat it myself even after it became infected and how sure I was that it was never going to heal. I glance at Mum, and she's staring at the burn mark, her jaw slack, her eyes wide – and no wonder, it's *ugly*. 'This was because I looked at Mayor Crouch for too long at a council meeting three years ago. David turned the lamp on and pulled the shade off, and then he pressed the hot bulb into my skin until it *shattered*. Do you think I'm sorry to leave that lamp behind?'

'Oh, Livvy… '

'And the couch? I was sitting on that couch when he threw a plate of food at me because a contract he was *sure* the dealership would win fell through.' I point to the couch, then my hand is shaking as I redirect it, over to the coffee table. I remember the cool wood against my face, and my knees hard against the carpet, and David's angry hands on my hips. 'He accused me of flirting with Sebastian at the Christmas party two years ago and we got into an argument, and he slammed me down on my face on that coffee table and he ripped off my dress—'

I was just going to tell her a few basic things and no detail – just enough that she could understand, and I thought I could do it calmly – rationally delivering her facts to grasp my chain of thought. The problem is that once I start talking the words fly out of my mouth of their own accord and even as I see the horror on my mother's face I can't bring myself to stop, not until she very gently cups my cheek in her hand. Her eyes are swimming in tears, and I close my eyes. I'm so disconnected from my emotions that the hiccupping sobs I hear coming from my mouth are confusing to me.

'Sorry,' I choke, and Mum pulls me into an embrace.

'Olivia, I can hear it if you want to talk about it. But if you think you need to tell me to convince me he hurt you, you don't. I *believe* you, sweetheart. I wasn't trying to pressure you to keep anything. I only wanted to make sure this is really what you want.'

'Okay,' I whisper into her hair. God, my mother smells good. She smells like clean – hospital antiseptic and soap and that tea-tree shampoo she's used since I was a kid. I let her hold me for a very long time, until even my feet are numb, but she doesn't move and I don't want to, so we just stay like that there in my prison of memories.

'I just wish we'd found a way to get you out, Olivia,' she whispers when I eventually try to move away. Her arms tighten around me, forcing me to stay close. 'We should never have let him isolate you once we realised what was happening.'

'Mum,' I murmur, and I force myself away from her to look right into her eyes. 'At that stage, you could have stormed in here with a SWAT team and I'd have found a way to stay.'

'But *why*, Livvy? I still don't understand,' Mum chokes, and I try to pull together words to express the mess of my thoughts over those years.

Sometimes, I think those sessions with Natasha are a waste of time, but then I realise that at moments like this, at least I know how to explain myself now.

'Because I thought that was *love*, Mum. I thought he would change – he always used to say it was the last time. I thought I deserved it, I thought I'd provoked it, I thought he was sorry. I thought I could help him. I thought he needed me. I thought he'd kill me. Later, he explicitly told me he'd kill himself if I left, and I *knew* it wasn't a false threat, I knew it all along. And after a while, I thought I wasn't strong enough to rebuild my life – he had *all* of our money, Mum – I didn't have a cent to my name. And I truly thought he was all I had left.'

'We let you down, didn't we?' Mum murmurs sadly, and I smile at her and pull her close for another hug – a different hug. This time, I'm consoling her.

'No, Mum. David Gillespie let me down.'

The day before the moving sale, I reluctantly move back into Mum and Dad's house. Mum, Dad and Louisa are all manning the sale so I stay at home alone while it happens. I watch television that day, but I don't see or hear a single thing that happens on any of the shows I watch. Natasha has told me that this is called disassociation, it is a simple avoidance of current reality – a protective mechanism, like denial. I'm not upset by the moving sale; I'm relieved that it's happening – but I can't bear to think of the people who are standing in David's house right at that very moment purely out of morbid curiosity. I can't bear it, so I tune out, and allow myself to cope in whatever way my brain wants to cope, which seems to be by going into a state of semi-sleep.

When Mum comes in just after sunset, I look up at her in surprise. I have almost forgotten where I am, and I'd almost forgotten what was happening. Now I panic – because I also forgot about Ivy and Wyatt, and what if the house has been cleared out and it's too late for them to see if they wanted to take anything?

'Mum… did you ever call Ivy?'

'Of course, lovey. She came past this morning before the sale, they took a few mementos – photos mostly.'

I exhale heavily, 'Thanks, Mum. And how did the rest go?'

'We sold a lot of stuff, but there's still a lot left. I've talked to the op shop. They're going to pick the rest up over the next few days.'

I walk across town with Zoe to go back to David's house the next morning to take a look. The bones of our life are scattered everywhere in that house now. Most of them have been picked clean by the vultures during the moving sale, but there seems no pattern to the things that remain. I can't figure out what the buyers were thinking. Some hideous modern furniture is gone, but many expensive pieces remain. In the living room, there is a large oak bookshelf – Mum and I had put a ridiculously low price on it, and I can't understand why no one has taken it. I stare at it, and memories rise to the surface of my mind.

There was a time when I sat the book of our wedding photos on this bookshelf, and arranged it so that the beautiful photo of us kissing at the mountain on our wedding day was on display. I remember the time when David ordered that huge stone sculpture in from Turkey, and it cost hundreds of dollars and I loathed it and couldn't fathom how or why he'd even found it. He sat it right there in the centre of the bookshelf – and I used to stare at it sometimes, and wonder whether he actually liked it, or he just liked the idea that he could afford it.

I used that statue to smash a window the day I escaped. I've not noticed in the weeks I've been back here, but the statue is back in place. David must have picked it up from the lawn and put it right back on the shelf after I left.

This bookshelf is just a piece of furniture, but it has been a silent witness to everything that has happened in this room, in this life that I have led. I wish that the bookshelf was gone but I'm also suddenly unsure that I should let it go into someone else's house. I know that an inanimate object like this can't absorb bad vibes, but I still feel guilty. What if the op shop picks it up tomorrow, and some innocent person buys it, unaware of the awful history that it has witnessed? What if they put it in a child's room, or if the evil that it's been exposed to somehow leaks out and taints an innocent family?

I walk on autopilot out to the garden shed and I find the axe and I take it back into the house. I push the bookshelf over, and it lands with a huge, echoing thump on the carpet, shelf-side down. I pick the axe up and I raise it above my head and I bring it heavily down onto the back of the bookshelf. I'm not *crazy* – I don't use the sharp edge – that would surely destroy the shelf quicker, but it would also damage the carpet and I don't want to have to organise to replace it. Besides which, I somehow enjoy the feeling of my muscles straining as I raise the axe over my head, again and again, until I am drenched in sweat and the bookshelf is little more than a pile of huge chunks and splinters all over my living room floor.

When I'm done, I rest the axe against the wall, and I survey the mess I have made. David *hated* mess and disorder. He was the kind of man who wanted to replace the fridge if there was a scratch in the door, and he wouldn't tolerate disorganisation – my chaotic toiletries drawer used to drive him crazy. I think back to the brief days we had together as a family after Zoe was born, and the endless tension that came from me being unable to keep up with her care and the housework. I spent more time worrying about David than I did even enjoying my new baby.

She's sitting in the Bumbo on the floor in the kitchen, well away from all of the commotion of her mother smashing the bookshelf in a fit of confused rage. I look over to her, and I think back on those first few weeks of her life. It suddenly strikes me that in all of the weeks since her birth, not a single day of her life has been about *her*.

As her mother, I have wasted all of those days, and there is not a thing I can do to get them back.

'I'm sorry, Zoe,' I say, and I rush to her and pick her up, cradling her against my cheek. Those early days with her should have been so precious, instead I was caught in the grip of a bizarre depression – trying to keep David happy, trying to allay his paranoia, struggling to even get through the day – *never* managing to focus on a single precious moment with Zoe, moments that are actually lost now. My time with her has passed in a terrible blur. I try to think back to some pure moment with her as a newborn, but every memory is tainted by the tiredness and the worry and the fear as David's moods escalated.

I turn back to what's left of the bookshelf and I exhale.

It's not too late – it can't be too late. Once this transition is over and I'm in the new house, I'm going to be a better mum. I have to be.

✦ ✦ ✦

I'm walking to the furniture store that afternoon when I hear a car pull up beside me. Ingrid winds down the window of the passenger's seat on her logo-emblazoned Focus.

'Olivia! Hi! How's things?'

'Hi, Ingrid, I'm great thanks. How are you?'

'Oh, I am doing so well – I have a few new listings, sold another house last week… I've taken a few calls about your place, too. Things are looking up.'

'Fantastic!'

'Where are you headed? Do you have time to grab a coffee?'

'A coffee?' I repeat blankly, and she shrugs.

'I don't know many people around here. I figured it was time I made some new friends.'

'Oh,' I said, dumfounded. *Huh. Friends?* 'Thanks, but, sorry – I was just going to the furniture store… '

'Never mind then,' Ingrid smiles kindly. It suddenly strikes me that I haven't had a friend of my own in years – but I've wanted one. A friend like Ingrid. Someone positive and bubbly and fun and relaxed.

The realisation dawns on me that this is an opportunity to reach out for something I both want and need. *This is how you make friends.*

I had female friends at school and university – loads of them, but gradually, just as he distanced me from my family, David pushed away them all away and subtly cut off any attempts to make new ones. If I'd wanted to go out for a simple coffee like Ingrid had just proposed, he'd insist on joining me, even if he was the only partner there with a group of women. That made everyone so uncomfortable that the invitations gradually faded away, and even when they did come, I got very good at declining them to avoid the embarrassment of showing up with David inevitably in tow.

But there is no David now, there is only Olivia, and she likes friends. And she likes Ingrid. I grin. 'Actually,' I say, 'I'd like that. I can go look at furniture after.'

'Sure, hop in?'

I step towards the car, but then I stop and I look down at Zoe in the carrier against my chest.

'I don't have a car seat,' I say hesitantly.

'It's only half a block,' Ingrid points out, but still I hesitate, and Ingrid adds delicately, 'Or – you can walk and I'll just meet you up there in a few minutes? I can order for you if you like? It'll be ready when you get there.'

I don't want to be complicated. I like the idea of a simple cup of coffee with Ingrid Little – a simple gesture that doesn't require me climbing over a mountain of my own baggage to complete. I can see the coffee shop from here – it's probably only a few hundred metres. I want to get in the car. I want to do this ordinary thing. I want to be normal.

'I'm sure it's going to be fine,' I say, and I sit in the front seat and I strap the seatbelt over the two of us. I wrap my arms around Zoe and I brace my feet hard against the floor of the car as Ingrid pulls forward. She's chatting – aimless words – telling me all about her new clients and an amusing encounter with Todd she had at the petrol station – and then the car stops and we are there.

It is a short, uneventful trip – two fledgling friends in a car for less than thirty seconds – but I'm still not sure if I should even be *in* the car. Have I underestimated the danger of having Zoe in a car but not properly restrained, or am I overthinking a simple decision?

Well, it's done now. Was that an achievement to add to my list, or a stupid mistake that could have ended in tragedy?

'God, I'm dying for some cake – let's go,' Ingrid says as she slides out of the car. I fumble to unbuckle my seatbelt, and I step onto the footpath. It's quiet inside the café – and Ingrid points to a set of empty chairs and says, 'This is my treat, I'll write it off as a business expense since you're a client.' She throws out that musical laugh, and asks, 'What can I get for you?'

'A flat white, please.'

'And which cake?'

I look at the display cabinet and realise that I'm absolutely starving.

'Oh, that salted caramel tart looks amazing.'

'Good plan,' Ingrid says, 'I think I might have the same.'

A few minutes later, she joins me at the table with the coffees and as soon as she sits, she grins at me and says, 'So, you're a *vet*, that is so cool – tell me all about it.'

I laugh as I pick up my coffee. 'Well, I was that kid at school who fell in love with every animal she met... '

It's an ordinary day in an ordinary place, but as I chat with Ingrid Little over coffee and caramel tart, I am well aware that I am taking an extraordinary step – one that it had never even occurred to me to add to my shopping list of things to do in building a new life for myself.

I am making a friend, and the possibilities that might come from such a simple thing are virtually endless.

✦ ✦ ✦

On moving day, I wake at dawn in my childhood bedroom. I have asked my parents for an hour or so alone at David's house – one last chance to say goodbye before we meet Ingrid at the new place.

Mum drops me off at the kerb.

'You sure you don't want me to come in with you?'

'No, thanks,' I say quietly. 'I need to do this alone.'

I step out of the car and close the door, and take a step towards the gate. Mum winds down the window and calls hesitantly, 'Olivia, did you want me to drop Zoe to Louisa's now?'

I spin back to the car and look into the back window. Zoe is there, safely strapped in the capsule. I actually forgot her, and the thought makes me feel a little ill. But Mum offers me a gentle smile and she says, 'You do have a lot on your mind, love.'

'Mother of the year,' I sigh, and I step back towards the car and open the door. I kiss Zoe gently, and then I take a very deep breath. 'Mum, you know I haven't ever really been apart from her, not since… '

'I know, love. But we're going to have our hands full today. And Louisa will really take very good care of her. Call it practice for next week when you're back at work?'

I kiss Zoe again, then I straighten out of the car. This time, I don't turn towards the house until my mother has driven away with my daughter, and then suddenly it all feels very real. My arms feel empty and my gut is churning. I fumble for the mobile in my pocket, ready to call Mum back, but she's right – I do need to get used to this – and Louisa will be fine with Zoe – and God, it's just *time*.

I push the gate open and I march to the front door. There's a small hole in the grey paint, right about my eye level, and I haven't really looked at it today – but I know what it's from. He left the note here, hammered into the door for me to find; only *Ivy* found it, and she's never even told me what it said. I brush my finger over the hole in the paint and I wonder if he hesitated before he did it. Did he think at all about the pain he was about to cause? Was he scared at all? Did he have second thoughts? Did he pause here, just as I am paused now, thinking about the chapter that he was closing when he left that note?

All of these questions need to stay here, in my history, because there is no way to resolve them. I will never even begin to fathom what was running through David's mind that day, and in some ways, I don't even want to.

For the last time, I unlatch each of the locks and I let myself inside.

The house is finally empty – everything is gone. I walk into the living area and I'm struck by the sheer vastness of the space. There's no TV, no white-leather couches, even the splinters from the bookshelf have been removed. All that remains are memories – beautiful ones, horrific ones.

I have been one of the possessions in this house – nothing more than one of David's 'things', a status symbol. Just like a couch or a bookshelf, I had no autonomy – no right to say how I wanted to be used, or *if* I wanted to be used. I had a role to fulfil, and eventually that role was almost entirely about meeting David's needs.

Not all that long ago, I didn't even have access to my own money without David's authorisation. But today, I am moving into my own house – and only *my* name will be on the title.

Olivia Brennan. Owned by no one.

I am still bound in chains – chains of grief, lingering fear sometimes – but the shackles of David's control have broken and fallen to my feet. This will be the last time I stand in this house with the ghost of David Gillespie watching over my shoulder.

From now, I am a new person. I am a person who lives where she wants to live, in a house that looks as she wants it to look, with the furniture that she chooses, and the décor that she likes.

And then I feel the smile start to spread over my face. I *have made it* into this new chapter of my life, and no one can ever take that away from me.

Mum returns with Dad an hour later. They reverse the ute down onto the drive, and then the three of us carefully load the only items left in the house onto the tray. Everything we need comes down from Zoe's room – her furniture, and the few keepsakes that I've kept – although they don't even reach to the top of that laundry basket. If I hadn't spent a fortune on new furniture and incidentals to be delivered today, I'd be shifting from one empty house to another.

Once the ute is loaded, Dad leaves without us while Mum does a walk-through of the house to check for anything we might have missed. I walk slowly into the garage. It still feels odd to look at that space now and see only my car waiting. David's huge black SUV was always squeezed in tightly beside it. I wonder what became of that car? The police would have taken it, but what about once they were done?

'Right, love,' Mum says, and she joins me in the garage and pulls the internal door closed behind her. 'Ready to go?'

'*So* ready,' I murmur.

'Who's driving?' Mum asks. I'm holding the keys. I raise my hand and hit the button to unlock the central locking.

'Me,' I say, and I stride towards the door with confident, purposeful steps.

I reverse out of the driveway, and I lower the garage with the remote button, which I pass to Mum. She drops it into a zip lock bag for Ingrid, and I pull out onto the road.

I drive across town to my new house, and I feel like the most powerful woman in the world.

Ingrid meets us at the front of Mrs Schmitt's house – *my house*. She is beaming and in one hand she holds an enormous bouquet of flowers, and in the other a bottle of champagne.

'I hope you have the keys somewhere too,' I laugh as I approach her. She laughs too, and she brushes a friendly kiss across my cheek and passes me the flowers and the bottle.

'Let me take those things,' Mum says. 'You'll want to open that door by yourself, I imagine.' So I pass the flowers and the bottle to Mum, and my hands are empty. I miss Zoe for the first time since Mum drove away with her – it suddenly feels very wrong that she isn't with me. This thought in itself is quite shocking because it occurs to me that this brief separation from her is much easier than I had expected it to be.

And that, I recognise, is the magic of this decision that I have made to move on. My mind is full of progress; I do not have time to ruminate on my anxieties.

Ingrid passes me a small chain, with several keys of various shapes and sizes, and a little Perspex plaque. I look down at the plaque, and my eyes fill with tears. In hot pink, scripted letters, the plaque declares THE KEYS TO YOUR NEW LIFE.

I give a teary giggle and then I all but jog away from my parents and Ingrid, right past the hydrangeas and the gardens, all the way to the front door. I slide the key into the lock, and I listen to the clicks as the barrel tumbles. I push the door open, and the second I step inside I can somehow smell the cookies baking like when Mrs Schmitt used to babysit me after school.

I am *home*.

This house is empty but rather than feeling vast, it feels like a blank space – begging for me to make it my own. I walk from room to room, and I am crying softly but these are not sobs of sadness – these are sounds of pure relief. I walk into the room that Zoe will have one day, when I'm ready to move her out of my bed. I look at the beautiful, wood-framed window with the lead-light features at the sides, and the high ceiling with the ornate cornices. I walk across the hall to my room and I imagine that beautiful bed that will be delivered any minute, set right up in here. In the kitchen, there is a huge bunch of flowers and a bottle of champagne sitting on the cast-iron stove, and I pick up the little card beside them.

Olivia,

We are so glad that Mum's home is now your home. She was so very fond of you, and we are sure that she will be watching over you as you make a life here. All our very best wishes for the future,

The Schmitt Family

I look from the card to survey the kitchen and I remember warming my hands by the stove on cold winter days and licking the whisk when Mrs Schmitt cooked pancakes. Louisa used to tease Mr Schmitt about how much he looked like Santa Claus and he would chase her through the house to tickle her, and Mrs Schmitt would stifle her laughter as she told them not to run inside.

There is not one single bad memory here. There is no lingering ghost of fear here, no memory of having been trapped – just hope. In this house, I see a place where I can make myself confident and whole again. I will shower every day in this house. I will dress myself every day. I will leave that front door, every single day, if not to go work – then just to get some fresh air, then just to be healthy and *alive*.

The grey times after The Tragedy are now officially over, and I am ready and positioned to become Olivia 2.0.

'I had my doubts at first… but, Liv, this is a great move,' Dad says gruffly from the kitchen door, and I look up at him and I beam for the first time in months.

'I know,' I say, and I'm proud of myself.

I had almost forgotten what that felt like.

❖ ❖ ❖

I spend the weekend in my new house with my sister. Lulu insists on sleeping over, 'christening the spare room', she says – but I really don't mind the company. This is different to the times she wanted to sleep over at David's house with me – Lulu's presence in this new house is a sign that she *wants* to spend time with me, not an awkward proof that everyone fears I'm about to do something terrible to myself.

By Sunday night, my home is almost set up – all that's left to do is Zoe's room. I lie on my new bed and I stare up at the ornate ceiling and I breathe in the scent of the lavender in the garden beneath my window. I'm not happy yet – but I'm closer to a sense of peace. I sleep again without the aid of a sedative, but this isn't an exhausted sleep – it's an easy one.

When Louisa goes to work on Monday, I set up Zoe's cot in my room, and I promise myself that one day soon I'll actually move her out of my own bed and into it. Then I set up all of her clothes and the change table, and the pretty little cross stitch that Mum left on the doorstep for her after she was born – all of these things go into the room across the hall. Because when I am just a bit stronger, and it will happen one day – I will move Zoe's crib in there too.

But soon it is Wednesday, and that means it's time to go to work. I get up early, and Louisa makes me a coffee. I ask her to hold Zoe while I get dressed. She sits on the lounge beneath the throw rug with Zoe in her arms.

I pull on my Milton Falls Vet Clinic uniform, and I drag my hair into a neat, smooth bun. I even put on a little make-up – not much, just a scrape of mascara. The woman who stares back at me in the mirror is strong, capable and intelligent. She has a career that she takes pride in. She is so much more than her mistakes, as immense as they may be. She is even more than the sum of all of the parts of her history.

I strap Zoe in the car seat. I feel that odd shiver, the strange one I always feel when I put her in a car – but I know how to deal with it now. I wait a moment, I double-check her straps, and then when the sensation of anxiety passes, I slip into my own seat. Louisa climbs in beside me, and we drive in silence to the day-care centre. I park, but then I sit still, my hands tight on the steering wheel.

'Livvy, if you're not ready to do this, it's absolutely fine,' Lulu murmurs, and I look at her – surveying the sadness in her brown eyes and the flush on her cheekbones. I can't believe how many years went by without my baby sister in my life. I recognise that Louisa has been trying over these past few days to make up for lost time, and I love her for it.

'No, I can do it,' I tell her, and then I force out a sharp breath through puffed cheeks and I nod towards the door. 'You go to work, Lulu. I'm going to be fine.'

'No way, Liv – I'll come in with you, then I'll come to the clinic and just walk back over to my office.'

I shake my head fiercely, and then I fumble for her hand and I squeeze it, hard.

'Thank you for everything you've done, but I need you to go now so that I prove to myself that I can do this alone.'

Louisa's eyes fill with tears, but she offers me a smile anyway, and then she pulls me close for a hug. My sister's perfume is far too sweet for me; she smells like a teenage girl most of the time. I breathe that scent in, and it bolsters my confidence, and then I push her gently away and I tease her, 'Stop being so clingy! Get out of here.'

I watch as Louisa crosses the car park, and then begins the short walk down the street to the offices where she works. We will meet for lunch later, at a café between my clinic and her office – just as we used to, years and *years* ago.

I can't wait for that lunch, but first, I have to get out of the car and I have to take Zoe from the back seat, and I have to walk inside and hand her over to a near stranger.

I watch the other parents coming out of the car park for a few minutes. None of them are in tears, none of them look traumatised. They simply take their children in, say goodbye, and then go to work. I can do that too, and this is going to get easier. Like with everything else I've done in the last few months, I just need to take the first step. When I do manage to convince myself to get out of the car, I immediately begin to sob. Still, I unbuckle Zoe, and I walk into the office. Ellen is waiting right there, and she greets me with a smile and she pulls me close for a very unprofessional hug.

'I am going to personally look after her, Olivia, I promise you,' she whispers. I pass her Zoe, and then I turn immediately towards the door. I can't hang around because the feelings are only building – and if I leave it too long, my courage will vaporise and I'll snatch Zoe back and run home.

'You have my details, Ellen?' I fling the question over my shoulder as I take my first steps towards the exit.

'Yes, Olivia, it's all on your file,' Ellen calls after me, and I glance back at her as I reach the doors. She is rocking Zoe gently in her arms, and she is smiling at me.

This is the right thing to do. Still, I cry a little as I drive the short block to work, and I need to take a moment to compose myself before I dare to walk into the clinic. I stare at myself in the vanity mirror above my steering wheel and I tidy up the mascara that has run under my eyes, then I step out of the car and I walk inside.

'Livvy's back!' Gilly cheers as I step into the reception area, and there are greetings called from all of the rooms in the rabbit warren of the clinic. Gilly embraces me briefly as I pass the reception desk on my way to my office, and as I pass Sebastian's room, I glance inside to see him sitting behind his desk. He looks up from the computer screen and our eyes meet.

'Welcome back, Olivia,' he says.

'Thank you, Sebastian,' I say. 'It's good to be back.'

I sit at my desk and while the computer boots up, I take a photo of Zoe from my bag and I pin it to the clipboard beside my monitor. Ivy took it at the hospital just after she was born, but it's one of those images that just perfectly encapsulates a moment. The light through the window in my hospital room was perfect, and Zoe was asleep. Her eyes are closed, her eyelashes resting against her plump little cheeks, and her angel-kiss lips are curved upwards at the edges, as if she was *just* about to smile. The nurses had wrapped her in a little woollen blanket, and her tiny fists had poked out – they were resting up near her face. She had a little crocheted beanie on her head over the top of her patchy hair.

I smile to myself, and I touch the photo with my fingertip, and then I wade through the mess of six months of unattended email.

And just as I knew it would be, it is truly a relief to find myself back at work. I meet the locum – Stephanie – and she's polite and professional and proficient – which is exactly what the clinic needed her to be. The vet nurses have organised morning tea for me, and as we eat cupcakes and drink coffee, they catch me up on some town gossip that *doesn't* involve me or my family. Then I help Stephanie plan for a farm visit, and just as she leaves, the nurses take a call that there's an emergency coming in – a pet has been run over.

'It's the Thomas family... their three-year-old cat – from the sounds of things there's some pelvic trauma,' Gilly murmurs to Sebastian, and he looks straight at me and says mildly, 'Take this one for me, Liv? I've got bookings all afternoon.'

'Have you lost your mind, Sebastian?' Gilly gasps.

Sebastian's gaze doesn't waver; he continues to stare at me expectantly.

'I… I just don't know, Seb,' I whisper. I'm confused by the confidence in his gaze. He believes I can do this, and he knows me… better than anyone. *Is he right?* But what if I can't concentrate yet? What if he trusts me, and I let the family down? I succumb to the panic, and shake my head. 'No – I can't. I thought I'd just assist you and Stephanie… at least until I get back in the swing of things.'

'It's like riding a horse,' Sebastian says softly. I ponder this for a moment, then I laugh uneasily.

'I think the analogy is "riding a bike".'

Sebastian throws his hands in the air as he laughs too. 'See! You're already showing me up. Go wait in the theatre, let Gilly handle the family and the admission. You've done this a million times, you'll be fine.' He starts to walk away, but as he passes me, he whispers just loud enough for me to hear, 'If you need me, come and get me.'

I plan to do exactly that – I'll review the cat myself and then I'll brief Sebastian and have him handle whatever the treatment required is. But as I'm waiting in the theatre, Gilly opens the door, and I catch a glimpse of the owners in the reception area. I know this family and I've actually treated this cat before. I can't remember the parents' names, but I do remember their child – his name is Weston, and he's four or five. He's crying his eyes out against his mother's shoulder.

There are two things I have always loved about my job. There's the animals themselves; the fact that in my role I get to tend to them and bring them back to health. And then there's the families. There's no greater honour than to be entrusted with a family pet, and no greater responsibility than the chance to heal one.

I have the skills to give this cat a fighting chance and to dry that little boy's tears. I'm instantly emboldened and any lingering hesitance disappears. Maybe I'm a broken woman, but I'm not a broken vet. I trained for years to gain the knowledge and skills to help this animal and help these people. And just like that – I'm back. Confidence and *power* surge through me, and I feel like it's reinflating me – my shoulders straighten and my chin lifts, and I look Gilly right in the eye as she approaches with the cat.

'Can you call my sister and cancel my lunch date? Tell her I've had an emergency case come in and I'll see her tonight,' I say quietly. Gilly sets the fiercely protesting cat down carefully on a stainless steel table. The cat meows furiously, but when it tries to climb away, the sound turns to one of pain and she pulls herself forward with her front paws, dragging her back legs.

'Sure,' Gilly says. The surprise in her tone registers, but then I focus on the cat and I don't even notice as she leaves the room. Several hours later and with Gilly's careful assistance, I've set a pin in Fluffy's pelvis and she's slowly coming out of her anaesthetic while I update her case notes on the computer. The day has disappeared completely. I've thought of Zoe periodically, but my thoughts have been calm. Sometimes, I wondered how she was doing – but the thought was always quickly followed by an automatic reflex – a mental reminder that she must be fine at the day-care centre or Ellen would have called – and then my thoughts returned to the task at hand.

It's just past five when Sebastian appears in the doorway. He crosses his arms over his chest and leans into the doorframe. He's wearing a smug grin.

'Just like riding a horse, right?' he says pointedly. Our gazes lock, and the cheeky smile fades from his face. My world might have crumbled outside of this office, but here, just for just a moment, it's as if nothing ever changed. There's still comfort and pleasure to be found in staring into the eyes of the one person who truly understands me. Sebastian is *the* reason I can come back to work so quickly. He will push me, but never past what I can handle.

'Thanks, Seb,' I whisper, and it's more than a simple thank you. It's a declaration of gratitude from the bottom of my heart. 'Thanks for taking a chance... letting me try to handle that on my own.'

He offers me a different smile this time, a proud one.

'It wasn't a "chance" – there was no risk involved. I *knew* you could do it, Livvy.' I slide the keyboard tray back into place and draw in a deep breath, then I offer him a smile.

'So we'll see you again next Wednesday?' he asks.

'You bet your life you will.'

CHAPTER 26

Ivy

I certainly didn't expect it to be, but the day that David married Olivia was actually one of the happiest days of my life. I focused on it as an important milestone for my son as a man, rather than thinking too much about the significance of the day for *their* relationship. I wasn't losing my son to Olivia. Nothing was going to change, this was just a token gesture to formalise that things would stay the way they were, and a huge party for all of our friends and family.

Olivia helped me pick a soft pink suit.

'Beautiful,' she smiled when I modelled it for her.

'No one cares if the mother of the groom is beautiful,' I muttered, and Olivia hugged me.

'Of course they do.'

She had two bridesmaids with us at the boutique that day trying on dresses – both friends from university. While the girls were in having a fitting, I remarked with some surprise to Olivia that she hadn't asked Louisa to be part of the bridal party.

'Ah, we're not so close any more,' Olivia said awkwardly. She put a dress back onto the rack, and reached for the next. Her jaw was set hard and she hadn't so much as looked at me since I asked the question, so I knew she was hoping I wouldn't press any further, but I was too curious to drop the subject.

'Did you have a falling out?'

'We just grew apart,' Olivia said, and this time the stiffness in her voice was evident.

'But your family will be at the wedding?' I frowned.

'Yes, they're coming.'

'And Tom *will* give you away?'

Olivia shook her head.

'No, we're not doing that,' she said. 'We're not much for tradition.'

'Oh? Well, how's it going to work then? The father of the bride *always* gives her away.'

'David and I have been to plenty of weddings in the city that skip that part. I'll just walk down the aisle myself. It's going to be fine.'

I imagined the faces of my friends when Olivia appeared at the end of the aisle, and how confused they'd all be... how judgemental of my son's wife-to-be's funny, modern ideas. I frowned. That wouldn't do it all. What on earth was she thinking? Another selfish decision from this woman my son had chosen. Why couldn't she just *do* the right thing by him, without needing to pushed all of the time? It was maddening.

'But, someone *has* to give you away, Olivia. It's just not right for you to walk down the aisle alone. Won't you feel awkward? Lonely?'

She hesitated, then shrugged. 'I'm sure it will be the least of my concerns on the day,' she flicked me a glance at last, and a tight smile that I couldn't bring myself to return.

'In a town like Milton Falls, it's very important to do things the right way – particularly for someone with a high profile like David. If you don't let Tom walk you down the aisle, everyone will wonder why and the rumours will start. It's a matter of appearances more than tradition. You know he wants to be mayor one day.'

Olivia swallowed, then cleared her throat, and said weakly, 'I'll think about it.' She turned away from me then, and ruffled among the gowns again for a moment. I was getting ready to press on – to *insist* that she let her father her give her away – but then she held up a hideous purple gown.

'What do you think of this dress?' She laughed softly at my mortified expression. 'I'm kidding, don't worry. But… so many to choose from… ' This time she flashed me a genuine, hopeful smile, and she asked, 'Do you think you could you help me pick? You always look so stylish… '

I had no choice but to drop the subject that day, but I raised it with David himself a few weeks later.

'Olivia doesn't want to ask him. It's not a big deal. They're coming to the wedding; we need to leave it at that.'

'But everyone is going to wonder why, David, surely you can talk some sense into her?'

'Mum, her family is really *weird*. I know they seem like nice people, but there are good reasons why we don't spend time with them these days. We have to drop it, okay?'

At least everything about Olivia's look on her wedding day was perfect, and no wonder, since I'd helped her pick her outfit myself. Her dress had a simple beaded bodice but a huge hooped skirt and she carried an enormous bouquet of lilies. She looked beautiful – but I had to steel myself against a pinch in my chest, because despite the perfect appearance, I couldn't help but wish it was someone else in that gown, walking towards my son with shining love in her eyes.

As she walked down the aisle, I looked across to see Tom and Rita – both their faces pinched, Rita's arm through Tom's elbow. I assumed at the time that Tom was upset that Olivia hadn't asked him to give her away, and I felt so sorry for them. I caught her eye and offered Rita a smile, but the one she returned to me was hollow. This was bewildering, but also… infuriating.

As Rita's eyes drifted back to the altar where my son waited, I saw the unmistakeable signs of distaste cross her face. Her lip curled and her nostrils flared, and she clutched at Tom's arm harder. He turned to her, and I saw the grief in his eyes too. He brushed his lips over Rita's hair, and then his gaze met mine. He didn't even try to smile, and neither did I – because by then, I was incensed. I thought about David's comments about Olivia's 'weird' family and my anger surged. Rita and Tom were ungrateful and foolish. How could they not realise how *lucky* they were, to have their plain, selfish daughter marry a man like my son in an elaborate ceremony like this one? It was exactly the kind of wedding that I had dreamt I might have for myself once upon a time; so contrary to the courthouse ceremony that Wyatt and I had actually shared. David's wedding gave all the pomp and ceremony the townsfolk of Milton Falls could ever have imagined. Two hundred chairs were laid out on the clearing on the mountain, each one covered in white linen with a big pink bow around the back. There were flowers everywhere; huge bouquets along each aisle and enormous lily displays at the centre near the celebrant.

And Tom and Rita had the hide to look unhappy about it?! Every member of that family should consider themselves *lucky* to be there at all.

I turned my gaze back to Olivia. She didn't even seem to be crying; all I could really see was that beaming white smile from behind her veil, and I felt another burst of anger hit me – she should have been crawling down that aisle to kiss his feet. But then, when she reached the front, David stepped forward and he lifted the veil over her face, and they stared at each other. My anger started to fade at the look in his eyes – the adoration, the devotion, and the stare went on and on, until then they spontaneously embraced one another. I clutched Wyatt's hand tightly in mine, and the minister made some joke about them needing to wait *just* a few more minutes, and the congregation all laughed. But the gesture spoke volumes – and I set my frustration and anger down. Perhaps he could have done better, but he'd made his choice, and there was no denying that he was sure about it.

The reception was held at the golf club in a huge marquee that David had hired out of the city. The day cost him a fortune – Wyatt and I gave some money to cover the bar tab, but David's business was doing so well by that stage, that they really didn't need much else in the way of help. And Olivia, much to my surprise, went out of her way to make sure that Wyatt and I were included, and to make sure that I felt special.

I appreciated every gesture, from our names featured on the wedding order of service, to the seating arrangement she'd chosen – opting to include both her parents and us on the bridal table, although blessedly the bridal party were between us. I did worry that someone might notice the tension between the families, because Rita and Tom kept themselves to themselves the whole night, but I was also a little relieved, because if they *had* tried to strike up a conversation with me, things might have been ugly.

When it was time for the bridal waltz, David surprised me. He finished dancing with Olivia, and then as everyone crowded onto the dance floor with them, David crossed the floor and took my hand. I leaned into his shoulder, and I rested my head against it, and I whispered, 'I am so proud of you. Your life is everything I dreamed it would be.'

David kissed my hair then, and the photographer snapped a photo of it. I have that photo on the wall in my bedroom, and I stare at it some days now for hours on end.

That was the David I always knew he could be; a child who had grown into a man so special that *his* success made my own life worthwhile.

❖ ❖ ❖

I honestly don't know when I first noticed troubles. There were tiny things even in the early years of their relationship, but these

seemed more frequent after the wedding. There were occasionally odd bruises or sharp words – small things just vivid enough
for me to notice and catalogue somewhere deep in my mind, in
some list I didn't ever want to consider too closely. The one time
I did ask Liv how she got a bruise on her shoulder, she had such
a plausible story. A horse had kicked her in the field, and taken
in isolation, that might have been a very reasonable explanation. I didn't exactly doubt it, but something about it left me
feeling uneasy – the same feeling I got sometimes when David
and Olivia were having dinner with us, and I'd see him dismiss
something that she said.

She'd be talking about work, her face alight with joy, and
she'd mention Ryder – and David would scowl – and sometimes
he would change the subject in a brutal, completely unsubtle
way. I didn't actually know what to make of all this; I just knew
that on some level, something was off.

My consolation was the progression of their relationship.
They'd been together for well over ten years by then, and they'd
only recently been married. So even if I did sometimes entertain
the thought that perhaps David and Olivia had their private issues, I explained those concerns away easily to myself – because
she stayed, and not only did she stay, she'd chosen to become
even more committed to him. She was an independent, intelligent woman – why would she do those things if he was treating
her badly?

She wouldn't.

But then again, I told myself, nor would he treat her badly
at all. He positively doted on her. She was his whole world, and
he'd never do anything to risk that.

Ryder was seventy-four years old when he decided that he
was finally ready to retire from the Milton Falls Vet Clinic. I
heard on the grapevine that Olivia was going to buy the practice. David had recently been appointed to the town council,

and Wyatt and I went to see his inauguration. It was a typical Milton Falls event, held in the park in the centre of town, attended by an embarrassingly large percentage of residents – because there's *so* little to do, and everyone tends to go to everything. I clapped and cheered when David was given his badge, and then the ceremony was over and we walked across the street to have lunch at the pub.

'I heard you two might be buying a vet clinic?' Wyatt remarked, and David shot him what could only be described as a scowl.

'Where on *earth* did you hear that?'

'Everyone in town is talking about it. Livvy here's the most popular vet in the district. It makes sense.'

'We don't think now is the right time,' Olivia said, but the words sounded hollow, as if she didn't quite buy them herself. She pushed her food around her plate, avoiding our gaze.

Even Wyatt wasn't going to miss the tension between them after that. David barely spoke as we finished our lunch, and my hasty change of subject did nothing to dispel the awkwardness. We managed to get through the meal, but as we parted ways to go back to our cars, I glanced back at David. I saw the look on his face – the boiling sense of thunder – and I saw the way that Olivia was walking beside him, her whole body tucked up. Her shoulders were slumped, her arms were wrapped around her waist; she was almost cowering – but cowering close to him, as if yes, there was a threat – but David certainly wasn't it; in fact, he was going to protect her from it. All that was missing from the moment was for David to slide his arm around her shoulder, and tell her everything was okay.

But he didn't do that. He walked stiffly – his face set in that scowl, his gaze dark. I wondered what Olivia had done to cause his anger. I called into the dealership a few days later under the guise of looking at a new car, and I asked him about it. I kept my tone mild as I asked, 'You were so upset at lunch the other day… did we say something wrong?'

'I'm just pissed off with the way that rumours swell in this town. Of course Olivia isn't going to buy a bloody vet clinic. What would she do with the business while she was off having babies and raising children? If we bought it now, she'd just be selling it again in no time.'

It was not at all difficult to pluck the silver lining from that particular cloud.

'So you *are* thinking about having children soon, then?' I asked, trying to hide my glee at the idea.

David's smile was almost secretive. He laughed and pulled me close for a hug.

'When the time feels right – of course we are, a whole football team of them, most probably. All right?'

We heard not long after that that Sebastian McNiven had purchased the vet clinic. He was an out-of-towner – and when people moved to Milton Falls, there was always this awkward period where they weren't quite friends, but they weren't quite strangers. A close-knit place like our little village doesn't readily absorb new residents, but with Sebastian owning the vet clinic and in contact with so many farmers and pet-owners, he wiggled his way into the community much quicker than most.

Sebastian had been at the clinic for several months before I had cause to visit. That first consult, he waived my bill because I was Olivia's mother-in-law, which endeared him to me immediately. He was quiet and reserved but exceedingly polite; vastly more pleasant than Ryder had ever been to deal with.

'I met Sebastian last week,' I remarked to Olivia over our Sunday night roast dinner. 'How's he settling in?'

'He's a nice change from Ryder, that's for sure,' she laughed, and David sighed heavily. I glanced at him, and I could almost *feel* the tension emanating from my son. This was different to David's dislike of Ryder. This was intense.

'You don't like him?' I said, eyebrows high. And suddenly I was reconsidering every aspect of that interaction I'd had with Sebastian McNiven. He *did* have an odd way of speaking with his hands, and he seemed eager to please – *too* eager, in hindsight. Even the gesture of the waived bill seemed suspiciously generous now that I really thought about it. Just what was he trying to prove?

'I don't trust him. There's something off about him, I can't put my finger on it yet,' David said, shrugging. I glanced at Olivia, and saw the irritation and defensiveness in her eyes, and that's when it hit me: *was Olivia interested in her new boss?*

I was aghast at the idea, but once it had risen in my mind, there was no avoiding it. Sebastian was about Olivia and David's age, reasonably good looking in a bookish way... and he did spend all day, every day working alongside her. There was no denying that since his arrival, the tension between David and Olivia had seemed to increase exponentially. Over the following months I kept waiting to hear that Olivia had resigned – David certainly seemed increasingly determined that she should. But she hung onto that job so stubbornly, I started to wonder what the appeal *really* was for her.

'She should just leave. David wants her to, I don't understand why she doesn't.'

'David is just a traditionalist, like me,' Wyatt sighed. 'I did sometimes wonder if maybe he shouldn't have married a career woman. Liv loves that bloody job, but I do understand why Davey wants her at home. I love that you're at home.'

I looked at him in surprise. 'You do?'

'Of course I do. Why do you think I never wanted you to work?'

'I didn't give it much thought. Of course I had to stay home when David was young, but ever since... '

'There's just something really comforting to a man about knowing that his wife is going to handle the house. It means that I can really concentrate on my job, and being a good husband to you. I know that I don't always get it right... but I try, you know? I think David is like me. He wants to know what Olivia is doing during the day, and fair enough – she *is* his wife.'

I was confused by Wyatt's comments – both gratified by his surprising appreciation of the role I'd played in our household over the years, and somehow irritated by the implication that he had a right to know what I chose to do with my days. He'd never actually shown much interest, as long as dinner was on the table by 6.01p.m. I sat back in my chair to ponder this, then peered at him curiously.

'What would you have said if I'd wanted to get a career?'

'You *wouldn't* have, love. Back in our day, women didn't have to bother about working except where the husband wasn't doing his job right. Things were simple for us. We both knew exactly what we'd each bring to the relationship, and it made everything easier. That's what David is looking for, too.'

'Well, what do you think will happen with them?' I frowned.

'The obvious solution seems to me that he should knock her up and take the job out of the equation.'

'Women tend to work these days even once they have babies,' I pointed out, and Wyatt grinned and shook his head.

'Trust me, Ivy. *David's* woman won't.'

◆ ◆ ◆

Soon, whenever the subject of Olivia's work came up, David would tense. I found this fascinating. I made a point to ask her about it every time I saw them, just so I could study the odd tension between them.

'How's work, Olivia?'

David tapped his fingers impatiently against the table before she had a chance to answer.

'I am so sick of hearing about that bloody clinic. They're fucking pets, for God's sakes. Does any of it really matter?'

'It's going well, thanks,' Olivia said carefully to me, as if she hadn't even heard David speak. My gaze narrowed on her.

'What's the point of me working my arse off to build a business to support us if you're determined to spend the rest of your life working for Sebastian Bloody McNiven anyway?' David asked, and Olivia turned towards him.

'Can we talk about this later please?' she whispered, flushing.

'Let's talk about it now,' David leant back in his chair and scooped his beer up in his hand, bringing it to his mouth to down half of it before he said sharply, 'Why don't you look at my mother and tell her why you don't want to make her a grand-mother, Liv? You know we're her *only* chance to be one, right?'

'Ivy,' Olivia said, with forced politeness. 'I will make you a grandmother, one day soon. I'm just not ready to leave my job yet, and since we've decided that we won't have kids until I'm ready to leave work, it might be another year or two.'

'Don't leave it too long,' I said pointedly, and I flicked a reas-suring glance to David. 'Women these days so often put their career first then moan about how hard it is to have a baby. It's tragic, and I'd *hate* to see it happen to you. You're not getting any younger, you know?'

'That's right, Liv,' David said, latching onto my points with enthusiasm. 'You're not getting any younger. Did you hear what Mum said?'

'I did,' Olivia said weakly. Her smile faded all the way to nothing as she looked back to her meal. She'd flushed from her hairline down to her neck, and guilt was vivid in her gaze. I glanced at David, who winked at me. I was actually pleased at how uncomfortable Olivia seemed at my comments. I hoped I'd given her something to think about because David was clearly ready for children and it was cruel of her to make him wait.

And after seeing the impact my comment had on Olivia that night, I decided I'd actively look for other opportunities to help David get what he wanted.

❖ ❖ ❖

I took my car in for a service one day, and David happened to be free so invited me into his office for a coffee. He was so busy by that stage that it was rare for us to steal a quiet moment alone together, and I was delighted for the chance to speak privately.

'I was thinking about Sebastian McNiven,' I said quietly between sips of coffee. 'I really don't want to meddle but... there's something... I don't know... *off* about the way Olivia speaks about him, don't you think?'

David's gaze was guarded. He sat opposite me in the spare chair in his office but leant forward to lean on his knees as he asked,

'What do you mean?'

'It's really hard to say. Call it mother's instinct,' I shrugged. 'Just watch that one, won't you?'

'I am,' David said, and I saw the beating of a tic at his jaw and the slight flare to his nostrils.

'She really needs to leave that job and have a baby, don't you think?' I said quietly. David sighed and shook his head as he sank back into the chair.

'You know I want that too, Mum. She's just so stubborn.'

'Well, I'm sure you'll talk her round,' I said brightly. 'I just wanted to make sure you'd noticed too.' I took a sip of my coffee, then added quietly, 'I really didn't want to see them making a fool of you... you know, if something *was* going on.'

'That won't happen,' David said abruptly, but then his expression eased suddenly and he flashed me a soft smile. 'Thanks for calling by, Mum. I really appreciate it.'

'Of course, Davey. Absolutely any time.'

CHAPTER 27
Olivia

'So, you've told me that you've moved house and you've gone back to work this week,' Natasha summarises, ten minutes into our next session. 'You've even been driving again, and you're here by yourself today – no Rita in the waiting room, I notice.'

I grin. 'Yep.'

'It's all brilliant progress.'

'Thank you.'

'You haven't said a single thing about how you're feeling though.'

'I'm proud of myself. I'm taking control of my life and it feels wonderful. It's been scary, but I really think I'm over the worst of it. Now the pieces are all in place and I can get on with life again.'

'So… are you ready to talk about Sebastian?'

That wasn't the reaction I expected from Natasha today. I thought she'd let me bask in my progress for a few minutes at least. I frown at her.

'I *have* talked about Sebastian. I just told you five minutes ago, he gave me an emergency case to do right off the bat and I handled it well.'

'Why do you think he did that?'

'He understood why I wanted to go back to work so badly. He knew that I needed to fill my mind with good things again by being useful.'

'It sounds like Sebastian knows you very well.'

Far better than anyone else does.

I pick at an imaginary piece of fluff on my jeans, because I don't want to look at Natasha while she's staring at me like that.

'Sebastian isn't the thread you need to pull to make me unravel,' I say stiffly.

'We have to talk about it sometime, Olivia. Have you been thinking about your homework?'

'I have.'

'And?'

'It's complicated.'

'All of this is complicated. That hasn't stopped you from opening up before.'

'Fine,' I say flatly, and I cross my legs and I exhale, and I look at her with anger in my gaze. 'From the first time David met him, he was jealous of Sebastian. They are polar opposite sorts of men. David was always so image conscious, Sebastian usually looks like he just got out of bed and forgot to iron his clothes. David's hair was black, and he never left the house without product in it so that it sat *just so*. This year, David's hairline had started to recede and he was in something of a panic about it – he had a specialist's appointment in the city lined up to discuss treatment.'

I pause. Natasha leans forward. I look at her, and I'm suddenly stricken.

'What is it, Olivia?' she prompts expectantly.

'Did I ever cancel that appointment? Did they wait for him, or send a reminder text to his mobile, or call him at work? Or did they see in the media what had happened and did some clever receptionist at the clinic join the dots and cancel his appointment without a fuss?' I stop talking for a moment and squeeze my eyes shut. 'I'm being an idiot. I don't even know why that's so upsetting. It's just one of those things I forgot, you know? I haven't thought about it since he died and maybe other people were let down by it.'

'Does that really matter?'

'Seb wouldn't care one bit if his hair receded. He's just not at all concerned about that kind of thing. He conserves his energy for things he's passionate about – his friends, his staff, his patients – and I know he doesn't make as much money from the clinic as he should because he's forever giving customers discounts. But David's business success was his life – he gave *nothing* away, and if people were late with their accounts he went after them like a shark.'

'You said David was jealous of Sebastian. Can you tell me why?'

'He used to mock Sebastian, all the time, especially his body language. Seb is so quiet but has these really enthusiastic mannerisms – he's all hand-gestures and big facial expressions. But it's weird because Seb can seem very reserved in a group – he lets everyone else have their turn before he speaks up, and he never takes charge. David was the kind of man who never had to speak twice to get the attention of a crowd – he had a deep voice, and somehow always managed to find a way to take charge. But Sebastian is the gentlest, most respectful man I know. He has always wanted the best for me, even when it wasn't the best for him. Maybe that's why I fell in love with him.'

Natasha sits back in her chair and she stares at me, and she's clearly very satisfied by something I've just said. I rewind my own words in my mind and I'm gripped by an ice-cold fear.

Maybe that's why I fell in love with him.

As soon as I acknowledge the words, the shame looms – right on cue, guilt and disgust at my own behaviour threaten, and if I let them loose, they will completely overwhelm me. Love for Sebastian and guilt have always been too closely entwined to separate. I can't talk about my love for him without facing the shame.

By loving him, I broke my wedding vows.

By loving him, I dragged him into this mess.

By loving him, I made everything worse.

By letting him love me, I risked his safety.

By letting him love me, I took from him moments that he can never get back. Important moments. Moments he deserved.

I look down at my daughter and my heart starts to race. The panic is looming, and if I stay in this room, it'll quickly overwhelm me. Where has all of the air gone? I can barely breathe, and I stand and cuddle Zoe tightly against me.

'I have to go,' I say abruptly.

'We've still got forty-five minutes, Olivia,' Natasha says quietly. 'Stay. Talk with me. We'll ride this out together.'

I shake my head fiercely and step towards the door.

'Will you stay if we agree to talk just about the basic facts? I promise, I won't push you past what you're ready to deal with,' Natasha says. 'Say the word, and we'll change the subject to whatever you're comfortable talking about. You're *completely* in control here.'

I hesitate. I'm still standing between my chair and the door. I glance back to Natasha. Her gaze is patient and she's calm.

'Why is this so important?' I ask her, frustrated, and she smiles kindly.

'You've made leaps and bounds of progress in every other area in the last few months, Olivia. But this one relationship... well, there's a good reason why it's so hard for you to talk about. Let's at least *try* to take some baby steps?'

I swallow hard and return to my chair and sink into it. I keep Zoe on my lap, cuddled close against me.

'Your relationship with Sebastian wasn't just professional, was it?' she asks, so gently that I can barely heard her.

I shake my head. A tear falls onto my cheek.

'What can you tell me about that?'

I was disappointed and defensive the first time I met Sebastian McNiven, especially when I realised he was exactly my age and he was achieving the dream that David had denied me – the dream to own my own clinic.

I wasn't hostile – I just wasn't friendly, not at first. I was professional… I loved my job, and I didn't want to risk it. But for the first few weeks after he arrived, I couldn't help but resent Sebastian's presence at work.

All of that changed with a single display of gratitude.

'Liv?' he stuck his head into my office late on a Friday afternoon and I frowned up at him from the computer screen.

'Yes?'

'Can you follow me for a sec?'

So I walked down the hall after him into the kitchen. There was a box on the table, and when I peered at it, I recognised a high-end automatic coffee machine.

'The nurses told me how much you like your morning coffee, so I got this for the staff room. It's for all of us, but I mainly wanted to do something to say thanks to you. You're a brilliant vet – honestly, the practice would be nothing without you and I'd already be lost without your work. So… I just needed to make sure you realised how much I appreciate you. I hope you like it.'

I stared at him in shock.

'But… ' I was lost for words for a moment, until I laughed. 'You know, Sebastian – Ryder used to grizzle if I took a coffee *break* once a day.'

Seb laughed too. 'Yeah, well… Ryder was a tyrant by all accounts. I want to run this place as a team, you know? And you're the glue that's been holding it all together while I settled in so… *thanks.*'

Sebastian managed to take a fairly stale workplace and turn it into something of a family in a very short period of time, and despite his modesty – he was actually a very skilled vet. We fell into an easy rhythm together – collaborating on cases and diagnoses, but also, he'd come to me for advice about staffing matters or marketing or accounts. Often, I'd have no idea what the answer was, but that he thought to consult me at all was flattering.

We were a partnership of equals, and I loved it.

'We were just colleagues at first,' I tell Natasha. 'Then genuinely just friends for a long time. I had always eaten my lunch in the kitchen at work, but Seb and I naturally started sitting together and talking while we ate. Sometimes one or two of the nurses would join us, but even when they didn't, Seb and I usually found time to sit there together.'

At first, we discussed easy things… cases, the weather, colourful townsfolk. Gradually, the conversations grew deeper. We swapped stories from our childhood. We laughed about our naive assumptions about veterinarian practice during our uni days. Seb told me about the long-term relationship he'd ended just before he moved from the coast to purchase the clinic, and about his close bond with his father, who was battling cancer.

Gradually, on those lunchbreaks and as we worked side by side, I opened up to Seb. I shared hopes and fears with him, things I couldn't talk about with anyone else. It was a complicated task, because I'd share something I thought was simple… like the fact that I didn't want to have children with David just yet because I knew it would mean leaving work… and we'd somehow wind up talking about issues *right* on the edge of the dark side of my marriage.

'Why don't you just have a baby and come right back to work?' Seb shrugged. 'You can work whatever hours you want – giving you some flexibility will be easy.'

I cursed myself for bringing it up.

'David doesn't want me to work after we have kids,' I admitted, flushing, and Seb's eyes widened.

'Why on earth not?'

'He's kind of traditional like that.'

'What do *you* want?'

'I don't actually know,' I said, and I tried to laugh it off. 'Anyway, it will have to happen one day.'

'Will it? Do you even want kids?'

I was surprised by the question, because no one had asked me it like that before. David and I had talked about *how many*, but I don't think we ever really considered the possibility that a perfectly acceptable answer might be *none.*

'I guess so,' I said, but I was frowning by then. The subject of children with David had become so fraught with tension and danger that I no longer allowed myself to think about it in any positive light at all. Truthfully, by that stage, I would have foregone motherhood if it was the only way I could keep my career.

'Well, just because he doesn't want you to work, doesn't mean you can't,' Seb said, shrugging. 'That's why you're waiting, right? So you can negotiate these things and find a compromise?'

Whenever Seb would assume the best of my marriage, I'd lie – either with my silence or a simple nod. For the longest time, I thought I had fooled Seb just like David and I had fooled everyone else. I figured Seb thought I was happily married and that David really was the admirable man everyone else assumed him to be.

And for all of that time, I told myself Seb and I were just friends. Increasingly good friends, incredibly close friends – but *nothing* more.

'David had no idea how close Seb and I were becoming at work – I went out of my way to avoid talking about him at home, sometimes I even pretended not to like Seb at all just because I thought it might help. And I never *wanted* to be unfaithful to David. I would never have done it on purpose.'

'People rarely set out to have affairs.'

'It really happened very organically,' I say softly. 'We just became emotionally intimate. We learned about each other and we each liked what we found.'

'Did Sebastian feel safe to you, Olivia?'

'Completely. Nothing about the relationship felt safe once it became more overt, but whenever I was with Seb, I felt... ' I pause, searching for the word. I think about his confidence in my ability to handle the feline case on my first day back at work, and how Seb seems to understand what I need even better than I do. 'Even when I only gave him half of the picture of my life, he still seemed to know me better than anyone else.'

'Did you ever feel that safe with David?'

I shake my head immediately. 'It was different with David. He was always intense. But Seb is the most relaxed person I know.'

'So you and Sebastian were good friends... *best* friends... and then... ?' Natasha prompts.

Am I ready to talk about this? It's been easier than I expected getting this far, and in some ways, I'm almost enjoying the chance to look back on those times with Seb. They were certainly some of the happiest moments of my life over the past few years.

'A young family brought in a puppy one morning. They said it had been unwell overnight and they weren't sure why. Once Seb checked it over, he realised it was actually critically ill – later we discovered it had eaten a heap of dark chocolate which contains theobromine... toxic to dogs, particularly little dogs, particularly large amounts. It was just too late to help, and the puppy died. Pets die all of the time in our job – it's not pleasant, but it's also part and parcel with it... but that puppy... the mother had been eating the chocolate the night before and she left it out. The father had seen the puppy chewing it but didn't realise it was dangerous. So Seb had the whole family sobbing in the consult room with him. Once they finally left, he came in to chat with me and he was so upset.'

I saw the look on his face when he came to my office, so I rose and shut the door behind him. We sat together side by side on the edge of my desk while he talked – venting his frustration that there was nothing at all he could do to help – lamenting about how preventable the situation was if only they'd known or they'd called us sooner. I don't think I'd ever seen him so upset before.

Even Sebastian's self-awareness and openness with his feelings challenged me. It was bold – brave and deeply masculine, but in a way that was so unlike anything I'd ever seen, not in my father or male friends but especially in David. There was no loud testosterone blindness to navigate with an upset Seb. On this rare occasion that he was distraught, he sought to understand the emotions he was feeling, and he didn't try to hide them behind machismo.

Seb opened my eyes to the wealth of connection I could feel with a man who knew how to express emotions *other* than anger, and the revelation was life changing.

'If you'd told me once upon a time that a vulnerable man would be insanely attractive to me, I might have thought you were crazy,' I whisper to Natasha, and she laughs quietly.

'Self awareness and honesty are attractive traits because they make for pleasant partners,' she tells me. 'But they aren't terribly compatible with the kind of hyper-masculinity you experienced with David.'

'No,' I shake my head. 'Not at all. David would have called Sebastian a "sissy" or a "wimp". In fact, even without knowing Seb much at all, he often did.'

When Seb had finished talking, we slid off the desk to leave and he thanked me for listening. Automatically, I wrapped my arms around his waist for a hug – offering him only support and comfort. As I did, I heard him draw in a sharp breath. Then his arms closed gently around me, and my heart started racing.

It was that simple, and that complicated. A purely physical response to a relationship that was entirely more than that. In a single hug, Sebastian really was more than a friend.

'That's all it took for me to realise at last that my respect for him had actually grown into something deeper. I pulled away just a little – just so that I could look into his eyes – and I saw it there too. It wasn't lust. It was purer than that… just a mutual awareness of *something* more between us.'

'Did the two of you discuss it?'

'Not at that stage. Actually, I think he sprinted out of the office and avoided me for a little while, but we got over the panic of it and just carried on for some time. We stayed in this kind of in-between zone… more than friends, less than lovers. I knew I shouldn't let it progress, and I told myself I wasn't going to. But after that day, we touched each other more – innocent touches – the odd hug when we were alone, or we'd brush hands at the kitchen table but our hands would linger. It was dangerous but… it was nice.'

Sometimes, just for a moment or two when he walked into the room with me, I'd actually get a taste of what it would be like to be free, because for a few moments, I'd pretend that Seb and I were properly together.

'So given how close you and Sebastian were by that stage, did he ever notice anything amiss in your relationship with David?' Natasha asks me quietly.

'Yeah, he did.'

It was dozens of gentle invitations to talk that came in the form of casual comments, always when we were alone, and never delivered with any pressure.

Have you noticed the way he talks to you, Olivia? Why does he think it's okay to push you around like that?

That's a nasty bruise on your neck, Liv?

Is your arm okay? That looks like... it almost looks like a hand-print? How did that happen?

Why are you limping?

Of course you can take time off for the dentist, but if you chipped that tooth on a nut, why is your lip bruised too?

Is David really *coming to the vet conference again this year?*

'He didn't directly ask me. Not at first,' I whisper. 'He just gave me space. He'd mention things that concerned him, always when we were alone, and then he left the ball in my court.'

'Did you consider talking to him?'

'*No* way,' I say firmly. 'I couldn't risk dragging Seb into it.'

'So, Olivia,' Natasha says gently. 'Are you ready to talk about when Seb *did* get dragged into it?'

David gave me a black eye the night he made me go off the pill and I couldn't hide it.

And from there, everything spiralled completely out of my control, if I ever had any at all.

'Can we leave it there today?' I ask her. 'Please?'

'Okay, Olivia,' Natasha nods. 'That was a great start.'

CHAPTER 28

Ivy

On David's birthday, Olivia came to dinner with a ghastly black eye.

I tried to figure out if I should mention the bruise or not. She'd done a terrible job of covering it with make-up, and her entire face looked odd – almost deformed by the swelling around the bruise. But I didn't want to make things awkward, besides which, I told myself that there was definitely an explanation for it.

But the grinding in my gut did not go away as we ate dinner, and when I went to the kitchen to fetch the cake that I'd baked, Olivia followed me with the dirty plates. She slid them onto the bench, and I turned to her and I saw that purple-green bruise in the bright light of the kitchen and I couldn't stop myself. I asked her very quietly, 'That bruise looks painful. Are you okay?'

The flush crept from her neck all the way up to her hairline. It was a beet-red blush – and it left her looking both guilty and completely mortified. If I could have sucked the question back in, I would have done it in a heartbeat, because I had a feeling I didn't want to hear her answer.

'I opened the cupboard door into my eye accidentally. So clumsy,' she said, after a moment's visible panic.

'Ah, that's no good. Accidents do happen,' I remarked, and she nodded, and returned to the dining room.

The conversation with Olivia felt off to me somehow, and the instinct that something more was going on niggled at me. Even as we sang and shared the cake, I found that I couldn't stop staring at the bruise.

Even Wyatt commented it on it after she left.

'Looks like trouble in paradise,' he murmured. 'That bruise was terrible to look at.'

'She said she opened the cupboard door into her eye.'

Wyatt snorted derisively.

'You… you don't think… David did this to her?' I felt guilty for asking that question aloud, and then I felt defensive when Wyatt didn't answer me immediately. 'Wyatt! How could you think that about our son?'

'Ivy, you've got to wonder. She's not *that* bloody clumsy.'

'I won't have you say that!' I hissed. 'David adores her; he'd never hurt her. At least not on purpose!'

'Well, even if he is getting a bit rough with her, it's not exactly our business, is it?' I glared at him in frustration, and Wyatt sighed. 'Love, are you outraged because I'm thinking it – or are you thinking it too and you're just upset because I'm actually *saying* it?'

I stormed off to the kitchen, slamming the pots and plates and generally trying to take my frustration out on the dishes. After a few minutes, Wyatt joined me in the room.

'Don't be pissed at me, Ivy. I'm not suggesting we storm their castle and drag her out of there. It is what it is. Plenty of men get a bit physical with their wives, it doesn't mean he doesn't love her, right? David's always been passionate about his girls, and Liv has really pushed him lately. Things will settle down once they have a kid, you'll see.'

I gnawed at my lip and tried to process this. What did it mean for the way that I saw my son? Could he really be who I *knew* him to be if he was capable of giving his wife an injury like that?

'Love,' Wyatt said suddenly, and he reached across to squeeze my wrist gently. 'It's *their* business, not ours. Don't go getting hysterical about it, okay?'

I nodded, and told myself I wouldn't overreact, but it was all I could think about for the next few days. I told myself it wasn't a big deal. Wyatt had never raised a hand towards me, but I'd certainly known of other men who got a bit rough with their wives from time to time. And Olivia had surely provoked David – hadn't she been pushing and pushing him for the past few years? Forcing him to wait to become a father? Maintaining that job at the clinic even though I *knew* that David would have made it very clear to her that he wanted her to stop working so closely with Sebastian?

The more I considered all of this, the calmer I felt, until I'd digested and accepted this new fact I had discovered about my son, and I could even understand it. I'd known all along that David was intensely passionate about Olivia – I'd known all along that he would do whatever it took to keep his family together. Hadn't I admired that very trait? This was just an extension of his passion for her, a way to *stop* her destructive behaviours before they ruined his marriage.

In fact, the more I thought about it, the more disappointed I was – in Olivia. The story she'd given me was ridiculous, was she trying to insult my intelligence? Or was she hoping I'd see through it and help her?

By the time our next family roast rolled around the next Sunday, I had digested my discovery of this side to David's marriage, and I had even come to terms with it. By then, the bruise had faded a little but was still visible. I waited until Wyatt excused himself to use the bathroom. There was something I needed to do, and I didn't want him to accuse me of meddling.

'Olivia, darling,' I said mildly, as Wyatt disappeared down the hall. 'Would you mind checking on the stove? I have a feeling I left a hot plate on?'

She nodded and rose, and as soon as she left the room, I looked at David and asked calmly, 'That's some bruise on Liv's face. What happened?'

'She tripped on the stairs at home. She can be so clumsy, and she's always too tired after work. The sooner she leaves that job, the better,' David sighed as he shook his head.

There was a sound at the archway that led to the kitchen – a squeak of protest, the faintest of sounds. We both looked up, and Olivia was there, her jaw slack, her face deathly pale against the yellowing bruise around her eye.

She stared right at me, her gaze pleading, and I stared back at her. Did she actually think I would intervene? Chastise him? Call the police?

Did she *really* think I would betray my son – for *her*? I never would, and that's why I exposed her lie. Olivia Gillespie needed to understand where my loyalties were and where they *always* would be.

'I thought you said it was the cupboard door, Olivia?' I said lightly, and now there was a heavy silence that descended on my family dinner table. David looked shell-shocked – the glare he offered Olivia shifted into a slightly nervous glance toward me. I let the silence hang just long enough that *everyone* felt it, but when I saw David open his mouth – no doubt to defend himself or try to excuse the situation – I smiled thinly and chastised Olivia, 'You silly girl. I suppose you must have been *confused*.'

And then I looked right at David, and I raised an eyebrow at him, and his eyes widened. Olivia walked to the table and sat back down, but she barely touched her meal, and she was virtually silent for the rest of the evening. At the door, I gave David my usual hug, and while he was in my embrace I murmured, 'She provoked you, didn't she darling?' I knew he wouldn't deny it. There was no point. We *all* knew the truth now, there was no longer a need for secrecy.

'She pushes me, Mum. This shit about not waiting to have a baby… It just got beyond a joke.'

'Okay, Davey. Just be more careful, you can't afford to have people gossiping.'

'I know. It won't happen again,' David assured me softly.

'It's your marriage, son. You deal with it as you see fit, I'm just telling you – be more discreet.'

CHAPTER 29

Olivia

I wouldn't say I'm bouncing through my days with a spring in my step, but I do feel settled in my new home.

'*Now* can the unscheduled house calls stop? You can't even say you just happened to be driving past any more, I'm on the other side of town now,' I say to Dr Eric when he appears on my doorstep one afternoon.

'Well, this house is just so lovely, I won't mind calling in here from time to time.' At my confused sigh, he slips the stethoscope into his ears and adds gently, 'You'll know when it's time, Olivia. I don't think we're quite there yet, you're still definitely one of my special cases.'

'I really don't like the sound of that, Dr Eric.' I mutter. 'I *am* making progress, right?'

'Oh, you must certainly are, my girl. The entire town is proud of you.'

'And you'd bloody know what the "entire town" thinks too, you old gossip.'

Dr Eric grins at me. 'See? Your fighting spirit is returning. Yet another great sign.'

I can't help but feel surprised by the way that life marches on, and the inevitability of each new day I have to face no longer fills me with fear. Instead, I settle into a routine just as I hoped I would.

On Wednesday, I go into work and I feel like my old self again.

Even though on Thursday, I sit in Natasha's office and I feel fragile, as though if she presses just a little too hard, I'll crack altogether.

'Can we talk about Sebastian again?' she asks me, but gently now. There's no easy history left to fill her in on, only the painful parts. When she asks me, I do try tentatively to take my mind back to those days, but when I do, every part of myself braces as if I'm about to shatter.

'No.'

In spite of this, I feel like I want to work more than just that lonely Wednesday. I tell Sebastian I'll do two days a week from now on, and he doesn't say anything at all, he only nods.

I meet Lulu for lunch often, and sometimes Mum or Dad come along. It's a way of avoiding lunch with Sebastian, who inevitably sits in the kitchen with an empty chair across from him; an unspoken invitation for me to join him. But I have seven years of family time to catch up on, so I continue to meet with my sister and parents as often as they are willing.

People still occasionally take frozen meals to Mum's place for her to bring to me, but my new freezer never really fills up with them, and so I even start shopping at Gillespie's on a regular basis. It's not always pleasant – sometimes there are awkward encounters and uncomfortable reminders. One time when I'm walking the aisles after work, I say a polite hello to Michael Walters, a man I went to school with, and he gives me a slightly strained smile. I don't think too much about this – I'm often on the tail end of pained facial expressions these days, so I keep shopping and get all the way to the checkout before I remember I need bread and have to go back. As I'm walking back to the bakery section I see that Michael is just ahead of me in the aisle. His wife approaches him carrying a bag of flour, and after she sits it in the trolley she falls into step beside him and Michael mutters, 'My God, you're not going to believe who I saw in here five minutes ago. Olivia *Gillespie*. Shopping in here! The hide of the woman.'

'Where is she supposed to shop?' his wife shrugs, but Michael shakes his head disdainfully.

'I heard she was sleeping around behind his back.'

'Well, Peter Wallace's girlfriend works with her sister, and *she* said he used to beat the shit out of her, so God only knows what's true.'

'Please,' Michael scoffs. 'If one of the town councillors was beating his wife, *everyone* would have been talking about it. You can't hide secrets like that in a place like Milton Falls. Besides, even if it was true – I have no sympathy for her. If a man hits his wife once, she should leave, and if she stays – well, she deserves everything she gets after that.'

I feel like the brave thing to do would be to clear my throat and start a conversation with them during which I could lay some home truths on the table and defend myself, but I'm too mortified for that. Instead, I leave my half-loaded trolley in the aisle and ask Louisa to pick me up some bread on her way home from work. For hours afterwards, I wonder if I just happened to overhear a sample set of what the whole town is saying, and if so: can I *really* continue to live here? But by morning, I have calmed myself, and my thoughts return to balance. Most people in town have gone out of their way to be supportive, but of course people are curious, and of course rumours have swirled. It's not pretty, it's not pleasant, but I do need to learn to deal with it, and in the meantime, if someone upsets me and I walk away and leave my trolley, well, it's not the end of the world.

So I make a point of forcing myself to return to the store the next day with Zoe, and I buy the things that I was going to get the previous day. I make a promise to myself that even if I find myself in a situation where I *need* to take a step back every now and again, I'll always find a way to keep moving forward.

Ingrid and I walk in the park some mornings before she goes to work, and we catch up for casual coffees sometimes. One day, she invites me to the movies in Bathurst.

'It's a romcom,' she tells me on the phone. 'Please say you'll come, I'll look pathetic if I go to that kind of movie alone.'

'I haven't really left Zoe at night yet... ' I say, but then I think about how easy it is now to drop her off with Ellen and I say, 'Let me see if Mum can watch her on Friday night. It should be fine.'

Without too much anxiety at all I leave Zoe in Mum and Dad's capable hands. Ingrid and I watch her silly romantic comedy and I eat far too much popcorn, and on the way back, she drives right past the turn-off to the Bush Chapel and I notice that it's dark and exactly the kind of night it was when David proposed to me there. The observation itself isn't all that surprising, but the fact that I manage to make it quite calmly and without completely losing my mind is some kind of achievement in itself. Dr Eric might not think I'm ready to stop being a 'special case', but I know that I am recovering. I still don't exactly know what that means or if there will ever come a day when I feel 'healed', but for now, it's enough that I am definitely moving on.

Then I'm cooking dinner on Saturday night when I hear the doorbell sound. I flick off the stove, scoop Zoe up from the Bumbo chair on the bench and walk to the door to peer through the peephole.

Sebastian?

Something about this visit feels different to the ones he made back at David's house. Perhaps it's a sign that I'm healing, perhaps it's a simple consequence of me getting used to seeing him at work so often. But instead of being anxious about why he's here, I find myself quite delighted with the unannounced visit – and even more so after I swing the door open, and he gives me a sheepish grin as he presents a gift with a flourish.

It's a tiny chocolate Labrador puppy with a ridiculous purple bow around its neck.

'Housewarming present,' he tells me, and then he kicks a box of supplies out from behind the bush so I can see it. I don't know whether to laugh or cry, but I do know that the adorable and terrified looking puppy needs a hug, so I wordlessly pass Zoe to Sebastian and I accept the dog into my arms. I slip the bow off its neck and do a quick once-over along the pup's body out of habit. It's a female, and she's young – probably too young to have left her mother. I open my mouth to ask him, and he holds up a finger in my direction and says pointedly, 'And before you ask, yes she is only five weeks old and she's going to need a lot of care. I had to give the dam a C-section and she didn't bond with the pups, we've been trying to sort it out for weeks but the mother got a bit aggressive with them yesterday and the owners have decided to separate them. It was a big litter and they couldn't care for them all by hand so they asked if I knew anyone who could help out… *but* if you don't want her, I'll keep her myself. So absolutely no pressure.'

The pup cuddles up against my chest and then wriggles until she's found a way inside my hoody, just the tip of her nose visible at the zip. I can't help it – I giggle.

'No pressure from *you,* maybe, but she's made herself right at home. *Get* in here, you big idiot,' I sigh, and I move out of the doorway to grant Sebastian access. He steps around the box, but I point to it with my elbow. 'Bring Zoe in and put her back in the Bumbo, then come back for the box.'

'Does that mean you're keeping Princess Scratchy Paws?' Sebastian grins, and I shake my head.

'That is *not* her name. And I'm not sure yet, but I can definitely cuddle with her while I make up my mind.

Sebastian carefully sits Zoe into the Bumbo, then returns to the front door and brings the box in. He rests it on the table beside Zoe and looks around the kitchen.

'This house is beautiful, Liv. Congratulations.'

'I love it.'

'It has a perfect yard for a dog… lots of room, good fences… '

'I know. I was going to get one anyway once I'd finished settling in here.'

'And you could bring Princess Scratchy Paws to the office once she's had her vaccinations… '

'So I can't bring my baby to work, but I *can* bring my puppy?'

The smile instantly fades from Seb's face. He pauses, and he glances at Zoe, and then back to me.

'*Your* baby?' he asks me softly.

I feel the flush rise across my cheeks. I look away, and I whisper stubbornly, 'Yes, *my* baby.'

I hear Seb sigh a little, but he changes the subject quickly, 'How are you going with it all? It is working okay – with her at the day care?'

'It's hard. But it felt so good to be back at work that it was definitely worth it.'

'Good. It's good to have you back,' Sebastian says, and it's an innocent sentence spoken in an innocent tone, but I see the depth of feeling in his eyes, and I have to look away.

I turn my attention to the dog, who is resting against my breast, already drifting off to sleep. I gently pet behind its ears, then glance back towards Sebastian. The moment has passed, but I keep the conversation moving away from it by asking, 'What should I name my puppy?'

'Princess Scratchy Paws,' he says, and he lifts his hand to show me a long scratch from his thumb towards his elbow. I wince but shake my head.

'I'm not calling my dog "Princess Scratchy Paws". Besides, she was just practising for her illustrious future career as my guard dog.'

'You should call her Milo.'

'Milo?' I repeat blankly.

'You know, for the drink. I remember that you used to drink it all the time when you were pregnant; she's exactly the same colour as the granules.'

I'm actually amazed the Sebastian remembers me drinking the hot chocolate drink at the office, but he's right, I did drink several cups of it a day, and when I glance down at the puppy, I see that he's right about the colour too – her soft fur is exactly that shade of warm brown. There was seemingly endless tension in my life at that stage, but those quiet moments in the kitchen at work were brief glimpses of peace.

If I follow this chain of thought forward or back, I'll get to the ugliness that came before and after those moments, but if I consider that set of memories in isolation, they are comfortable – *comforting* memories.

'That's actually perfect,' I say, then I say softly to the dog, 'Well, welcome to the family, Milo.' I glance at Sebastian. 'She's such a thoughtful gift. Thank you.'

'I wasn't sure if you were ready, but she couldn't really wait to find a new mumma, so I figured it was worth the risk.' Sebastian stands and surveys the chicken fillet and vegetables half-cooked on the stove. 'I should get out of your hair… '

'No… ' I surprise myself when I say the word, and when I pause and reflect on it, I'm even more surprised to realise how much I want him to stay. Sebastian glances at me questioningly, and I try to maintain a nonchalant shrug. 'Stay a while. Let's order in pizza.'

'Are you sure? I don't want to intrude.'

'Any more than you already have?' I laugh as I gesture towards the pup in my shirt with my chin, and Sebastian shrugs easily.

'Exactly.'

'You can pay for the pizza then.'

He stares at me, and I see that Seb has aged in the last few months – just as I have. He glances away, only briefly, and I see him hesitate. I'm just about to claw back the suggestion – I feel embarrassment rising at the idea that he might reject my offer, and I'm about to apologise when Seb's face is transformed by a soft smile as he says, 'Deal.'

✦ ✦ ✦

I can't help but think about David as I share an easy, relaxed evening with Sebastian, but my thoughts are calm. I reflect on how impossible this would have been if David were still alive. Seb and I socialise – *gently*. He sits well away from me, and even when the pizza arrives he manages to serve it up on plates for each of us without so much as brushing my hand. He sits on the other couch when I put the television on, and although he relaxes into it, he even points his legs away from me when he stretches them out.

Our conversation stays well within safe territory – we mostly discuss work – but we are *alone together* outside of work. We've only ever done that once before; about this time last year, actually. I look over to Seb, who is engrossed in the terrible action movie that happened to come on the channel I picked, but *I* start to sink into the memory of that other time that he and I actually managed something like privacy.

My mental brakes slam on with force.

Don't go there, Olivia.

I have to resist those thoughts because I know that even letting myself recall what happened between us then might just open a Pandora's box of issues that I can't deal with just yet. But I do *really* like having him there with me, hanging out on the couch like old friends. Sebastian's presence still means happiness for me, and that's actually close to a miracle.

'Thanks for coming over tonight, Seb,' I say suddenly, and he glances at me and smiles.

'No worries, Livvy.'

God, how I've missed him. I've missed his quiet presence in my life for an entire year, because even though I worked with him for some of that time, we effectively hit the pause button on our relationship after our fateful night in Sydney. I missed connecting with him, intellectually and emotionally – Sebastian McNiven had given me a glimpse into what it would be like to be in a relationship with someone who was truly, honestly a good person. And it was just a glimpse, because we never even stood a chance. What would it be like to build a life with someone like Seb? To wake up every day in the arms of someone who trusted me to run my own life, but loved me enough to support me while I did it?

Do I even deserve that, after everything I've done?

Do I deserve it – after everything I've done to Seb?

And then comes the guilt, and it swamps me, and suddenly, my happy, contented mood evaporates, and all I can think about is getting up from my chair and going to the medicine cabinet and taking one of Dr Eric's sleeping pills.

I glance at Sebastian again, and although he must have no idea at all what I am thinking, he looks back at me and offers me a reassuring smile. My butterflies rise at the easy smile, and right on their heels is a tidal wave of shame that I know all too well could actually destroy me.

'Sebastian, I need to go bed,' I say, and I sit up, awkwardly bringing the dog and Zoe with me. 'You should go.'

Sebastian stands, but I can see the bewilderment in his gaze as he takes a step towards me. 'Are you okay?'

'I'm fine.' I shrug my shoulders to show him that my arms are full and it's going to be awkward to stand and walk him to the door. 'Could you see yourself out so I don't have to disturb these two? Thanks again, and goodnight.' My tone is dismissive, but that somehow makes *him* look guilty, which isn't fair and it's not right because he's virtually blameless in all of this.

His only crime was to love me, and even then, he never put demands on me.

'I'm sorry, Livvy,' Seb says, and he looks so awkward now, reaching up to cup his neck in the palm of his hand. 'You've got so much on your plate – the last thing you needed was for me to come here tonight and upset you.'

'No, I liked you coming over, and I am *not* upset,' I protest a little too hard, and when I look at Sebastian, his expression twists. Now he brushes both of his hands through his hair; he's increasingly distressed with every second that passes. Suddenly I see that it's all too much for *him* to bear, and while that's sweet – it's also bewildering.

I am heartbroken, and I'm still shocked, and I'm still grieving – but all of that is natural, and given what I've been through, I *am* exactly where I need to be.

'Really,' I repeat myself because he looks so devastated and I want to console him. 'I just need to go to bed, I'm not upset.'

Sebastian bends and he brushes a soft kiss against my forehead, and then just as I asked him to, he walks right out of my house. I am alone with the puppy and my daughter who might just be *our* daughter, and even as I let myself think that thought, I become quite disoriented. I'm there on the couch in my daze when Louisa unlocks the front door and lets herself in as she calls, 'Hey, it's just me. Thought I'd have a sleepover.'

My sister walks into the lounge room and I see that she's already in her pyjamas. I shake myself a little, and I sigh as I ask her, 'Why are you really here?'

She contemplates this for a moment, then she admits, 'Sebastian rang me.'

'Jesus, Louisa. Do I have *any* privacy?'

'He said he upset you.'

'He *didn't* upset me.'

'Well, *he* sounded pretty upset. Do you want to talk about it?'

'I distinctly do *not* want to talk about it.'

'No worries. Cute puppy. Can I hold it?'

While Louisa cuddles with Milo, I take Zoe down the hall, intending to rest her in my bed. As I'm lowering her down into the sheets, the cot catches my eye.

Milo is going to cry all night if I don't hold her close to me, and I can't really have the baby *and* the puppy in the bed at the same time. Just for a few nights, Zoe won't mind being demoted back to her own bed. I walk over the cot, and for the first time in two months, I lower my daughter very gently onto her own sheets.

❖ ❖ ❖

'… talk about today?'

I feel like Natasha is talking to me through a wall on Monday morning. I don't usually see her on Mondays, but I wasn't sure I could go to work on Wednesday if I didn't talk to her first, so I called and I asked for an emergency appointment and now I'm here and I'm not sure why.

'Olivia, are you okay?' she asks me carefully, and I shake myself and sit up a little straighter.

'Thanks for seeing me today.'

'I just asked you what you wanted to talk about today. My receptionist said that you sounded a little distressed on the phone, that's why I squeezed you in.'

'I wasn't distressed,' I insist. 'I just… I have a dog now. Her name is Milo.'

Natasha raises an eyebrow. 'Congratulations.'

'Sebastian gave her to me.'

That gets her attention.

'Oh?'

'He came to my house and we had pizza.'

'And how was that?'

'Absolutely wonderful right up until I asked him to leave.'

'Oh.'

'It's only the second time I've ever seen him outside of work. I mean, there were Christmas parties and that kind of thing, but David was always there – always *right* at my side if Sebastian was around.'

'Do you want to talk about Sebastian some more today, Olivia?' Natasha asks me gently, and I panic a little.

'I don't know.'

'Why don't you just start by telling me a little about that other time you saw him outside of work?'

'Okay,' I say. I'll just tell her the basics; try to stick to safe territory like I did last time we discussed Seb. I'll talk until I need to stop and then I'll just go home. I am in control of this discussion, Natasha won't push me past what I can handle – she's proven that now. 'It was this time last year, at a vet conference in the city. I needed to go – it was always hard to get enough continuing professional-development points for my registration because David never wanted me to go away. So I went to that conference every year, and David usually went with me. But not that time.'

Sebastian had messed up the dates on a holiday he'd planned with his brother – he'd double-booked himself, he said. He told me he wasn't going to make the conference, and once he knew that I was going alone, David decided to stay home. When I walked into the opening session of the conference and saw Sebastian seated right near the entrance, I was bewildered.

'Aren't you supposed to be skiing with Alistair in Japan?' I asked as I took the seat he'd saved for me. My heart was racing, because I knew what this meant.

I *could* flirt with Seb when we were at the office because I knew it couldn't go anywhere… But now we had three days alone together, four hours away from David.

'I got back yesterday,' Seb shrugged. I stared at him.

'Did something happen?'

'No,' he said.

'But… why didn't you tell me you'd be here?'

'It just slipped my mind,' he said, but I didn't believe that for an instant. I was anxious, but I was also pleased because I was greedy. I wanted to see Seb more. I wanted to *be* with him. I wanted the chance to see where things led us, if only we had the chance. But had he manipulated this? Was he expecting sex?

What would I do if he was?

'Dinner?' he said casually, when the day's formalities drew to a close, and I nodded silently.

We agreed on the restaurant in the lobby of the hotel, and over entrées I took a deep breath and asked, 'Seb, why did you tell me you wouldn't be here?'

He hesitated, then he silently poured me a glass of wine, and pushed it across the table. 'I knew if I told you I'd be here, David would come to the city with you, and I needed to get you alone.'

'Alone?' I'd whispered, and I took the wine into my hand but had to immediately lower it back onto the tablecloth because I was shaking. When I looked back to Seb, he was staring at me, and I started to feel sick.

He was either going to directly address the way our relationship had changed, or he was going to directly challenge me about David.

I wasn't sure which was worse.

For all of Seb's gently probing questions about my minor injuries over the year or so before that, there was one he had never asked. David had given me that hideous black eye just a month or so before that very conference, and Seb had never mentioned it once, which had confused me at the time. I'd seen the question on his lips every time we spoke for the entire fortnight it took to fade.

'Olivia, I'm scared for you,' he whispered over dinner, and the rawness in his voice was unbearable. I was mortified – and I just couldn't hear it, so I tried to brush the conversation away before it even began.

'Seb, I am absolutely fine, please—'

'No. Hear me out,' he choked the words as if he was struggling to breathe, and that disarmed me completely, so I sat in silent horror as he brought my secret shame right out into the open, there in a crowded, candle-lit restaurant in a five-star hotel in Sydney. 'Didn't you wonder why I didn't ask how you got that black eye, Livvy?'

I stared at him, and he stared right back at me. Our gazes spoke of all of the things we couldn't quite say yet. *I'm worried for you, Liv. I'm scared too, Seb. Please, can you trust me, talk to me? No, I can't. It's too dangerous.*

But I didn't answer his question aloud, and after a while, Seb whispered, 'I just couldn't bear to watch you lie to me again.' I looked away then, until Seb continued quietly. 'You don't just bruise easily and he doesn't come with you when you have overnight emergency calls because he's protective – he does it because he's controlling. I've seen the way he treats you, I've heard the way he talks to you – and I've tried to mind my own business but I swear to God I just can't stand to see one more bruise on your body, Olivia.' Seb was shaking too by then, and there was a desperate pain in his gaze as he whispered, 'Help me understand – why don't you just leave him?'

'It's not that easy,' I said, and Seb reached across the table and he rested his hand over mine, very gently and very tenderly. I looked down at it, terrified, and then I looked around the room – half expecting David to storm in out of nowhere.

Seb dragged my gaze back to his when he squeezed my hand lightly and breathed, 'Of course it it's that simple, Olivia. If you want to get out, I'll help you get out.'

I withdrew my hand all the way to my lap, to hide it beneath the white-linen tablecloth. 'He'd kill you, Seb – he'd kill me. He's already jealous of you—'

'I'm doing this as a friend, not as anything else.' I wasn't sure how I felt about that statement, until Seb sighed and admitted uneasily, 'Look, I'm not going to insult your intelligence by pretending I don't have feelings for you – I know it's become pretty obvious that I do, but I promise you, that's not what this is about. I just can't keep silent any more – but there's no ulterior motive for this intervention. I only want for you to be safe.'

'I can't,' I choked, and Sebastian leant forward over the table and he stared right into my eyes as he repeated, 'Help me understand, Liv. Do you love him?'

'Of course I do,' I said, and even now I don't know if I was lying when I said it that night. The love I'd had for David had faded over the years, and what was left was a habitual closeness and a confused resentment... a tired acceptance, some kind of variation on Stockholm Syndrome. I was so convinced by then that I was the cause of all of David's anger issues that I no longer even resisted his fits of rage, because at that stage, I honestly believed I both deserved and inspired them. That was part of the way that David played me like a puppet – transferring the responsibility and then guilt to me for *his* behaviour by always, always reiterating to me after he hurt me that I had provoked it.

'But he does hurt you, doesn't he?' Seb had whispered urgently to me, and I started to cry. No one had ever directly confronted it before – not even Ivy, although she'd made it *clear* that she knew and wasn't going to intervene. Hearing the words aloud filled me with a shame so intense that I almost couldn't stand it. Sebastian tried to comfort me, but when the tears turned to sobs, he gently led me back to my room and arranged for our meals to be brought up to us. We sat at the little dining room table and it was awkward at first, because I felt so ashamed that I could barely look at him.

Until that night, I had actually convinced myself that I'd hidden it all so well, but Sebastian had seen right through me, and he was the last person in the world I wanted to know what really going on. I wanted him to respect me and admire me, not to see me as the pitiful, weak woman I really was.

'Explain it, then,' he said, when I eventually pulled myself together. 'Explain to me why the smartest woman I know would put up with that shit.'

'He doesn't mean to; it usually happens when I provoke him—'

'Bullshit.'

'Seb,' I pleaded with him to understand. 'I—'

'Don't waste your breath, Olivia, because there is nothing you could say or do that would ever convince me that statement is true.'

'He loves me so much that sometimes he loses control of himself.'

'That is not *love*!' Sebastian gasped.

That realisation was depressing, and I slumped in my chair and admitted, 'I can't leave, even if I wanted to. Where would I even go?'

'I can think of half a dozen places off the top of my head. The refuge in Bathurst. Your mother's house. Louisa's apartment. Gilly's house – fuck, any of the nurses would take you in. And then there's my house, and you would *always* be safe there. If you want to get out, there'll be a way. And you won't be alone, Livvy – I'll be with you every step of the way.'

'I'd lose everything, Seb. He has all of our money – everything is in his name. I need his authorisation for a *bank balance*, for God's sakes.'

'So you'd start over. I'd help you. It would take me two minutes to move your salary payments to a new account. Livvy – surely you realise that I'd *give* you money if you needed it.'

'I'd have to leave town. I'd have to start over alone.'

'Why?'

'David *is* Milton Falls. He's on the town council – he's the president of the football club – his dad owns the supermarket – he's got a finger in every pie – everyone knows him – everyone loves him—'

'No, they don't. I see through him, and others will too – especially if you leave. You have nothing to be ashamed of, Olivia – none of this is your fault. You can rebuild your life. Let me help you.'

'I *can't* let you get involved in this.'

Seb sighed, and he raked his hand through his hair, then he looked right into my eyes and he whispered, 'Olivia, I'm already involved in this. There is nothing in the world more important to me than knowing that you're safe.'

I couldn't face the depth of his feelings for me right then, and he didn't try to force me to. Instead, we talked about David, and my options. For every obstacle I threw up, Seb would talk me through how I could get around it; until each of the things that I had convinced myself were insurmountable over the years suddenly felt like holograms. I realised that night for the very first time that the biggest obstacle to my freedom was going to be my own mind.

We talked for hours, and just as the sun started to rise, the periods of silence between our words grew longer and longer and our eyes were gradually sinking closed. I'd moved to the bed and was lying against the pillows, Seb was stretched out on the couch. Just as I started to fall asleep, I thought I heard a sound at the door, and I sat up in a rush – my chest tight, the room shrinking in around me – my terror and my panic coursing through my blood.

Seb was on his feet in an instant, and he approached me on the bed. He silently wrapped his arms around me, and pulled me gently against his chest.

'He's not going to hurt you, Livvy. Not ever again. I'm going to keep you safe.'

I texted David a little while later and told him I was at an early breakfast meeting and I'd call him later in the day between sessions. Then I slept in Sebastian's arms, and when I woke at lunchtime, we ordered room service. I had an eye on the door at all times and, eventually, I knew I had to call David so he wouldn't get suspicious about my silence.

We sat at the little table with our dirty lunch dishes in between us and Seb stared at me while I spoke to my husband. On an ordinary day, at least via a phone call, I'd never have been afraid to talk to David, but that day I was, because my whole perspective on my fucked-up marriage was shifting back into focus. I hadn't let myself question it in so long – but Seb had forced me to rethink everything I thought I knew about David and I hated what I saw. So while Seb stared at me, I stared at the food debris on my fork and my lunch churned in my stomach and I tried to keep the fear from my voice as I lied about the sessions I'd been to that day and the breakfast meeting I had supposedly shared with other female vets. When David said I must be bored and lonely at night without him there, I said yes, yes I was, and when he told me he loved me I echoed it back and then I hung up the phone.

And I knew then that I couldn't do it any more – that there were countless alternative futures for me – and that they were actually all just within my reach, if I dared to stretch out towards them. As I thought about that, I sat the phone down on the table next to my plate, and then I reached across the crockery and I took Seb's hand in mine, and I said, 'I need to leave him, don't I?'

He didn't say anything at all, he just lifted my hand and he pressed it against his cheek, and there were tears in his eyes, and then there were tears in mine.

Later, we finished the bottle of wine from that first night's dinner, and he cuddled me until I fell asleep again on the bed. We hadn't left my hotel room in twenty-four hours by that stage, and we'd somehow run out of words – we were just together, and it was gentle and sweet and completely innocent.

The next morning, Sebastian went back to his room to change, and I dressed too, and we went to the final day's session of the conference as if nothing had even happened. That night, we went to the banquet and we networked with colleagues and then when the night was over, I followed into the elevator and I pressed the button for his floor level.

'I'm going to stay with you tonight, if that's okay.'

'Of course it is,' he said, but I saw the way that his eyebrows knitted and I knew that he was nervous about my intentions, right from the start.

Sebastian wasn't a reluctant participant in what happened that night, but he was very concerned that he was taking advantage of me – constantly breaking away from me to ask me if I was sure – to try to talk me out of it – to say that maybe we should wait until I'd had a chance to think. But I'd done so much thinking already, all I wanted to do that night was feel, and my God, did I do that. It wasn't even about the pleasure, it was about the freedom of being with someone who *saw* me and the power of initiating it all myself – the thrill of controlling the direction it took and the things we did. Sex with David had gradually become a punishment by that stage – something he took from me. But sex with Seb… maybe I was the abuser that night, because perhaps I did love him, but much more than that, I was using him to make myself feel powerful again.

'How do you feel about Sebastian now, Olivia?' Natasha asks me. My throat feels sore because I've just spoken and sobbed more in the last fifty-four minutes than I have in *all* of our sessions over these past weeks.

'Numb,' I croak. 'Scared. Ashamed. What do I *say* to him?'

'Are there things you need to say?' she asks me softly.

'I'm scared once I start putting those things into words, everything is going to fall to pieces.'

'What happens if you don't say the words, though? What does it feel like when you hold those things in?'

'It feels like *surviving*.'

'Surviving is an action, not a feeling.'

'Do you think I should talk to him?'

'Only you know if you're ready to do that, Olivia. But I think realising that you might *want* to talk to him about this is something of a breakthrough for you.'

It's incredibly unprofessional of me to do so, but I go directly from Natasha's rooms to Sebastian's office in the clinic. His door is closed, but I peek through the window and I see he's just staring at his computer screen. He's not even typing, he's just staring, his gaze vacant.

I push the door open and say, 'I used you that night in the city. You should hate me.'

He looks up at me in shock. 'I could never hate you, Olivia.'

Seb rises and he walks behind me to gently push the door closed, and then he steers me very carefully towards the visitor's chairs. There's one right next to me, but he doesn't take it – instead he perches on the edge of his desk, away from me.

'Zoe… ' My throat constricts, and I can't even force myself to say the words. 'Seb… Zoe… she… '

'Livvy,' Sebastian speaks very gently, and then a sound comes from his throat – a slightly strangled sob. He clears his throat and gives me a helpless look. 'Sweetheart, I figured it out for myself, I'm not an idiot.'

'I just… I wasn't sure… I still don't know. She could be his… '

When I told him I was pregnant, I lied to Sebastian about how far along I was. I had no choice. Zoe was due on a Friday – exactly forty weeks after the Friday we spent together in city. If I'd given him the true due-date, he'd have known for sure. Still, he wasn't an idiot and he'd had his suspicions anyway.

'She wasn't born two weeks early, was she?' Seb whispers, and I shake my head and admit the truth.

'No, she was late. They were going to induce me.'

Seb draws in a sharp breath, then he slowly exhales. I wait, battling the part of myself that wants to brace for anger with the part that knows Seb would never hurt me. After a while, he simply says, 'Okay.'

'Is that all you're going to say?'

'What do you want me to say, honey?'

The endearment doesn't move me – the way he says the word does. *Honey*, like I'm the sweetest thing in the world to him, and I don't deserve that kind of affection.

'Be *angry* with me, Sebastian!' I exclaim. 'I've kept your daughter from you!'

'Olivia,' he says gently. 'I am *not* David. Even if I felt angry with you, I'd *never* take it out on you. And in this case… ' he breaks off, and I watch his Adam's apple bob up and down as he swallows several times. 'Liv, I have nothing but compassion for you. After what you've been through, I can't judge you.' He shrugs and shakes his head. 'I just can't.'

Compassion. Oh God, he is just too wonderful, and I owe him so many apologies and explanations that I don't even know where to start. I stare at Sebastian, and there is real *love* in me for him – it's strong and it's beautiful and I can actually *feel* it, it's broader even than the permanent numbness I'm still conscious of some days. And when I think about that love, I realise I have to start somewhere to at least *try* to explain, and so I take a deep breath and admit, 'I tried to leave him.'

Sebastian is staring at me with fear in his eyes, as if this conversation is spinning out of control and he's scared of where it might land. I know the feeling all too well – it's exactly the same way I've looked at Natasha every time she's said the word 'Sebastian' in our sessions. But just like all of those other times with her when I dared to speak about Seb, I know it's safe for me to press forward with this chat now.

Because just like with Natasha, when I talk to Sebastian, *I* am in control of where the conversation goes.

'I came back to Milton Falls the day after the conference, and I went to the police,' I say steadily, and Sebastian slides from the desk and finally joins me in the visitor's chairs. He doesn't touch me – there's still distance between us but he's closer now – close enough that I can catch a hint of his scent when I inhale. He's staring at the floor.

'Why didn't you tell me that?' he asks eventually.

'I wanted to take out a restraining order. I wanted to do it by myself, I wanted to prove to myself that I was strong enough – I knew that was the only way I'd get *and* stay away from him. But the police… they told me I should try to sort it out with him. The sergeant on duty knew David from the football team, and he really didn't want to know… he said it was a personal matter. Then they called him, and he came to the station, and they left us alone in the interview room to talk.'

'Christ, Olivia… '

'David didn't hurt me that time. He just told me that if I tried to leave him he would kill himself. He'd threatened me with a lot of things, but he'd *never* said that before. He cried, and he begged me to stay, and I just didn't know what to do. He promised me he was going to do better. And I was always scared after that, because, well – what if he *did* hurt himself, and I had to live the rest of my life knowing it was my fault?' I laugh. I'm trying for wry, but the sound escapes unevenly and I sound a little hysterical. Seb looks at me in alarm. 'Well, that kind of guilt would be enough to drive a person insane, wouldn't it?'

'Liv, none of this is your fault.'

'I stayed, Seb. I stayed with him. That's what makes it all my fault. Not what happened between you and me, but because I didn't have the courage to leave him.'

'And now?' Sebastian asks me unevenly. 'Where are you up to *now*, Liv?' His gaze drops to my arms, where my daughter – maybe *our* daughter – is safe against my chest. There are tears on his cheeks, rolling down towards the tidy hair of his beard, and his gaze is wild – he's desperate. The depth of his feelings catches me by surprise, and I wish I could comfort him, but I can't. I don't know how to or if I have a right to, because all of his pain is my fault. David only cried when he wanted to manipulate me. I know that these tears Sebastian is shedding are without agenda, and that makes them completely and utterly heartbreaking. I stare into his eyes, and I recognise grief there – *grief*. He's not grieving for David – he loathed David. Is Seb grieving for me, and what we might have shared? Or is this pure empathy for my pain and for *my* loss?

The thought strikes me suddenly, and I sit up straighter, tensing. Seb is beside himself – and that makes *no* sense at all. *Why is Sebastian crying?*

Natasha's words float through my consciousness.

I want you to think about that shame, and ask yourself what's behind it.

'I don't know,' I say, and then I stand as the panic overwhelms me. He watches silently as I walk to the door, almost tripping over in my haste to leave the room.

I want you to think about that shame, and ask yourself what's behind it.

Not yet. I can't yet.

My hands are shaking. It takes three increasingly jerky attempts before the door swings open for me. I stand in the doorway and I cuddle my daughter tightly against me and I mutter, 'I have to get her home; I've been out with her all morning.'

'Okay, Livvy,' Sebastian says quietly, and he rises and rubs his face with both hands. I can't look at him any more, so I angle my body halfway into the hallway.

'You know where I am if you need anything,' he whispers. I meet his gaze one last time, and there's an agonising twist in my gut.

'I'll see you Wednesday.'

CHAPTER 30

Ivy

A few months after David's birthday, Olivia and David had news.

'All aboard for grandparent station,' David announced.

'I thought you weren't even trying yet!' I gasped.

'Kicked a goal on the first attempt,' he winked at me. 'I have champion swimmers.'

'We're not telling anyone else yet,' Olivia added hastily. 'It's still very, very early days.'

'Totally understandable,' I said, but I hugged her tightly. 'But I am absolutely sure everything is going to be fine. Just let me know when I can let the cat out of the bag.'

I was so excited for the future. With Olivia and David and their baby just around the corner, I knew I'd see my grandchild often – maybe every day, if they invited me to babysit, and I was *really* hoping they would. I offered, explicitly, on more than one occasion. I so vividly remembered the early months and years with David, and how fulfilled and how happy I had been with him toddling around behind me. I imagined doing that all over again – with his child.

Olivia seemed so happy, too – she visited me on her own a few times, for the first time ever. Her relationship with her parents was inexplicably distant, and had become more so over the course of their marriage. I knew she was missing her own mother, and I was more than happy to fulfil the role when she let me. The last of my ill feelings towards Olivia disappeared during those moments. For the very first time, instead of feeling like I'd lost my son to her, I felt like I'd gained a daughter.

We talked about pregnancies, she shared with me the woes of morning sickness; I told her that it would pass. When the baby started moving, I wasted so much time trying to feel the tiny kicks, long before they could be felt from the outside. She'd come and sit at my kitchen bench, and I'd make her a Milo, and she'd sip it slowly – sometimes over a whole hour – and we'd talk, if not about the pregnancy, then about all of the trials and tribulations that were coming ahead of her – about the early days of having a baby in the house, about the challenges of toddlers, and the joys of parenting. I loved that she thought to ask me questions, like suddenly all of the wisdom I'd acquired – wisdom that seemed to go to waste because I'd only had one child – well, maybe it was going to use after all. Olivia listened intently, and I felt valued and special that they were including me in the pregnancy in this way.

As the months passed, and her belly started to grow, she moved from her clinical role into a more administrative one. It was no longer practical for her to be lifting pets, or working with livestock – but she was still unwilling to leave her job. David muttered and mumbled about this, but perhaps the truce between them was fragile – because he never again raised it in any visible, difficult way – at least in front of Wyatt and me. When Olivia announced her intention to continue in this new role right up until the birth, I saw the thunderous look on David's face, but he held his tongue. I knew I had to intervene.

'Olivia, you really should reconsider that – you'll need a break before the baby comes.'

'I'll think about it,' she said.

We heard second-hand that she'd broken her wrist. One of the nurses who treated her at the emergency ward saw Wyatt at the store a few days after it happened and asked how she was going, and he had no idea what she was talking about but managed to bluff his way into gleaning at least a part of the picture. It was a startling breach of confidentiality, but not at all a surprise in a town like Milton Falls.

'Do we go see her?' I asked Wyatt.

He shrugged. 'No idea.'

We went for a walk together with the dogs that night and stopped in to ring the doorbell.

'Oh, hi,' David answered it, but he stood right in the doorway as if he wasn't going to invite us in. 'What's up?'

'Hello, darling,' I said brightly. 'We heard Olivia had an accident… just thought we'd come to see how she was going.'

'Who told you that?' David asked.

'One of the staff at the store saw you two at emergency,' Wyatt said quietly, and I glanced at him, confused about the half-truth.

'Yes, it's fractured,' David sighed. 'Terrible timing, but at least the cast should be off before the baby comes.'

'Was it the stairs again?' Wyatt asked, and David glanced behind him, then nodded.

'I told you – that job was exhausting her. She's clumsy at the best of times. Look, she's quite tired tonight – I'd better go keep an eye on her.'

'Well, let us know if you need anything,' I said, and David nodded curtly as he closed the door. Wyatt and I walked to the edge of the driveway before I murmured,

'Why did you tell him one of *our* staff saw them?'

'Did you see the look on his face? He's got a black cloud floating over his bloody head, Ivy. I wasn't about to get that poor nurse fired just because she wanted to make sure Liv was okay.'

'Do you think he did it?' I asked Wyatt quietly.

He shrugged. 'We've been over this, love. My position on David's marriage is unchanged. When it comes to their personal business, I don't think anything.'

❖ ❖ ❖

For the remaining three months of her pregnancy, David and Olivia's relationship seemed to settle down completely. Those signs of trouble all but faded away, and we were all completely focused on the anticipation of the birth again. But the due date came and went, and to everyone's frustration, two weeks later there was still no sign at all that Olivia was going to go into labour.

'They've booked me in for an induction tomorrow,' Olivia called me one night to let me know.

'And how are you feeling?'

'Fat, tired, and impatient,' she laughed.

'Curry for dinner, sex before sleep and *good luck*, Olivia. I can't wait to see that grandbaby tomorrow,' I breathed, and Olivia laughed again and said goodnight.

David called us at 7 a.m. the next day to tell us that Olivia's water had broken and that they were in the hospital. He sounded exhausted, and we assumed at first that he'd been up all night with her.

'So how many hours has it been?' I asked urgently, and Wyatt was on the other side of the phone, both of us trying unsuccessfully to press our ears against the earpiece at once. At first, I missed David's answer, and so I pushed my husband away, and pressed the phone fully to my ear.

'It only just happened,' David said, and then he groaned. 'Mum, she's already in so much pain – I don't know what to do. I didn't think it would be like this.'

'She's going to be fine, David,' I said firmly. 'Women have been doing this for millennia. Olivia will find her instincts, and she'll get through this.'

'I want her to take the drugs,' David muttered, and I laughed.

'Well, that's up to her. But there aren't any drugs available for you, so you better pull yourself together and get back in there.'

I paced up and down the hall so many times that day that I'm surprised I didn't wear a hole in the tiles. I was more anxious than I'd ever been in my entire life, and when the phone rang again just after 1 p.m., I answered it before it had a chance to even ring a second time.

'Is everyone okay?' I asked, without waiting for David to identify himself.

'We are,' he laughed weakly. 'And *she's* beautiful, Mum – come on – get down here. Meet your granddaughter.'

Zoe Joy Gillespie was a work of art from the first moment I laid eyes on her. She was plump, at nearly nine pounds, with a thin sprinkle of hair on her skull. I sobbed hopelessly as I took her into my arms for the first time. Olivia, resting on the bed at that stage, had that exhausted, satisfied look on her face that I remembered myself from David's birth – the feeling of having sprinted up a mountain only to find that it was actually the entrance to a brand new world of love.

David hovered close to me, staring at his daughter almost in disbelief while I took dozens of photos of her on my phone. I looked between my son and his wife and for the first time, I thought about all that they had, and I was simply happy for them. I was no longer jealous of Olivia, I was grateful to her.

I had a new role to adopt, and I'd been missing that sense of importance ever since David had grown to the point that he no longer needed me. This little one was going to need me, she was going to need her nan when she needed consolation after she hurt her knee, she was going to ask me endless questions that would make my mind hurt, she was going to rush to me and ask for a lolly as soon as she came in through my front door – because I could, and I *would* spoil her rotten. I looked forward to babysitting her overnight so that her parents could have some alone time, I looked forward to long afternoons with her while she played with my pups, or frolicked in the garden. I looked forward to the Christmas mornings, when she would be so lost in a sea of wrapping paper, and birthday parties that we could make into world class events – particularly given that I'd recently discovered Pinterest and I couldn't wait to spoil her with over-the-top celebrations.

Zoe was the future – *all of our futures* – and she was here, and she was safe. As I walked out the door of the hospital that day, I was positively floating on air.

I hadn't felt so alive in decades.

CHAPTER 31

Olivia

'And how was yesterday at work?' Natasha asks me on Thursday morning at our regular appointment.

'Professional,' I say. 'I shouldn't have had that conversation with him in his office on Monday, so I went out of my way to keep things proper yesterday.'

'So I think you only told me half of the story before we ran out of time on Monday. You said that you and Sebastian spent the night together in the city, and then you came back and tried to go to the police – you didn't tell me how Sebastian handled you going straight back to David.'

'He tried to call me while I was driving back from the city to the police station. I deflected his calls, but he kept calling so I turned the phone off.'

'Why was that?'

'I wanted him to be proud of me. I wanted to be able to ring him to tell him that I had taken out the restraining order and that I was leaving David. I knew it was all going to be terrifying – but I'd been terrified for so long – all I wanted was to get myself back into Seb's arms, because I hadn't felt that happy in forever.'

But then after that plan went to hell, when I was back home and things with David in such a delicate, fragile balance, I turned the phone on only long enough to send Seb a text message which I immediately deleted.

It was a mistake, Seb. I'm really sorry. David is my husband, and I love him. Please, can we just forget this ever happened? I'm fine, and I know what I'm doing – respect my decision. Please don't text back.

'*Did* he text back?' Natasha asks me quietly.

'No, but… David was so clingy to me that day, he wouldn't let me out of his sight and when he saw I had the phone he took it,' I whispered.

'Did he do that often?'

'Always. I was so used to David going through my phone, it didn't even occur to me to ask him why or to resist. I just sat there frozen and I prayed that Seb *could* resist the urge to call me or text back – I wasn't sure what he'd do. David went through my phone for a while then he told me it needed an update and he went into the office to download something, and I spent the next half hour sweating through my clothes because I thought David would find some magic way to undelete text messages.'

'What was David doing with your phone, Olivia?'

'I didn't know at first. I thought he really was updating it. He came back later and he gave me the phone and he cuddled me and he told me that he thought things were going to be better between us – that we were about to start a whole new era of our lives.'

When I got to work the following Monday, Sebastian flicked me a quick glance, but he didn't hold my gaze. It was awkward for a while, but he didn't try to change my mind.

I knew he'd respect my decision, even if he hated it.

'And when you realised you were pregnant?' Natasha asks me now.

'Well, Zoe really could be David's *or* Sebastian's baby. I had no way of knowing, and I knew I couldn't leave David. So for all of our sakes, I just had to pretend there was no doubt she was his.'

I kept the pregnancy a secret for as long as I could, and when I finally told everyone at work, I did it over morning tea so that I didn't have to face Seb alone. While the girls all cheered, Seb stared at me in shock, and so then I made a point of telling them all that my due date was a month later than it really was.

'Did he have doubts?' Natasha asks.

'I didn't think so at first. But then one day he just walked into my office and he shut the door and he asked me point-blank if the baby was his.'

'What did you say?'

'I lied about my due date – I told him I was four weeks earlier along than I was. He made me look him in the eye and promise him.'

'How did you feel while you were doing that?'

'Pretty much like I feel when I think about it now,' I admit miserably. 'Like the worst person in the world.'

'Did you think about telling him the truth?'

'I knew if I did that he would convince me in seconds to leave David, and that Sebastian would find a way to keep me safe.'

Natasha tries to hide her surprise, but fails. 'So why *didn't* you?'

'I was scared that David would go through with his threat – and you know, as much as he was a nightmare – he was also my husband, and I didn't always *hate* him – the idea of him doing that to himself… ' My chest tightens, and I reach for a tissue. I hold it in my hands while I calm myself, and then I whisper, 'I was just stuck. If I told Seb, I'd end up leaving with him, and the best case outcome was a bad one because David would harass us forever anyway, and the worst case scenario was… well, what happened.'

'When did you leave work?'

'It was that day, actually, because later that night, David was working in the study while I cooked dinner and Seb sent me a text. It just said something like *I don't believe you, we need to talk*, and I deleted it and told myself I would deal with him the next day at work. But then I heard David's footsteps on the stairs – he was running – and he ran straight to me, and he grabbed my wrist, and he pushed me up against the wall. I felt the pop of the bone as it broke.'

His grip was too hard and the angle was all wrong and my ulna snapped clean through. But David was beyond rationality – still holding my wrists in his fists and shaking me as he shouted and I was in too much shock to feel the pain at first – focused purely on his bewildering rants.

Who does he think he is, texting my fucking wife? He has no right to talk to you outside of the office, he's fucking lucky I even let you work there – you're mine. And what the fuck was that even about?

'I figured out a few weeks later that David had set up my iCloud account on his laptop, so he saw Seb's text as soon as it came in,' I tell Natasha softly. 'The stupid thing is that at the time, I didn't even wonder how he knew about the text – because in our house, David was all powerful. It was no surprise at all to me that he might have developed an omniscient knowledge of every little thing going on in my life.'

'You were pregnant when this happened?'

'Yeah… six or seven months.'

'Didn't that raise alarm bells at the hospital?'

'He told them I tripped on the stairs and landed badly. They didn't buy it at first – the nurse took David away for paperwork and the doctor asked me point blank as soon as I was alone.'

Olivia, this injury just doesn't look like the result of a fall. Is there anything else you want to tell us?

'Were you tempted to ask them for help?'

'No. Because they'd call the police, and I knew from experience that wouldn't work.'

'So – how did Sebastian handle the fractured wrist?'

'He didn't,' I sigh. 'He probably still doesn't know exactly what happened, I didn't tell him and I didn't see him, I barely left the house for the rest of the pregnancy. David told me to call and resign the next morning, and I did call but... I just told Seb we'd had a scare with the pregnancy and I had to go on maternity leave early.'

'Did Sebastian have his suspicions?'

'He didn't buy it for a second,' I whisper, staring at my wrist. I wore the cast for two months. It only came off at the end of April, and Zoe was born in May. 'As soon as I told him I wasn't coming back, Seb suspected David had seen the text. But what good would it have done if I told him the truth?'

'How did you convince him?'

'I was a bitch, just like David always said I was. I was cold with him, I wanted to hurt him and to push him away. So I told him I was fine and that my welfare or the welfare of *my* baby was none of his business.'

'That must have been so difficult for him to hear. Particularly looking back now and seeing where things wound up... '

'I know I hurt him so much, and he has this way of wearing his pain on his face. Even yesterday when I was at work and I was trying to keep things normal, every time I caught him looking at me, he looked like his heart was breaking for me and I don't understand it and I don't know how to deal with it.'

Natasha has her notepad on her lap, but she lifts it now and carefully rests it on her desk before she turns back to me.

'I have some new homework for you, Olivia.'

I stare at her warily. 'What is it?'

'The next time you're speaking to Sebastian and you see that pain in his face, can you think really hard about what might be behind it? And I know – I *know* it's easier to stop when it hurts so much, but... when there's a tragedy like this, there really are phases of grief. And contrary to popular opinion, everyone works through grief in their own way and in their own timing, and there's no *right* way to deal with it. But I do think there comes a time when the methods we use to cope in the early days after a trauma can start to hinder our progress if we hang onto them too long.'

'What does all of that mean?'

'It means' – Natasha takes a deep breath, and she says very gently – 'denial is only going to get you so far, Olivia. You are going to need to look Sebastian in the eye sometime soon and face what's happened to you both.'

I sit up thinking about Sebastian that night, and in the end, I need to take one of Dr Eric's sleeping pills just to get some rest. This means I sleep in – and I wake up feeling strange. My head aches, and it's a struggle to get ready for work. I'm flustered by the time I get Zoe to the day-care centre. I kiss her and pass her to Ellen, who gives me a concerned look.

'Are you okay? You're awfully pale this morning.'

'Just running so late,' I mutter. 'Couldn't sleep last night – then I couldn't wake up this morning. But hey – Ellen – I keep meaning to ask you, I haven't had a bill from you yet for Zoe's care?'

'Oh, we can sort that out later,' Ellen assures me, but I see the odd way she pauses. I wait for her explain herself, and she smiles at me. 'I'm just very happy to help you out for now.'

'I don't need your charity; I really can afford to pay for her care.'

'I know, Olivia. Why don't we sit down and figure something out soon?'

I drive the short block to work and park, but my head is still pounding and now I'm thinking about Ellen's awkwardness when I reminded her about the bill. I go to the kitchen for a coffee and Sebastian is there, and he greets me with a polite, 'Good morning.'

'Hi.' I say, and I reach for my own mug and slip it under the coffee machine. 'How's your week been?'

'The same,' he says. 'How are you going?'

I smile at him and echo, 'The same.'

'Are you doing *any* better, Olivia?' The words seem to burst from his lips, as if he's been holding them back for weeks. I try to reassure him with a smile.

'Of course I am. Being back at work is helping me more than you could ever know.'

'And… Zoe?'

'She's settled into day-care well.'

I can see from the way he's staring at me that Seb desperately wants to say something, and so I pause, waiting expectantly – and then my eyes widen because it suddenly strikes me that maybe he's going to ask to come around to see her – or to start to get to know her? There's really no reason why he shouldn't… not now.

Could we be a family one day?

I wait, but he only stares at me, and I feel myself soften towards him. Maybe he's finding it difficult to ask. Maybe he feels awkward.

'Seb,' I say gently. 'Do you want to spend some time with her? To start to get to know her?'

Sebastian picks up his mug and he leaves the room abruptly. As he passes me, I see that his eyes are glistening, and I'm taken aback. Why would he react like that? I know it's late – but it's not *too* late. Maybe this is our chance? Maybe everything can still be okay?

I stand there for some time, but I can't untangle the mess of thoughts in my mind, and I decide I'll try to go into my office and prepare for the day. I'll talk to Seb again later. In the meantime, I have to de-sex three pups this morning, then lunch with Ingrid, and then this afternoon Gilly has booked in a few routine procedures – a feline tooth extraction and the excision of a mystery mass from a prize bull.

It's a busy day, but as the morning passes, I'm constantly distracted by the thought of Sebastian in that kitchen. I keep picturing the tears in his eyes, and it doesn't make any sense at all. *Why does he keep crying?* He's a sensitive man and he cares for me, so perhaps it's natural on some level – but this isn't my mirrored grief I'm seeing, it's his own. Is it because there's a very good chance that Zoe is his, and he's never had a chance to spend time with her?

Is it because he's angry with me about hiding the truth from him? Well, if that's the case, fair enough. My options had just felt so limited. I felt like I was trapped in an impossible situation from which there was no safe way of escape, so I took the route that seemed the least dangerous to *him*. But maybe when I transferred the risk to myself, I transferred the cost to Sebastian.

If that's what he's upset about, we can fix it. Zoe is only a few months old – it's nothing at all in the scheme of things.

But despite my attempts to console myself, that unsettled sensation in my chest just won't ease, because every explanation I can come up with for Sebastian's odd behaviour just doesn't convince me. There's still something else going on here and I *just can't see it* and it's starting to frustrate me. It's almost like everyone is looking at me with a knowing look in their eyes all of the time and I have no idea why.

It's a good thing I've done hundreds of pup castrations before, because I'm barely concentrating as I perform the procedures. My hands work methodically, but I lose time in my thoughts, trying to figure all of this out, like it's a puzzle I can solve. I feel like I'm just a heartbeat away from an *Aha!* moment that will make all of this make sense, but it's maddening – my heart keeps right on beating but my mind can't connect the dots.

'Liv, Seb's had to go home sick,' one of the nurses says as she appears is in the theatre room doorway, and she grimaces. 'Must have eaten something bad I think. Just wanted to let you know.'

I look up at her and nod. Maybe that's all it was, he was sick.

That makes sense, but somehow, I can't convince myself that's what really happened.

CHAPTER 32

Ivy

Olivia left the hospital a few days after the birth. Now, our proximity became such a blessing – I called in with pre-cooked meals for them to reheat, in exchange of course for cuddles with Zoe several times a day. After a few days, their immaculately kept house had rapidly dissolved into the chaos that comes with a newborn, and I took loads of laundry for them in the morning and returned it clean and dry in the afternoon. Zoe was absolutely adorable, but it took Olivia some time to get the hang of breastfeeding, and the new family had suffered through increasingly unsettled nights.

'Thanks, Ivy,' Olivia sighed, and she rubbed her eyes wearily at the end of the first week at home. 'I had no idea how exhausting this was going to be.'

I couldn't help but smile.

'That's what I'm here for, Livvy,' I said, and I was pleased at the thought of still-more time with my delicious little granddaughter. I glanced at David, and caught him staring off into space. 'When are you going back to work, Davey?'

'Tomorrow,' he said, and he gave himself a visible shake and straightened in his chair.

'Everything okay?' I prompted.

'I'm just tired,' he said, and I smiled.

'Goes with the territory I'm afraid. It gets easier.'

I was weeding the garden at the front of my yard later that afternoon when David walked along the footpath, pushing the pram.

'Hello!' I said, delighted. 'Oh, Zoe's come for her first visit to Nan's house. How wonderful.'

'Liv needed a sleep,' David said, but I saw the huge bags under his own eyes and frowned.

'Looks like you could join her.'

'I just… ' David started to say something, then glanced down at the pram and I saw confusion on his face. 'I just can't help but wonder… '

He trailed off, and I could sense his mounting frustration. Zoe started to cry again in the pram, and I bent and automatically lifted her into my arms to hold her close.

'Wonder?' I prompted gently, once I'd settled her, but David sighed and shook his head.

'Never mind.'

'Is something troubling you, son?' I asked, frowning.

'She looks… do you think Zoe looks like… ?'

A moment of understanding passed between us somehow, and I suddenly realised what David was really asking. I looked down at my granddaughter in the afternoon sun, and played the game I'd been playing since her birth – scanning for features like mine. When she was born, her face was all scrunched up as newborns often are, and in those earlier days it was hard to find any resemblance to anyone at all. She had the dark blue eyes most newborns have, not yet the cool blue David and I shared, although I was hopeful that might come with time. Her hair was fair, as were her eyelashes, and I'd assumed that came from Olivia's side – Louisa was quite blonde too. Now though, as I stared down at her, the sun caught her hair and I stiffened.

'Her hair,' I murmured, and I raised my eyes to David. 'Her hair.'

'What about her hair?' he asked. His breathing was coming faster… heavier… and every time I looked into his eyes the darkness there seemed deeper.

Oh, God. My poor baby. What has that woman done to you?

'It looks… '

I stopped myself right there, and I took a deep breath before I spoke. The chill in my chest had become something hot – pulsing anger, an infuriation deeper than any I'd ever felt before in my life. If we were right, Olivia had made a betrayal of the highest order – against *all of us*.

'It's not quite blonde, is it?' I asked him, but the tension had tightened until I could barely breathe. I lifted the baby into the sun, and she screwed her face up in protest, but I stared at her hair. 'It's more of a… '

Still I hesitated to say the words. I knew I was playing with fire, but honestly – if the baby that we were all so excited about actually belonged to Sebastian McNiven…

There'd be hell to pay.

Well, so there should be.

If Olivia had been making a mockery of David… she deserved everything she got if David found out. That wasn't my problem. My loyalty was to my son, and it *always* would be. I had to bring the baby back tightly against my chest to hide the way I was trembling because the very thought of it – the *very thought* that she'd made fools of all of us – it was just too much. I was so angry I couldn't even bring myself to speak for a moment.

I'd finally welcomed her into the family with open arms and it was all for a lie?

I'd spent all of those hours playing stand-in mother to her over this pregnancy and it wasn't even my son's child?

I cleared my throat and looked right at David and I said flatly, 'It's more of a strawberry-blonde, you might say. Maybe even going to be *red* when she's older.'

David nodded slowly, and I could see the barely restrained frustration in the way he held himself. Even so, I could see he was uncertain – he didn't want to believe what I was coming to accept more with every single second that passed. David leant forward to stare at Zoe's hair, and his face contorted – his gaze shifting from fury to uncertainty and then back again with every second that passed.

He didn't want to believe it.

Well, neither did I, but now that I saw it in the sunshine, there was no denying the definite red tint to that baby's hair.

'Well, Olivia has brown hair,' David said, and I could tell he was trying to convince himself. But then he trailed off, and his eyebrows knitted. I tilted my head as I stared at the baby, then back to David.

'And your hair is black,' I said. 'So surely the baby should have black hair too.'

'I don't know if genetics works like that,' David murmured, but when he raised his eyes to me, he was stricken. He reached for Zoe abruptly. 'I better take her home.'

'Okay, son,' I said quietly. I watched as he sat Zoe back into the pram. He moved very slowly, fiddling with her blanket and then adjusting the sun visor with much more care than the short journey around the block really required. And all the while, the beating of my heart grew loud in my ears and I was so angry and scared for him that it took every shred of energy I possessed not to scream.

'Do you think it's possible?' I blurted, as David moved to walk away at last. He raised his eyes to me, and now the swirling anger had drained from them altogether. He was simply devastated, hurt beyond repair.

'I don't know,' he said, his tone dull. 'I didn't want to believe it. I still don't. She's… ' His voice broke, and my heart broke with it. 'She's everything to me, you know? She's *my* wife – if she did this—'

He broke off, battling for control. His breathing was ragged, and his hands were fists around the pram handle. David swallowed, hard, then he glanced at me. 'I better go.'

'Okay, son,' I said, nodding. 'You just… just let me know you're okay, won't you?'

David nodded silently, and then I watched as he slowly disappeared from my view. I felt lost after he'd gone – achy and confused and angry. I picked up the shovel I'd been using before his surprise visit, but the garden blurred when I tried to focus on it. I stood, and threw the shovel into the dirt, then walked inside to pour myself a wine.

✦ ✦ ✦

I texted him a few hours later.

Davey, are you okay?

His reply came a few minutes later.

Working through things. Best to give us space for now.

I didn't like that at all – was he pushing me away? That wouldn't do, not at all. I sought for an excuse to text him again, just to keep the conversation going.

Are you still going back to work tomorrow?

David's reply took longer this time, and it was several minutes before my phone sounded.

I have to at least for a while – wages need authorisation.

As the afternoon passed, I thought about David's house around the corner, and tried to imagine what was happening there. Were they arguing? Had he raised his voice… ?

Had he raised his fist? Had Olivia confessed? Did she have anything *to* confess? What if she didn't? I'd never even have noticed that red tinge to Zoe's hair if David hadn't raised the subject. Had I overreacted? What if I was wrong about Zoe's paternity, and David lashed out at Olivia, what then?

I resisted anything like guilt that rose inside, until all I felt was anger and frustration. I just wanted to know what was going on in my son's house and his life; I felt I had a right to. My helplessness was maddening, and by the time Wyatt came home, I was a mess.

I greeted him at the door.

'David thinks Zoe might not be his,' I blurted, and my husband stared at me incredulously.

'What bloody nonsense! Did you tell him he was being ridiculous?'

That wasn't the reaction I anticipated. I thought Wyatt would be outraged right along with me. I crossed my arms over my chest and frowned at him.

'I just don't know, Wyatt. I mean, she was *so* determined to keep working with him…'

'With him? With who? With Sebastian McNiven? *Christ*, Ivy. She liked her job, that doesn't make her a whore! Bloody hell,' he exhaled, shaking his head at me. 'Look, you need to stay out of this. I keep telling you. *Their* marriage is not *our* business.'

'But he's our son, Wyatt.'

'And he's a grown man!' Wyatt exclaimed, then he ran his hands through his hair in frustration before piercing me with a look. 'I mean it, Ivy. Stay *out of it*.'

I wasn't happy at all about Wyatt's reaction, but I felt too frazzled by that stage to argue with him, so instead, I nodded and kept my thoughts to myself. Later, after Wyatt was settled with his dinner in front of the television, I texted David again.

Worried about you, son.

I suffered through a fitful night's sleep, checking my phone every few minutes only to be disappointed by his lack of response. When the morning came, I tagged along with Wyatt to walk the dogs, but David's house was peaceful – there were no external clues at all as to whatever was going on inside.

'Ivy,' Wyatt said abruptly. 'Stop staring. It's *none* of our business.'

I sighed and nodded. And then we went home and Wyatt went to work and I looked from my phone to the front door and I twiddled my thumbs and then I decided.

I'd go see her myself. David would probably be at work, so I could look her right in the eye and confront her. I told myself I wasn't going to check that she was okay – that wasn't my responsibility, my loyalty was to my son.

So I walked back around the corner and I rang the doorbell, and when that went unanswered, knocked on the front door. The house was completely silent, and I started to feel an inexplicable anxiety. Was Olivia taking an early nap? I debated giving up and going home, and then I had a last-minute impulse to go check the back door. It was as I walked around the side of the house that I saw the broken window. It had been shattered, and the glass all around the window frame had all been knocked out onto the grass. I panicked and fumbled for my phone, and I called the police first.

'I think someone is robbing – or has robbed – my son's house. I'm not sure if my daughter-in-law is still inside. She has a baby… '

The police instructed me not to go inside, so I paced on the footpath as I called David.

'Don't panic,' I said carefully, 'I think someone has broken into your house.'

'What do you mean?'

'There's a smashed window… It's a bit of a mess.'

'Mum, where's Olivia?' David asked me. The dark edge to his voice sent a shiver down my spine, and I stopped pacing and stared back at the house as I said carefully, 'I'm pretty sure she's not home, but the police told me not to go inside.'

'Why did you call the fucking police?' David gasped, and I could hear his footsteps echoing over the line – he was running to his car. His anger was directed at me, and that stung and confused me.

'You have a smashed *window*, David,' I said stiffly. 'Clearly the police need to be involved. What if you've been robbed?'

'Call them back, and tell them not to come,' David said abruptly. 'Tell them you were mistaken. I'll be there in ten minutes.'

'But I wasn't mistaken. You should see it; the whole window is gone.'

'Would you fucking listen to me for once in your fucking life, Mum! Call the police back!'

My son had *never* spoken to me like that before, and I was frozen in shock – although not numb enough to avoid the wave of hurt that washed over me. And then David hung up on me, and I stared at the phone in my hand, and I had absolutely no idea what to do. I tried to call Olivia's mobile several times but it rang out and there was no still no movement from inside.

I was sweaty and sick to the stomach, and that big house loomed there so still and so silent, and nothing about the moment felt right at all. How could David speak to me like that? I was only trying to do what was right. I was only trying to help him.

Eventually, I called Wyatt.

'You need to come to David's house,' I said, uneasily. 'Something is really wrong.'

The police arrived first. They went into the house through the open window, and then came back and told me there was no one at all inside and no other signs of unrest. But then they also said that the window had definitely been broken – and from the inside – and just as I was trying to make sense of this, David's car pulled into the driveway. He was flustered – his face red, his forehead beaded with sweat.

'There's been a mix-up,' he said, and then I could see that he was searching for an explanation, but all he could come up with was, 'This was an accident, this morning. I've already called a glazier. They're coming to fix it later today.'

'But where is Olivia?' I asked. 'And where is Zoe?'

David looked at me through narrowed eyes, and then he said, 'They're fine, Mum. They'll be home soon.'

I got the impression the police didn't buy David's story, but they left anyway – after all, it *was* David's house, he was insistent that his wife wasn't missing, and if he wasn't concerned about the smashed window, there was no reason for them to be. Just as the police car left the driveway, Wyatt arrived. David gave Wyatt his version of events as I walked to look closely at the window. Now I saw the stone statue up against the fence. It had been thrown *through* the window, and the glass all around the edges of the frame had been knocked out with great care.

As if someone had busted their way out, and they were being extra cautious to make sure there were no sharp edges as they did.

As if someone was trying to get out of the house while carrying something particularly precious.

As we reached the front door, the first thing I saw was the new lock. It had been crudely installed since my last visit the previous day, and once we were inside I saw the matching lock on the internal garage door and I knew then that I'd find a similar lock on the back door. Suddenly, everything almost made sense.

'Darling,' I said, as I tried to force the pitch of my words back down to their usual level. 'What happened here today?'

'There was an accident,' David said, and he was sweating again, and Wyatt cleared his throat.

'Son, is Olivia okay?'

'Of course she's okay. We talked about Zoe last night and she got upset, she was threatening to leave and I just… ' David broke off, and he looked at me – his eyes wild. 'Mum, she was going to take my kid away. What else was I supposed to do? I had to keep her here just long enough to sort this all out. I didn't think she'd be fucking crazy enough to smash her way out.'

'It's okay, darling,' I said, and I drew in a breath, and then I started to think things through aloud. 'Everything is going to be absolutely fine. Olivia forced your hand, didn't she, Davey?'

'She did,' he said, and his gaze was pleading. 'What am I going to do?'

'She was threatening to take your baby girl away. Threatening to keep her from you. You love your family and you had to do *something*.'

David nodded.

'It's just a lovers' tiff, right?' Wyatt said quietly. 'No one's business but yours and Olivia's. No one needs to know.'

'No one's business but ours,' David repeated, but then he linked his hands behind his hair and exhaled, and his face contorted. 'What am I going to do? I *have* to get them back. She can't just fucking *leave* me like this.'

'She had no right,' I said tightly.

'Look, what's done is done,' Wyatt said heavily, and he shifted his attention to David. 'Get the window fixed, and take a breather, hey? Calm down – give her some space, she'll come back.'

David looked at Wyatt blankly, and then a red stain swept along his cheeks.

'But I don't even know where she is,' he snapped. 'I'm not going to give her *space*, I'm going to find her and make her come home. For God's sakes, Dad, you don't know anything about what's been going on around here—'

'Do you want the whole town to know you locked your wife in the house, David?' Wyatt interrupted him pointedly. 'Because if you go after her and give her a hard time right now, word is going to get out. The smart move here is to lay low and wait for her to make contact.'

'But what if she's gone to Sebastian! The whole town will be laughing at us!' I cried, shaking my head. 'No – that won't do, Wyatt, we have to try to find her. I'll call her parents and see if she's there, okay, Davey? That way at least you'll know if we have anything to worry about with him.'

Wyatt threw his head back in frustration and sighed. 'Let *me* call Tom, Ivy. You're hysterical, you'll only make things worse.'

'Maybe we need a lawyer, David,' I said suddenly, and David peered at me.

'In case she calls the police?'

'No, so you can still see *Zoe*,' I said pointedly. 'She's a newborn. Every hour you miss is precious, you can't let Olivia take it *all* away from you.'

'Ah… ' he pondered this for a moment, then he nodded. 'Okay. That's what I'll do. You two try to find her, and I'll contact the lawyers.'

CHAPTER 33
Olivia

'Two houses, Liv. Two bloody houses! In the one week!'

I'm at lunch with Ingrid, and she's positively glowing with excitement. It's impossible to avoid getting caught up in her joy, and I've managed to push all thoughts about the odd moment with Sebastian in the kitchen all the way out of my mind.

'You'll put Todd out of business soon,' I remark, and Ingrid grins at me.

'The day I do and I move from my pokey little shithole office into that beautiful big building, promise me you'll come and dance on his desk with me.'

'You've got yourself a deal,' I laugh.

'How's work?'

'Going well. I'm well and truly back in the swing of it now.'

'Still doing mostly theatre work?'

'Yeah, Seb is still really weird about me dealing with the human customers,' I sigh. 'I think I'm nearly ready for it, but he's still… I don't know. Things with him are pretty complicated.'

Ingrid's phone begins to sound, and she grimaces apologetically as she picks it up.

'Ingrid Little Real Estate,' she says, 'You're speaking with Meg.'

I press my fingers into my mouth to stifle my giggle, and Ingrid grins at me for just a moment before her eyes widen. As she wraps up the call, she gives an excited squeal.

'You're not going to believe this. Those people who went through your old house last week want to see it again right now. They said they're ready to make an offer.'

'Oh, fantastic!' I say, and she stands.

'I'm so sorry – I'll need to get over there—'

'Go, go,' I insist as I wave my hands at her. 'Three houses in a week? You really *are* on fire.'

Ingrid laughs, then she grimaces as she glances at the door. 'So sorry to cut this short, Olivia.'

'We can do it again next week. Good luck!'

I've got half an hour before I'm due back at work, so I finish my wrap without rushing, and then wander across the road to the post office with a bag of accounts Gilly asked me to post for her. I join the end of the line, and I'm looking around the random assortment of envelopes on the shelves—

And then I realise that Ivy is two customers ahead of me. For a moment, I consider leaving – she hasn't seen me, if I turn away now, I could back away before she does. But then I realise she's talking to the owner of the town pub, Gwen Grayson, and they are talking about David's death. I still want to leave, but like watching a train wreck happen right before my eyes, I find I can't tear my gaze away.

'How are you doing, Ivy?'

'Ah, I'm okay. You know, you have to keep your chin up.'

'I can't even imagine… '

'Yes.'

'Have you… are you any closer? To finding out why?'

'It was a complicated situation.'

'There are rumours… '

'I'm *well* aware of the rumours. You knew David too, do you really think he could have done such things to Olivia right under our noses and we wouldn't know?'

'No, no… of course not.'

'I mean… my God. Just look at her lately. She's clearly not a well woman, who knows what David was putting up with in that house? My son was a *good* man, Gwennie. Everyone knows it, that's why he was elected to the town council twice. And yes, clearly he snapped, but she *did* try to take his daughter away from him, so if we're going to ask ourselves who's fault all of this really is… '

She trails off, and my heart is racing, and I want so much to run away but I feel frozen in time.

'Is it true?' Gwen asks, her voice a scandalous whisper. 'What they say? About the car?'

'It was an accident,' Ivy says stiffly. 'The whole thing was a terrible, unfortunate accident.'

'How exactly does someone *accidentally* hook a hose to an exhaust pipe, Ivy?'

I'm embarrassed for whoever has shouted that sentence because it was inappropriately loud in the confined space of the post office. My throat is sore. It takes me a moment to connect the two concepts, and then I realise that I'm standing in the post office and I'm unravelling and all of the progress I've made in the last few weeks has been for absolutely nothing because I'm two minutes away from running back to my house and locking myself away again.

David was a good man, and perhaps he snapped.

Is that the story we'll *always* tell ourselves about David? Is that a true story? If it is, why does it make me so angry that I feel like my entire body is turning to stone with the effort it takes to hold my rage in?

Ivy and Gwen have both turned and they are staring at me and I am conscious of their horror – of the blood draining from their faces and the way Ivy's jaw is hanging loose. But if the whole town is saying this and the whole town believes it then I am a victim of their excuses for him, just as I was a victim of his violence. There is no escape from it – I am trapped here, and I've been kidding myself.

My vision fades, tunnelling around Ivy and Gwen, and I drop the bag of envelopes and I start to back away from them.

'How exactly does one wind the exhaust pipe to the window of the car, above *my baby's car seat*—' I'm not just shouting now, I'm screaming – spitting with rage and hate and pain. But I can't continue. I can't say it. The words nearly choke me, and I stop mid-sentence and I make a sound like a wounded animal.

The brave thing to do would be to explain myself, to stand up for myself, and to face their judgement and their assumptions and to tell them all just how it was. I have a captive audience – the whole post office is staring at me, enough small-town gossips in this space today to get a message to the far reaches of the district by sunset.

But I have never been good at standing up for myself, not since David convinced me I had no right to. And I've never been good at making a scene, not since I spent fifteen years under his thumb trying to avoid them.

So I spin on my heel and I run. I run all the way out of the post office and down the street to the day-care centre. By the time I get there, I am red faced and exhausted and I can't feel anything but hurt. Ellen takes one look at me and she ferries me into her office and she gently guides me to a chair and Zoe is already in her office waiting for me – but shouldn't she be in the nursery? How did Ellen know I was coming?

The hose above her capsule. The swirling fumes in the car.

No, no, no.

I push the thoughts and the images away frantically. I can't face this yet. I won't.

No! No! No!

Ellen pulls a blanket around my shoulders and tucks Zoe into it too and then I see her on the phone. She whispers into the handset as she stares at me. Her gaze is gentle, and when she hangs up, her touch on my shoulders is soft and comforting. But I am in a bubble of shock, and I sit right there within it until Mum and Dad come through the door and they gently guide me to their car and take me and Zoe home.

'Darling girl,' Mum whispers to me. 'You've been so brave, my darling.'

'Don't say that, Mum, I can't hear you say it,' I say. My lips feel fat and stiff. 'If I was brave, I would have gone to Seb earlier. If I was brave, I could have saved her.'

I try to gasp those words back in, because I'm not ready for this. *Not yet, not yet. Just one more day before I face it. Push it away. Bury it deep.*

'Darling, none of this was your fault,' my mother says, and the pain in her eyes actually echoes my own and I can't even look at *her* now. Why is my grief so magnified when I see it in the eyes of people who love me?

Because they haven't found my magic weapon.

They don't have my denial.

Rolling sobs break over me and I curl up into a ball over my daughter in the back seat of my mother's car and I wish that David had taken *me* that day, because it doesn't matter if I managed to pretend otherwise for a few weeks; I am as good as dead anyway.

✦ ✦ ✦

I wake with a start and the sun is already up. I'm confused – I can't figure out what day it is – my eyes feel gritty and my mouth is dry and I recognise the Stillnox hangover as soon as it hits, but I can't remember getting home from the day-care centre, and I'm guessing that Dr Eric came to sedate me, but I can't remember seeing him.

Something feels different inside – I can't figure out what it is, only that my pain feels raw all over again. I need to get out of bed. The urge to keep moving forward is still right there within me – so I go with the impulse. I sit up and reach for Zoe, but my hand meets cold, empty sheet and I panic for a moment until I remember she's sleeping in the cot now.

But then I look across to the cot, and find that it's empty too. My heart starts to race.

I run now towards the chatter of the television on low in the living area. I find Mum sitting at the dining room table. She's got a pink teddy bear against her chest as she reads the paper. There's a steaming coffee on the table in front of her, and my baby is nowhere to be seen.

'Where's Zoe?' I demand, and Mum looks up in surprise and gives me a quizzical smile.

'She's right here, love. Are you feeling any better?'

I scan the room again, and then narrow my eyes on Mum. I'm not in the mood for games. I haven't been in the mood for games for months now, maybe longer. Right here? I don't see her. I need to see her.

'*Where*, Mum?'

Mum lifts the teddy bear towards me, and I stumble backwards, as if it's a danger to me. I stare at the teddy and I'm absolutely sure that I've never seen it before in my life, but it's familiar anyway – really familiar – how is that possible? It's a deep pink bear, with a light pink bow with a tiny silver heart on it, and there is white embroidery on its round little belly.

Zoe Joy Brennan
21ˢᵗ May 2016 – 5th June 2016

My knees give way and I stumble again – this time my back hits the doorframe at the edge of the kitchen – and I shake my head violently and I hear this loud, wailing sound coming from somewhere far away but it's echoing in my head as if I'm caught in a tiny space, and then somehow… I am. As Mum shoots to her feet and comes towards me, I scamper backwards – away from the bear, away from the truth – pressing myself into that dark little space between the pantry and the fridge, pressing myself all the way back in till I'm tucked inside it and I want to curl into a foetal position but there's just no room and I'm stuck. Mum is reaching in towards me – I see her lips moving in slow motion – but I can't hear anything but the wailing. The pain is coming – it's a pain so great that I have run from it for months, pushing faster and faster to try to convince myself that I could avoid it forever – running so hard that I couldn't feel my feet moving at all – but it has caught right up to me. I am crushed now – destroyed by it – Olivia Brennan is gone forever because Zoe Brennan is gone forever.

So many things that just didn't add up. The intensity of Sebastian's grief. Ingrid suggesting I bring Zoe in the car without the car seat. Ivy's strange comments about letting go. Natasha… so much gentle prompting from Natasha.

And the way that everyone just keep staring at her, and I thought it was because she was so beautiful and they were so sorry for David but it wasn't that at all.

It is only an urn – an urn inside a teddy bear – my perfect little baby's ashes in an urn inside a teddy bear. The bear was Mum's idea, I remember now her talking to me through her sobs in the days after The Tragedy when I needed to make decisions about Zoe's body and I just couldn't. Mum thought the bear would bring me some comfort, she said maybe it would help if I had something to cuddle against my body.

And it did. It was a false comfort, but comfort nonetheless.

I squeeze my eyes shut – wanting to block out the sight of the bear – but as the darkness closes in I see her face – as if she could have been sleeping peacefully, but she wasn't – she was grey and purple and still and cold and—

And I can pretend my life will go on, but it won't, because on a cold winter's day the very best part of my heart was taken away from me.

◆ ◆ ◆

Dr Eric comes yet again to my home, and he sits patiently at the edge of the gap between the fridge and the wall. I see him, and then after a while, I hear him talking to me in soft, fatherly tones that are not professional at all any more and haven't been since The Tragedy.

I had to call it The Tragedy, even to myself. I couldn't even bear to think the words *murder suicide*.

Dr Eric cares about me and he, like everyone else, has been so patient with me. Today, he's patient enough to wait however long it takes me to find the strength to climb out from my hidey-hole – which I only do when the tears run out and my mouth starts to feel cottony and I need a drink of water more than I need to feel enclosed.

'I know it doesn't feel like it,' Dr Eric says gently, as he takes my hand to help me to my numb feet, 'but this is real progress, Olivia.'

Progress? What 'this' feels like is humiliation and devastation all rolled up into one mortifying and overwhelming ball. I flick my gaze towards the bear which now rests on the dining room table and a sob wracks me all over again, because the idea that my beautiful baby is gone and all that remains is ash is completely, undeniably *wrong*.

And oh God… *Sebastian*. Perhaps he lost his daughter too, but he never even got to hold her or meet her, and he hasn't even had the basic right of having his role in her life acknowledged. Oh, what I have put him through…

Unforgivable.

I see it now, clear as day. This *is* why I couldn't talk to Sebastian and why I just couldn't bring myself to talk *about* him. In his story, I am surely the villain – the person who made the decisions that mean he'll never get to know his own daughter.

And if I talked about Sebastian, eventually I was going to talk my way up to the part of the story where the shame hit, and my guilt is now for *his* loss.

Mum and Dr Eric sit with me for a while – until they eventually decide that they should sedate me again, which I suppose is probably the right course of action because once again I cannot stop shaking, and once again I cannot stop crying. In those awful days between discovering her body and her ashes being returned to me, I knew the truth then… but it was unbearable, and then the urn arrived. The thought of her inside it was too much for me to contemplate, and so I simply didn't. I just continued on as if it had never happened. I accepted what I could deal with – that David was dead – that he had taken his own life – that in some undeniable way, my infidelity had caused this whole godforsaken scenario – and that was bad enough. I had enough to deal with in that.

I hear Natasha's careful words, and finally I understand what she has been pushing me towards for all of these weeks.

Denial isn't something you know you're doing. It's subconscious.

But the coping mechanism has failed now… and I have to face this. I don't have it in me. There is already nothing left of me, nothing like the strength that I would need to face the fact that my daughter is gone.

I let them sedate me. I let them pull me back into the bed, and once again, Mum touches me tenderly, as if I am the child. She brings the bear and tucks it in beside me, but this time as sleep overtakes me I stare at it, and I am suddenly angry even with the bear, because what it represents isn't my memories – but my loss.

✦ ✦ ✦

'Livvy, Sebastian is here,' Dad is standing at my door late in the evening. 'Do you want to speak to him? He said he understands if you can't.'

I am lying on my side with the bear hard against my chest, and Milo is asleep, cuddled right up beside it. I hear Dad from the doorway, but I'm facing away from him, and I can't really find the energy to sit back up. I want to stare out the window at the hydrangea plants all day and go back into that state of denial where I truly believed Zoe would pick the blooms with me one day.

'I'll see him,' I whisper. My voice is hoarse and I have no idea what day it is. But I do know that I owe Sebastian McNiven at least a million apologies, and my grief and my pain is no longer any excuse to delay the first. He comes very quietly into the room, and he crouches down beside my bed to stare into my eyes.

'How are you going, sweetheart?' he whispers.

Why is there still love in his eyes? I don't deserve it – I never did. I can't even lift my head off the pillow at first, it's all I can do to force myself to meet his gaze. I'm ugly crying and I have been forever – my nose is raw from it. I must look disgusting.

'I really wasn't sure,' I say. 'She truly could have been his, and I didn't want her to be, but I also didn't want her to be yours because if she was… there was no way out anyway, you know? It just made everything worse if she was yours, because if she was *his*, then I could almost keep you out of it.'

'You were in an impossible situation, Olivia.'

I sit up and shuffle over to make room for Sebastian. I lift Milo up into my arms, but I pass Sebastian the teddy bear, and he sits it on his lap and wraps his arms around it and his jaw tightens. He takes a moment, staring away from me, but then his gaze returns and he asks me gently, 'Why did you finally leave him, sweetheart?'

'She wasn't sleeping well and I was exhausted. He took her for a walk one day, and I fell asleep… I woke up choking. His hands were around my neck,' I tell him. I sound numb, but I'm not – it's just that if I let the emotion into my voice, he's not going to be able to understand me. 'He kept screaming at me about her hair being red – asking me if she was yours, and I denied it over and over again, then he'd choke me until I blacked out, wait until I woke up and start all over again. He'd been angry before, but that was the first time I realised he was actually going to *kill* me if I didn't leave. So I was looking for a chance to go, but he was doing his usual thing… the remorse, the pleading, this time even worse because things had never gotten so out of control before. Later that day, the doorbell rang and it was one of the mechanics from work, dropping off some locks David had asked him to pick up. He put new locks on all of the doors so I couldn't get out. He took the phones and the modem. I was trapped. David had to go to work to authorise the staff payroll, so as soon as he left, I smashed a window and I wrapped Zoe up and I ran.'

'I'm so sorry, Livvy,' Seb whispers. 'I'm sorry I put you in that position. You were vulnerable that night in Sydney. I should never have—'

'Seb,' I say, and I start to cry. 'I don't regret it. I can't regret it. You and Zoe have been the only good things in my life for so very long.'

'I know, sweetheart. But… I should have protected you… I should have been there for you.'

'I didn't let you. I *couldn't* let you. I was scared he'd hurt you too and I couldn't have lived with that.'

As the conversation has progressed, we've somehow, naturally shuffled closer to each other on the bed. Now we are touching – Seb's arm around my shoulder, his head resting against mine.

'So after you broke out, what did you do?'

'Mum and Dad's house was too far to run on foot, so I ran to a stranger's house and I begged them to hide me and let me use the phone. Dad came and got me.' He took one look at me and the bruises around my neck and he burst into tears. I was terrified of how my parents would react to me calling them for help after so many years, but the minute I saw my father in tears, I knew they *only* cared about my safety. 'So Dad and Mum hid me at their place. I knew we couldn't call the police again – not after the first time. So instead, I sent David a text from Louisa's phone later that night to tell him I was never coming back.'

You have to let me go, David. I'm not coming home, and if you try to force me to, I'll have to go to the police again but this time I won't be able to let it drop. I'm never coming back. Please just let me go.

We sit together for a while, the silence punctuated only by the echoes of our breaths as they fall in and out of sync with one another. After a while, Sebastian whispers, 'So, what happened? How did he get his hands on her?'

'He went straight to a solicitor and within a day of me leaving he had an order issued for visitation rights. I didn't have a choice,' my words are strained as I plead with Seb to understand the unforgiveable. 'The lawyer said it would make things so much worse in the long-term if I refused him reasonable access to her. I had ordered a DNA test but there was paperwork coming that never showed up and anyway… until I had proof that she wasn't his, the lawyer said I had to give him something. So that's what I agreed to – one single hour.'

It's just one hour, Olivia – not a lot to ask, the lawyer had said. *Let him spend some time with her this week, and we'll rush the DNA test next week. It's one hour of her life, and then we can make some more permanent moves to keep him out of yours – okay?*

I made Louisa hand Zoe over, because I couldn't even bring myself to see David. She said he was polite, and he said to give me his regards.

Give Olivia my regards please, Louisa.

It's just one hour, Olivia.

CHAPTER 34

Ivy

David was so depressed and angry in the days after she left, but it gave way quickly to a deathly calm and defeat. I saw him every day; he came by for dinner with us. He'd play with his food, his face set in a miserable mask, but I was full of energy all the time. I could barely sit still during the day and I couldn't sleep at night. Olivia had devastated my son, and I wanted revenge so badly that it was all that I could think about.

'Liv promised me Zoe's mine,' David whispered one night. 'But… I just don't know.' He raised his eyes to me. 'You saw the red in her hair too, didn't you? I looked the genetics up online. It's possible we could make a baby with red hair but… '

'Grandpa Gillespie had a red moustache,' Wyatt said flatly. 'You need to stop this talk right now. Things are bad enough without adding to the drama. We need level heads now.'

'Well, whether Zoe is yours or not, Olivia was simply never good enough for you, David,' I snapped. 'That girl was—'

'*Ivy*,' Wyatt groaned, and I broke off but clenched my fists. Our gazes met and locked, and Wyatt's became pointed. I looked at David, and his eyes were shining – tears were threatening again. The urge to lash out at Olivia was so strong in those moments that it was all I could do to stop myself from storming away from the table and going right across town to her parents' house, to give her a piece of my mind. I knew I couldn't do it. I knew it would only make things worse for David. So instead, I reached across and squeezed his wrist.

'David, we love you, whatever we can do to help – we will,' I said, and despite all of the insanity, I mostly felt like my heart was going to break for David. 'She just shouldn't have provoked you. She shouldn't have forced you into this position.'

'I just need to keep this all quiet, you know? My reputation is everything. If this gets out... the business... the town council... '

'Has she told anyone?' I asked. 'I mean, no one *knows*, do they?'

'Her family for sure. And she has a lawyer.'

'Did she go to the police?' Wyatt asked quietly.

'Not yet. I have a mate looking out for me at the station. If she tries, he's going to call me.'

'So... have you spoken to her?'

'No, but her lawyer has agreed to let me see Zoe on Friday. I'll pick her up and bring her round for a visit if I have time.' His lip curled, and he shook his head in disgust and looked to me, his gaze somehow pleading. 'One hour, Mum. That's all they've given me. One fucking hour a week with my daughter.'

'It's only for a while, isn't it?' I said gently. 'Surely you'll be able to get some more access once the dust settles a bit.'

'Who knows?' he whispered, and the anger drained out of him and he stared at the table again, and his gaze vacant. I curled my hands into fists at the defeat in his stance. It was so *unjust* that she could do this to him! This was all Olivia's fault – whether Olivia had been unfaithful to David or not, it had been her decision to leave. David was a good man, and it incensed me that his wicked, unfaithful wife could have all of the power in a terrible situation of her *own* creation.

Every time I saw David that week, I hated Olivia just a little bit more. She'd taken things from my son that could never really be restored – his trust, and those innocent early days with Zoe. And perhaps Zoe really was his daughter, my granddaughter –

how was I to know for sure? But I knew one thing: if Olivia really loved David, she would never have left him the way she did.

The day came for his afternoon with Zoe, and David was suddenly over the moon, positively glowing with excitement. He had taken the day off work to run some errands in the morning before he picked the baby up at lunchtime. He told me he'd call by with Zoe in the afternoon, and when I heard his car on the drive I ran out to see him – but I could see in his eyes that he still wasn't right. There was a joy there, but behind it lurked a breathtaking depth of pain.

I told myself that made sense. After all Olivia had done to him...

Inside, I cuddled Zoe as I took her inside and sat on the recliner with her. She was sleeping – so chubby, so healthy, so well. It was a cold day and she was wearing a pink jumpsuit that I had bought her – I'd given it to Olivia when she was in the hospital, and although less than two weeks had passed, it *felt* like a lifetime ago. I wondered if she had chosen it specifically, knowing David would be likely to bring Zoe to my house. I wondered if it was a hidden message, some taunt to me. I pondered this and stared at the baby and for a while, paid too little attention to David as he sat opposite me, watching me. But eventually, his silence began to unnerve me, and so I smiled at him and I tried to distract him by refocusing his energy on the baby.

'Thanks for bringing Zoe around.' He smiled back at me, but there was still ice in his eyes, and I felt another cold shiver run down my spine. I held her closer – tighter – so tight that she squirmed a little in my arms. David stared at us, that odd smile still fixed on his face, and finally I asked the question I did not want to ask. 'Are you okay, Davey?'

'I'm happy. I'm relieved,' he said simply, and I exhaled and looked back to the baby.

'So will this be the start of regular visits, then?'

'I'll be seeing much more of her now.'

'Every week, you mean?'

'No, Mum. I've decided not to settle for an hour with her a week.'

'Have you and Livvy reached a compromise then?'

'After today, things are going to be sorted.' I raised my eyebrows at him, but he pressed his finger against his lips. 'I'm still working out the final details. You'll know soon enough.'

I had seen my boy laugh and cry and dance and run and sleep and learn and grow and change over his lifetime. He had been my sole focus and my greatest privilege for almost forty years. I knew him inside and out, better than I knew myself.

I knew then that he was going to do something to get at Olivia. I thought maybe he was going to run away with Zoe – or that he'd found some new lawyer who was going to pull some sleight of hand and switch the custody arrangement.

They were both frightening options, but I somehow still felt sure that David would do the right thing for Zoe. So maybe if he was going to run off with her, it would just be to prove a point, or maybe if his solicitor had found a loophole, it would force Olivia to reconsider the situation and be less restrictive with his access to the baby.

It didn't occur to me for a second that he would do anything permanent. I knew my son. He just wasn't like that.

Zoe was tired and started to fuss, and David told me he needed to take her home for a little nap. When the time came for him to leave, he pulled me close and hugged me, and I was sure then that he was going to run away.

'Whatever you're planning, David—' I started, and he smiled at me. He was at peace. All I could think was – well, if Olivia was going to make this difficult for him, then maybe he really had no choice in the matter. Maybe running off with Zoe would show Olivia just how deeply David loved them both. Maybe that was just the way it had to be.

'It's okay, Mum. I know what I'm doing.' And then for the first time in decades he said casually, 'Love you.'

'I love you too, son.'

He kissed me on the forehead, with Zoe caught between our torsos, and then he unlocked his car.

'You aren't walking home? She'll probably fall asleep as you go around the corner.'

'I'll need the car, Mum. It's fine.'

He sat Zoe gently into her car seat, then he closed the door, and I let him leave.

I let him leave.

I went back inside. I sat down to finish my cross stitch, and my hands were shaking. I rose, and I started to pace. I picked up the phone to call him, then I sat it back down again.

I told myself I was being silly. I told myself I was overreacting, being a hysterical, foolish old woman, just like Wyatt always said I was.

I put the dogs on their leads and I went for a walk. It was cold – my fingers were icy, my lips felt numb – and I remember the warm flush of relief that ran from my head to my toes as I turned the corner and saw David's car in the garage at his house. The roller-door was open, and Zoe's door was open, and I imagined him getting home a few minutes earlier to find her asleep, and him lifting her gently from the seat and carrying her inside.

I felt instantly ridiculous at the sight of his car right where it belonged. David had made some mistakes – but my son was hardly a lunatic, and he'd never do anything to jeopardise his chances of continued access to Zoe in the future. I turned around and went home.

✦ ✦ ✦

By the time my phone rang an hour and a half later, I had sufficiently distracted myself from my earlier concerns. I'd pottered around the house as if I didn't have a care in the world. But then the phone rang. I answered it mildly.

'You're speaking with Ivy.'

'Ivy… ' Olivia sounded uncertain, and in a single instant it was back – the ice-cold chill down my spine. I gripped the phone tighter in my hand.

'What do *you* want?' I snapped at her. I heard her sharp intake of breath.

'David hasn't dropped Zoe back and he's not answering his phone… Have you seen them?' I didn't answer her – I wasn't sure how to. She cleared her throat, and then she added in a confused whisper, 'He was due back an hour ago, Ivy.'

The instinct sounded – the icy grip of fingers of fear around my mother's heart – I *knew* then that he was in trouble. I hung up and dialled my son's mobile number. I held my breath and felt myself tense with every ring that sounded and passed, and then I dropped my handset and I ran from the house, stopping only at the hall table to pick up my mobile phone.

I saw the note on David's front door as soon as I rounded the corner. The garage door was closed now, so I couldn't see if the car was there, but I could see the paper that had been fixed to the very middle of their large, charcoal front door.

I leapt up the steps two at a time and then I tore the papers from the nail that held it against the door. There were two pages there – an official looking form at the back, and a note at the front.

I looked at the form first.

Request for DNA Analysis – Paternity Confirmation

The form was pre-filled for Olivia and Zoe and addressed to Olivia at her mother's address – but what was it doing here at their house, and *dear God* – here was the proof, if she'd ordered this test, she *must* have a reason to suspect that someone else was Zoe's father! I couldn't wait to tell David – but just as that thought struck me, I saw the handwritten note. It was folded over – and the word *Olivia* was written in thick, heavy black letters on the front. The paper felt ridiculously heavy as I unfolded it – as if its weight was so much greater because of my fear.

You made me do this. See you at the mountain.

I stared at the note, completely bewildered. What on earth did he mean? Olivia's number was still on my speed dial, and that was fortunate, because as I tried to call her my hands were trembling so hard that I might not have managed otherwise.

'Ivy?'

'He… ' I was still holding the note; its meaning slowly penetrating the fog in my brain. 'At the mountain, Livvy. He said he's at the mountain. At the Bush Chapel, I guess.'

'Oh, okay… but… ' I heard her relief give way to confusion, then she asked me hesitantly, 'Did you speak to him?'

'No… he… there's a… ' I closed the note again and saw the harsh marks of the letters of Olivia's name.

David hadn't written that note – he had scrawled it, his hand in a fist.

'Olivia – we need to go there. Right now.'

❖ ❖ ❖

As I drove, I tried to imagine the scene that would be waiting for me. David had probably planned some romantic gesture just like his proposal – yes – surely that was it. I would arrive and find myself somewhat awkwardly in a field of flowers with David on a picnic rug with Zoe in his arms. Perhaps he was going to propose again. Perhaps this was their fresh start. He did so love Olivia.

You made me do this.

My foot flattened against the floor and I drove faster – the closer I got, the more panicked I felt. When I finally pulled into the lookout clearing, I saw a car at an awkward angle beside David's – I saw Olivia's sister was right beside it on the phone, bent at the waist and *screaming* into the handset. Louisa too had been speeding, she too had stopped abruptly – her car door was wide open, and it reminded me of the moment just hours earlier when I'd seen David's car in his garage with the door open and that beautiful warm rush of relief.

But there was no relief for me now, because this was not the scene I'd been hoping for at all. There was no picnic. No flowers.

Only David's car, and the garden hose taped into the exhaust pipe, winding its way lazily to the back window of the car – the window right above Zoe's seat. The windows were all fogged up – frosted almost, as if they'd been tinted with some kind of swirling grey tint. I surveyed this with a confused kind of horror – all of my thoughts gradually slowing until they fell like heavy raindrops instead of in a steady flow.

Smoke in the car.

David in the car.

Zoe in the car.

Olivia with a rock. A huge rock. How could she even lift that?

Oh God. She was aiming it at the driver's side window. What if the glass shattered and hurt my David? I screamed and leapt from my car before it had even stopped moving. As I ran from the car, my ankle twisted on a thick tuft of grass and I fell to my knees but kept moving forward – clawing my way across the ground towards the other cars. I tried to stand – but my ankle gave way immediately – and so I continued to crawl, one hand in front of the other, my knees scrambling across the rough ground.

'No! *No!*'

I kept screaming the word as if it could stop the nightmare unfolding before me. I heard Olivia's desperate, unbearable cries too – but they washed past me because I saw the boulder hit the glass that was probably right beside my son's head. The glass sank in – but the window didn't shatter – and the rock fell to Olivia's feet. She picked it up again and even as I scrambled towards her I marvelled through the numbness of my shock at her strength to be able to lift it. She was red faced and determined and she threw it all the way through the window this time.

Oh God. It surely landed on him. What if it hurt him? Oh God. Oh God.

Olivia unlocked the car and went straight for the backseat but all I could think was *my baby – my baby – my baby.* I was staring at the driver's side – my focus fixed solely on David – at the exhaust fumes still pouring from the car through the open door – and it was only when I saw Olivia fall to her knees too with the baby in her arms that I looked to her again.

Zoe was still wearing the pink jumpsuit I'd given her.

Olivia lowered her to the ground and began to perform a frantic CPR. Her tears ran down over the baby's face and she was shaking and framing her daughter's tiny cheeks with her palms in between each compression. I thought for a moment I saw Zoe move, and I sobbed in relief and resumed my scramble towards David.

But then as I came closer, I looked towards Zoe and Olivia again, and I knew then. Zoe's tiny, perfect face was grey, but her lips were a startling, sickening plum colour. Olivia was screaming and shaking her daughter now but it was all in vain. It was all too late.

I reached David just as the police arrived. I was completely unaware of the wailing of the sirens and the tyres on the gravel – but I felt an officer wrap his arm around my waist to pull me away from my son. I struggled against him and managed to break free – and scrambled up into the car to stare at David.

He was a baby just a minute before that; a newborn in my arms, fresh and new and perfect. And then he was a toddler, chubby and curious, and a pre-schooler with questions so big my mind ached from the endless barrage of them. And then he was a school kid, and his enthusiasm delighted my heart, and he was a teenager with growing confidence and individuality – and a young adult who knew where he was headed – and then a man who made me so proud.

And then I touched the grey shape of his cheek and he was none of those things, because he was cold to my touch, and everything I had ever lived for was lost.

CHAPTER 35

Olivia

'Everyone in town thinks I'm a lunatic,' I whisper to Seb. We'd moved closer and closer to each other as the hours passed and the words and the tears flowed freely, and now we are lying wrapped tightly in each other's arms, the bear resting safely between us. My parents quietly left us alone, giving us privacy to grieve our daughter together at last.

'You certainly have been a hot topic of conversation,' Seb whispers to me. I make a sound that's both a sob and a laugh.

'Why didn't *anyone* tell me?'

'Your family tried in the beginning, but you just couldn't deal with it. Then Dr Eric and Natasha agreed it was better to let you face it when you were ready.'

Now that we've finally laid everything on the table, I'm surveying what's left of my life and realising just how much I've lost, but strangely, I'm also conscious of how lucky I've been. Maybe the only reason I've survived this at all is that I had the space to be crazy for a little while. Looking back on those days after Zoe's memorial service, I remember nothing but the agony and the confusion, and a total lack of *hope*. I truly felt like David had taken everything in my life worth breathing for.

But as humiliating as these crazy weeks may be, at least the denial gave me time and space to shuffle myself here – into my new place, into my new routine, even back out into the world. And the best part of all, back here, into Seb's arms.

'You never even got to hold her,' I press the words out around sobs.

'No, I didn't,' he says, and it's the darkest, most miserable phrase I've ever heard.

'I took that from you.'

And just like that, sobs overwhelm me again, but his arms are around me even though I don't deserve them.

'We're going to be angry, and we're going to be sad. And we're going to hurt, and we're going to feel her loss forever. All of that is true, Olivia. But if you want to know the secret to how we're going to carry on, I *can* tell you what it is,' he whispers to me hoarsely. 'We're going to learn to leave all of the blame where it belongs, with David Gillespie. He made the choice to take our baby's life, and only *he* can be held responsible for it.'

I think about this for a very long time. It's dark when I'm ready to get up, and then I go to the bathroom and I wash my face. When I come back, Seb's still on the bed, the bear in his arms. The echoes of a thousand lost moments are there in the sadness of his gaze, and I hesitate just a little at the thought of leaving him alone.

But there's something I just have to do.

'Could you stay here with her?'

Sebastian frowns at me. 'Where are you going?'

'I need to talk to Ivy.'

Seb looks at me in alarm. 'Can I come with you?'

'Seb,' I shake my head. 'I need to do this on my own.'

I drive back to Bathurst Street and I park on their driveway. I stop for just a moment to collect myself. The last few days have been exhausting, and I know this isn't going to be a pleasant conversation. I remember Natasha asking me if I could ever confront Ivy, and how terrifying that idea once seemed.

But now, the idea of *not* doing it seems even more terrifying. If I never challenge the lies she tells herself and those around her, then I am forever a victim. I know I won't change her mind, but this conversation needs to happen. I need to do this. *For Zoe.* And for me.

I walk to Ivy's front door and I knock without hesitation. She opens it a moment later and I brush straight past her into the house.

I have disconnected from my feelings again – inwardly, an odd calm has settled, but I'm achingly conscious of the fact that my whole body is shaking. Oh God, I so hope this isn't a mistake. Wyatt is eating his supper in the recliner – a sandwich I know Ivy will have made for him. He's watching the news as if the world hasn't ended – as if everything is as it always was.

He looks up at me with a confused frown. I probably look crazy – little does Wyatt know this is actually the *least* crazy I've been in months.

Ivy follows me into the living room, and she stands at a distance away from me, as if she's scared of me. I look from Wyatt to his wife, and then from Ivy to her husband, and this seemed like such a good idea only seconds ago, but now I don't even know where to start.

'Zoe is dead,' I say softly.

I see the look Ivy and Wyatt exchange, the frenzied, panicked look of two people who were just going about the evening, and then their poor, bereaved ex-daughter-in-law barges into the living room in order to state the bleeding obvious. But I'm enraged by the normality of the evening; I know they are in pain too, but why does life get to go on for them? How can *they* live with what has happened?

Ivy approaches me, slowly, cautiously. When she is close, she extends a hand towards me, and I slap it away furiously. Ivy's face contorts, as if she can't bear to see me suffer like this – but I'm cynical, and I wonder if the pain on her face is actually because I'm making *her* uncomfortable.

I could understand her rose-coloured glasses for most of these years, at least until she learned that he was hurting me. She was a devoted mother, and she adored her son.

But surely now… surely if *I* have to face what has happened, then Ivy has to as well.

'Zoe is dead. And that is David's fault. David *murdered* her, and even if I made mistakes, there is *no way* the responsibility for his actions lies with me. And I can't let you say that to people any more, Ivy. I can't even let you think it.'

Now, Ivy's face reddens, but she's staring at the floor. Has she heard my words, and is she having one of those moments that I have had lately, where life just shifts into a different kind of focus? Is she hurting? For a moment, her pain actually gratifies me. I want her to feel the guilt too – the same guilt that I feel whenever I think of Sebastian – but I want it to consume her, and destroy her, because she *made* David.

She made David, and now David made the mess that's left of me.

But then she raises her gaze to me and I realise that she's not lost in her pain at all. She's furious and it's all directed at *me*. I'm not the victim here; not in Ivy's mind. I'm the enemy. Maybe I always was.

'It was an accident,' Ivy says flatly, and then her nostrils flare and she glares up at me. '*My* son would never harm—'

'*No!* I shake my head furiously as I shout the word, and Ivy's eyes widen. 'Your son… ' I say, but the words come out as an incredulous accusation and I break off, shaking with rage. I take a deep breath, and I force myself to continue.

She deserves to hear this.

And *I deserve the chance to say it.*

'Your son made the last ten years of my life a living hell.'

Ivy is almost vibrating with her fury and frustration. I can see the cogs of her mind turning, but she's not thinking about what I said. Her gaze keeps flicking back to the hallway, back to the front door – she's trying to figure out a way to get rid of me.

But I'm not going anywhere. This is my moment. It wasn't on my whiteboard list, but this is the final step I need to take, and as I stand there before Ivy, with Wyatt blustering but impotent in the chair behind me, I suddenly feel empowered.

'I will not have you come in here to *my home* to make these unfounded accusations about my son.' Ivy is shouting now, and she raises her fist and points her finger right in my face. 'David was a good boy... a good *man*.'

I silently raise my wrist until it's right near my face, and I simply stand there and stare at her. She's confused, and her gaze flicks between my wrist and my eyes.

'What? Are you going to *hit* me?'

I shake my head, and I say flatly, '*Look* at it.'

Ivy's jaw is set hard. She shakes her head, and I move the wrist closer to her face and I whisper harshly,

'Do you know how hard you have to twist a wrist-bone to break it? Do you know how long he made me wait before he let me go to the hospital? Do you know how terrified I was? Do you know that he choked me the day that I left, over and over again, until I passed out *each time*?'

'You provoked him,' Ivy hisses. 'If you'd been a better wife, a *faithful* wife, he'd never have raised a finger against you.'

I remind myself that this is Ivy. It is not David. I am not saying what I always wanted to say to my husband to the right person, but somehow... those eyes confuse me. Her icy blue eyes are the *same* as his, and this is as close as I am ever going to get to confronting David.

'There is nothing I could have done. Nothing I could have said. Nothing I could have *been* to deserve his abuse. It was his problem. His decision to treat me as a possession instead of a

human being! And my daughter? How do you excuse that, Ivy?
He *murdered my daughter!*'

Ivy is still shaking her head, but she starts to cry, and Wyatt
finally gets up and approaches us, blustering and panicking but
left useless by his outrage. He makes noises if he's going to speak,
then loses courage, and instead goes to the telephone table. Is he
going to call the police? Dr Eric? My parents, most likely.

I do need to leave.

But there is one more thing I need to say to this woman first
so that the words are *out there* in the universe – even if it's too
late, even if she doesn't hear it. I step closer to Ivy until my face
is close to hers, and I whisper fiercely,

'And *you* let him do it. The blood of my beautiful, perfect
baby girl is on your conscience too because *you knew* who he was
and you knew he was hurting me and you knew I couldn't leave
and *you never said a word.*'

I spin on my heel and I walk out of the Gillespie house for
the very last time. When I step out into the night air, I draw in
a desperate, enormous breath, and I fill my lungs all the way to
the top.

And then I walk to my car, and I slide behind the wheel, and
I point towards home. When I walk back into my bedroom,
Seb is sound asleep on my bed with his arms wrapped around
the bear. I climb in behind him, and I pull the blanket over all
of us, and I sleep.

CHAPTER 36
Ivy

When Olivia leaves, Wyatt and I return to our recliners. We move stiffly and at first, we don't speak. The television is still on; the sports segment on the nightly news comes on just as we settle in exactly the same positions we were in before her arrival. Wyatt even picks up the sandwich I made him earlier. He didn't like the rice pilaf I made. My fault, I should know his tastes by now, but I put too much onion in it.

'You don't think she's right, do you?' he asks me suddenly, and the question is so unexpected that I startle a little. But I glance at him, and I shake my head violently. Then I take a deep breath. I straighten my hair, and I wipe carefully at my nose with a tissue from the box beside my chair. Finally, I clear my throat, and I say, 'I think we all knew all along that Olivia was a damaged, troubled woman. I just wish we'd gotten her away from our son before she... ' My voice breaks, and I clutch the tissue harder and clear my throat again. 'Before she did him any harm.'

We sit in silence for a moment, before Wyatt murmurs, 'It looked bad... you know. Even the police said he probably *meant* to... I mean, the car... the hose... '

'It was an *accident*, Wyatt,' I snap, and I'm furious with him for even *suggesting* otherwise. 'I'm sure of it. He wanted to give her a scare, and he probably didn't realise how long it would take her to find him. He would *never* hurt an innocent... '

I can't speak any more, and so I don't. Wyatt drops the subject too.

In our hearts, *we* know the truth about who our son really was and there's absolutely no point entertaining any other possibility. I am comforted by this thought – it's my *only* comfort... just enough to hold further tears at bay.

Wyatt reaches across the recliners suddenly and squeezes my hand. I squeeze back, and we turn our attention back to the news.

CHAPTER 37
Olivia

On Wednesday morning, I park in the Milton Falls Long Day-Care Centre car park and I look to the passenger's seat beside me. I have the bear sitting on the seat, and not strapped into the capsule on the back. I feel guilty about that, but I don't want to put her back into the car seat, because I'm scared if I do I'll slip right back into denial all over again.

I know it doesn't feel like it, Olivia, but this is progress.

Seb suggested I could take some time off again. He hasn't really left my side this week, except when I've asked him to. We are grieving together now, and the shared burden really does feel easier to carry. I want him around as much as possible, but there are moments when I need to and do take my space. Moments like now.

I step from the car and I carry the bear inside. Ellen is behind the counter where she always seems to be. She sees me and she smiles.

'Morning, Olivia. How are you today?'

My arms contract around the bear, and my throat works as I try to figure out how to apologise. Ellen rests a manila folder onto the counter and approaches me cautiously.

'I just came in to say sorry,' I blurt, and she raises her eyebrows at me. 'I'm so embarrassed, Ellen. I know... I know about... ' I can't bring myself to say my daughter's name – how messed up is that? I clutch the bear tighter and I force my lips to form the sound. 'I know about Zoe.'

'*Embarrassed*?' Ellen repeats, and without asking me for permission, she embraces me in a huge hug. 'Olivia Brennan, you have nothing at all to apologise for. Life dealt you an impossible set of cards, and you simply had to turn them over one at a time to survive them.'

'It's just so humiliating,' I whisper into her shoulder, and I choke on a sob. 'Everyone thinks I'm crazy.'

'Actually, we think you're brave, that's why this whole town has rallied to care for you these months. You've been through enough, my girl. The last thing you need now is to beat yourself up because you just had to take your time accepting this.'

I sniff and pull myself away from Ellen's embrace. She extends her arms towards the bear, and I look at her in confusion. 'Well?' she prompts. 'Are you going to work, or not?'

'I can't keep leaving her here now that I know.'

Ellen smiles kindly. 'Are you ready to leave her at home on her own, Olivia?'

I shake my head mutely, and Ellen indicates again for me to pass her the bear, so I do – carefully extending my arms and watching as she cuddles the pink bear close against her body.

'Isn't this weird?' I blurt, and Ellen shakes her head with some determination.

'It's weird for a mother to want to keep all that she has left of her daughter safe? Of course it's not.'

'But... what do you with her all day?'

'It's just as I told you, love. I look after her as if she is my own. I rest her on the visitor's chair in my room, and if I have staff or parents in for meetings, I move her right onto my desk. I even talk to her sometimes while I'm working, she's a great listener,' Ellen says wryly, but she immediately sobers. 'And I will continue to do so until the day comes when you tell me that my services are no longer required. Your daughter's story touched me, Olivia Brennan. I never got to meet her, but I'll never forget her, and if I can do this one small thing to ease your pain as you rebuild your life, then I'll consider it an honour.'

I'm beyond moved by Ellen's generosity towards me, and so relieved that I have a way to avoid leaving Zoe at home alone until I'm ready, that I can't quite figure out how to express my thoughts. I don't need to, in the end – Ellen raises her arm and points towards the door.

'Get out of here. Don't you have sick pets to tend to?'

'I wasn't sure I was going to go to work today.'

'And now?'

I take two steps towards Ellen, kiss the pink fur on the bear's head, and I turn to walk away.

As I step out into the morning sunshine, I am conscious of the warmth on my face, of the sweet lightness of blossoms on the breeze and the morning birdsong beginning to sound. I'm going to drive down the block to work, and I'll see my colleagues and clients and the animals I always hoped would one day bring me back to life. And I'll work right there alongside Sebastian, and he'll be kind and supportive and I'll feel his gentle love ready to catch me; a safety net beneath my feet.

This brutal winter is fading away into the past, and soon it will be only memories – the inevitable spring will slowly take its place. I find no joy in any of those things or even in the passing of time – not yet. All I have at the moment is a flicker of strength… the quiet voice inside that reminds me that I am a survivor, and that one day I know that I'll be able to look back on all of this as a part of my past, because I will have *survived* it.

And for now, the hope of that is more than enough.

EPILOGUE

Two Years Later

'Okay... a little more, Olivia... nearly there, and... oh! *Congratulations.*'

The baby slides into Sebastian's gloved and waiting hands and the second the pressure abates I start to collapse. The midwife has been waiting. She catches me beneath my arms and lowers me down onto a thick mat, and suddenly there's a huge foam cushion behind me, holding me into a sitting position even though I've become a giant ball of jelly the second the baby left my body.

I can't tear my eyes off my partner and our daughter. Sebastian is sitting on the floor. He's holding the baby in his outstretched arms, staring down at her in shock – his jaw hanging open, his face drenched in tears and his breath coming in tight little pants. Euphoria is already washing over me and I feel amazing, but Seb looks *terrible* – his ruddy hair is sweat-slicked and standing at crazy angles.

The baby is protesting furiously at all of the fuss, but Sebastian is silent. His eyes are locked on his daughter. I watch all of this patiently – I'm eager to hold the baby, but more than happy to wait my turn.

Soon enough, Sebastian shuffles closer, angling the umbilical cord cautiously as he lifts the baby onto my chest to rest her against me. I cradle her and I marvel at the slightness of her tiny body, and the perfect shape of her little nose... the squishy lips... the long eyelashes. She's a miracle; a living, breathing miracle. Seb and I stare down at her together, and now we're sobbing in stereo.

'My God,' Seb chokes. 'You were magnificent. And she is… ' his voice catches again, and he's completely overcome. It's a long while and several unsteady sobs later that he finishes with a croak, ' …she is just so beautiful.'

I wipe the tears from Sebastian's cheeks, and he presses his lips desperately against mine, and then we're laughing and we're crying together over our furiously protesting daughter. The midwife has been hovering, closely monitoring the baby but giving us space – just as I wanted, just as we'd planned. I've been in complete control of this birth, from the first contraction four hours ago, to this moment now – everything has happened as I wanted it to. We had contingencies in place of course, in case anything went wrong but… nothing went wrong, and I can barely believe how strong I was.

And she's here, and she's perfect. Now, the midwife gently presses a sheet over us – over the three of us. Over my whole *family.*

Well, most of my family. We're missing Milo and Milkshake, the three-legged Maltese we adopted last year. They're at home on guard-dog duty.

'Does she have a name?' the midwife asks. Her voice is a little hoarse, and when I glance at her, I see the tears that she's tried to hide. There's no sympathy there in her eyes. Only joy.

'Asha Zoe Brennan,' Seb murmurs.

My baby's last name is Brennan, and so is mine. When I told Seb I didn't want to get married again, he shrugged and suggested we could skip right to the honeymoon. We are equals. We share the driver's seat in our lives. He is mine, and I am his… but only because we choose to give ourselves freely to one another. We have a beautiful, peaceful life in the cottage… Seb and me and the dogs and now…